A WORD FROM THE AUTHOR

MERCY OF THE CROW is the first novel of an intricate series, threading through generations with cruelty and grief. The themes within this story are extremely heavy and, at times, expressed through content that may be disturbing to some readers. Themes of abuse—particularly SA—are prominent in this book. Please proceed with care.

MERCY OF THE CROW

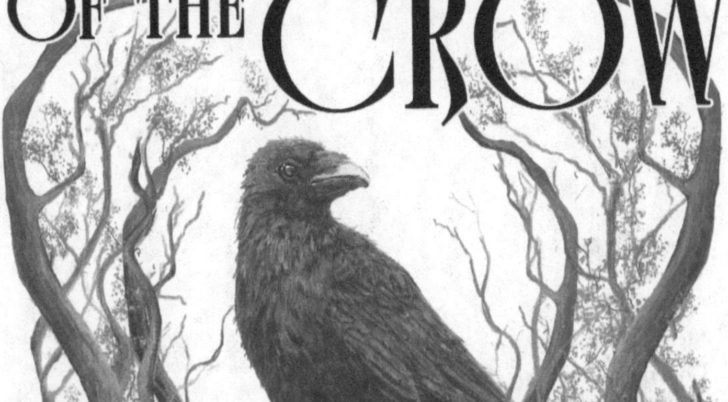

STEPHANIE ESCOBAR

TRILLIUM PRESS

Mercy of the Crow
Copyright © 2025 by Stephanie Escobar
Trillium Press

Book and cover design and illustrations by Maple Projects, LLC
Edited by Friel Black from Grey Moth Editing

ISBN 978-1-7357380-3-1

For *Harrison* and *Jacquelyn*,
for without their support this novel may not exist.

CONTENTS

PROLOGUE

The night Sirilda was born, the high moon cast an animated glow upon a mountain of forest, filling the crooked spaces between trees with brilliant silver light. All within the forest was still and silent, except for the cloak-shrouded woman who staggered uphill, crunching upon a floor of fallen leaves and needles of pine. Until, at last, the trees thinned, and she came upon a vast circular clearing. Here, the moonlight bathed unobstructed upon lustrous grasses flowing in a frigid wind, and the woman fell into a squat, a pained moan escaping her throat.

The woman raised the hem of her cloak. Her naked belly, silhouetted against the moonlight, was swollen with child. With a strong heave of her every muscle and a strangled whine,

she used all her strength to push out
the child who was ready to be born
this night.

She had done this once before.
Two summers ago, she had given
birth to a healthy, beautiful daughter.
However, the last time, she was not
alone, squatting beneath the stars as
she was now. Last time, she was in the
comfort of her home with her lover's
hand to squeeze as she delivered their
daughter. Both the memory of such
love and the loneliness of its absence
made her cry out from a sharp stab of
grief among her pain.

"Let it be his." She lifted her face
and implored the moon. She felt its
light upon her skin, dazzling in the
tears upon her cheeks. "Let me see his
face again in this child."

And as with every time she

remembered him, her lost lover, even in the agony of childbirth, she recalled the scene of his death—how he lay on the floor across from her, sprawled in his own blood.

No matter how tightly she grasped the memory of his bright eyes and hair of gold, his features always faded into those of his murderer. Her lover's warm gaze of brilliant hazel was replaced by cold black eyes—the predatory eyes of he who looked down upon her that night as he made his conquest over her body, her life, her future. Still she could feel the man's weight upon her as he pressed himself within her, against her every raging will. His black eyes haunted her now and would always.

The memory made her whimper with fear among her cries of pain, for she did not know what she would do if this child resembled the man who had

destroyed her life rather than the man whose memory she lived for.

"Please," the woman pleaded to the night before giving another wrenching push, her panting breaths becoming that of the rhythm of impending birth. She soon could feel the familiar flare of fiery pain as the child's head crowned, however slighter than that of her former, and then the ease of the expulsion from her body. Her hands went between her legs to catch the slippery prize, and in her practice of having delivered several babies, both human and that of the forest animals, quickly unwrapped the cord from the child and cleared its airway, so that the baby's gurgling wail echoed across the mountain.

The mother—glistening with sweat and stilling her uneasy breaths—was first unable to look upon the identity of her newborn child

who cried and flailed for the warmth of her breast. Instead, she looked up to the quiet sky stirring with moonlit clouds. She did not quickly bring the babe to her chest, to cradle it lovingly and nurse it as she had with her first, but rather waited to look down upon it, terrified of what she would see, terrified she would despise it. Slowly, her gaze lowered to the wriggling shape of her newborn's shadowed body, its scrunched, screaming face obscured by the shadow of the tall grass.

With her heart pounding with exhaustion and fear, the mother lifted the tiny body up into the moonlight. She saw the thick whitish vernix coating some of the baby's limbs and part of the gleaming, wet face, as was to be expected—and genitalia belonging to that of another daughter. With the babe's dampened hair

slicked back, the mother could not tell its shade, and still held her breath as she inspected closely for the fateful answer.

"Let it be his," the mother pleaded again, this time in a tremulous, agonized whisper—and at the sound of her voice, the baby opened her eyes and looked up at her mother for the first time. Her eyes, they were black slits, shiny with the moon's light, liquid and deep—no doubt the same eyes that had haunted the mother for so long. The mother shuddered a gasp and looked back upon the child with revulsion.

Without thought, the mother lowered the child into the cold grass and sliced the pulseless cord with a blade from her pocket, wiped her slippery hands off on her cloak, and turned on her heel to leave.

She started back down the

mountain at a walk, but as her guilt soared along with the fresh, hearty cries of her naked child wriggling alone in the grass, the mother broke into the fastest run she could without tripping, tears falling out of her eyes with every pounding stride.

The baby's wails faded the further the mother ran back into the forest. Branches and sharp brambles whipped at her as she sprinted through them heedlessly. Soon, her own wailing was nearly as hearty as the babe's, and she stopped in her tracks to sob into her hands that smelled sweet of her blood and juices.

Almost every fragment of the mother was pulling her onward to the home she could now see through the entwined branches of trees: a small, round cottage with the cracks of shuttered windows glowing yellow with firelight. *Home,* where she could

return without another thought of the newly born child, the child's father, or the suffering he'd caused her all this time. If she went forward, she could try to continue as though this tragedy had never been. But the innate maternal force pulling her backward was stronger.

The mother finally hushed her own whimpered breathing enough to hear that the distant forest had gone silent. What a powerful, hungry wail the baby had cried with—and now it cried no more. Unbearable it was for the mother not to hear its sound. Unbearable for her not to sate the cry with milk.

Despite how badly she did not want to feel this instinct, the mother ached for the babe she had left to die in the grass. And the babe would die soon—of the cold, if animals did not prey upon her little body first.

As suddenly and thoughtlessly as she had before, the mother turned on her heel again and began racing back up the mountain to the clearing. In the black trees all around her, watching eyes of animals reflected shards of moonlight. Their chatter hissed with the autumn wind that stirred the leaves. She heard them; she understood their little squeals in the dark:

"The human gave birth."

"She abandoned her young."

"Its wails have ceased."

"The wolves have caught scent."

The mother ran as quickly as her weakening legs could carry her, sweat dripping down her brow and tears streaming from the corners of her eyes. She did not stop running, even as the heavy-hot placenta squeezed from between her legs and dropped, steaming, onto the cold, brittle leaves

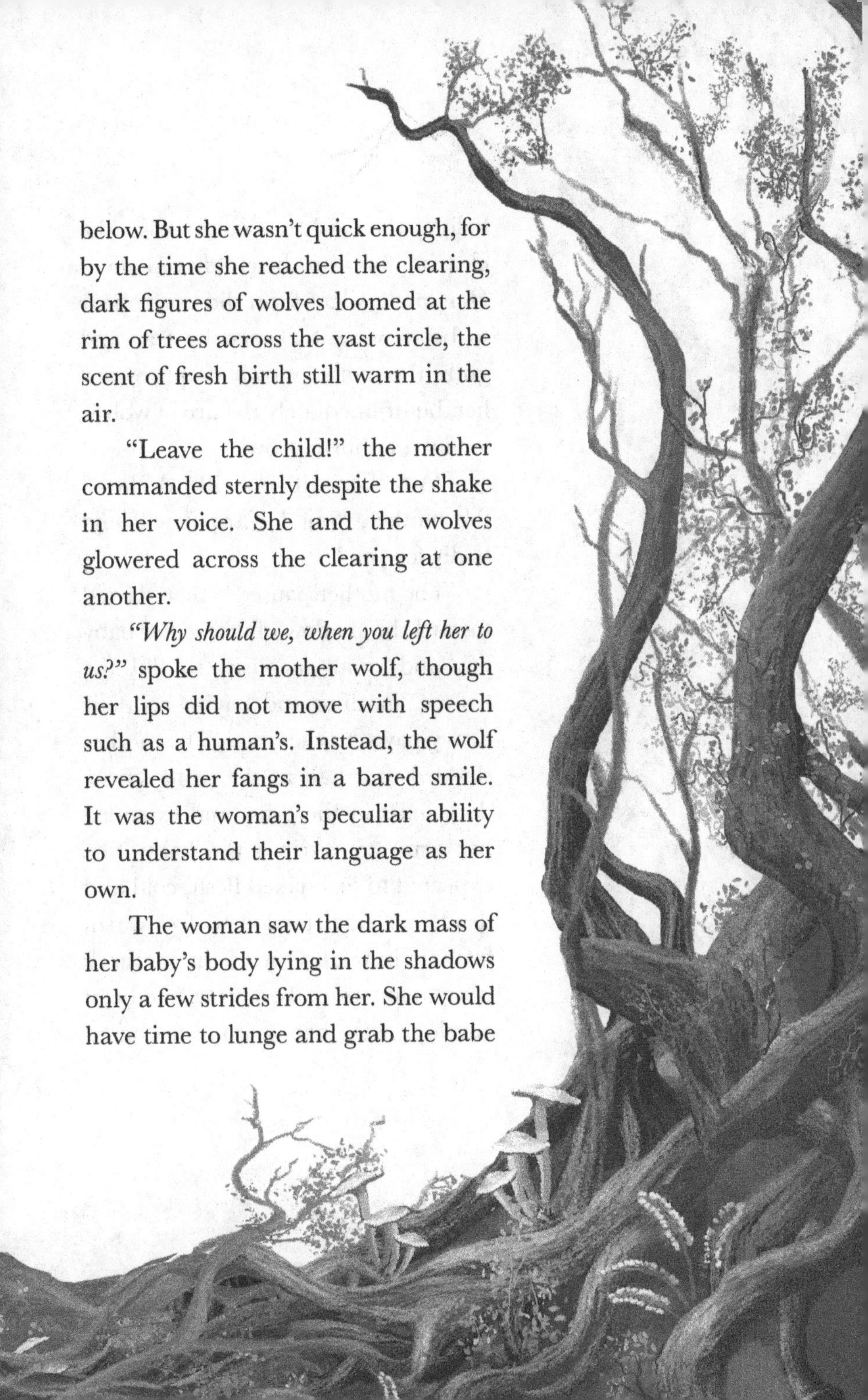

below. But she wasn't quick enough, for by the time she reached the clearing, dark figures of wolves loomed at the rim of trees across the vast circle, the scent of fresh birth still warm in the air.

"Leave the child!" the mother commanded sternly despite the shake in her voice. She and the wolves glowered across the clearing at one another.

"Why should we, when you left her to us?" spoke the mother wolf, though her lips did not move with speech such as a human's. Instead, the wolf revealed her fangs in a bared smile. It was the woman's peculiar ability to understand their language as her own.

The woman saw the dark mass of her baby's body lying in the shadows only a few strides from her. She would have time to lunge and grab the babe

before the wolves could cross the clearing, but was the child even alive? Her small, silent form did not appear to be moving. Sickened by fear and guilt, the mother slowly crept toward her, but immediately the arc of wolves let out a uniform growl.

"Attack me, if you will," declared the mother, "but I warn it will end badly for you."

The mother paused—then darted toward the shadow of where her baby lay, and simultaneously, so did the wolves, snarling and baying as their heavy paws hit the grass. The mother skidded to a halt as she came to the dark mass in the grass and extended her arms to retrieve the baby. She expected to feel naked flesh, cold and dead, but was startled to feel warm feathers instead. One of the mother's companion animals, a crow, had been enveloping the babe with its feathered wings, keeping her warm in the saving embrace.

The crow flew away into the night, and the mother snatched up the warmed, wriggling baby into her arms. She held the babe protectively to her chest with one hand, and with the other, reached hurriedly into her pocket. Inside was a drawstring bag, containing a powder of her own creation that she always kept with her. Her fingers parted the bag and enclosed around a fistful of the powder.

Just as the wolves reached her, so close now she could feel the wind of their motion touch her face and smell the meaty steam of their breath, she tossed the handful of powder in a precise motion so that it would hit each of them, and instantaneously the vicinity before her exploded into flames, causing her hair to billow back

in the hot gust of fire.

Each of the wolves were swallowed in a rage of orange light. The mother staggered backwards, covering her frantically rooting babe now with both of her hands, watching the blazing bodies of the wolves struggle to walk away, then collapse upon the ground. Their fur like torches, she could smell the hair burning along with the grass, hear the crackling of the fire as it ate the meat off their bones, and then their final whistling whimpers before the silence.

She stood there until the fire was extinguished from the blackened ground and from the sizzling remains of the wolves, watching how the smoke billowed in mesmerizing curls up into the starry sky.

"It's all right," the mother whispered tenderly to the babe as she pulled open her cloak and offered her breast at last. "I have you now."

The babe, wriggling with an eagerness to suck, latched upon the mother's nipple with ease. The mother nursed her as she walked, slow and shaking with exhaustion, down the mountain, back to the warm cottage she called home. She lost her balance and rested against a tree as the child drained the colostrum from her. Hazily, she looked up into the spindly boughs and saw that the crow was perched there, watching her.

"Thank you," the mother said up to the bird and staggered on.

Dawn had turned the sky pink by the time the mother came through the front door of the cottage; she was glad to see the body of her golden-haired first-born daughter, Lirinda, slumbering still upon the makeshift bed they shared. But at the first sound of her new sister's nursing grunts,

Lirinda startled from her sleep, sat up, and rubbed her eyes—bright eyes that reminded the mother instantly of the lover she'd lost and lost a second time tonight when the child was not his.

The mother shuddered with revulsion again at the thought of whose child it was, so strongly that she wanted nothing more than to rip the suckling child from her nipple and toss her away. But though she could not stand the feel of the child, she vowed never to forsake her again. Forcing away her memory of his dark eyes, she maintained a forgiving breath for the baby so as not to spoil her milk with hatred.

"Lirinda," the mother addressed gently but gravely, with still a shake in her voice. "I have something to show you."

She sat beside Lirinda upon the bed and parted her cloak to reveal the

small baby, now illuminated by warm candlelight to reveal a full head of curly-wet black hair suckling hungrily upon her breast.

Lirinda's large, luminous eyes grew even larger as she inspected her little sister, then looked up at her mother with awe.

"You now have a sister."

Lirinda gingerly reached out her hand to pet the tiny shoulder of the babe.

The mother had not thought of it yet, but the child's name easily came to her lips.

"Sirilda."

As the mother looked down upon her two daughters who belonged to different fathers, she was conflicted with love and pain. The peace she now felt was being eaten away by guilt, and even fear, for she knew she could never fully love Sirilda—that

her runtish, black-eyed and black-haired daughter would never amount to the love and glory that beamed like summer sunlight from Lirinda. Because of this shadow cast upon her child, and the damnation of who her father was, the mother feared that if she was not careful, Sirilda's life would surely stray toward a malevolent path.

CHAPTER ONE

Mother's bones are cracking, which means a storm is in the wind. Feeling her ankles and knees snap like leaves in the strengthening breeze, she tells my sister and me to hasten to her garden where we must hurry to collect the ingredients for a potion she's been awaiting a storm to concoct. A potion that she will sell to her customers in the capital city market tomorrow and guarantee us enough provisions to last the cold months.

I'm the first to listen. I take my cloak from off its antler hook upon the cottage wall, throw it about my shoulders, and slip my harvesting basket up to my elbow. When I open the door, I'm greeted by a swirl of autumn air still warmed from the sun with depths of cold emanating from the shadows of the surrounding forest. The leaves have only just begun to be touched by red; still Mother's pumpkins haven't properly attained their uniform orange rind, nor are the carrots ready for their second harvest. It is a season of transition, as I am still dressed in my summer frock and bare of foot. However, the colder nights have made the soil less pliant beneath my toes, and Mother warns of a freeze soon to come.

Lirinda follows me out the door with her basket, too, but she dawdles. She has never been driven by the same urgency as I, and I wonder if all elder sisters are lazy. She takes a careful moment to arrange her long gold-silk hair so that it hangs smoothly down the back of her cloak, unlike mine, which is a long, tangled mess of black curls, caught beneath the tie of my hood, which I fasten at my throat.

Sometimes, I think my sister and I are more unalike than we are similar. Considering that we come from different fathers, both of whom we've never met nor heard anything about—unable to even know their unique traits we may have inherited—our differences are understandable.

But when Lirinda hitches her skirts into her fingers and skips to my side at last, twirling in an excited dance in her joy for our little quest, a rogue leaf falling from the sky and landing upon her clean-swept hair, and her bare toes caked with soil just as mine are, I cannot help but feel we are the same after all. For we are both the daughters of our mother, and together we are bound to this wild life within a sprawling expanse of forested mountain—a sacred, secret place unbeknownst to anyone but us three, where only the plants and animals are our kin and company. This place, our home, we call Haven.

Wild indeed Lirinda and I are, for Haven is all we have ever known and will ever know. For Mother warns us of the world that lies beyond the Boundary that she made for us with her magic, and how those who dwell beyond the safety of Haven cannot know of us—cannot know what we are. So long as we remain in Haven, we cannot be harmed by man.

We have been beyond the Boundary, my sister and I, but only when Mother has deemed it most safe. When she travels to the city to sell her potions, herbs, fermentations, fungi, syrups, bones and feathers and pelts, we are sometimes able to accompany her. Especially now that we are older—Lirinda nineteen, and myself, soon to be eighteen—Mother trusts us more with our own careful duties in the city.

We have gotten quite good at selling the wares ourselves, while Mother meets with her secret customers in the shadowed rooms of the inns—women in need of medicines, poisons, and men in need of virility. She trusts Lirinda and me not to stray from the sunny, safest streets with always our hoods drawn over our long hair, casting shadows over our faces and throats, keeping ourselves from being known, discovered, while we trade our harvests and creations for coin.

As treacherous an environment as it is, in the busy streets full of turning wheels, clattering hooves, and rowdy folk bartering chickens for sacks of grain, there is something about the world beyond Haven—the realm of paved stone and wrought iron—that feels so very like another home to me, as though in a foreign lifetime I might prefer it or even belong. But not this lifetime.

I am contented to live here, in Haven, for all my life; to grow old and gray-haired alongside the pines and the fauna who will give birth to generations of young who'd skitter past me in my journey into old age; to learn all the potions and enchantments Mother knows; to abide in this forestine seclusion without ever knowing another human beyond kin. But Lirinda is not so content. It is Lirinda who dreams, Lirinda who longs for romance and babies, Lirinda who gazes a little too long at the handsome farm boys as they roll their dirty carts of turnips along the market square. Always, of course, with her hood secured over her lovely head. Never to be noticed in return.

There was a day, the summer of last, when Lirinda and I dared remove our hoods. While Mother was consulting a customer in one of the inns, Lirinda and I had been entrusted to sell our wares beneath the blistering hot sun. My nape sweltered and itched with trickles of sweat beneath the sunbaked wool of my hood. Still, I was afraid for what would happen if I disobeyed Mother and let my hood down. I had always been told that we wore our hoods for two reasons: one was so that the slave-takers would not notice us for our young beauty and sell us into the trade, and the other was so that there would be no invitation for anyone to know Lirinda or myself and discover that we were not as they were, but of a lineage of man-and-magic, long-since purged from the realm—and by Glindian law, to be slain upon discovery. I'd thought taking down my hood would instantly bring about my murder or capture, so I did not commit the act without fear.

Lirinda was the first to do it. Perhaps it was because it was her eighteenth birthday that she felt more brazen to defy Mother's command, but she seemed to have made her decision when she saw a handsome Honorable, perhaps a young lord, passing us on horseback upon the cobble-paved street. He spared not a glance to us two ragged, cloak-wearing folk, not until Lirinda's hood came down, and suddenly the summer sunshine brightened tenfold as her golden locks reflected prisms of color, blinding him with her radiance, her outrageous beauty. And her large liquid-green eyes beamed, too, as she smiled coquettishly up at him.

The Honorable man dismounted from his horse at once and ran to Lirinda, asking her name and where she'd come from, for he'd never seen her before. Never in the capital, never at the royal court. He would have remembered.

Against my every protest and plea for her to replace her hood, to retreat from this stranger before Mother returned from the inn and saw us, Lirinda allowed him to kiss her hand and indulged his every question with a mysterious reply that only enamored him more.

The three of us ended up in a stone passageway off the street, where the handsome man courted my sister as any gentleman out of a tale might, clasping her hand in his and begging to see her again. All the while, I nervously watched the street for any sign of Mother's familiar green hood and cloak sweeping into view—for her ever-fearful eyes to rake the crowds like a mother cat for her wayward young.

It was there, in the shade of the passage, where the thundering of horse carriages could be heard upon the road above us, that I succumbed to the temptation of removing my hood, too.

Did Lirinda feel exposed as I did? As though my very flesh sparkled with the secret power I had thrumming through me at all times? It was appalling the man so close to me could not see it, or feel it like a gust of icy wind, but then, he was so besotted by Lirinda's full bosom, so prettily framed by the tie of her cloak at her neck, that he would not notice a tremor of the earth bringing down the buildings all around us.

It did not appear Lirinda felt any fear for her exposure at all, how she tossed her long hair back as she tinkled a pretty laugh. It seemed in that moment, Lirinda had never known our secret life of potions and pine-silhouettes, only the world she often constructed in her fantasies; a world of sweeping ball-gowns and pastel parties. But never was Lirinda so committed to our wild life as I, nor did she show the same magical traits. She was not burdened as I with a constant burn of magic thrumming through her. Never had Lirinda shown any signs of magical inheritance at all, aside from her beauty, so it must have been easier for her to forget—to pretend.

And though in that moment I willed myself to forget, I could not. For I felt strangely as though my magic had never been more potent than it was right there, standing exposed as I was in the city, though none but the man courting my sister could see me. It was like a cold drink of water upon a tongue touched by peppermint—a rush, an arousal, an awareness, almost too much to bear.

I had always felt different in the capital city, but that day I was keenly aware that there might be a reason why. For now, as I hike up the long, twisting path to Mother's garden, hearing but not listening to Lirinda's insubstantial prattle amid the deafening chittering of birdsong, surrounded by a fortress of wind-shaking trees, I feel only what I've always felt: an urgent pulse of my own unique magic, easily disturbed into a dangerous rage that I work constantly to control. But nothing like in the capital, where I felt almost…*purposeful.*

I sometimes allow myself to wonder: *But what purpose could there be beyond Haven?*

"Oh, Sirilda! Are you there, Sirilda?"

Removed from my thoughts, I see Lirinda walks backward ahead of me so that I look at her, at last.

"Did you not sleep well again?" she asks. "You're distant in your own head! Haven't you been listening?"

"Sorry." I feign a yawn into my hand. I had tried long ago to share all my many curiosities with Lirinda but found it easier to simply keep them to myself. She does not understand how all-consuming my power is—how I fear I'll never even begin to explore the surface of its abysmal depth. Whenever I attempt to explain to her, she alters the conversation into something she can understand—usually her many fancies and daydreams.

"What I was saying was…I had that dream again last night!" Lirinda smiles as she dances further along the winding forest path. Dappled shafts of strained autumn sunlight sparkle down through the treetops upon her as she spins about, one arm extended gracefully outward with her basket swinging off the crook of her elbow, her other arm bent to hike up the skirts of her dress. I follow at a slow walking pace.

"Which dream?" I cannot keep a laugh out of my voice. "You have too many."

"The one I always have! The one where I turn into a dove."

"But of course." I purse my mouth to keep the smile from my lips. "And where did you fly this time?"

"*Up.*" Lirinda indicates with a flourishing arm held to the tangled branches above. "Into the clouds. Only they weren't clouds at all. They were bundles of white linen, fragrant and soft. And when I flew into them, they spread into fine tablecloths smoothed over long tables, laden with shining pewter plates and cups. I was sitting, all of a sudden, in a chair before my very own place at the table. Out of nowhere appeared delicious steaming food to eat and ruby-red wine to drink!" She smirks, stopping her dance to reflect fondly. "I woke up with drool beading down my chin."

"So that's why my sleeve was all wet this morning," I muse, crouching down before a great knotted tree and collecting the tiny bones from an owl pellet. Mother will be asking if we'd seen any along the way; I try to predict the things she'll request so that I may avoid her withering stare that sometimes makes me feel useless to her, even if that is not her intention. Lirinda never seems to suffer this as I do, I've noticed. Which would explain why she goes on dancing without a care or a thought as to anything other than herself.

"No dashing gentlemen this time?" I prompt Lirinda, though I do not really listen to her reply. "No handsome strangers to dance with?"

"I woke too soon." Lirinda sighs over her shoulder. "I always wake too soon."

Mother's garden awaits us upon the sunniest, flattest peak of Haven.

For all the day-long sunshine here, it is warmer and more abundant with wildflowers pocking the outside of Mother's gigantic square of neatly sown flora. Although it's warm, I can feel the storm in the air, wet and cold but distant. I'm certain if I were to climb a tree, or hike to a higher peak, I would see the dark clouds rolling in from the west. Already the trees bend to the wind, growing stronger with each gust. A wind that promises change, for winter and death are imminent. It is the time of autumn where one wonders if this is the storm to bring about the great change, the shriveling of the last of the leaves, the bearer of frost, the killing of the crops. It makes my cloak flutter behind me as I get to work, picking from the rows the exact herbs and measurements Mother requires and setting them neatly into my basket.

Life blooms fiercely here in a diverse array of color and size— medicinal plants of all varieties which provide our customers and us with remedies for our ailments; fat, delicious fruit and vegetables to sustain us through the seasons; and magic flora of which the realm of Glindor will never see. For even such plants are forbidden—plants from centuries ago, before all the magic in the realm was burned to ash and the ash buried beneath the new earth. Such magic, even in nature, is forbidden…as are we.

It is a pity these plants are unknown to all but us, for they are so pretty—far prettier and more fascinating than the ordinary flora of the new earth, like the tiny white moonbells that chime sweetly when agitated, even in the softest breeze—or the massive lilac-colored scryflowers, ribbony as peonies and larger than sunflowers, so soft and luscious I always long to press my face into them but do not dare touch their pollen to my skin. Scryflowers provide visions upon burning, and sometimes they emit euphoric, hallucinogenic fragrance in the summer's sun. I never have such vivid dreams as I do the nights after I extract scryflower oil and stopper it. Mother says scryflower is one of her preferred essences in her euthanizing potions.

Of all the spectacular plants Mother grows, and their curious properties, it is the blazing orange-red fire lilies that are Mother's favorite, for when dried and crushed into a fine dust, they create a most useful Flame Powder, which can ignite a persistent and precise flame even upon a river's surface. There were times when Lirinda and I set leaves aflame with the powder and watched them sail down the stream like fiery boats, until after a long while they would catch upon rocks, overturn, and sink, the flame crackling and dousing at last. I pick some fire lilies now—careful, as always, not to burn my hands upon the red-hot stamen.

Indeed, all the loveliest, deadliest, most useful flora of all the realm curl and tower with color and vitality here in Mother's garden, but also wherever her hands will such growth. The entire expanse of Haven blooms with all Mother has touched and nourished with her plant magic. She can even construct the trees and vines to grow to her own intricate design. There are staircases of vine and tree-limb she's constructed for us to travel across over the steep ledges of Haven and bridges woven like lace across cliffs. Garden walls of curling, low-reaching branches allow the climbing plants, like blooming pea and vines of squash and grape, to thrive. Even our own cottage is a living work of continually growing boughs and leaves that have interconnected into a livable dwelling. Mother says that once our cottage had been a mere tree. Seeing how small it is, with rounded wood walls and a moss floor, it is not difficult to imagine.

"Oh, Sirry!" Lirinda calls to me in a taunting sing-song voice from the perimeter of the garden. I look to see that her basket has been discarded and set a pace away from her, empty, and that she stands before the bark of a tree, smirking at me over her shoulder. "I found something for you!"

"Can't it wait?" My impatience for her is difficult to keep folded away after so long. I can feel my power rising in its urgency—a *glug-glug* that thumps with my pulse—as it does whenever there is a flare of my impatience, anger, or jealousy. Seeing her now, my lazy sister, how she ignores her work for constant play and would not receive the disappointed glare that I would if we were to not complete our task, rouses my furious power.

I close my eyes against the urge to release it now. Sometimes when I feel this way, something breaks in the distance. I listen for it, the sound of a branch snapping, a pot shattering, a sunflower slicing halfway down its stem.

"Please, Sirry! Before it flies away."

I drop my basket, exasperated, and walk to her. Of course, it is a large furry white-and-black spotted moth resting upon the tree that she gestures to, and without her explanation, I know exactly what she intends for me to do with it, as it's something she's had me do hundreds of times since we were very young.

"Only for a moment. Mother's expecting us to hurry." I bare my teeth at her as I speak, the frigid-turning wind gusting long black tresses across my face as a reminder of our urgency.

As I focus my gaze upon the moth, it is lifted from off the bark of the tree, and without even a motion of its wings or furry antennae, is levitated into the air opposite where Lirinda stands, expectantly poised to begin a dance, with her knees bent in a curtsy and her hands at the hem of her skirts. As if there's music playing for the pair of them, I maneuver the moth around in the air as if the creature was a willing dance partner to Lirinda. It is a beautiful scene, and I'd imagine if any magicless human were to stumble upon it, they might agree, how she spins opposite the moth amid the tall grass and wildflowers. Like something out of a dream.

Though I'd never admit it to Lirinda, I'm glad she called me to do this, for in order for my power to not become so overabundant that it forces itself unpredictably—and dangerously—out of me, I must exercise it. And I've been feeling the throb all day, growing painfully with each long moment spent too close to Lirinda, which is perpetual. For even at night do we share the same too-small bunk.

So often do I long to be alone, but even in a secret forest like this, privacy is scarce. Lirinda's playful energy bounces around me even when I long to escape it, and Mother's suspicious gaze seems to follow me, even through the eyes of her watchful animal companions, as if she knows I am desperate to expel my power in a wrathful way.

Only a few times has she caught me being wrathful in the past, a state I've only reached at my angriest: felling trees in a fit of rage, even possessing Mother's beloved crow companion to shoot up into the sky and immobilize in the air just before smashing back to the ground. Mother has cradled the exposed roots of sapling trees and called me monstrous for desecrating life, not knowing that sometimes there is nothing I can do to stop it—that tearing trees from the earth is a far better alternative to tearing Lirinda's golden hair from her scalp. These wraths of mine are the only instance, in all my years, to have provoked Mother in such a way that she is so unspeakably disgusted by me that she will not look at me for days. So I do my best always to quash my fury before it rises high enough for Mother to see—and to never dare reveal to her the slightest bit of power that burns at my behest.

She doesn't understand that this power is not a choice for me—not an aggressive trait I can easily pacify by idly weaving baskets, stitching patches upon our clothing, or sniffing a bundle of lavender as she has so suggested. Using it—channeling it—is a necessity just as vital to my existence as using my lungs to breathe. I must release my power, quell its fiery blaze from my aching bones, and I must do it more and more often, for I feel it growing in urgency and strength as I mature into womanhood.

The moth as I maneuver it now is hardly enough weight to sate my burning pulse, so when I release it from my tendrils of power, and its frenzied flutters take it confusedly away from Lirinda's dancing embrace, I still feel my magic boiling beneath the surface. It would satisfy me much more to use it upon something heavier… like raising large rocks into the air or commanding an owl into flight. If only Mother would allow me to better aid her in her city tasks, I may be of use with extracting teeth…especially molars I would love to pull upon. But for now, the rage of my power is satiated enough, and it must be under my control, for tomorrow when we accompany Mother to the capital city, my power cannot be volatile in any way.

As it does every time my power's been spent, the familiar trickle of warm blood oozes at the rim of my nostril. Lirinda sees, but does not truly see, how I wipe it away—wipe away any sight of what burdens me constantly within.

CHAPTER TWO

Cold rain strikes the earth as Lirinda and I scurry back down the path to the cottage. Being far nimbler than my sister, I easily dodge the low-hanging branches and leap like a stag over overgrown fronds of fern trembling in the downpour of rain. The closer I come to the cottage, the more I can hear the wood-and-metallic chiming of Mother's many dangling baubles of stones, tarnished-old pieces of ironmongery, moon-shaped pieces of flotsam and driftwood, all tied on cords from the branches of our roof. By the way they jangle and spin is how Mother tells the direction and speed of the wind, and I see her now standing before the wildly thrashing chimes, the front door of our small rounded cottage thrown wide open. Her arms are crossed at her breast, and she stares at us unforgivingly. Her dark red hair, streaked at her temples with silvery white, hanging long down her back in a plait stiff enough to be a thick rope, is a vivid shock against the greenery. And her dark green cloak swells formidably behind her, her very stature making me wish I could disappear.

"I thought I asked you to make haste," is all she says as

we run by her and into the dry shelter of the cottage, which is hot with steam, the cauldron bubbling upon its hook in the hearth. We set our baskets upon the single table we share for both concoction and meal making.

Quickly, we prepare our ingredients and stir them in the cauldron once it's brought to boil residually upon a cloth on the table, leaving marks of soot, which we always accidentally streak across our cheeks as we wipe our hair from our sweating faces. After only a moment of being inside, our frocks are damp with our perspiration, for a fire rages in the hearth hot enough to make us feel we're burning a fever and have a stomachache, and the bubbling cauldron makes the air too humid to breathe.

It does not help that the cottage is so small, merely a single room of curved wooden walls. Small though it is, it houses all the things the three of us need, with a floor of soft moss at our feet and a ceiling of tightly woven leaves and branches above our heads. And I, being the tallest while also the youngest, sometimes fear that if I were to grow any more, I would have to crouch so as not to hit my head upon one of the branches. It is not so easy for the three of us to walk around in this small space, especially when we hurry to brew potions as we are now, scuttling around like frantic hens, bumping into one another in our haste for ingredients.

At one end of the cottage is the hearth, and before the hearth is Mother's workspace—the table on which the cauldron now rests, bubbling violently. The rounded hearth wall is lined with shelves—shelves of tree-root protrusions climbing up the wood wall, filled disorderly with stoppered glass bottles of all sizes containing assortments of curious organic findings, from preserved owl eyes to fermenting frog spawn. Dangling from the twig-woven ceiling is a multitude of herbs, both the leaves and blooms being hung to dry, making the cottage always smell of a myriad of sharp-and-sweet fragrances, blending into one potent perfume I associate with home. Ladles, spoons, scalpels—and other utensils used for cooking, potion brewing, and even the skinning and butchering of animals—hang from hooks made of antlers and bones. Hanging beside the utensils are the fur pelts we use so often in winter, along with our wooden snowshoes and traveling cloaks. Upon every surface possible are beeswax and pine resin candles we've crafted ourselves, crooked and dripping wax in twisted rivers down the shelves.

The rest of the cottage is a crammed area of storage beneath the loft Lirinda and I share as a bed, constructed of yet more gnarled tree roots growing off the wall. There is no bed for Mother; an old chair facing the fire is where she chooses to sleep…not that I've ever witnessed her sleep, though many times I've tried.

In through the open door flies a flurry of black feathered wings. Lirinda squeals and prances aside as a large crow flies in past her and lands upon Mother's forearm, balancing on a single, scaly foot.

"Yes, Crow, what is it?" Mother asks of the bird distractedly as she reaches her fingers into a clay bowl off one of her shelves. She pinches a tiny amount of Flame Powder between her fingers and sprinkles a delicate amount upon the potion, which shimmers suddenly with low flames upon the surface.

Crow replies in a series of loud, obnoxious caws that make me wince. Lirinda and I pass one another a mutual expression of dislike for the bird. Of all the creatures who come to visit Mother, we find this one-legged crow to be the most irksome, although Crow is the most loyal of all. She is Mother's favorite companion, though I can hardly understand why.

"Thank you," says Mother to the bird and tosses her a mouse tail from the shelf, which she catches in her beak before taking flight back out the door.

"What did she say?" Lirinda asks.

"That it's time." Mother reaches above her head for a dried leaf hanging from the ceiling and crumbles it into the cauldron, which then emits a mushroom of smoke and the smell of burned herbs, the low flames having crackled into a mud-like paste which Mother strains to stir. "The storm is properly placed above us."

After quickly stirring in a final, silvery vial of moonbell extract, which makes the potion shimmery and fluid, Mother instructs us to each wrap our skirts around our hands and heave the heavy iron pot into the rain, now so heavily falling that it drips down our lashes and noses, making us squint our eyes to see. We haul it over to a flat stone upon the ground and lower it upon it.

"Now stand back." Mother holds out her arms to us on either side of her, like a shield, forcing us to step away from the cauldron. She holds us back protectively, just as a blinding-white bolt of lightning pierces down from the heavens and strikes the cauldron so radiantly that I can feel its heat bloom upon my flesh, the booming rupture of atmosphere strong enough to make Lirinda stumble backward. Even with my eyes squeezed closed can I see the flash of light fill the cauldron. Once I open my eyes, squinted with half-blindness and the rain that beads my lashes, I look to the glowing cauldron and see that the liquid within has scorched from metallic to white-hot, then cools slowly to translucent as though it is mere water.

Only when we've heard thunder crackle further east does Mother release us, the earth booming, trees rattling with sound. Lirinda and I try to blink away the searing white of our vision, standing there in the pouring rain while Mother unties her apron and throws it over the cauldron so as to keep the rain from diluting it.

"It's no wonder this potion will earn us enough to last the winter," I say quietly after a long moment, my voice hardly audible above the cacophony of rain pelleting Mother's apron like a drum and jingling all her many baubles hanging from the cottage.

"How dire your customer's need must be, Mother," mutters Lirinda, a little shaken.

With every potion Mother has us brew, we know the graveness for whom it has been made. The more difficult the process, the more desperate the customer. Mother has told us some of the requests her customers have brought to her feet, the tragedies they suffer—the deep losses, abuses, broken hearts—and many a night have I lain awake with my throat choked for them.

"We are right to pity them, my customers," Mother has said tenderly in the past. "But do not let pity ebb your gratitude."

I recall her words when first she explained her transactions to us: a younger Lirinda and me listening with rapt faces as she bottled a bleeding-heart potion for lovesickness. "My services, alas, are for the sorrowful. Without their sorrows, we would not profit enough to survive. That is the way of this world, down to the blowfly born out of decay. Nature is but a cycle of suffering and pleasure; loss and gain; death and life. We can only strive to live gently within its balance."

Now, as Lirinda and I take the ends of our skirts to help carry the cauldron back inside the cottage—the forest echoing with the loud chatter of birds rejoicing upon the cold rain— gratitude fills me for the quiet peace of our life in Haven. How here, in our safe seclusion, we need not be so exposed to the tragedies of man and love.

Lirinda and I spend the rest of the rainy evening simmering a grouse carcass for bone stew, while Mother accounts for all her inventory and prepares for tomorrow's delivery. She pours today's potion into a large flask and labels it with a wax seal. Once we finish supper, I am the one who volunteers to wash the pot in the stream, so magnificent is the rain-washed twilight, and even more magnificent it is to spend it alone. Lirinda prefers to remain indoors, dry and warm, humming as she strings up all the collected fire lily blooms from our baskets to dry from our twig-woven ceiling.

It goes on to rain the rest of the night. The storm stimulates the forest's release of its every scent, and even the soil itself is rich with fragrance. The chill-fresh air makes the cottage warmth all the more welcoming when I return from the stream, my cheeks flushed from the autumn cold. The flickering candles, low-burning hearth, and the warm, savory smell of supper lingering against the cold invigoration seeping in from outside smooths away my gooseflesh at once. As I enter through the door and hang the cleaned pot and my damp cloak upon their antler hooks, I find Lirinda seated at Mother's feet before the fire. She's having her long, pearlescent hair braided. I cannot help but watch how Mother's fingers wind themselves so easily through Lirinda's clean, pretty hair—in such a way she cannot do with my coarse, tangled locks that irritate her so when they snag upon her fingers. I know my hair will be braided next, reluctantly, in an attempt to make it more manageable tomorrow, but my grooming never looks so peaceful a scene as when Lirinda and Mother are together, truly, mother and daughter.

The intimacy between them is something that, for some reason, always makes me feel a pang of hurt. I feel strange, foreign, like I do not belong. But I say nothing as I brew a pot of dandelion root tea for us all to drink before bed. Always, I say nothing. Too tight is my throat, I do not think I could speak if I wished.

As with every time Lirinda sits before the hearth, with Mother's tender fingers at her hair, a rare, delicious giggle shared between them in their low conversation I cannot discern beyond the crackling logs in the hearth, she toys with a shining necklace at her throat, and watches how the facets of the pendant's jewel dances with a fiery glare. For as long as I can remember, my sister has worn this necklace. It is as much a part of her as is her every other golden feature.

"Mother says it belonged to my father," Lirinda once told me, in the singsong braggery of a child still growing in teeth. "Don't you think it the most beautiful treasure in all the world?"

To me, it has always been a most enviable treasure. A dazzling, delicious-looking ruby the size of a cherry stone, set within a rhombic plate of gold, embossed with symmetrically patterned filigree like spiraling willow leaves. The pendant, while exceptionally ornate, is still simple and small enough to hide delicately at Lirinda's breast beneath her frock bodice. The chain at the back of her neck, the same glittering gilt as her own tresses.

Never has a day passed that Lirinda has not stroked the pendant with her fingertips, admiring its shine in the sunlight, firelight, or moonlight by turning it this way and that, and kissing it always before slipping it back into her bodice. Always, her eyes fall starry as she thinks of him, her father, fantasizing about who he must have been to have once possessed such a jewel as a ruby, a stone neither of us have seen except upon the hats and fingers of the wealthiest folk of the capital.

Of course, Lirinda knows nothing more of her father than I know of mine, for Mother has never uttered a detail of either of them. But to have a treasure to hold, to ponder—proof that such paternity exists—is a gift I ache for with the very marrow of my bones.

"Mother must really have loved him, my father," Lirinda had said. "To have kept it all this time…and given it to me."

I once wanted Lirinda's necklace so badly for myself that I would beg her to let me hold it, to slip the delicate gold chain around my thick hair and feel the weight of the cold pendant upon my sternum—to study it as if that might somehow answer riddles of my own mysterious father. And once, when Lirinda had continually refused me out of a sisterly quarrel, I'd been so angry that I had used my power to raise the necklace into the air from around Lirinda's neck, high beyond her reach.

Lirinda had wailed, tears streaming from her eyes, as she jumped in an effort to reach it. I laughed at the struggle, my nose oozing blood into my grimacing teeth, and finally, when I had tormented Lirinda enough, I'd let the pendant plop into the stream. Lirinda scrabbled into the water to retrieve it, her frock soaked and heavy when she climbed out with her prize gripped tightly in her fist, her long hair a silken mess around her reddened face. She pushed by me as she ran off to the cottage to cry to Mother.

Once Mother knew I had used my power to torment my sister, she had me work all of Lirinda's chores for a sennight while Lirinda was able to laze around more than usual, stroking her necklace with even more infuriating fondness; for days Mother would not look at me nor speak to me. I've not used my power to offend Lirinda since.

I look away from the necklace now, to avoid the jealousy I always feel for it—that I have nothing, not a clue to the mystery of my own father except the stark blackness of my ever-longing eyes.

"I've decided something," Lirinda says to me. Mother has stepped outside, as she does every night, to bid goodnight to the animals in their trees and burrows and see that everything in Haven is tucked away and in order. Lirinda and I undress from our dirty work frocks and into our nightshifts, our long hair plaited and our feet bare upon the moss floor.

"What is it?" I ask patiently.

"I'm going to fall in love tomorrow," says she with honey-sweet certainty as she climbs up into our bunk and slips under the patch-leaf quilt stuffed soft with feathers, dandelion seeds, and thistledown.

I want to laugh and scold her all at once, but instead I say nothing as I blow out the many candles one by one, until the low burning flames of the hearth are the only source of dim orange light, throwing everything into long, quivering shadow. I can see her eyes in the dark glinting with her fantasy.

There is so much I want to say to her, but it is all contradictory. I wish for my sister to be happy, and I wish she could so easily fall in love with someone who might provide her with all the love she requires and a comfortable home somewhere. She deserves romance, to be a mother, and to entertain parties and wear gowns like she so desires. Even if she were to be a poor fisherman's wife, she would be better suited to loving and mothering than never knowing such things. After all, she's nineteen, and to wither away in Haven would be a waste of her vibrant will. Perhaps that is her greatest fear—to wither away without ever being known.

I am also afraid. I'm afraid for Lirinda to reveal what she is—that she'll bring about a tragic end before these dreams of hers can ever begin. I'm afraid that, although Lirinda desires more than Haven can give, it is the safest place for her. For all of us. And it does us harm to ever think of another life beyond this one.

I climb up onto the bunk and lay beside her. The sewn mattress of straw, feathers, leaves, and thistledown yields to my long, bony body as I struggle to find a position that is comfortable. The longer my limbs have grown—having made me taller than any of the women I've before seen in the capital and even some of the men—the more I realize there is no comfortable position beside Lirinda.

I wonder, sometimes, if I will ever sleep in my own bed. But the thought is so foreign that it terrifies me. To not sleep here, like this, is as unimaginable as it would be to sleep upon the moon.

"Do you think we will ever not be here?" Lirinda asks after a long while of silence, looking above at the ceiling of living interwoven branches; a pretty orbweaver busies herself with her web just above our noses, irritated with how our sleepy exhales flutter the silk like a caught moth.

Lirinda and I have thought of this so often that I know just what she means. Of course, we've both been curious to know more than the limits of Haven, but the thought of ever knowing another sound than the constant pulse of forest noise around our cottage is a concept we cannot imagine. Thrilling though it is to try to think of sleeping beneath another ceiling, perhaps one of dead dry-wood boards and no spiders, we both know it would be frightening. Never have we not closed our eyes to the chime of crickets like soft bells, the soothing rush of distant streams, and the sweet chatter of Mother's animal companions in the dark. Indeed, I wonder, too, if ever there might ever come a day that I reflect upon these nights of such unchanging sameness and long for them.

"Where else could we be?" I answer, turning upon my side to see that Lirinda is already nearly asleep. So easily she dozes—so easily she falls into dreams. I wonder what it would be like to not have thoughts and compulsions to keep me awake all night.

Mother returns to the cottage, and I feign sleep as I do every night, and only when Mother takes her seat before the hearth do my eyes open again, watching the unmoving shadow Mother casts upon the gnarled ceiling. From years of this routine, I know Mother will go the entire night without moving, except to add another log to the fire or prod the embers for a flame.

Except for, once every few months, when Mother thinks me as deep in slumber as Lirinda, and she collects her needle and thread and works at her embroidery upon our cloak hoods. With the change of season, she cuts out the old thread and stitches something new: designs of lovely flowers and leaves to complement the season at hand, like clover for summer and snowberry for autumn. With each new embroidered design, I have witnessed how she pricks her finger with the needle to draw blood and weaves in the shining, sacred droplet with every purposeful stitch so that the thread gleams in the firelight.

I dwell not on this strange habit of hers as she has too many of them to inquire about, and the ones of which I have asked have scarcely received answers themselves. So I have learned to accept that my mother is peculiar, especially at night, and she guards her many mysteries and secrets like an egg guards its yolk.

I know better than to pry after any of them.

From the times I have crept a peek at her through the dark, I know there is no emotion to be read upon her shadow-draped face all the night long when she sits before the fire, and that her staring eyes are heavy as always—heavy with memories, perhaps. Painful or pleasant or both all at once, I've never been able to tell, but I wonder every night what images dance in the fire that she watches so intently.

I don't know much about her, my mother. Only that her name is Mora, and that she was raised by her own Magic mother—a cruel woman, she often says—who taught her most of the things she knows. But what happened from that point, wherever and whenever it was, is all mystery. Though we've asked, she's never once told us what her life was like before Lirinda and I were born, or where our anonymous fathers fit into the story, whoever they were… and whether they're still alive.

My gaze returns to my sleeping sister. How beautiful she looks, her features blurred in the shadows except for the faint outlines of her soft lips and long lashes. She seems to be smiling; another lovely dream.

I can almost feel them, her dreams, just by looking at her shadowed face. Sometimes, if I focus on a point where our skin touches, I feel as though I can visualize Lirinda's dreams, or see her memories flash before my very own eyes. I focus now upon where Lirinda's warm knee wedges between my rib and protruding hip, feeling my power move a little at my command, like a breeze running through me and into Lirinda, so gently that it would only make a blade of grass flutter. In my mind's eye, I see Lirinda in an outrageous frilled gown, dancing amid a group of others dressed like her. The floor beneath them is polished, reflecting their synchronized spins; the swirling of the skirts; the delicate placing of slippered feet. I can almost hear music.

When at last I retract myself from Lirinda's vision and simply melt into the warmth of our slumberous embrace, taking in the comforts of our home in the shadow-flickering dark, of Mother sitting so near to us I can sense her protective presence, I am seized suddenly by a cold, dreadful feeling. I look to Lirinda's innocent face again so close to mine and am filled with a grim awareness that life may not always be this way. Surely it cannot. If ever Lirinda manages to leave our life, I will never sleep so near to her like this again; the sacred life the three of us share would be broken.

I cannot imagine such a fracture of our life, yet I also sense one is soon to come. Too old Lirinda and I are becoming for this life of our childhood to continue. I wish I could halt time, stopper the sounds and smells of this moment in one of Mother's potion vials, for I feel imminent grief for this moment surrounds me. Perhaps it is the quiet crispness of autumn I sense that fills me with the terror of change. Yet as cold and fearful as the feeling makes me, I am equally curious for what a destiny could look like for us all.

CHAPTER THREE

A cloud has settled low over Haven this morning, and we walk through the wisping white air with our baskets of carefully packaged potions hooked upon our arms. The fragrant sacks of dried herbs, leaves, and blooms we've harvested over the months hang from straps slung over our shoulders, as do the rolled-up pelts we've skinned from the creatures who've died over the summer. The potions in my basket clank; I stop walking to adjust the cloth surrounding the glass vials so as to keep them secured.

Lirinda exhales a deep breath of steam. In the early light, still gray but for the first glow of dawn gilding the silhouettes of eastern trees, I can discern that the reddening of leaves has deepened since yesterday.

"Such a cold morning." Lirinda breathes another hot gust, this time into her cupped hands. "I ought to have brought my mittens. Mother, might we go back for them?"

"No, no, no." Mother nearly smiles. "The day will be warm soon enough, and you will regret having to carry them."

Lirinda and I have walked along this path enough to know

that Mother is right, although the rising sun will not seek out the cold shadows of forest for hours yet. The peaks and open ground surrounding Haven will be touched first by the ascending sun's warmth and have their mist evaporate into gold sunshine, but still the wet-cold crevices we'll meander through in our mountainous descent, between crags of dripping rock and damp-dark understories, will keep our noses running with the still-frigid air. For these first hours, I will be glad for the heavy wool of my cloak and the deep hood over my head, but once we descend from the labyrinth of damp shade and come out where we are at the mercy of the brilliant autumn sun, I will not be so glad of it.

Morning chirrups of birds echo across the mountain and sweeten the misty air. We talk not, for Mother is too concerned with what the birds are saying, and Lirinda breathes more hot steam upon her hands. I am glad of their silence. Walking the long path to the edge of Haven is one of my life's delights, for I so enjoy the sights of the changing trees who feel to me like kin, going through their seasons as we humans tend to do, too; the deer I see, grazing up the grassy mountainside, lifting their heads to acknowledge us, flicking their ears and chewing their cold clovers, are our generous friends. Most exciting to me is that, with every step we take from home, the more intense a deep, magical sensation becomes, swirling unseen within the tufts of mist, emanating from the surrounding trees. It is a magic like dark wet soil, of flowers yet to open, of powerfully spreading roots and the whispers of the deepest, most ancient trees; a magic I would recognize anywhere upon the earth—the magic of my Mother.

The magic of Mother's Boundary radiates around us through the tangle of trees. Even before the Boundary can be seen can I feel it, and so bone shudderingly strong it is to me that I wonder if Lirinda, or even Mother herself, feel it as I do. For even my teeth seem to rattle the closer to it I get, and I feel I may weep. It is almost as though a song plays through the plants, so eerily high-pitched in its whining that I doubt any but the insects could hear it.

Why, then, am I so affected? I wonder if, perhaps, it is but another depth of my power I may never understand. A sensitivity of my own curious magic.

Mother's magic, though far more developed and understood than mine, is still such a mystery to me. Capable she is of plant magic, as naturally as if she was a plant herself, as well as her possession of animal tongues and ears, being able to commune with the birds in the sky and even the bears lumbering through the berry brambles. These things I know so well. But what I do not understand is how Mother enchanted a boundary around Haven, a wall of magic that prevents so much as a sound from entering or exiting, so that no man can ever trespass upon our sacred home, and likewise, so that Lirinda and I can never willingly leave.

Perhaps the answer lies in another kind of magic Mother has refused to teach us, such as blood magic or shadow magic. I have heard her, offhandedly, mention such practices, but when Lirinda and I have asked about them, she claims to know nothing of them—although I suspect she does know.

Now that I am nearly a fully grown woman myself, I'm beginning to notice there are several things Mother refuses to tell us sisters, which may play together into some greater secret. Such as why she's never told us of our fathers, or why I feel more powerful in the capital city, when contrarily I am to be kept from it.

We have reached the Boundary wall when I feel so overcome by Mother's magical essence that I am rendered immobile—incapable of moving any further away from Haven, and the only possible motion is to cower back toward home. Such is the purpose of the Boundary.

Mother easily strides to the invisible wall that surges with her magic. She holds her hands out to one of the great trees before her—a thick, tall pine towering into the mist above: the tree she uses as the doorway to the Boundary, which sends her power thrumming through a circuit of trees surrounding Haven. It is with this tree that she releases and restores her enchantment. She then closes her eyes in the serene, characteristic way that means she is connecting to a plant, either willing it to grow or healing it. As she focuses, the humming of the Boundary diminishes until the intense radiation of magic is all but gone, and I am relieved of my agony. Mother opens her eyes and releases her embrace upon the tree, the signal that we may step forward.

Always, it is strange when we take a step beyond Haven. For Lirinda and myself especially, our gait is precarious over the opened Boundary. The side beyond, the outside world, is unsettlingly foreign to us. It even feels colder, fresher, sweeter, so much noisier.

Once we've all cleared the threshold of the opened Boundary, Mother returns to the backside of the same tree as before and replaces the enchantment throughout the entire perimeter. I feel that bone-buzzing radiation restore once again and surge down the line of trees that make up the Boundary; the inaudible whining-song makes me wince. In the same instant, the familiar feeling of home, the smells and sounds I know so well have seemingly gone from the earth. And how vulnerable it feels to be at the whim of the world now, unprotected in a realm that is bloodthirsty for my and my family's demise.

Just as Mother likes, the capital as we come upon it is slow running, the market square uncrowded, and the folk about it the usual merchants selling wool and wine, pottery and spices. The rowdier crowds linger in the dingier streets outside the pubs and brothels, drunk still from the night before. But where Mother has us go, the stone-paved streets are swept clean but for the leaves falling upon them and skittering in the chilly sea breeze, faintly whirling in from over sun-bleached rooftops and between the maze of streets and passageways from where the sea crashes at the edge of the city. I've never seen it but have always wondered what it must look and sound like, and from the salty taste of the air, I think I would quite like to see it for myself one day if I can.

Few people have come today, fewer than usual, and I wonder why. But when I overhear a conversation at a beekeeper's table, about how they are setting up their wares early for the festival tomorrow, I understand today is the calm before an uproarious storm and think Mother clever for her timing.

"Which festival is tomorrow, Mother?" I ask of her, and Lirinda, who had been wishfully eyeing some ribbons at a cart, whips her head around to me.

"Did you say *festival?*"

"None that would be of any benefit to us," Mother answers quickly. Then, in almost a whisper, she adds, "If there is one day a year that we ought to stay as far away from the eyes of others, it's tomorrow."

"Why? It's not some ancient Magic-killing celebration, is it?" Lirinda muses, and to our surprise, Mother nods.

"That is precisely what it is."

Lirinda and I are quiet then, Lirinda looking sullenly down at her feet, stung yet again by another prospect for fun being lost to her. I glance curiously around me, so bewildered that these people I see would ever celebrate such a monstrous thing. I wonder if they've ever given it a thought.

"It's the Gillin's Day festival," Mother mutters over our shoulders as we continue to walk toward the great fountain in the center of the market square, where we usually depart one another and meet again. The rush of water drowns out her voice from any eavesdroppers.

Our eyes find the metal-plated armor of a Glindian guard walking along the adjacent street, glaring in the sun. His gaze through his helmet is sharp, as though searching for any sign of magic. We hold our breath collectively until he passes, sparing no glance to us, the three hooded women at the fountain with bags of dried flowers on their backs.

"The day honors the first king of Glindor, *Gillin*," Mother begins quietly as she unfastens the pelts and sacks slung from around her shoulders and sets them upon the wide rim of the fountain.

Fortunately, Gillin and his history is not among the information Mother has withheld from us before; I know enough about Gillin to understand he is the very reason for the hood over my head; I know that he was the one who had long ago usurped the land from the Shade King Rinma, and began the eradication of our kind from the realm; that Gillin's descendants, the kings who have inherited the throne after him—the Glindians—have sought to destroy any of us who remain, and succeeded.

It has been centuries since the purging of magic, and even still, the people of Glindor celebrate its removal from the realm. 'Purity' they call it—pure from any fleck of magic. They remain vigilant for any sign of magic remaining, even down to the quality of the soil and the flora that grows from it, such as

Mother's fire lilies and moonbells, flowing with the breeze in her secret garden now, protected, of course, by her Boundary.

Not long ago, the Pures used to string us Magics up in the streets and perform a 'Burning of the Blood' ceremony, but none have been caught in years, unless of course…we are the only ones left. Mother once explained that perhaps there are more of us, but they hide as we do. We would not know otherwise.

"Is it truly so horrible?" Lirinda asks, her eyes wide and heavy with both fear and the foolish hope that, perhaps, Mother is simply being paranoid as usual—that the festival is actually quite accommodating, even to us. And that she may find herself among it one day.

"I suppose it's not so horrible for the Pures. It's a most glamorous, ridiculous holiday. In the capital, there is a parade and a cavalcade of the king and his court. Then, in the castle, the king hosts a grotesque party that spans for days, celebrating the blood spilled, that even thousands of jugs of animal blood are poured and burned in some revolting ritual," Mother whispers, then adds, "Or so that is what I have heard."

Mother once explained to me that the Pures think magic is only eradicated if blood is first drained from the body and then burned for hours until only ash remains, then the ash washed away by water that has been prayed over by a Receiver, a priest for the Pures. And that over the centuries, the Pures painstakingly bled, burned, and rinsed the blood of every magic human and animal alike from the face of the earth. Even the trees of the ancient forests had been burned similarly. The ground itself was burned and blessed for the Pures to reconstruct this land in the way they wished, and with the plants and animals they themselves selected.

I am reminded, as I look around at the immense city and all its towering buildings—even the landscapes in the distance—

how everything in this new Pure world was built over what had been burned away before. Always I have wondered what the Magic realm would have looked like. Mother had once heard from her own mother that the trees were so gigantic that many humans dwelled in them like vertical villages, and so wide were the trees' canopies that the understory was a world of constant twilight. And that before Gillin upheaved the earth, reshaping it to his design, the climate of the realm was a mild one. So much colder it is now, with abnormal patterns of weather, that it supposedly snows here upon the sea.

There is something about that ancient world I sense, especially when I am in the capital. In that same sensation, I feel something within my power flare delightfully. How much more strongly would I feel it without my hood, I wonder.

Lirinda and I stand in our usual place beside the textile merchant with our baskets of feathers and herbs and await our usual customers. Dressmakers love the selection of feathers we bring, so taken they are with the fine quality of the plumage and bright unblemished color—all collected from where they've gently fallen upon the forest floor—that they usually buy the whole basket's worth. Apothecaries appreciate the perfectly dried leaves and blooms for their tinctures and teas as they've been harvested at the peak time for potency and are so fragrant even now, filling our corner of the street with perfume, competing with the soiled hay from the pig and sheep pens.

Mother sees that trade today is slow and predictable, so she allows us to sell the rest of our wares—the pelts, the oils, the fungi—within the safe, open breadth of the market square while she precariously sweeps into the nearest inn, glancing at us over her shoulder several times, ensuring the street is still drowsy-paced before the heavy doors close behind the final swirl of her cloak.

Today, she'll likely be hours long with her secret consultations, taking potion orders for the spring. Perhaps while she is there, meeting customers in the shadows of the back room, with her hood halfway concealing her down-tilted face, there may be an illness to attend—a festering wound to be cleaned with a frosty-cool drop of potion, a growth to be dissolved with an oil compress—or an expectant mother in need of midwifery. Lirinda and I know not to expect her until the sun has crossed more than half the sky.

This time, as she disappears from our view, I am filled with anxiety that something terrible may happen in her absence. But Lirinda's tugging grasp upon my wrist lurches me into playfulness, forgetfulness, ignorance.

"Let's go, Sirry!"

People on ladders hang banners across the street for tomorrow. I see a cart of fireworks being pushed into the market square and overhear excited talk for where they will be lit at sundown tomorrow—how they will explode magnificently in front of the castle so that the royal court can see them all the way from the highest windows and balconies. It is King Gastlin's wish, they say.

I glance up to the sky, where I can always find the towering spikes of the castle looming like a threat over me. Over the years, I have trained myself not to look up at it, not to acknowledge its influence, but it is always there with its sharp turrets and towers of glaring-bright pale stone.

When I look up at the castle, so high atop a mountain and piercing up into the clouds, I feel a strange, forbidden twinge within myself. Acknowledging the castle's obvious beauty is not why I feel strange, however. Nor is it the fact that Gillin was the one who had it built, and that his descendants, the Glindians, the very enemy of the blood in my veins, reign there still. What feels most strange to me is that, despite all these horrors, I have always felt a pull toward the castle. A desirous sparkle of my power. Almost as though something deep and dark beckons me there, and perhaps me alone.

Surely, what I feel is anger, revulsion. And my power...my power surely longs to destroy the castle, not seek it.

It is when we have distanced ourselves far enough from Mother's potential gaze that Lirinda's hands tentatively go to her hood and slip it from her head. It seems in that instant that everyone upon the street, who had paid her no mind before, each swivel where they stand and breathe in the beauty of her beaming gold locks and demure, sweetly pursed smile. They watch her raptly as she passes them by.

I shake my head at her. "You're mad."

"Oh, Sirry, it feels so lovely to have the warm sun on my hair. The sunlight here isn't so cold as Haven's." She spins as she walks ahead of me, trotting into a little dance that a group of children giggle at.

I glare around suspiciously as the people around us cheer and praise her.

"Rinda, stop!" I hiss desperately after her and realize as I do so that I'm being ridiculous as Mother. Lirinda is simply smiling and twirling as usual, and no one suspects a thing of her or me. Though it's unsettling, I refuse to kill what little fun my sister has.

One of the children offers her a dandelion they've picked from growing between the stone flanks of the street. Lirinda bends down graciously to take it from them, offering a curtsy that the people of the street applaud at.

My mouth twitches with the urge to smile for her, but it is a pursed frown I bear. My teeth grit with my anxiety.

An idly standing musician has caught sight of Lirinda's playful dance and has brought the bow of his instrument to its strings, creating a vibrating, joyful song that fills the street. Seeing her long, glossy hair bounce in the sunlight makes my own scalp desperate for me to remove my hood, to feel the fresh sea breeze and warm autumn sun. To free myself.

But I stay my hands. I am not the sister who is able to flounce about so easily. Lirinda is the one who is entitled to play. Lirinda is the sister who fears no consequence. And I am the daughter who must bear the fear and worry for our mother, the secrets of our family. Always, it is me who watches and waits while Lirinda is fawned over. I stand back from the gathering crowd that begins to energize in dance along with her, a watching shadow, a dark-hooded wraith in comparison. Am I forever bound to be the one in the hood while my sister dances?

Though I long to break free of my restriction, I do not trust what removing my hood would do, for last time it awakened my power tenfold—and just now, I have begun to feel that power sting in my fingertips, simmering with rising urgency with my pulse.

Not now, I plead with myself, squeezing my fingers into fists beneath my sleeves. I bite my lip with anxiety, for I know that once my power has begun to rise, as it does so easily when I am agitated, there is no ridding myself of it without its violent release.

In vain, I attempt to calm myself while Lirinda dances and giggles among the children, but my power only rises more with the infuriating heat of the sun, my hood roasting me like an oven. And, perhaps, with that unknown, insistent force I feel simmering so strongly around me, here, in the capital— so much more strongly than in Haven. Interminable is this moment. I cannot stand here, near to bursting, for another breath of my lungs.

Without another thought, I weave nimbly between the dancers and reach Lirinda in the center.

"Rinda, we have to go," I growl urgently to her once I reach her side. She hardly sees me as she looks up into my hood-shaded face.

"But why?" Her voice cracks with dulcet plaintiveness, so like one of the children she dances for. "We've only just begun down the street! Mother won't be out for longer still."

I glance around at the surrounding people who would soon see my power if I did not flee from them now.

"*I* have to go," I plead out of my desperation. In what little attention she pays me, I believe she understands what I insinuate. Comprehension trickles through her and she nods.

"I will meet you back at the fountain," she promises. She tucks a stray strand of hair behind her ear; I see the dandelion has been placed there. She blinks at me with her full attention now. "Before the sun reaches the tower of that chapel building just there." Lirinda indicates with a quick flourish of her fingers to an ornate stone building towering over the timbered structures around it. "Surely Mother won't be out until then. We'll still have plenty of time."

I nod curtly back and storm away from her down the street, wringing my hands desperately beneath my sleeves. I feel my dark-gray cloak swell behind me as I weave aggressively between merchants and street corners, and I take myself as far away from the open sunniness of the market square as I can, but not quickly enough. I hear a ceramic pot crack down the street—and another and another. Suddenly an entire stack of them shatters, to the merchant's audible roar, and I turn and sneak down a dark tunnel, following a series of lonesome, dark streets. With my hands gripped

into trembling fists, I slither hastily through them until I am
perfectly alone.

CHAPTER FOUR

By the time I have woven myself deeply between dark and seemingly abandoned stone buildings, my burning power is at its absolute cusp before it ruptures from me. I have ensured that I am somewhere unseen, somewhere safe and far enough away from Lirinda and Mother so as not to relate myself to them in any way should I be caught. A dead-end at a stone wall is where I stand and wring my hands painfully, sparkling with pain in every measure of my meat and flesh, trying with all my might to hold it in a little longer so I might find something, an object, through which to expel it—but the scene around me is barren but for buildings; no trees to uproot, no animals to levitate.

I can only close my eyes and cower inward before the squall erupts.

White-hot power seeps out of me like the breaking of a dam, a slow rush at first spilling through, then gaining into a crash, an explosion of energy. I can feel the ground rumble at my feet, like a dozen horses cantering by. I hear the stone buildings tremble around me and heavy matter clatter to the ground and break. Then, it is over. The pain, the blinding of my senses, all of it is alleviated as though it never was.

I open my eyes, fearful I'll see a crowd of people before me, gawking at me with horror, shielding their children from me and pointing me out to the massively armored Glindian guard with crackling screams. But all I see is dust rolling through an empty alleyway and broken stones littering the ground. I glance up to see that a chimney upon one of the weak old buildings has collapsed, and that it was the source for the tumbling stones. But there is no one, not even the sound of a voice.

I let my head fall back against the wall behind me and close my eyes again, sighing my relief. When I inhale again, it is with a gasping cough from all the dust. I wave my hand before my face and storm back through the alley, escaping the scene of my destruction for another empty street I turn down to walk, dusting the evidence from my cloak, furtively glancing around me for anyone who might be watching. The toe of my boot kicks aside some broken stone and its echo against the surrounding brick walls is the only sound for many streets yet. I wonder where I am, how many streets I hurried through past the market square. It did not seem as though I had gone so far, but so insistent I was to escape, I spared no attention to my route.

The decrepit stone buildings in this part of the city are crooked in their age, and their darkened filth makes me aware of how clean the market square is kept. Yet another tactic of Mother's. How well she seems to know the capital, I muse, down to its cleanest most predictable streets, culture, and trends. It rouses my curiosity for Mother's life before my own, and I wonder whether she's walked these same streets before. It isn't so difficult to imagine her green cloak meandering between dirty buildings, her crimson hair falling in strands before her cautious eyes.

A warm tickle at the rim of my nostril compels me to wipe at my nose with my sleeve. I see a smear of red and hear the drips strike the ground with my walking stride.

I wipe at it again, feeling the blood smear up my cheek, where the sea breeze is cold upon it. I try buffing it into my flesh, and hope any trace of it is rubbed away, for Mother knows what my noseblood means—what I've done, what I've been unable to control. If she knows I've released my power here, in the city, I know she'll never allow Lirinda or me to accompany her here again.

Dogs bark down the next street. People shout from out their windows. Rather than banners, laundry is strung across the street to dry, but the laundry is not whole and fresh, but shredded-worn garments still stinking of filth. Rather than tanneries and baked bread I smell cooking grease and the faint ammonia of urine. I grip the thorn-and-rosehip embroidered hem of my hood with my fingers, pulling it further down over my head before I turn down the next street.

My eyes are downcast as I walk coolly past a group of raucously laughing men. I do not allow myself a glimpse of what they look like, but they smell of sweat and feces. Further down, there are women who call to them in nasty, sing-song voices. These women do not smell much better. As I pass them and ignore their calls to me, too, I recall what Mother has told me of prostitutes. *Slaves with the illusion of a choice,* she'd said. I sneak a glimpse at their faces, seeing rotted teeth, sore-pocked cheeks. The legs they reveal from under their skirts are bare and smattered with bruises.

Perhaps they had been stolen into the slave trade when they were young, and when they were older and discarded from their masters, they felt the whoring of their flesh was their only choice to survive. As I ignore their taunts to me, I pity them. I wish that I could help them, but all I am capable of is destruction.

With each street that I don't recognize, my throat tightens. I think of Lirinda who is alone and waiting for me. And Mother, who will soon be finished with her errands in the inn and will wonder where I've gone—why I've left Lirinda alone.

I hope that, if I've not returned to her in time, Lirinda will have replaced her hood and come up with a clever excuse for Mother as to my whereabouts. I squinch my face at the unlikeliness of this. Oh, foolish Lirinda. I wish we'd discussed a plan beforehand. Always this was bound to happen, and unless I somehow learn to control my power, will likely happen again.

I raise my gaze to the sky to judge the sun's placement, curious how much time has passed, but see the sun has vanished behind a thick, steely cloud. The sea breeze blows colder now, ushering clouds across the blue sky, and I find it ironic that the cooler day could not have arrived sooner. If not for the agonizing sunshine as I watched Lirinda's ridiculous twirls, I may not be in this predicament.

Still, I scan the sky for a glow of sun, a clue as to my direction, but see only innumerable rooftops and buildings undulating like hillocks around me. Dizzyingly narrow, disorienting me, so unlike the forest where wind and shadows quake and contrast every last surface with clear direction— where moss and birdsong will always lead me home. So close are the roofs, buildings, and interconnecting bridges and tunnels here, that I cannot see my mountain, the mountain of Haven. I turn in circles as I walk, trying to distinguish east from west. The only fixed landmark in the sky that I have to guide me are the glaring white turrets of Gillin's castle, stretching impossibly high into the darkening clouds. I could not escape them, hide from them, even if I wished.

I glower up at it from beneath the hem of my hood with disdain, untrustworthiness, and curiosity—as if the castle itself was a sentient stranger who knows me, what I am, wandering the streets alone.

Yet, I feel not alone. For there is a constant presence, here in this chaotic maze of walls and street. It is that ancient feeling I have felt when I have come to the capital, but never have I wandered this far, experienced it this strongly—a hum of power unrelated to my own, that courses like a current through the stone all around me. The deeper into the capital I unwillingly wander—or perhaps it is willingly—the stronger it becomes.

I hunger to follow it, this feeling. I wish I needn't return to the fountain, to Lirinda, or even to Mother. I wish I could wander like this for hours into the evening, allowing only the keenness of my magic to guide me.

But what ever could it be? Something ancient and secret? Something benevolent to magic…or perhaps even a malicious lure to our capture? I am not fool enough to think I could trust it, but I wish I could discover it all the same. A creature or an object or a nameless entity of open space, calling like a beacon to the flecks of magic in my blood.

The pull is stronger than ever before, and I am tempted to remove my hood. To receive it. What would it feel like to surrender? To relinquish my urgency; to feel my hair lift gently from my nape in the cold wind and flutter behind me like the many white flags of Glindor I see; to feel the true guidance of that mysterious force. Wherever would it take me if I let it?

Lirinda removed hers just moments ago. Why shouldn't I?

My hands go to my hood. I glance cautiously over each of my shoulders, seeing no one around me in this empty, barren alley, then I let it slip over my coarse-curled black hair, allowing my tresses in their freedom to unfold and flop down to my lower back and flow with my cloak in the delicate wind.

The jolt of power that runs through me is instantaneous. I gasp with it; so painfully aware of it I become. Is this how I truly am? Unfettered? This strength I feel, is this mine or it is a gift from my invisible benefactor? And how strange that my power's pulse is beating again, a slow drum, not out of fury or jealousy as usual, but in a way that is almost sensual, and pangs me pleasurably in ways I've only briefly fantasized that I might feel with a lover. Caressing hands of magic pull me into this sightless embrace, urging me on, to find its source.

But when I hear a man's voice so near to me, the voice as clear as the tolling of a bell on a bright day, I am removed from my pleasure with a sharp intake of breath, and quickly I throw my hood back over my head.

A group of men descend at the end of the street from a flight of stone steps. I hide myself behind a wide column of brick before they can see me as they walk up my desolate street.

I can smell the fine leather of their doublets and knee-high boots from where I hide, my back pressed to the column, and already I can guess they are very wealthy lords, if not Honorables. Honorables, who might as well be royalty; their families favored by Glindian kings for centuries; their forefathers having aided Gillin in his overtaking of this realm. As their lineage can be traced to the beginning of Glindor, and they are thus proven to not have any trace of magic, they are deemed the purest of the Pures besides the king himself.

"Shall we go for another round?" asks one of the men brightly. "Didn't you say there's a tavern down here that brews an especially dark ale?"

I cannot resist a careful crane of my neck to spy upon them as they come closer to my view, my hood casting shadows over my curious face.

So importantly poised they are, the swords in their scabbards dangerously long, perhaps only for the purpose of killing someone like me. There is something caught on the cool autumn wind, a spice of their masculine essence that intoxicates me like I imagine a hot drink of liquor might. Compelled I am to watch them—one of the men in particular, the tallest of the three, and... I realize with a flush that is not quite lust, but a fascination that deprives the breath of my lungs...the most beautiful.

I'm unsure why I feel so drawn to him, to study his face as he smiles among whom I can only presume are his friends, for they make him grin, commanding his strong-chiseled jaw to flex. He flicks curled, shoulder-length dark-brown hair from out his eyes, also brown but shining copper with the scarce fractures of sunlight beaming from between the shifting clouds above. His eyebrows are dark and bushy, ferociously expressive. Years of athleticism are revealed through his strong girth, visible from the wide shoulders of his intricately laced doublet and his close-fitting breeches handsomely shaped with his strong legs.

He is the one who speaks next, and it is his voice which rings like bells with such clear authority, my eyes threaten to smart.

"Aye. None of the court, other than you three, know of it, and I hope to keep it that way. So we oughtn't tell anyone who we are."

"You don't think they'd recognize their own king walking up to their bar?"

"You would be surprised at how few know me by face alone," is his reply.

I slink my back to the column and bate my breath. *The king?*

"Shall we go there then, Your Majesty?"

"I shouldn't like to be drunk so early. Still, there is much revelry to be had into the night and even the morrow. I should not like to have it spoiled."

"Aye, Your Majesty. If we're stupid-drunk by nightfall, how can we properly amuse ourselves with all the beautiful women until dawn?"

They laugh together, obviously already feeling light and joyous from drink, and disappear down the next street.

I stand there breathing, rigid, frozen, with the exception of my heart, which pounds hot with fear and interest. *The king.*

King Gastlin, descendant of Gillin.

He who, like his fathers before him, keeps this realm free— *pure*—of magic. He, who has likely seen dozens bound and hung for the Burning of the Blood and has likely been the one to spill it himself. That sword in its scabbard, bouncing with his proud strides, has certainly touched the innards of those not so different from me. Women… children. Innocent.

My frozenness thaws with a feeling of sickness churning in my belly. My hands at my sides tremble, and my breath comes in, shuddering, like I might weep and laugh all at once. I'm disgusted enough to vomit. Why then do I feel tempted to follow him?

Though I peer around the column for him once more, I, of course, cannot slink as I want to down the next street, watching his progress from behind columns and alley corners. I must hurry to meet Lirinda. How she will gasp delightedly when I tell her what, *whom,* I've seen. I smirk at the thought of how, for the years to come, we will whisper in the shadow of our bunk as I recount to her the image of the King of Glindor.

At last, after wandering through still more streets, I ascend a staircase, which leads me to a higher level of the city, lending me a broader view of all I've passed and have yet to go. I am able to find the market square and memorize a path to reach it.

I slither between peddlers, families, musicians, and

merchants to reach the wider streets that seem so clean now in comparison. I check at the sun's place in the sky and am relieved to see it is only a hair's breadth from reaching the tower. However…when I run to the fountain at last, its sparkling spray of water and rumbling noise a relief to my senses, it is to find that Lirinda is nowhere in sight of it.

CHAPTER FIVE

I have always been able to sense my sister.

Half-sister though she may be, I am tethered to her essence in such a way that whenever she would hide from me in our seeking-games throughout Haven, by climbing trees and between crevices of rock, even crawling into the moist-dark dens of our animal friends, I have always followed that nectar-sweet trace of her and found her instantly. Like how Mother's essence is of fresh damp soil and fragrant herbs, Lirinda's is honey and flower pollen warmed by a midsummer sun. No matter where Lirinda has been, every one of her hiding places far beyond my reach of sight and sound—for even sometimes I've blindfolded myself and covered my ears to test my senses— her essence I have easily been able to perceive, to follow.

But now, as I stand at the rim of the fountain, searching in every which direction from the market square for a glimpse of her dark, daisy-embroidered wool hood, or even a flash of her yellow hair, if she is stupid enough to have it revealed here, or even a familiar tinkle of her pretty laughter like a chime, I am blind to her. For nowhere in the vicinity can I sense her presence.

Dark spots of rain appear upon the stone of the ground. The faint, irregular percussion of it striking upon my hood lends to the newly chill, lonesome air.

"Lirinda," I seethe quietly between my teeth. "I am going to kill you."

Why would she not be here? My belly begins to roil again with dread. Sickness trembles cold and sweaty in my palms. Has she forgotten? Has she truly been so daft as to forget?

Or has something happened?

I visualize her where I left her: the dancing flower maiden, flouncing her beauty before everyone, and hardly paying mind to me, what I had said, what my needs were. Perhaps she had not listened at all and is still dancing in the faintly sprinkling rain. But I feel, with chilling terror spiraling within me, that she is not.

Something is different…

I glance around again, hoping beyond any desperate hope I've ever felt that I have been the fool and that Lirinda is simply within plain sight. But it feels desolately cold without her warm presence. A cold I have never before felt.

With my heart thundering in my sick-bloated throat, I hurry down the market street, looking down every intersecting street, every alley, hungry for a glimpse of her hair, a tinkle of her laughter, a scent of her honeysuckle perfume. Lirinda is an unmistakable figure even in her hood, and there are none who resemble her in the slightest.

I race against Mother's progress, pleading against the gaining shadows that Lirinda will be looking for me, too, and that while we both look down the alleys for one another, we'll ironically collide and fall onto our asses, laughing, gathering each other's hands into our own, and setting off to meet Mother at the fountain. But even as the market street thins to the shabbier streets such as I'd ventured before, where a chill of danger lurks behind filthy timbered walls, still there is no sign of her. Until, down one shadowed alley, a slight and crumpled clue lies discarded and wilted upon the cobbled street.

My heart freezes in its pulse.

I run to it, bending down to take the dandelion that had been behind Lirinda's ear into my fingers. And it is the same dandelion, for I feel the slightest trace of her upon it, but now it is crushed and broken, and her essence upon it fading like a flame. She was here, so far from the fountain. So far from everyone. *Why?*

I look from the dandelion out to the passersby who seem so far away and foreign. I hadn't noticed before just how sinister some of them look: hooded men prowling alongside families walking by, eyeing the young women, even the children. I see one man regarding an adolescent girl, still young enough to be wiggling a tooth at the side of her mouth with her tongue, as though raking in her value, as though she is merchandise to be bought or sold.

A new sickening horror crawls up my arms. Why hadn't I thought of it before? How have I been so stupid as to leave Lirinda alone, when a slave-taker might glimpse her bouncing gilt beauty in all its unrestrained glory and see it as an opportunity.

Without debate or any thought toward the imminence of Mother's wrath, I weave myself forcefully back up the street until I am at the fountain once more, and perfectly, as if this has all been coordinated in some ironic play, the door to the inn opens and Mother's hooded figure emerges.

I find my mouth is agape and my hands shake as I stand before her. Alone. Without my sister, as I have never been before.

As soon as she notices me, her darker daughter standing solitary with a quivering countenance, she seems to understand her worst fear has come true.

"Where is Lirinda?" she demands, emerald eyes flaring with fear beneath her hood. Her breath catches in her lungs. The horror upon her face makes her look aged and almost demented.

I know not where to begin. But her eyes furiously take notice of the smear of blood that must be so bright upon the pale of my cheek, that her first notion is that whatever has happened is my doing. And perhaps it is my doing.

I bow my head as my face squinches with the painful urge to cry.

"I do not know," is all that I'm able to say.

She places her hands on my shoulders, her grip not maternal or stabilizing but vicious as her fingers dig into my skin. *"What's happened?"*

I try to speak through my sickness. Guilt, along with my fear, renders me even more speechless.

"I left her alone," I force with great effort, swallowing hard through my drying throat, trying to speak above a whisper. "I had to. But now I cannot find her and—"

A sharp slice of pain slashes across my face as Mother slaps me. I stand frozen in place, numb, the slash echoing on my face as Mother storms past me.

Over my shoulder, I see how she slithers through the gaining crowd, growing thicker with those who wheel in their carts for tomorrow's celebration, some folk already yelling and rowdy with drink, unnoticing or uncaring of the misting rain. To my surprise, she pushes back the hood from her head and reveals her fire-red hair, her long braid swinging with her determined strides.

I hurry to follow her, trailing like a dog at the flowing hem of her green cloak.

"Where last did you see her?" Mother demands when I've caught up to her side. And though I am unable to stop looking at her, my mother, and how she looks in this sober light, in this world, she will not look my way. She spares not a glance for me, not even to cast her anger. Those sharp green eyes instead scan the faces of the street just as I had done, but with a mother's precision, which makes her look all the more fearsome.

It's as if I've never truly looked at her before. To me, she has only ever been a master of plants and creatures, surrounded by ferns and fire lilies, but here she seems as commanding of the brick and timber as any Pure around us.

I know it is an inappropriate time to feel such a thing, but I am thrilled by this boldness of hers. Never did I know she could be so quick and fierce, so brave. But I am equally disturbed by the removal of her hood; that to her this situation is severe enough for her to discard her constant caution.

I am tempted to remove my hood again, too, but think it unwise. I would not like to be slapped a second time.

"Just over there." I point up to where the children had been, where rebellious patches of dandelions have forced their way through the stone ground. "She'd been dancing. And I...I had to leave her there...I had to go..." My voice shrinks with the words.

"She'd said she'd meet me at the fountain, but she never came. I searched for her down every street, then I found this." I brandish the dandelion for Mother to see, but she only stares hawklike down the street, refusing what I show her. But I continue, "She'd been wearing it. I found it down a road—that one, way down there, by the alehouse." I gulp uneasily.

Everything around me is hazy, as though I am in a feverish, sickening dream from which I hope I will soon wake. My body insubstantial as vapor, I cannot feel my flesh or bones, only my heavy-feeling heart pounding in the pit of my stomach.

"You don't think... She hasn't been—" I can't finish the words, but Mother finishes them for me.

"Taken for a slave?" Her voice is broken, a hoarse crackle just above a tormented whisper. I realize her staring eyes have pooled with tears that snake down her freckled, capillary-etched cheeks. Never have I seen my mother cry, and that unsettles me perhaps more than anything else. "It is likely."

By the scarce light of burning lanterns upon street corners, Mother and I wander the capital in the unwelcome darkness of night. Rain has slickened the streets; the stone flanks are glossy in the faint amber glow of lamplight. My senses rendered slow and faint, what with the filmy darkness and the din of downpouring rain upon street and rooftop, and, too, upon the wool of my hood, deafening me. If Lirinda calls for us, though I do not think she does, I cannot make out a sound.

What people had filled the streets over the hours have all complained of the rain and cowered indoors, rolling carts of fireworks beneath awnings or within storerooms to keep them dry. Now, they have all gone. Now, at this timeless hour of night, still and silent but for the infinite splashes and cacophony of falling rain, Mother and I haunt the streets alone, our loss so palpable and heavy that our pace has gone slow.

We dare not say it aloud, but we both seem to know we will not find Lirinda tonight.

Hours we wander, until the steely heavens relent with only a slight trickle of rain like the tears I wish I could cry. Sound restores to my ears but there is nothing to be heard, not until

Mother and I both make out a chilling noise slicing through the forlorn quiet: the clanking metallic strides of a patrolling soldier of the Guard. We slink as silently as we can down another street so as not to be seen. Our eyes meet beneath our hoods in the shadows, exchanging a mutual understanding that it is not safe for us here anymore.

Down the narrow stone streets that run with dark rivers of sewage is the nearest inn, the Gander's Gullet, with the wooden sign above the front door the cutout of a gruesomely painted goose having its head axed off.

I have never been inside an inn before. Earlier, Mother was the one to check inside each of them in our search for Lirinda while I waited outside, keeping a watchful eye for her upon the streets, asking the passersby if they had seen a fair young woman with hair like spun gold. But now as Mother and I saunter in, shrouded in our dark cloaks in a room full of firelight and the din of half-a-hundred voices, I understand Mother's caution against such establishments as these.

My roving eyes take in the large men gambling at tables, spilling ale, and wrestling over their gravy-soaked trenchers of half-rotten meat. A pretty barmaid is taken into the powerful arms of one brutish man as he tries kissing the plump overflow of breast over her low-cut smock, and though she is disgusted by him, still she giggles politely, pushing herself off his lap. I overhear several tables celebrating early for Gillin's Day, crashing tankards together for Purity, and singing old rhymes of burning blood and pretty witch women slain.

I trust Mother's judgment as she pays the shaky old innkeeper from her sack of coins, and we follow his small hunchbacked figure up the narrow stairs into a room that smells sharply of a full and calcifying pisspot. It is dark in the room until the same pretty barmaid from downstairs lights a fire for us in the hearth, and Mother and I are both grateful for the warmth. Beneath my hood, my eyes search Mother for an explanation for this unexpected lodging, but her face is impassive and hard, and she utters not a word until the innkeeper and his daughter leave us alone with the door closed behind them.

"We will not be sleeping here," she says at last, doffing the many satchels and baskets she'd been carrying. I take the cue to set mine on the stained bed as well. "We will not sleep at all until she is found."

My eyes, burning red with exhaustion, my feet, broken open with blisters, and my mind, which had gone numb hours ago, long for rest, but I feel I could not sleep ever again if I tried. Not without Lirinda's dreamy warm breaths at my cheek or the nudge of her presence at my side. My throat constricts at the thought I might never feel those sisterly comforts again.

"Then why rent the room?" I ask, too exhausted to frame my curiosity with my usual fragility so as not to shatter Mother's patience, and it is visible how such a blunt question brings her rigid mouth to twitch.

"We will keep our wares here," is her tight-lipped response. "This is where we will continue to meet, you and I, after we've gone our different ways looking for her."

We are silent, equally exhausted and strained with our panic. The plinking of rain dripping through the roof into a pot upon the floor startles us from our misery.

"And if not tonight, then the next night and the next." With emphasis, Mother slams her final sack of heavy rolled pelts upon the ground. As she considers the weight of what this means, the nights of absence of her beloved daughter, the light that illuminates her Haven-green eyes dims.

Neither of us speak, but I believe we both envision

similar horrors of Lirinda being bound in fetters and dragged throughout the dripping, clandestine tunnels we'd wandered through—perhaps with a gag between her teeth to keep her silent, perhaps abused. The shame I feel is so deep, I do not know whether my power rages or if it has gone from me forever. I feel nothing—nothing but the hollow of regret.

"But first we will need to nourish ourselves. We'll be needing our wits about us. You stay here; I'll go downstairs and bring up a plate."

In her absence I wade sluggishly over to the window. I unlatch the shutters and look out into the dripping, abysmal night, all dark except for the pinpricks of lanterns like orange stars throughout the capital, and, with a surprising jolt of magic I had not felt in hours, I look up to see the castle dazzling with diamonds of light up into the black sky. Each window in each tower is alight and sparkling with internal firelight. Their celebration mocks my grief.

My mind flickers, briefly, to the image of King Gastlin. How I'd seen him only hours before, striding with ordained confidence, yet now it feels like a lifetime ago. I should never have been there, should never have seen him. I regret so painfully wandering from Lirinda as long and far as I did—how I had secretly longed to be away from her. But I do wonder what he, the king, is doing now. What it looks like within the castle where he is, dancing, feasting perhaps.

Deeply, deeper even than my grief, do I feel myself being pulled to the castle. To the echoing, cavernous halls within. I have never seen them, of course, but in my pulse, I envision tall, vaulted corridors like arteries of a beating heart, illuminated by fiery torches. So taut is the string connecting me to its mysterious call, I feel I could rise off the floor and fly there if I surrendered to it.

"What are you looking at?"

I spin from the open window to see Mother has returned with a wood plate for us to eat trenchers off and a tankard of ale to share. She glares at me with suspicion.

The castle, I almost answer, but think better than to upset her with the truth. Carefully closing the shutters, I swallow down my honesty and say, "I was looking for Lirinda."

Mother knows too well how often I would gaze at the castle as a child. I have never been one to admire beauty, not in the way Lirinda would, but the castle has always been an object of fascination to me. She knows how I lie, the glittering ostentation of the castle having been perfectly framed in the background of the window. She shows me the same withering, almost fearful, glare as she's shown me all my life whenever I reveal any part of myself which isn't subdued in her soils and herbs.

Now, however, is not the time for her to scold me. Nor even for me to feel the ache of her lifelong resentment for me, which I've never understood. We ought only to think of our Lirinda.

We sit on the floor to eat; the moldering, stale bread is ash in my mouth, and the ale, so like piss, warms me not at all. But I eat and drink still, for I have not realized how thirsty or hungry I've been—how dry my mouth and stingingly empty my belly. Mother and I sit in mournful silence, chewing, swallowing hard, and I wonder if Lirinda, wherever she is, has eaten.

If she is even alive.

My throat tightens upon my dry food, and I choke a whimper of a cry.

"There will be slave auctions," Mother murmurs aloud her thoughts. "Perhaps not tonight or the next, but soon." She sips the froth of the ale and winces with disgust. "Usually, they are every sennight. We will have to be clever if we are to find them. Their whereabouts will not be disclosed publicly."

"You've been told this?" I ask her, my voice throaty with my bread-choked grief.

But she does not answer. Perhaps she does not hear me. She looks at the ground, thoughts absorbed in her scheme. Her mouth frames words she does not utter.

A loud bang from a nearby room makes me jump where I sit. There is shouting, a woman crying. The walls rattle around us with danger, violence. I had always known the world beyond Haven was treacherous at every turn, but never did I think I would feel scared by it—*within* it. *My sister*, I think mournfully. She is alone in it, wherever she is.

"What do your senses tell you, Mother?" My quiet voice, which I have used so little today, crackles pitifully. "What do you feel—now, in this very moment? Where is she?"

Her weary gaze is fixed upon the wood plate between us, the grain blackened and growing hairs of mold. The only living flora in our vicinity—the closest thing to home.

"It is difficult for me to sense anything without roots or leaves in this hard world. It is all the harsh mortar of man. It blinds me, makes me feel weak. Like I have no magic at all."

So deeply I have been imploring my surroundings for a hint of Lirinda's honeyed essence that I have paid no mind to Mother's. Indeed, her usually potent spirit of fresh earth is diminished.

"Has it not helped to remove your hood?" I ask, not realizing my folly until Mother's eyes glance up at me, large and suspicious.

"No, it has not," she says harshly. The way she looks at me, her emerald gaze burning with accusation, tells me she can read my treachery from my very posture. With her furious wisdom, it is as though she can see hours into my past—see that I have removed my hood within the maze of city streets and felt the whirls of the unseen world pull and thrash pleasurably within me. It is written upon my shameful features as blatantly as the castle glowed at my back.

"Has it helped you?" she asks of me poisonously.

I inhale deeply through my nose. There is little more I can do to upset Mother, so I might as well share with her information that might be useful to us.

"Yes," I answer as rigidly as I can. "Twice now I have removed my hood within the city, felt my magic swell and heighten more powerfully than ever before. Perhaps, if I could remove mine again…I might better sense her…"

She rises to her feet. "So, there is more to this tale! How many more secrets will you spill until this yarn has unraveled? You've been running amok with your hood removed—leaving your sister unattended among predators. Now tell me, was Lirinda's hood removed, too?"

I feel my power rise at the injustice of this. How wrongly she has wound these truths into a story. I look away from her, my hands clenching into fists. My power throbbing.

"It was."

She snorts out of her nose. I look not at her directly, but I see the face she bears at me is the clenched expression of disgust, her chin and mouth squeezed, eyes burning with irreparable hurt. I've betrayed her—her and Lirinda both.

"She wished to be seen," I contest bravely, squaring my gaze upon Mother's at last. "There was nothing I could do to stop her, though I tried."

"You left her," Mother reminds me, and now all spite has gone from her, leaving only her sorrow, hanging heavy over her shoulders like a mantle of iron. Her sorrow, I cannot bear. I look away again.

"You speak of secrets, Mother," I snarl sweetly, my pulse

thundering with fear for challenging her honesty. "When will you tell me why you insist we keep our hoods secured over our heads?"

It is still her sorrow that paints her face, and the fire as she now faces it casts long shadows beneath her eyes and cheeks which make her appear to me all the more haunted by grief, too old for her age.

"There is a protective enchantment," she says at last, her voice deep and weary. "A similar enchantment to what I've woven through the trees of Haven has been woven upon your hood with threads of my Mondril fibers. The embroidery of your hood keeps your magic from being discovered."

I think of the nights I have seen her stitch the pretty leaves and blooms upon our hoods, stabbing herself with the needle so blood would weave with the embroidery.

I nod, understanding. "Why then has removing your hood not helped you to sense her?"

"I weave no such enchantments for myself," she explains, scowling at me. "I do not value my safety so much as that of my daughters. But even if I had, I would feel nothing in removing my hood. It is as I told you, this city is barren to me. My senses are blind. I feel…nothing. My magic thrives in the forest, not in such a dead environment as this. I removed my hood not for some rush of power, but to reveal myself to Lirinda should she be searching for me."

I swallow hard. *So it is only me who feels awakened here, after all,* I think with a chill.

"But you…" she whispers. In her tremulous hiss there is accusation again, the slightest twist of disgust with her tongue. The same disgust as when she saw me stand before the window, the castle. "You feel powerful here, do you? You feel life in these dead-stone streets?"

I refuse to look up at her now, but I nod, and she says nothing more. A grave silence stretches, thick, between us. For the first time, we both realize how very different our magic is.

CHAPTER SIX

I f even we had slept, there would be an early call to wake before dawn. As soon as we hear the first commotion of early-risers setting up their wares in the dark of morning, Mother and I slink from the Gander's Gullet and continue our red-eyed, restless wander. In the waning darkness, the streets of the capital clot with folk of all status and cloth, chattering, boisterous, eager to celebrate, the chill autumn wind having blustered away the leaden clouds of rain, leaving only puddles upon the road, and residual droplets hanging from the eaves of buildings, shining silver to gold with the slow radiance of dawn. A brilliant autumn sun ascends to the sky, promising a clear day for us to search for our Lirinda.

There is a spark of hope with each golden head of hair I find in the gathering crowd, but there are no such golden heads as bright as my sister's. Nor can I sense her unmistakable essence. I've searched and searched for it still.

"Perhaps it's best if we cover different areas," I suggest in a yell to Mother, for otherwise my voice would be lost in the thousand voices and the merry music that commands dancers in circles, but Mother is reluctant. I wonder, with a swell of hope, if her reluctance is due to the worry of losing me as well.

The masses, how they swarm around us like currents of a river. Mother's face is pale, far paler than ever I've seen it.

"You must be careful, Sirilda," she resigns hoarsely. Her eyes meet mine. In her gaze I understand that she trusts I am capable of protecting myself, but that I am capable of a great many other things, too—things that make her leer at me with mistrust.

"And keep your hood on."

We agree to meet back at our room at dusk. The sun-soaked hours of being jostled between shoulders seem interminable. Still, it is only morning, and my tongue clicks in my mouth with thirst. My eyes, burning-tired, lose their keenness upon the blurry faces that pass. Mother had said she will spy within the establishments and haunt the filthier alleys for information of the slave auctions while I search still for a glimmer of my sister's features upon the wider paved streets, unlikely though I know it is to see it here.

In the middle of the street, I stop in my stride, allowing the currents of the crowd to stream around me. I know I am only wasting my energy wandering like this, using my exhausted eyes and ears when there is another force within me that I can call upon that is far more powerful.

"Sorry, Mother," I whisper as I slip my hood from off my head.

My eyes close with the rush of awareness that sparkles into my blood. My power's pulse no longer a painful throb but a smooth and exhilarating force as natural as gravity or light.

Where are you, Lirinda? I implore as I focus upon the pulls and releases given and taken by the world. In Haven, I have been good at this, sensing the transactions of energy between plant and animal, sun and moon, but never in such an environment as a crowded city where foreign factors are at play. I try dismissing all the interference: the external smells and sounds; the internal ice-cold fear pounding in my heart with my rapid pulse; the ever-constant magic coursing like a stream of white-hot starlight. And in my focus, I feel something tug at me. It feels like the times I've cast out my childhood makeshift fishing line into the stream and felt a pull at the other end.

I feel something, I think, and open my eyes excitedly, but my expectant face falls when I see it is only the castle, again, looming before me like a familiar presence, magnificently sprawling into the sky above.

I scoff disgustedly and turn away from Gillin's castle for another street, one which blocks it from my view.

Lirinda, I chant in my mind. *Sister.*

My cloak swishes behind me as I weave between shoulders and wagons and the columns of buildings, having no purpose to where I turn or go, only allowing my body to decide rather than my mind.

It is nearly midday when I find myself standing in my exhaustion at the main road of all the capital, wide and clean and neatly manicured with trees and flowerbeds that blaze brightly in autumn's colors. I smell a sweet waft of bread from a baker. If only Mother had given me a quarter yeor for a roll. I am hungry enough for even the nasty waste the Gander's Gullet deems edible.

Tempted I am to abandon my search for my sister to search, instead, for a coin upon the ground or shimmering in a fountain basin, when I hear a strange fanfare of instruments blare from up the street where I stand. The chaos of the crowd around me goes suddenly orderly with rapt attention, and the people divide to the sides of the street, leaving the cobbled stone clean and open as though it had not been overcrowded just moments before.

I scurry to one side of the street, too, stretching my neck for a glimpse of the source of the music and the cheers that have begun faraway down the curve of the street out of view. The men around me remove their hats from their heads, some lifting their eager children onto their shoulders. Excited prattle buzzes around me, and I am nervous, sweat trickling from the pit of my arms, for whatever Pure affair this is. I remember the monstrous things Mother told us that are done on this day—the grotesque rituals, the celebration of the purging of magic, the pouring of animal blood. And I realize, with my sickest plummet of dread yet, that I have now left both Lirinda and Mother alone, here, in this terrible city…and if there is a Magic the Guard has found to execute before all today, on this Gillin's Day, it is likely either of them.

Could this be what has happened to Lirinda?

The sweat that drips down my neck is ice-cold; the vomit that threatens to rise is hot. I tremble where I stand. My legs compel me to slip through the crowd and escape for my own safety, but the rest of me is immovable, my heart pounding faster than ever before, my eyes locked up the street for the first sign of my sister or Mother being dragged down the cobbled stone by the ornately armored guards. My mind, once numb, now races with the hundred plots for how I could attempt to rescue them. My fists close so tightly, I may have caused myself to bleed, for my power now rages readily, thumping, preparing to destroy all who may oppose me in my effort of saving them.

But how would we get away? I know it is all impossible, the crowds would close in on us—we would be seized, or the city gates would be closed before we could hide in the cool solace of the trees I wish we had never left.

The crowd around me begins to cheer when a procession of decorated white horses walks proudly into view, the royal standard held high by liveried riders; dark blue banners with the embroidered design of a white elderflower upon a single upright sword, the silver thread gleaming in the direct sunlight of midday.

More riders follow, the Guard's metal armor glaring bright in the sun. The crowd cheers for them but the guards are too severe in their helmets to so much as look at them.

And more riders... I do not look at them. I do not hear the cheers of the people around me. All has gone silent in my head. My body numb with fear. Except for the rush, suddenly, of something familiar, like tendrils of spice and summer reaching for me across the crowd, just as the royal carriage—a spectacle of magnificently carved scrolls of gold, pulled by eight massive, slow-treading horses—rolls gracefully into view.

Everyone around me has folded into a bow. But still I stand, immovable.

I stare boringly through the open window of the shining gilt carriage at the king and the shadow-obscured figure beside him who waves their hands merrily. The closer the carriage comes, the better I see the handsome, perfectly carved face of King Gastlin smiling out at the reverently bowing crowds. He wears a dazzling crown, his dark-brown hair curling round his ears and resting at his broad shoulders, copper-brown eyes alight with youthful joy.

I am no longer afraid. Fear ebbs from my veins as another sensation pounds scorchingly into my heart. For I seem to know everything already; I can feel it on the cold wind, primroses nodding in a summer breeze.

The figure seated beside him is a woman. Luxuriously

dressed—dressed for a queen. And her face, the one I've been so desperate to see, comes into the light of the sun—the laughing, beautiful face of my sister—cheeks flushed with happiness, a tendril of her golden hair slipping stylishly from beneath a bejeweled headdress, a swan-feathered cape over her shoulders with a diamond brooch in the center.

Jewels of all colors sparkle prismatically from the pair of them. And I simply stand transfixed, unable to feel my relief, my anger—standing like a statue among the crowd that bows for them, confusion and understanding wrestling in my fury.

There you are, is all I am able to think, and powerful enough is my revelation that it cuts all the way to Lirinda and makes her turn her head to face me. Lirinda's light, jovial gaze sweeps across the reverently bowed heads until it meets my furious face.

"Sirilda," Lirinda mouths silently, swallows, then stands in the carriage, gathering the massive skirts of a cream-and-gold patterned silk gown into her hands. "Sirilda!"

The king is aghast at how she clambers over his lap to the carriage door, hollering out the window for the riders to halt the horses. The entire procession comes to a clumsy, confused stop, and she exits the carriage to the surprise of everyone and trots straight for me, her gown gripped delicately in her hands, a beaming smile upon her face. The king steps out of the carriage, too, an expression of concern furrowing his dark brows.

All has gone horribly quiet but for the clapping of her footfalls upon the ground as she runs to me. I look around me now, how every face upon the street gawks curiously at me, the haggard peasant in a dark wool cloak, for whom the king's pretty, gilded companion has stopped the procession.

"Sirry!"

Lirinda's warm, perfumed embrace envelops me in a crash. I feel soft feathers brush against my face. Lirinda smells clean, like roses in bath water, not hearth smoke and the herbs of our cottage. My fists, squeezed against my sides in Lirinda's embrace, touch the silk folds of her gown; never have I touched something so luxurious and foreign. It is all I can feel.

"Sirry, I've done it," she whispers in my ear. The familiar comfort of her breath so near me, my sister. I do think I am dreaming after all. Are we truly not in our bunk right now? Have I only been sleeping and will open my eyes to our twig-woven ceiling; Mother's figure before the dying hearth; the sweet morning sounds of Haven?

"I've gone and married the king!"

I say nothing but pull out of her grasp. Gravity pulls so heavily upon me I fear I will collapse. I am not dreaming; the ground at my feet sucks me down. The cold breeze on my cheek true, as is the warm sun. How it glistens upon my sister… I look at her as though I've never seen her before.

"You've what?"

"Lirinda!" calls a voice I've heard not so long ago. A voice that makes the tolling of bells sound diminutive. A voice I cannot help but turn my gaze to.

King Gastlin, surrounded by other concerned guards, hurries toward us.

I step back, shying into the crowd that stares at me, murmuring their curiosities, but Lirinda only grabs my hand playfully, like this is one of our silly games, not letting me go.

"It is my sister!" she calls over her shoulder to the king. "I am telling her the good news!"

Like an amused parent of a darling child, the king chuckles indulgently at this and so do the guards and those surrounding him who have stepped forward in their concern.

Lirinda turns back to me, bringing her face so near to mine as though we are mutually gleeful and prim, finding my other hand and taking it into her grasp as well. "I'll tell you all about it! Sirry, you must come to the castle! You and Mother both! Where is she?"

"Looking for *you!*" I hiss. "This is where you've been?"

"Yes!" she says breathlessly to me, squeezing my hands in hers. Her eyes, those ever-starry orbs glistening, and at last they suit her queenly dress. "Just this morning, we had a small ceremony in the chapel. Oh, it is love, Sirry. Truest love! We could not allow a day to pass without us being married! And soon I will be coronated as his queen! *Me*, Sirry. Queen of Glindor!"

I am immovable still. I cannot speak. I fear I'll faint before all these inquisitive gazes.

Over Lirinda's feathered shoulder, I inadvertently lock eyes with King Gastlin. I had indeed felt strange looking at him before, overwhelmed by a tingle of connection just as he had passed me by, but having his gaze met with mine, a stream of acknowledgement passing between us, has made something within my very spirit shiver.

"Come with me to the castle now!" Lirinda urges me toward her, toward the carriage—toward *him*. "There are closets of gowns to choose from for the ball tonight. And you'll live in the royal apartments as one of my maids. Mother, too, of course."

I peel one of my hands away and hold steadfast against her tug. "I cannot come," I declare, my voice tremulous with emotion. I wish to say, *and you should not go, either!* But by the proximity of others who may find my words treasonous against the king, I do not. Instead, I only say, "I cannot leave Mother, too."

There is a bite of venom in my voice, but Lirinda is oblivious to it.

"Then you will go to her and both come?" She beams with

her usual vacuous innocence that always sets my jaw to clench. Has she forgotten that we are prey to these Pures? That one blunderous word from her mouth, which is inevitable, would have her slain by her husband's sword, no matter how pretty she looks in her feathers?

Does she realize we have been looking for her, thinking her enslaved or dead, but she has been betraying us by doing the worst possible thing she could ever do?

I try to express this all to her through my furious eyes, but she does not receive it.

"I will try," is all I am able to whisper, peeling my other hand from hers.

Before Mother can return to the Gander's Gullet at dusk, I am already there. I ask the innkeeper's daughter, Malinne, the pretty barmaid who is constantly wrangled for sport by the drunkards at the bar, to unlock the door for me, for Mother is in possession of the key.

Kindly, Malinne brings in a tinderbox and kindling for the fireplace and lights it for me, though I could have done it myself—even without Mother's Flame Powder—if I was not so numb-minded, staring off in a daze of horror at the wall. As Malinne works, I can hear crowds outside the window, and even downstairs in the pub, roar with their celebration for Gillin's Day. She refills our pitcher of water before bidding me good evening and sweeping back downstairs to her duties at the rowdy, overcrowded tables. I attempt to thank her but cannot utter a word. My grief, somehow, has only grown more terrible even though Lirinda has been found alive and safe. At least, for now.

I am sitting on my heels before a flourishing fire when Mother enters the room. I hear her sigh heavily with grief and exhaustion, a cry not so far from the surface of her breath. I cannot bear to reveal to her my stony expression, for I know she will see in my dry, staring eyes that I know something. And I have not yet decided how I will say it. How I will utter such nonsensical truths into the world.

"I did not think you would be here before me. I came early to let you in," Mother grunts, her voice dry with thirst. Two days we have both gone without sleep and ample food or drink. I would have ordered a meal for us to share but Mother carries with her the sack of coin. I think of how it has grown lighter, almost empty, with the payment of this room and for our nourishment—and how Lirinda wears diamonds.

I clench my eyes closed to resist the image.

"What is it you know, Sirilda?" Mother asks, always surprising me with her wisdom. I can refuse her no longer.

I turn to reveal to her the uncomfortable knowing in my eyes, but my eyes instead widen with alarm at the sight of her. Mother has gone even paler than before and looks somehow as though she'd shrunken in her weariness, her hunger. She puts a hand against the bedstead to keep herself steady. Her breathing heavy.

"Mother…" I breathe. "You must eat something."

"I've already ordered it downstairs. They'll bring it up." Even speaking those words is difficult for her. "I'm afraid we will soon be out of money. We'll have to sell more…have to work to earn a wage, depending on how long…"

I wince at the discomfort of this. The truth escapes me before she can say any more.

"I've seen her, Mother."

So feeble she is, it takes her a moment to realize the enormity of what I've just said.

"What?"

"I've seen Lirinda."

The silence of her mind working at what I could mean by this, and why Lirinda is not here with me now, is painfully loud. I turn back to the fire, bowing my head.

"She is well," I add quickly, before Mother can think her ill-treated or dead.

"What do you mean by this?" she seethes in an incredulous whisper. "You've seen her? She is well? Where is she, then?"

A rap upon the door interrupts the tension. It is Malinne again, carrying the plate of a trencher and another tankard of ale. Her smock and corset sopping with spilled beer, she sets the plate down upon the bedstand and nods to us.

"Thank you," Mother acknowledges weakly, then in Malinne's departure, turns her fury back upon me.

But I cannot remove the wedge that chokes my throat. I think I'd rather say Lirinda was restrained and imprisoned than reveal how deeply she has betrayed us. How she is not with us due to her own choice.

"I know not how it happened," I force the words. "But she has not been taken for a slave at all. She has met someone… someone she has fallen in love with…" I cannot will my tongue to say whom.

I hear Mother's back slide down against the wall until she has seated upon the ground.

"Did she see you?"

"Oh, yes." Here comes the grief, choking my voice. "We spoke…"

"And?" Mother breathes a painfully sharp breath. "She knows how we've looked for her? She would not return with you?"

I shake my head.

"Who is this person?" Her voice is an agonized growl. I lift my face, studying the ceiling as I ease my throat to speak.

"King Gastlin."

She is silent. I had been expecting a gasp or a wail. But nothing. I turn again to look at her, to make sure she has not fainted or died, and find her frightening face has gone slack. She only looks at the flames as she always has done. Haunted, demented, far away from here.

"Mother…"

"No," is all she says. "It cannot be."

"I know…but it is." The throatiness of my misery is deep and crackling. "And that is not the worst of it."

"What more could there be?"

My throat refuses the words to come to my mouth. I speak only air at first. When my voice comes, finally, it is broken and pitiful.

"They are wed, Mother."

Mother gazes at the flames, as she does every night, but this time, their writhing dance of orange light illuminates stark defeat upon her sagging, weary face. It looks to me as though whatever she has battled in silence all these years has won.

I swallow hard. The crackling of logs and the yelling from the other rooms and the streets outside are the only sound for a long, grievous time.

"She says…she wishes for us to join her at the castle. To live there with her."

"Never," she swears in a low growl. "She will come back to us. She will come home."

"But they've been married…"

"I do not care!" she roars. "No oath is greater than the one to your family."

We are silent again. A long time, the silence stretches, which is not so silent at all but filled with noise. Laughter, yelling, the stomping of feet overhead, scraping tankards and chairs down below.

Then, there are explosions booming from outside. I jolt where I sit, prepared to flee, to take cover. But the cheering of crowds confuses me.

"That would be the fireworks," Mother croaks bitterly.

I fling open the window shutters and see that, indeed, there are colorful explosions of light in the sky. Just before the castle, reflecting brightly off glassy windows. The castle where my sister now dances as always she's dreamed. The castle that still beckons to me, beating dark with my pulse. And with a chill, I have an overpowering knowing that I can deny its call no longer. Somehow my fate has been threaded into its very halls, so much so that I have even been offered an invitation.

I know now that I must go there. It is inevitable.

CHAPTER SEVEN

Sleep glazes over me, but my mind whirs with color—a poisonous garden of emotion. Pains, pleasures, and endless questions sprout from the earth, blooming.

Why would she do this? I turn to my other side, groaning feverishly in my sleep. The stained mattress beneath me yields in a sickening way that keeps me partially aware that I am so far from home. Still, I smell the stench of the pisspot, and hear the yelling of the other rooms, still not quieting even into dawn. So exhausted I am, even in my sleep I achieve no rest.

How *could she*? I toss my body the other way. *How did this happen?*

Lirinda's bouncing figure fills my dreams. Gowns of pastel blues and pinks and pretty cakes to match. I cry for her in my sleep, my sister with whom I once spent long winter days with nothing to do but weave bones and feathers into each other's long hair. Telling the stories of what the creases meant upon the tenderness of our palms, making guesses at our futures. My sister, who braided clovers into coronets for me to wear and wove stories of gallant princes and their maidens when we would sit in our patch of wildflowers in the tranquil spring sun, Mother working in her garden not so far from us.

Those days are forever gone; the cold suction of loss slurps at my heart. My sister, no longer my sister, but a wife. Soon to be a queen.

The ache I feel manifests in visions of fiery torches within reddened halls. A pulse, deep and dangerous, emanates from the stone walls and from my very heart. The further into the torch-lit labyrinth my rage takes me, the more I understand it is a depth within myself I have always known existed but have never explored.

I jolt awake, feeling my power escape me but not knowing where or how. My heart thundering in my throat, sweat dripping down my brow, I look around, gasping for breath, to find the room just as it had been before.

Mother, I sigh with relief. Mother is still there, slumped upon the ground from which she refuses to move, still alive. I have not accidentally harmed her. Putting fingertips to my nose I check that there is only a slight residual smear of blood. It was only a dream, after all.

Mother has not noticed me, how aggressively I've woken. Still her wasted face sags in the shadows of the lingering firelight, her eyes sleepless, consumed in thought. Her thoughts must be far louder than my jagged breaths—than my delusional cries for my sister in the night.

I look to the ground to see the portion of food I'd left for Mother to eat is still untouched. A mouse skitters along the wall and, sniffing tentatively into the air, ensuring no big creature will come to harm it, goes to nibble at the stale, rotten meat. Likely that of a cat.

Once it's had its fill, the mouse goes familiarly to Mother's slackened hand upon her lap, slipping easily between her fingers, and resting upon her palm to wash its face with tiny paws. Comfortably together they sit, as perhaps they've done all night.

I hunch forward, taking my knees into my grasp and holding myself.

"Mother." My voice is broken still; perhaps she will not hear it above the crackling of dry kindling, but I know she hears all.

"Mother, you need to eat." But even as I say the words, I know they are foolish, for what awful sustenance this is for me to suggest. What my mother needs is hot broth and fresh garden vegetables and lovingly harvested meat for her lifeforce. Not cruel food, long since dead.

We cannot stay here, I think. I bow my head into my hands, kneading at my thick, tangled hair. Either we must return to Haven or go where we have been called to. And I myself do not know which is better. For I long desperately for the sweet familiarity of home, but without Lirinda, and with Mother in this ill state of desolation, I know it is no home to us anymore.

The dewy ferns I think of, swaying gently in cold forest air, are foreign to me now.

I clear my throat. "What are we to do, Mother?"

"She must come back to us," she answers distantly, proving that though she is faraway, she is immediately aware. Yet, still, she will not look away from the glowing coals.

I wonder if Mother knows Lirinda in the way that I do. That Lirinda has already made her decision, that she had made it long ago. Mother did not see how well suited she looked for the gilt carriage she rode in as she waved her hand to the crowd with such majesty, I found it difficult to believe she was not raised to be royalty. But I was there, beside her, for all the years she had practiced—*by the gods, how she practiced!* This has always been her heart's grandest intention, though she never knew it could come to be.

There is no use in arguing this with Mother. No use in telling Mother that Lirinda will never return to us willingly. Mother, how she rests without ever resting, is too fragile.

"She will not come back to us if we only remain in this room, doing nothing," is all I say, a plea for Mother to eat, sleep, and rise.

When Mother does not acknowledge my words, I stand from the bed. My hood has slipped off my head in my sleep, and still I've not replaced it, but Mother has not looked at me to notice anyway. Or perhaps in her acute awareness of everything, she has indeed noticed but no longer cares for anything I do.

I walk past her, testing her. I go to the door and place my hand on the handle. The sack of coin jangles with pitiful emptiness as I slip it into my pocket; I hang one of our baskets from the crook of my elbow, but still she does not acknowledge me.

"I'll be back," I mutter and leave.

The capital is quiet this morning. Rubble from yesterday litters the streets, and still a few folk are drunk and weary for their bed, cold and huddled in the almost-wintry air, but no longer is there energy for merriment. It feels it is not just me who carries a heaviness here.

Chimneys from every building issue smoke, and the smoke is no contrast against the clouded sky. I breathe in the perfume of woodsmoke with pleasure, but it pangs me for the scents of Haven, of our cottage where it sits alone, growing cold without a fire in the hearth. Will I ever walk along that familiar path to see its firelit windows again?

My voice as I ask one street merchant for potatoes, onions, and herbs—and another merchant for a cut of meat—is loud, and my breath is steam. When I walk back to the Gander's Gullet, the basket upon the crook of my arm heavy with ingredients, I avoid looking at the castle where my sister is or how beautiful the pale structure must look in this early gray light. So much had it haunted me in my sleep, I dare not give it any more power to torment me while I am awake. Not until I must face it.

Yet again I am haunted by the eerie sense that the castle stares upon me, as though with a pair of eyes. With my free hand, I reach for my hood and pull it back over my wild mane of damp-curled darkness. But the protection of my hood, the instantaneous block of external senses, is not as strong as it had been before. Still, I can feel the world beyond, the swirl of power and danger, and that uncanny call I do not understand, beckoning from the crevices of stone. Mother's protection, the enchantment upon the threads, has grown faint. I understand now why Mother has replaced the embroidery of our hoods with every time we return from our ventures in the capital. Simply existing here, in this environment of such tumult, all but sucks the protection away.

I think of the Boundary of Haven. Mother admitted to it being of a similar protective magic to that of our hoods. How often must Mother weave her magic into the interconnecting branches of the trees? Does it still hum now, with that bone-panging force, though we are so far away from it? Since I suspect Mother of using blood magic—pricking her finger with her embroidering needle—might that mean our Boundary is the product of blood magic, too?

As I walk, I spread my cold fingers, wriggling them. My own power I've not felt since Lirinda's disappearance. Fear has made me numb to it. Except for last night, in my strange, sick-whirring dreams, where it was all I could feel, guided through those reddened halls. I seek it out now, the throb beneath the surface. I ignore my worry for Lirinda, for Mother, straining to silence my woeful thoughts and feel only what surges within. And it is there—I've found it. A river beneath ice. My constant current.

My Current, I think with a faint smile. That's perhaps what I shall call it.

When I return to the Gander's Gullet, it is almost empty but for those who have fallen asleep over their table, a tankard still in their hand, or those who drowse sitting upright in their chair. The fires have all gone to ash, and the cold from outside has seeped in through timbered walls. Not even Malinne is down here to wipe down the tables with her greasy rag.

Over the bar, I peer into the kitchens to find them empty, too. Hanging within an ashy fireplace is a pot I would need to cook Mother a stew. Looking over my shoulders and seeing no one, hearing only distant slumberous breaths and the grunting dreamery of a sleeping dog, I use my Current to lift the pot's handle from the hook in the fireplace and levitate it across the kitchens and over the bar to where I stand.

As I maneuver briskly up the stairs with my arms full of supplies, I feel the tickle of noseblood, and wipe it with my sleeve to ensure there's not a smear of it left for Mother to see.

"Three and a half-yeor, was it your father said?" growls a man's voice from within one of the rooms I walk past. I hear the clink of coins and then a woman's soft, morose voice thanking him. I hurry along the landing before the door opens, and Malinne exits the room. She looks as weary as Mother, her face red and raw-looking from being abraded against, her mouse-brown hair more disheveled than before; she tucks it insecurely behind an ear with one hand as the other hand adjusts the coin in her bodice. I fear I know what she's been doing and feel a sick pity for her. Had it been her father who orchestrated this? By the haggard misery heavy in her features, Malinne does not appear to have chosen it for herself. In this life of hers, what has she chosen?

It does make me tingle with strangeness to think of carnal intimacy between two people, romantic or not.

Mother has hardly explained it beyond the obvious process of reproduction. I have seen the birds flitting in the spring, the frenzied rabbit bucks mounting the does, and even the bucks upon the bucks and the does upon the does. I know, mechanically, how it works for humans, but wonder how it might look or feel. I try to visualize what it must look like for Malinne, stripped of her dirty clothes, performing for a gruff traveling man she may not know. Who may not even be kind to her. Then I think of Lirinda, what she must be doing these nights and early mornings alone with the king. A contrast to Malinne—perhaps with passion and play, perhaps even laughter and kisses. Do they share a bed? A massive canopied bed, surely.

Of course, I think, *she has consummated this ridiculous union of theirs!* My sister's plump, soft body—naked—a body only ever seen by me, our Mother, and the sun itself, when she would bathe always so delicately in the stream. He has seen her, then? His hands have touched her, then? His hands upon her, wanting, insistent—warm.

I feel a flush of heat that's both anger and another unnamable sensation as I thrust open the door to our room.

The door opens upon the sight of Mother in the same place, her head gently tilted to its side as she sleeps, at last; her breaths rising and falling, too exhausted to maintain her constant rigidity. She's covered herself in some wooly blanket, but I see the bed is still clothed in its same filthy, stained-and-torn cover from before. The blanket Mother wears smells sharp of earth, and it makes me wince and cough slightly. I look closer upon it and realize she has formed a blanket of the furry black mold from the wooden plate, growing it to her will to comfort her in this room that has gone cold with autumn's wintry chill seeping through the cracks of the window.

I build a fire, my thoughts on how I will express to Mother when she wakes how I know what we must do. With her blade taken carefully from her cloak pocket, I begin to carve the potatoes and vegetables to craft her a stew in the pot for sustenance so she might feel well enough to accept the truth we must face.

The wind that carries clouds of heavy rain brings with it the severity of autumn's tipping point, that life has begun to die, and there is no stopping it. I feel it whistle past my ears as I open the window shutters to the cold, letting it in, for the room has become so hot and humid with the fire I've allowed to rage for hours with the boiling stew while Mother has slept.

I know that, in Haven, the trees are flexing with the powerful wind; that the pine needles percuss with the cold pelleting rain and fall gently, amber and sodden, to the forest floor. How strange to not see evidence of autumn here, for nowhere in view from the window can so much as a plant be seen amid the dark timber-and-stone maze of buildings. There is no foliage, no color at all.

Oh, but in Haven, I sigh and close my eyes with yearning of the imagery. In Haven, the deciduous trees and bushes would be brilliant in their shades of yellows and reds, the wildflowers still blooming vividly, contrasting so beneath darkened clouds bearing cold rain—cold rain which only makes the grasses greener before the coming of snow.

Mother's pumpkins will be fattening, ripening. And with those pumpkins would be pumpkin soup simmering in the pot; pumpkin seeds roasting over the fire; the smell of honeyed pumpkin cakes, the ones Lirinda used to beg Mother to bake, filling the cottage with sweetness. I remember Mother's green cloak, how it would trail behind her as she walked between rows of pumpkins and squash, and how their rain-washed orange flesh was so bright against her cloak, though nothing was as bright as her hair. So red like fire, not even the pumpkins could rage as brightly as she. Her only competition was with the reddest leaves in the trees, but even they were soon to crumble and fade.

I glance at her now, bundled beneath her mold, and I know it in my every sense that Mother will never be so strong and brilliant ever again. Will anything ever be?

Lirinda, how could you do this to us?

As I stand at the window, something black and massive soars past my peripheral vision. Its shape and motion I've seen a thousand times before, countless times throughout my life, but seeing it now is surreal and ominous. It is Crow.

Our Crow.

There is no mistaking the large black bird with its single leg, its iridescent feathers more unruly than any other crow I've before seen. She alights upon the roof of the building opposite the Gander's Gullet, gaze of inky-black eyes upon me. And I hear her sound, that cringe-worthy awful noise. *Aww-aww-aww!* she gesticulates her open beak at me. Then she takes flight again and lands upon the ledge of the open window where I stand.

"Mother!" I kneel to her at once, shaking her gently awake. "Mother, you would not believe who is here!"

"Lirinda?" Mother croaks painfully from her slumber, and I hate myself even more as I shake my head.

"No..." What a feeble, inwardly crumbling sound I make. "...It is Crow."

Mother's eyes open as slits and they find the black bird upon the ledge, silhouetted against the pale, wintry sky. She seems to understand something I do not.

"How could she be here?" I whisper. "Your Boundary..."

"There must not be a Boundary anymore. I think it's diminished...as I have begun to."

I think of the whirring power that weaves through the pines of Haven, Mother's fresh, earthy essence strong with it. Her essence that I have not sensed from her since Lirinda's disappearance.

If the Boundary has grown weak, the animals may be wandering past their usual borders, pricking their ears at the new sounds beyond, Crow having taken flight beyond Haven, searching for a sign of us amid the harsh world of the capital.

The longer we sit here in this room, the more likely there will be hunters or wandering men who come close to Haven and, for the first time, perceive beyond the pines and brambles a cottage with a living roof of twigs and leaves, overgrown with spindly branches bearing windchimes and baubles. And beyond it, a meandering path to a garden flourishing with forbidden, magical flora...

Anxiety grips my throat.

"It's because you will not eat, Mother," I scold in a hiss, going to the pot, only simmering now, and dipping our tankard into it for her to sip from. Oily juices drip off the side, and I wipe it off on my cloak. "Sip, Mother. I've made it for you. The vegetables are not as fresh as ours but it's better than rotten food."

She takes it into her hands but does not look at it. Her eyes have already found the fire. Irritated, I step before her gaze so she cannot be lost again.

"I am going to the castle," I say outright so that the shock of it may bring her attention to me, enraged as it might be. But she simply shakes her head.

"You will not."

"Then *you* will?" I challenge.

"It is a place of great evil," she whispers painfully. "I could not bear to set foot in it. It would kill me. I am killed enough being so far from our home…"

"That is why *I* must go!" I breathe desperately. *It is not too evil for me*, the words come to my mind, but I do not utter them. I am surprised by the flush of eagerness I feel. The determined pound of my heart.

"You would be lost, too." Finally, Mother's eyes find mine. Weary and diminished though they are, still they blaze as green as her plants, her ivy, her fronds of fern that dance in a breeze so far from here. They are a warning… a desperate plea for home, for safety, and I am chilled by it.

"I would not."

"You would." She looks away from me. "I have always meant to keep you far from this place. Always I've known what it would do to me…to her, to *you*. And already it has begun. I will not consent to you being lost to it as well."

"Mother, I am strong!" I kneel at her side and place a tentative hand upon her forearm. "You know how I have my power. I am capable, I am cunning. You know I am not so easily swept as Lirinda…"

"Never has it been weakness I've feared for you, Sirilda."

I lean back, away from her, onto my heels. She does not look at me, so she does not see the hurt upon my face as I realize that Mother does not fear for me; she fears…*me*. She cares not if I would be lost from her, only if I were to be lost in another way, a worse way. Tempted by my own strength and power. She fears of all things that I am dangerous.

Amid my disappointment, a cold swell of excitement swirls dark with my Current, something sinister like the castle's mysterious pull, but I close my eyes against it.

"I'll not be gone long." I rise to stand.

"You are both gone already," she mutters in little more than a breath, and I ignore her. The sooner I am out of this inn, rapping upon Lirinda's pretty, queenly door, the sooner we can be finished here, and Mother may not be so pathetic.

I have hope that, once Mother is surrounded by forest again, she will rise from this illness of grief. She may never recover fully but any earthen solace is better than this. I need only deliver her there.

I go to the window to close the shutters against the rainy wind of outside, seeing that Crow has already flown to another roof where she watches me with her ever-ominous stare. I give her one uncomfortable look before closing the shutters between us.

"You have food, a pitcher of water, a pot for pissing, and a bed if you decide to use it. Try not to let the innkeeper's daughter Malinne see the pot I've stolen from the kitchen if she comes in. But she'll likely not come by before I return. I'll be back in the morning."

I arrange the filthy tatters of bedcovers so they might be more appealing to Mother, rather than her superiorly vile blanket of mold, which appears to have grown in mass and length since I have been in the room with her. I look at Mother a long while, my mouth tightening with disgust, pity, and annoyance. How wrong it is that she is here in this hard, sunless room—this woman who seems sometimes to be more plant than human. A flower in a wood crate.

"Should our Lirinda refuse to return with me," I utter into the quiet of the room, hearing the crackle of dread in my otherwise certain voice, "you and I will return home without her."

With a cool swish of my cloak, I heave open the door to leave but pause to look over my shoulder at Mother for one lingering moment. Still she sits with her hands cupping the steaming tankard of stew, her face weighed by an even heavier sorrow than before.

"I really won't be gone long," I promise, but in my words I mean a wealth of other promises, too, such as that she mustn't fear that I will stray as Lirinda has.

But as I close the door upon her, the finality of the wood separating us, I can feel how very alone I am without either influence of my mother or sister, for the first time in my life. My solitude is realized as I exit the Gander's Gullet, holding my wind-jostled cloak around myself, with nothing to carry but my own fleshly burdens. My fear pounds with my heart for what awaits me, but so, too, does a secret excitement.

Swirling between buildings of the capital, an icy wind plays with my loose, uncovered hair like a lover, and my Current dances with the tendrils of the mysterious power I feel reaches for me across time, memory, and the expanse of city streets, beseeching me for something I do not understand but know I possess.

The castle looms pale in the stormy sky above. *I am coming,* I say in my mind, and as I stride resolutely up the main road to the castle, my cloak flapping with my black hair in the violent rain-spraying wind, I find I say this not to my sister but to the castle itself.

CHAPTER EIGHT

The castle, as I near it, is even grander, more terrifyingly imposing than ever I thought from a distance. I stretch my neck to look up to its highest towers, but they are lost in the dark, rapidly swirling clouds.

Armored guards stand sentinel at the massive iron gates of the gatehouse and look me over scrutinizingly through their helmets as I make my way up the steep inclining road. How must I look to them, I wonder. Through their eyes, I imagine myself: a haggard peasant, dressed in a rain-drenched cloak with her hood blown down to her nape, black mane wild around her gaunt and pallid face. My eyes—I know they are frantic as a cornered rabbit's, large and wary at the sight of them, at the metal spikes upon their shoulders, the fatal weapons hanging off their belts.

I close my fists out of habit, as if squeezing my fingers closed might prevent any magic seeping from me. I wonder if they can sense it at all. Do I look ordinary enough as any Pure woman? Or does my magic glean rebelliously in my black irises?

I open my mouth, preparing to yell through the wind the

speech I've come to memorize in my journey here—that I am Sirilda, sister to the king's bride, and that I have come as invited. But before I can make a sound, the metal gates screech slowly open for me and the guards nod approvingly.

I gulp down the unspoken words and nod back to them as I saunter on.

As the road ascends the swell of mountain, I am at such an elevation to see over the tallest roof pitches of the highest level of the city and am allowed my first breathtaking view of the menacing dark sea beyond. From my distance, the churning waves look small but no less deadly, frothing so far below the cliffs at the castle's edge. The nearer to the castle's fortifying walls I climb, the more potent is the smell of brine, algae, and wet stone upon the wind, and the more monstrously large the waves I am able to distinguish. I see that there are balconies upon the castle that overlook the water, and I am suddenly chilled to imagine such a view.

"You must be Mistress Sirilda!" hollers a pompous-sounding little voice, straining against the roar of wind.

So absorbed have I been in my surroundings that I've not noticed a small man descending a stone stairway from off one of the fortifying walls, dressed in the dark blue and white livery of the castle with a fine cape fastened neatly at his throat. He grips his petite hand to his plumed cap so that it does not blow off of his head, the ostentatious feather upon it thrashing.

Mistress Sirilda? I stand resolute, stricken with awe at the title.

I wonder what this man is thinking as his small bulbous face squints down at me in the rain. Surely, he is surprised at how much different than my sister I look—not prim and elegant, but unruly, scowling back at him as I drip with rain, my tattered hems soaked with mud. Perhaps he is most surprised at how I've walked here, all this way, in this weather, when horses and carriages pass me by on the wide cobbled road. Whatever his thoughts may be, he keeps them guarded carefully beneath a practiced mask of composure. I do my best to mirror him.

"We have been watching the road for your arrival. I am Tafton, a groom to Lady Lirinda. It is my duty to see to your comfort and lodgings here in the castle. Shall we hurry inside, then?"

Lady Lirinda? The words sound so strange…but only for an instant. So often had Lirinda called herself this in our tales and revels that I nearly grin despite the rain dripping down my lips. I nod to him.

A walking path perpendicular to the main road leads me to the stairway upon which he stands. When I reach him and he walks ahead of me, guiding me, I find that his progress is quite slow compared to mine. Upon his small legs, Tafton staggers side to side, like a young child still imbalanced on his feet. Too easy it would be for me to overtake him with the vast strides of my long legs, but I dare not be so impolite. So I follow him with tiny, measured steps, and he leads me through a series of walkways and staircases within the limestone fortifications of the castle.

Such as with the sea, I am equally startled by the amount of green I see once I am offered a generous view of the castle grounds. Opposite the cliffs that jut drastically into the sea is the rest of the mountain upon which the castle perches. Luscious lawns sprawl across the mountain, bordered distantly by forest. Small ponds glint between folds of landscape, perhaps bearing fish—and gardens, so many colorful gardens there are to behold, stretching far up sloping hills and neat terraces that go beyond my sight, vivid beneath the storming sky, with strange statues and beastly topiaries scattered throughout.

I see the vague figures of people at work within the faraway orchards, harvesting bright apples into baskets. Never have I seen so many neatly groomed trees grown in perfect rows. My tongue thirsts for the sweet cider.

So serene are the willows in their autumnal hues of yellow, dipping into shimmering pond water, and the lonely rose gardens I long to wander off to and smell, I feel I might forget everything I've come here for. The more I admire the surreal loveliness of this haunting place, the more I forget that it is treacherous to me. It is like something out of a dream—an enchanting nightmare.

As we ascend the highest, final-most fortification, I can see the smooth stones of the castle's exterior, forbidden and enticing to me as the flesh of a beautiful enemy; I am both repulsed and aroused at once. Impressed I am, at how each window, all the way even to the impossibly high towers above, is arched and mullioned with identical tracery of an elderflower design. *The Glindians,* I muse, *aside from being murderers, are also lovers of great beauty.*

I have chills, suddenly—chills unrelated to the whistling cold wind—as we come upon a paved semicircle of space before a massive arched door; the grand entrance at last. Guards stand unmoving before the imposing doors with their lances intersected. When they see Tafton and me, the metal of their lances slink as they uncross them and allow us passage. Unseen servants within pull the doors apart for us, and I am given the impression of a great, hungry mouth opening for me.

Tafton goes on through, but I halt in my tracks.

It is all so eerie…so impressive. Sentient, almost. The stone around me feels as though it breathes and watches. The statues of men carved into the front walls look upon me with blind white eyes as if they know what I am, why I've come, and that it's hardly for my sister…but for another purpose I've yet to discover.

In my trance of gazing up at the perilously tall entrance and the fearsome statuesque faces, the guards in their helmets break their composure to look me over with suspicion. I see that Tafton, in the chamber beyond, has turned where he stands, surprised I am not at his heels, and quirks a brow at me over his shoulder.

With a bracing breath, I pull my cloak's hood over my head; useless though it is, I am desperate for whatever protection remains. Still do I feel the cold, dark beckoning from the mysterious source, and my aroused power eager to meet it, but it is subdued beneath my pounding fear.

I force myself forward between the doors, the immense passage consuming me as I walk on through.

Such a fool I am, I think. *Treading willingly into the belly of my predator.*

Before I am able to take in the chamber beyond, I am blinded by the sheer brightness of the muted daylight filtering in through tall, pointed windows—windows as tall as the highest trees. The light beyond filters in and reflects brightly off walls of luminous stone. My eyes smart, and I blink like a stupidly squinting child, up and all around me at the grandeur I cannot comprehend.

Hardly aware I am of the servants who come forward to offer Tafton and me fresh towels to dry ourselves with, or that I absentmindedly dab myself with the fragrant cloth, for my attention is up, at the impossibly high vaulted ceiling and all around me in every which direction, for there is nowhere I can look that is something simple enough for me to recognize. There are no plants here, no herbs strung from ceilings, no hearth fires—only white marble, carved in hundreds of different forms from the enormous columns and grand staircase to the many sculptures of lithe naked men on pedestals, receded into archways within the walls. It is all so ornate it is almost grotesque.

An entire field could fit in this one chamber, I think, taking in the breadth of the entrance hall, how it seems to echo with my quickened breaths.

An indulgent chuckle comes from Tafton beside me. I pry my gaze from a sad, wimple-wrapped matronly bust to look down upon him, and see that he is evidently pleased with my bewilderment.

"Brilliant, isn't it?" says he. "Even on a dark day as this does the hall so brightly shine."

He removes his cap from his head and wrings the rainwater from it before replacing it atop wiry graying curls. I gawk with awe how servants instantly kneel to mop up the water, and how, without a word to them, Tafton leads me onward again, through the middle of the entrance hall. I follow closely, up to the staircase of yet more ornamented white marble, veined luxuriously with pale silver.

"King Geldan was responsible for the marble renovations more than two hundred years ago," Tafton explains, indicating a stubby hand to the too-pale chamber. "You'll find that the great hall and throne hall share in this style. However, before he could renovate more of the castle, he regrettably passed, and his son, King Gledden, did not complete his vision, nor have any of the Glindian Kings since."

I swallow hard and hope that Tafton does not invite me to speak upon the history of his kings, for I know nothing of them other than their mutilation of magic. Up until days ago, these kings were a reality I considered so distant, they were almost mythical, forbidden, never to be known, and seldom talked about. But now I am here, walking past remembered statues of them, a guest in their home…

With a chill, I wonder if their bones are buried somewhere near. I muse that my own bones can feel them, their wicked marrow. Their dust. Is that not what this entire hall smells of? Bones and dust? For how clean it is, my lungs itch with an urge to cough. I long for fresh air. Too still is it here, too many echoes. Our still-damp shoes squeak slightly upon the polished marble stairs, and I presume that just as soon as we are out of sight, the servants will come with their rags and polish them again.

At the top of the staircase, a grand door opens to the side of us, releasing an explosion of sound into the silent hall. The sound is of chatter, laughter, and merry music. I slow in my pace so that I might steal a captivated glance through the open door that a smartly dressed musician has entered through, carrying a heavy wood string instrument. Beyond, I glimpse another vast hall, perhaps more vast than the entrance hall from what I can see, and just as ostensibly wrought of marble. I crane my neck for a greater view before the door closes again and silence is sealed by the door once more.

Beyond the entrance hall, the high-arched corridor that Tafton leads me through is a stark change in atmosphere, and I know at once what he meant by King Geldan's unfinished renovations. Here, the walls are of rough, ancient, dark stone— the original walls, free without veneer, and they continue for the rest of the castle through which we pass. I feel rather like a mouse sauntering carefully through skeletal bellies of colossal monsters, for the intricate rib vaulting of the high ceilings remind me so of bones, of spines and ribs of great stone carcasses.

Relieved I am by the old stone, the cool darkness, exposed and vulnerable to me. Treasures of kings long-since dead glinting in the low light are much less insufferable here, but historic and interesting, reminding me of the centuries past of kings and their courts existing among these halls just as I am now. The stone makes me feel awakened, aware, not only to the past, but what still emanates from an era long before the velvet draperies, the woven rugs, the oak polished tables, the bronzed busts. A whisper from an era of unfathomable antiquity, seeping from between and beneath the Pure treasures.

It is in these raw halls that I begin to feel it, stronger than ever before. The ancient force that beseeches me, seeks me.

The Source.

It is here… I think wildly to myself. *I've come to it at last.*

I feel tempted to lay my hand to the stone wall, just to know if it's as hard and cold as I imagine it would be—or perhaps to reciprocate the greeting I profoundly feel, emanating from the Source that somehow, somewhere, I feel aching deep within the stone—but I instead fold my hands together.

Painful it feels to defy the mysterious beckoning for Tafton's guidance up several stairs and down numerous corridors, for the higher we climb the castle's towers the more distant that beckoning aches in my marrow.

How is it I'm not revolted by this place? I ask myself, staring up at a magnificent tapestry of a sword—no doubt a depiction of the same sword I've seen so often already—and I wonder what its significance is. Likely something horribly Pure, I muse. Same as the elderflower tracery I see everywhere, within every curvilinear window glowing with the diffused light of rainfall. Before I can admire these things as well as I would like, my hooded form is forced to move past them, flames of the gold candelabras as tall as myself fluttering excitedly in the breeze of my passing.

This is Gillin's Castle—the home of my enemy, I attempt to justify within my own mind, despite how strangely comforted

I feel being here. It feels to me almost as though I am existing within a pleasurable embrace, the corridors hugging me more profoundly than even the tangly branches of Haven, beating with the pulse of Mother's magic; I wonder if it is that I am finally here, the place that has been beckoning to me my whole life, that makes me feel strangely as though I belong.

"That is the sword, Hallath, of course," explains Tafton once we pass yet another artistic rendering of the sword I have seen so much of; this time, it is the subject of a mural stretching across a long hall. Tafton pauses a while for us to admire the detailed, time-faded painting; the pigments are oxidized and, in places, peeled or smeared with moisture. The sword Hallath is gigantic in the foreground, illuminated with a beam of sunlight shining down from cloud-parted heavens. The background of the sword is the beautifully intricate design of a wild green world with noble fauna in a great surrounding arc, showing the sword reverence. Deer and elk, bowing their antlers to the flowery ground. An eagle standing, rather than in flight. Horses and bears with their heads to the grass. And in the center, just behind the sword, appears to be a shining pond, muddled brown over time. But I realize with a jolt of remembered hatred that this had once been red paint, intended to be blood.

I needn't have an imagination to assume whose blood it must be.

"Our modern world knows no art like this." The little man clicks his tongue disappointedly. "Look closely, there, in the ray of sunlight. Do you see the Watchful Eye of the Goddess Mavet?"

I wince my eyes to make it out, and I suppose I do see a feminine, long-lashed eye painted within the sunlight of the heavens; a shared thread of gold shines down from it to the sword itself.

I feel my mouth open with the urge to ask about her, this goddess, and the story of her watchful eye these Pures must hold dear, but know it would reveal my ignorance. Instead, I force out the words, "It is beautiful."

"Yes, of course it is," replies Tafton smugly. He continues to walk on. "Honorables from across the realm come before the painting on Gillin's Day, just for the glimpse of her, to thank her for Hallath. They say that only to the most virtuous maidens can the painting move with the blinking of her eye." He glimpses up over his shoulder at me, suspicious of my reaction, if perhaps I've been blinked at, and if not, that it must mean to him that I am without virtue. But my expression beneath my hood is one of cringing revulsion, and so he looks forward again, guiding me on.

In our progress through the castle, there are many whom we pass. From maids, grooms, and liveried pages to the luxurious Honorables of the court, each of them slow in their strides and gawk after my hooded figure, watching how I follow Tafton in silence.

I avoid most of their incredulous gazes for the sake of keeping my identity from being exploited, but there are certain scathing Honorable ladies, looking over me cruelly, who I cannot resist but give a glimpse of my challenging black stare from beneath the hem of my hood. A stare that makes them gasp, for surely they never have seen a creature so wild as me that was not on their plate for supper, nor have they witnessed a being so unwilling to fawn after them.

Each of them, even the servants, speak in whispers to one

another once I have passed them. Fear thunders through me at what they might be saying. If perhaps I am a little too strange a stranger, and their minds wander to that forbidden and deadly place of magic.

I mustn't stay long, I plead to myself, though contrarily the magic thrumming within me begs never to leave.

It is when my gaze is over my shoulder, staring after a grand tapestry of maidens dancing among swans I pass, that Tafton comes suddenly to a halt before me, and I nearly crash into the backside of him. When I come to a halt, it is to see that he has folded into a low bow before me, for a group of Honorable men come parading arrogantly toward us down the corridor.

Before I can make out their features, my eyes lower, as though it might make me invisible to them. But I can feel their arrogance, like a hot day, scorching, and I realize it is not simply arrogance I feel like the other Honorables I've passed, but something greater—*power.* It is not unlike magic, power, how it can compel the world against nature and make the skin of my nape melt with nervousness. The intensity of it makes me shiver with fear, and perhaps, too, fascination.

In the red glow of the torches, my periphery sees a blur of jewels and metals glaring in the light. I make out outlines of fur upon broad shoulders and strong statures upon tall men. And then as they near, I catch the scent of one man in particular. An autumnal spice; a girthy, strong whip of action and passion; chopped trees and woodsmoke; an exhilarating run through a cold forest; a raging fire devouring wood.

My avoidance of their gaze is futile, for I feel their stares burn upon what can be seen of my chin and lips from beneath my hood, and, unable to resist the furious flare of curiosity I feel, I raise my face for my eyes to meet them. When I see it is the king who passes me, brown eyes just as curiously studying me, thick brows furrowed with what I can only assume to be displeasure, which I mirror perfectly with my own brows, I find we cannot remove ourselves from a mutual stare of one another.

"You must *bow* to His Majesty!" Tafton snarls at me with a jab of his elbow to my hip. That is enough to help me to remove my eyes from the king's, and for that I am thankful. But now that the king comes to a halt so near to my side, with his men slowing behind him, staring at me more intently, I am wishing I had simply surrendered to fold into a curtsy and hid myself from them properly.

"Your Majesty." Tafton turns to face the king where he now stands and bows again. "I beg your forgiveness. This girl— she…"

"It is all right, Tafton." The king's voice booms so near to me, up my neck. My frantic eyes know not where to look, so they fall furiously upon the ground at my side. "This is the Lady Lirinda's little sister, is it not?"

Get my sister's name out of your mouth, I wish to hiss at him. And being so near to his chest, his radiant masculine heat, the smell of him, I cannot help but return to my earlier thoughts of his naked knowledge of my sister. I hate him for it. For everything.

An inexplicable bubble of rage rises to my flesh, and I feel even hotter than before, I ought to be red-colored, but I shiver still with the sickening feeling of his power so near to me, sweltering me. A power I very much dislike. A power that brings my Current to burn in my palms, which I wriggle my fingers in my sleeves to resist.

"It is, Sire. This is…Sirilda," says Tafton with obvious distaste for my name.

At this moment they all seem to expect me to amend the situation and curtsy, apologize even, but I am frozen, my hood covering my rigid expression from the king and his men to see.

Just curtsy! I beg of myself, for fear that I am endangering Lirinda and myself both with my disrespect. Giving them all the more reason to suspect me, or worse, Lirinda. Slowly, I thaw from my terror, and my Current aids my muscles to slip into a very small and rigid curtsy.

A ripple of laughter erupts from the king's chest. "There is no harm in not knowing manners, so long as one learns, Tafton. Particularly with her, I have heard she is most uncivilized."

My eyes squint with the realization that he's heard this from Lirinda. Which, of course, is the truth, yet although the king says it without mockery, but as rather a cool statement, it is a sting nonetheless that Lirinda would speak of me as lowlier than herself.

"I assure you, Your Majesty, it will not happen again," Tafton swears, and with that, the king and his group of gentlemen continue on past us down the corridor. Although I feel the king's eyes upon me even as he walks away, and I sense his interest upon me lingers long after.

As soon as he is gone, I feel my eyes burn with the ridiculous urge to cry, but I twist my mouth so that I do not. My underarms, how slick they are with sweat; my palms cramp with the vicious clenching of my fists, straining to keep my Current from slipping from my grasp. Had I been forced to endure another moment in the king's presence, it certainly would have.

"That was very stupid of you," Tafton says to me, and I do not disagree. In the midst of the king, every move of mine was chosen sloppily, without enough heed. I close my eyes briefly, for I cannot bear to imagine how things might be now, had I performed any worse; had my Current slipped from me as oft it does.

If I had any sense, I would leave now, I tell myself, yet my legs continue to carry me after Tafton's progress.

Our journey through the castle comes to an end at last when Tafton and I arrive at a simple door offset from one of the more modest corridors.

"In here," says he, still disgusted with me for my failed courtesies with the king, but still maintaining a falsely polite air with his chin held high. When we enter, I am astonished to find it is a bare room of clean-swept stone, with only a plain bed and a tub for washing, save the lonely window in the center of the room, Lirinda's gilt figure nowhere to be seen.

"Where is—" I begin to ask, turning on the spot to interrogate the small man, but his answer rolls promptly and coldly out his mouth before I can complete my sentence.

"Presently, the royal court is preparing to dine for supper. Seeing as you have not yet taken oath to join the Lady Lirinda's royal household, you are not to attend. The Lady Lirinda will be notified of your arrival and will send for you when she is able. Until then, I am to invite you to make yourself comfortable here." He indicates to the simple room—simple in contrast to the luxurious halls through which I had just been guided, yet a room still far finer than any I had ever been in, or dreamed of being in, before. "Supper will be brought up once it is ready. And a servant will be in to light a fire for you."

"I can build my own," I contest.

His eyes linger upon me, the wild image of a wide, dark hood swallowed over a head of damp-frizzled hair and untrusting black eyes. A false little smile perches upon his wry lips as perhaps he grits back his impatience.

"Yes, I am sure you can," says he with a bite of poison. "This chamber is yours for as long as it takes for your oaths to be sworn. Should you care to bathe..." His eyes rove over the obvious mud soaking the hem of my cloak, the worn wool of it which has been gnawed at by years of hard work and grime, and perhaps he has even seen how dirt and ash rim my fingernails. "You need only ask the servants and they shall bring up water for you."

I nod in acknowledgement, and he flicks his head forward in return, eager to be rid of my presence, before exiting the room and leaving me alone with my whirling emotions and Current at last.

A hefty sigh releases from my chest once my solitude is realized. But a stone of anxiety chokes my throat so painfully, I take a hand to my neck and knead my fingers at the tense sinews.

Still, my heart pounds with panic for the king being so near to me. Rage like burning-hot acid swirling my Current to a soft, pulsating ache for release.

Why do I not hate all of this as I ought to?

It takes me a long moment to hear anything beyond the tumult of my mind—to hear how rain pelts upon the castle exterior and drips across the outside of the window opposite me. It is a narrow mullioned pane of glass through which the storm's gloom illuminates the chamber with a somber glow. Such stony percussion I have never heard, but it soothes me from my alarm. Unlike rain upon trees and soil of the forest, it is an unyielding, hard sound. The cold, sterile gloom of this chamber brings me to shiver as does my rain-drenched hair that I feel again now that I have nothing to distract me, and the cold water, which has seeped down the neck of my cloak and soaked my frock beneath. Soaked my blistered feet through the holes in my shoes.

I cross the chamber to the window. I expect I am very high in the castle, perhaps within the clouds, yet once the horrifying view of the earth so far beneath me—beneath even the mountain the castle perches high upon—reaches my eyes, I sway on the spot and grip the window ledge to keep me from falling faint.

Blurred by the falling rain, and far beneath the strips of rapidly drifting clouds, the entirety of Glindor is spread before me like a vast quilt of farmlands, towns, and hills. The capital looks to me like a brick-and-timber patch of tiny etches of streets—a city for insects, small and irrelevant from all the way up here. I think of Mother in the Gander's Gullet, but I do not allow myself to think of how she likely has not moved from her spot upon the floor; I do not allow myself to worry if she has allowed her stew to go cold.

A tatter of mist sweeps before the window. I focus my gaze upon the snaking beads of rain upon the glass to steady me.

My breath as I whisper to myself is fog upon the glass. "Did you ever think that you would be here? Standing at one of the windows I've looked to, marveled at."

I shiver at the impossible thought. And I am aware of the magic call, beckoning to me again, deep from somewhere within the ancient stone walls. I am aware, too, of the eerie feeling that, somehow, it has found me and delivered me here— all this way, from my years of having looked to the castle from between the ferns of Haven.

The door opens at my back. I turn with a jerk of fear that the Guard has come for me here, that this has been a trap, but I soften when I see that it is a young serving girl. A basket of tinder is held off to the side of one of her hips while with her other arm she carries a tray bearing tarnished pewter domed lids and a drinking cup, likely the most tarnished pieces of metal in this whole castle, but still very beautiful. She offers a small nod to me, and I nod my head curtly back to her.

Without a word to me, she sets the tray upon a table then gets to work, lighting a fire in the stone fireplace. Indeed, she is more trained than I at lighting the kindling with these castle tools. I watch her from beneath my hood, grateful for the bloom of orange light in the chamber that has already darkened with evening, the smallest comfort and reminder of home. She nods again to me before exiting the room.

When I am perfectly alone again, I go delicately to the tray of pewter as if I might startle it away if I am too rash, too greedy. Not until I breathe in the aroma of cooked fish and greens from beneath domed platters, and golden honey mead in the chalice, do I allow my empty stomach to gurgle upon itself with excitement.

I feed myself pieces of fish with my fingers, licking the juices savagely as they drip down to my wrists. Realizing my extreme thirst, my slippery hands cup the chalice, and I slurp from it, feeling the cool liquid spill down my chin, to my neck, down into my cloak. Never before have I drunk from a metal cup, and never has a drink been so fresh and sweet; the thought of drinking from carved wood at home again makes me drink all the heartier. When I use the back of my hand to wipe the juices from my lips, it's with knowing that I choose to refuse the cloth upon the tray, for the sake of whatever wildness I may possess still—a wildness which feels so unwelcome here in this barren chamber.

Uncivilized, I recall Lirinda's word with a bloom of anger.

Slowly, for longer than an hour, the room fills with heat from the fire. Perhaps if I felt more comfortable, I might go to sit before the fireplace as I long to do, to warm myself properly, remove my boots and warm the sodden flesh of my cut and blistered feet from days of walking. But instead, I stand still before the darkening window as I wait for Lirinda, unmoving from my rigid stance. My Current is prepared to flare from me at any moment that danger may present itself; my hands wring together in an anxious massage. I know that I should expel it here in a slight amount to be safe. For I know the one cause in all this tumultuous world for my Current to flare most dangerously is the person I am soon to see.

The set of iron pokers near the fireplace rise from the ground at my command. They are heavy enough to tug satisfyingly at my Current as I spin them around before setting them down again, but it may not be enough. So unpredictable my Current has grown to be, I do not know what is enough anymore.

When the door is rapped upon again, it is Tafton who greets me. "The Lady Lirinda is ready for you now."

CHAPTER NINE

The windows we pass to Lirinda's chambers are black with night, and as I wearily come upon a corridor arrayed with pieces of feminine art, with a massive, tall guard in full helmeted armor standing before a tall arched door, I am filled with a tired longing to wake from this splendid, horrible dream and find myself easily climbing upon the gnarled bunk of branches where my sleepy sister awaits me. But as the huge guard steps aside for Tafton and me, and I see a long candlelit chamber beyond the opened door, elegant and decorated for a queen, I know the dream is far, far from over.

The long room is beautifully furnished with an ornately woven carpet the length of the room and upholstered chairs before a grand fireplace of marble scroll. Vases overfilled with autumn's flowers decorate every lovely, polished surface. No one is here, not Lirinda nor any servants—and there is no bed to be seen, not even a washing basin—so I assume this space is simply for leisure. I imagine it filled with the fanciful women of the court, playing their instruments, or doing whatever else they deem delicate enough for such a room.

Tafton guides me through this long chamber, which he calls the ladies' gallery, and through another door at the end of the room. We walk next through what is called Lirinda's presence chamber: a beautiful stretch of room with time-faded murals of swans and flowering elderberry trees upon the plastered walls, certainly centuries old, bordered with flowery molding. Here, there are servants within, measuring the floor and long dining table, surely for the furnishings they will have crafted to fit the space in Lirinda's tastes. Through the next and final door is her bedchamber, at last, and here there are even more servants taking measurements of the lengths of the room, the dimensions of her enormous four-poster bed, and even of my sister, Lirinda, who stands in the middle of it all, while her waist and bust are measured by whom I can only assume to be the royal dressmaker.

Seeing her so comfortable here, knowing she has been well cared for, should soothe me of my anxieties, but instead I feel a burn in my chest quite like the disgust I felt for the king. A great part of me wishes that I had not come here—that I had simply gone back to Haven without ever seeing my sister so decorated in her selfishness.

"Sirry!" Lirinda beams over her shoulder at me when she sees us enter. "You've come at last!" She makes to step down from the stool on which she stands to be measured, but the dressmaker urges her not to move for the sake of his measurements. "Come here, sister!" she calls to me when she must stand still, and when I do, a little reluctantly, she takes my hand into hers as she smiles excitedly down at me.

"I am so glad to have you here with me now," she breathes with emotion, her eyes shimmering with sisterly adoration. "And what good timing you have! You can tell me what you think of the dressmaker's design for my coronation gown. He will make a collection for you as well once you've joined my household as one of my ladies. And Mother, too, of course..." Her gaze surveys the bustling bedchamber behind me as if she might see our mother among its fineries. "Where is she?"

She would not dare come, is what I open my mouth to say, but think better than to expose our mother's unwillingness to attend the castle to the servants around us, should this make them suspicious of our loyalties.

"She's not here," I say as blandly as I can. "And I cannot stay."

"You're not staying?" Her eyes widen with despair, her voice diminishing to a squeak. "Why ever not?"

I swallow down my urge to speak plainly to her before all these Pures. "I was hoping we might have a bit of privacy as we spoke."

"Yes, we're almost done now. There is just so much to be done before the coronation. I have been preparing for it all day, choosing this and that, and vowing myself to the Glindian Oath. And really! To be measured for my gown after such an indulgent feast is truly unkind!"

"It is always to be done this way, My Lady," replies the dressmaker with his chalk behind his ear, which he removes to add a sketch of detail upon his drawing board. "The Queen of Glindor must always have her gown made to fit widely, in the hope that she may be with child at the time of the ceremony."

A blush heats upon Lirinda's cheeks, and she smiles demurely. "So soon? I can be hopeful." She leans to me with confidence. "Already the king's advisor has asked me if I feel I'm with child yet. It has hardly been more than a day! I do not think it works that way, does it?"

Any humor lingering in my face, in my eyes, is sucked away at the confirmation that my sister has reason to believe she may be with child.

"No," my voice crackles with animosity. "No, it does not."

"I wish Mother was here," she says as she is rotated on the spot, and her back is to me. "She would know. Sirry, please tell me she will come here soon. You must bring her here. I must have you both in my household."

The image of Mother being forced to wear a gown and sit among Honorable ladies is almost laughable enough to bring the scant humor back into my face, until I am stung with the horror of where Mother truly is and that I must not dawdle here while she awaits us in her growing shroud of mold.

She will never come, I wish to say. *If we are ever to be all together again, you must come with us,* but I know I cannot speak in such a way in front of these servants.

I am glad when the dressmaker states he has finished his measurements and will begin Lirinda's coronation gown overnight. As he collects his supplies, Lirinda kindly commands the servants out of the chamber with him, and we are alone at last.

The room is warm and lovely with the light from the many candelabra flickering against pale walls of flowering molded plaster. So dark is the moonless night that I cannot see out the wide mullioned windows; only the reflections from within the bedchamber shimmer upon the glass, but there is a rhythmic rushing sound I hear and can subtly feel from beyond. I assume it is the sea, so near, crashing against cliffs. How I would like to see out these windows in the day, and witness such a sight, to be mesmerized by the sea's enormity. In the sterling morning, the sea must be especially beautiful.

But I know I cannot be here still to see it. If I am successful, Lirinda will not be here either. If I am successful, we will be walking together to the Gander's Gullet to retrieve Mother, and then the three of us ascending our mountain to Haven, where we can begin to forget the folly of Lirinda's marrying the king. But the thought of it, now, as I am here surrounded by castle gold, seeing Lirinda's rosy face flushed with pleasure and the wine from supper, I know that to rip Lirinda from this life and bring her back to our crude forest living will be as easy as forcing a swan into a birdcage.

I take a deep steadying breath for the feat I must attempt.

"Sit with me!" Lirinda takes my hands into hers and gently ushers me to sit with her upon her pretty silk-embroidered counterpane, our shoulders pressed together. So close we are, for a glimpse I feel we are back again in our bunk.

Since it is only the two of us now, I feel comfortable enough to take my hand to the embroidered hem of my hood and push it back so that Lirinda may see my whole face. She smiles at the gesture and takes a loving hand to tuck still-damp curls behind my ear. I nearly close my eyes at the relief of her presence. My golden sister, the sun to my shadow, my warm counterpart—how I have needed her. How I cannot bear to have her stay here, for her to become queen, for us to never to spin with our harvesting baskets in Mother's garden again. Never to dance our moth's dance.

"Oh, sister," she says softly, "There is so much to tell you."

"I want to know it," I say with a croak, my eyes wide with my anxieties and emotions wavering at her. "Why don't you begin with how this all came to happen."

Lirinda takes my hands into hers once more and rests them upon the soft velvet of her lap. "It is the most wonderful story," she recalls with a deep inhale and her eyes going starry.

"While you were gone, I was looking at the pretty trinkets," she begins. "I had not wandered too far from the fountain in the market square, just a few streets down where I found an old woman selling braids of cord and leather for jewelry. So simple, yet I had thought them pretty. There was one like a circlet, to be worn upon the head, with a bead like a pearl dripping down to my forehead. She insisted I try them on—really, quite assertive she was! So of course I did as she asked. I thought I was alone in trying it on, until I heard a man's voice beside me, suddenly, tell me that a crown suited me."

At this, Lirinda's smile broadens, and her grip upon me tightens.

"I turned and saw him, a man more handsome than I'd ever dreamed! He had these brown eyes, so captivating and warm, and this smile—a dimpled, gorgeous smile that made me forget how to breathe! He was well dressed, but I hadn't an idea of just *how* well dressed he was! I thought him an Honorable at the most, and you know me. That was enough to rob me of my voice and make me feel like falling where I stood.

"He didn't tell me he was the *king*. I hadn't an inkling—and how would I have known?" She squeals with incredulity, and I recall seeing the king that day, striding through the dingier streets of the capital with his gentlemen, wanting not to be recognized in his pursuit of tavern beer.

"He wore no crown, no jewels," she says. "He was disguised, and I loved him all the same. Still, I looked at him as though I had never seen anyone so ideal, because I truly hadn't! And I think that is what made him so fond of me: my feral innocence, my wonder for all things grand. There I was, in a homespun frock, my hair tumbling free without decoration but for a silly trinket I could not afford. And I looked at him with wide eyes, knowing I could not go on through life without being with him.

"The merchant asked if I would buy it, and I—a bit humiliated, really—said I could not, but my handsome stranger flicked her a gold piece and told me he would like to find me *true* jewelry, of precious metals and gems… no offense to the old woman. We walked alongside one another down a few of the streets, exchanging dulcet flatteries, until he took my hand and kissed it, and asked if I would join him in a celebration at the castle. I was just about to say that I needed to go find my sister and mother to ask them, when a group of his men strode down the street to us, telling him he was being looked for by his royal advisor. That they had to go at once.

"When they addressed him as 'Your Majesty', my mouth fell open, and as soon as I could force my body to move, I made myself curtsy the best I could. It made him laugh, how unlearned I was, but charming to him, still. He said then that he had no time to wait—his advisor would have his neck if he was not there to attend his own party—but that perhaps one day we might find one another again. With a gentle touch of farewell to my cheek, he turned to leave, and I had a moment to think what would happen if I let him. My whole life I had dreamed of such a moment, and it was slipping away. I knew you and Mother, if only you had known, would understand why I had to go with him then. And so I did."

I had been looking at her intently, but now I look away.

"And, oh!" Lirinda sighs. "It was the most wonderful night of my life. We danced to musicians in the great hall, drank deeply of his finest wines, and laughed *all* the night, never daring to release one another's hand. And that night, when I went to his chamber with him," she says this now a little demurely, and my already taut stomach rolls at the thought of her bedding the king, "he dressed my nakedness in his silks and jewels, and I lay with him, so deeply in love. I never would have thought then that this would be my life!"

I squint my eyes to refuse the imagery of them lying

together, of her naked in the king's silks, and him, naked, too. My head pounds with my aching pulse. I touch my hand to my temple. It is all too much. Lirinda is too much of a fool.

"And you know my necklace, Sirry, don't you? The one Mother says is from my father?"

"How can I forget?" My voice is stone.

"The king recognized it! At one time it was all I had on, and he took it into his hand and marveled at it. He asked where I had gotten it. When I told him, he said that such a necklace was an ancient heirloom of the Fairfellow family—one of the most highly regarded Honorable families since the beginning of Glindor—and had last belonged to the eldest heir, Lirrus Fairfellow. And he said that I was the image of him, his daughter."

I pry my eyes open now to look at her.

"An Honorable, Sirry!" She bites her lip with a smile. *"My father!"*

"You cannot be certain," I hiss. My eyes wince at the incredulity of this. "It cannot be so. Of course not... Mother would never... Not an Honorable..."

"Oh, but it *is!*" Lirinda smiles widely, tightening her grip upon me. "I share his every feature! Just this morning, a great portrait was brought in from the Fairfellow family. I was compared with it, and the necklace is even in the portrait. My father's own brother confirmed it! And it is me who this necklace has been passed down to—*his* necklace, Sirry! The necklace of Lirrus Fairfellow, my father!"

As Lirinda goes on excitedly, I cannot listen. I sit with my mouth agape and my brow furrowed, staring at the rug upon the ground. I hear her mention the words *'secret'* and *'mistress'* in regard to our mother, to which I feel myself shudder as if they cut me with a blade.

Lirinda's father—*an Honorable?*

And Mother—a mistress?

No. It is implausible. How could such a dastardly union come about? And if this bears any particle of truth, what audacity had Mother to keep us, her daughters—Lirinda especially—from this wicked world of Pures? A world that Mother has known and to which Lirinda partially belongs?

Has anything of our youth been true?

Everything about my body, about my surroundings, feels surreal as though I am in a sickening dream. I wish to wake from it—awake in our bunk to the sweet forestine sounds of morning, our hearth glowing with embers. But now even Haven seems a lie.

"The king then told me that, before my father died, he had been Captain of the Guard in service to his own father, the king before him. Both our fathers had been lost to the same massacre—something the king is most distressed about, even all these years later. Talking about it with me made him tender to me, for we have so much in common, he and I."

I quirk a brow. "Do you?"

She does not hear my scathing irony, but goes on in her excitement, "The king then knew I wasn't an ordinary commoner, but half an Honorable, and it changed something in him. I think, before, he wasn't certain a marriage would hold between the king of Glindor and a simple girl from the forest who could not even curtsy properly—but half an Honorable, a *Fairfellow,* that seemed to reassure him.

"That very night, he asked me if I would be his wife! As we lay there, talking for hours into the morning light, he said he wanted me for his queen. Of course, I told him that I would! It was all I would ever do, ever want! So we rushed to the chapel and married that very morning, our hair still a mess from his bed! And since, there has been hardly a moment we have not been partaking in some revel. Feasting or drinking or dancing! Oh, and to think that this is only the beginning! I'm not yet queen and already my every day has been such a pleasure!"

Lirinda slips off the side of the bed and begins to dance in the middle of the room, leaving me alone upon the bed to stare at her.

"Dance with me, Sirry!" She reaches for my hands to pull me to her, but I do not move.

"I'm not feeling well." I retract my hands to my lap.

"Oh, why won't you stay?" she moans despite her prance across the room, spinning in place before a gold scroll looking-glass, where she stops to admire her reflection. Coquettishly, she examines herself over her shoulder, admiring her beauty with an air of victory. Her fingers go to her hair, and she shakes the luscious sunny curls down her back then fixes the crownlike headdress atop her head so that it is straight.

"Rinda," I force from my throat in a growl. "You mustn't stay, either."

She looks from her reflection to me, and blinks with confusion.

"What?"

"You mustn't stay here," I try to summon as much pity for her as I can, but still my voice is hard. "You know it is foolish, don't you? Have you once thought of the danger you are in?"

"Gastlin would never harm me." Her voice rises with indignance.

"No?" My brows raise. "Does he even know you, sister?"

"Well enough, he does." She reaches for a pearl comb from the dressing table and takes it insecurely to her hair. "As well as anyone need know another to love them, to promise themselves to them."

I rise to my feet. "You know very well what I mean, Lirinda. You may be half an Honorable. But what of the other half?"

Her hair has become as luminous as the polished gold fixtures of her bedchamber with how frantically she drives her comb through it. She says nothing, but not to ignore me, for I can see in her face that her mind is working for an answer that will convince me.

I walk to her and rest a hand upon her shoulder. "Sister, it brings me much pain to deliver reason to your fantasy. But it is only a matter of time before you are discovered for what you are. What *we* are. That is why Mother will not come here, why I cannot stay, and why you must come home with us. No amount of jewelry or fine gowns can change the fact that you are a Magic in a Pure's court."

"*Shh!*" Lirinda hisses at me in a frenzied whisper. "You mustn't utter such words!" Her fear-widened eyes check at her bedchamber door, then meet with mine, sobering slowly from her mania. "Besides"—she softens, combing her hair again, slowly and with care—"I've never been… I've never shown any sign of it…"

I raise a brow, a furious grimace twisting my mouth. "You would deny yourself, deny us, so easily? You are a Magic whether you care to acknowledge it or not, because Mother is, and so am I. Are you not our kin? Did we not spend a lifetime together?"

"Of course we did," she seethes, albeit with a calm countenance. I realize she is practicing for being queen, how she raises her chin. "But it was not the same for me, and you know it. And now I know for certain why that is. I am a Fairfellow. I belong here. And now I am married to the king."

All I can do is nod. My jaw clenches, and I lick at my teeth.

I have lost, as I knew I would.

She sees my surrender and softens, bringing her free hand to the side of my face to cradle my cheek.

"I will be all right, sister. I promise you. Gastlin *loves* me! I have never been more certain of anything. He is not the cruel king we have always been told. He is a most tender man, my one true love in all this life. To be away from him would be a sentence worse than the most brutal death."

"Then at least you know what looms over your shoulder," I say severely. "You will ever be cutting your words carefully from your mouth, never to speak fully of who you are, where you've come from. Fearing the slightest slip of the tongue. And watching with fear for anyone who might smell your lies." I peel her hand from me and wish to drop it in my furiousness, but I cling to it instead, squeezing it in my palm. "Please do be cautious, sister. Already Mother is losing herself to madness for fear of our enemy."

"And what if we have no enemy to fear? I will protect you, Sirry. You and Mother both, if only she will come here."

"Mother will never," I swear. "And the longer I am here, the more she slips into that shadow of hers that has fought to claim her all these years, if ever you've noticed it. I fear she will never recover."

"I cannot live for Mother any longer," Lirinda pleads in a whisper, and it stings me with a shiver, for I know she is right. "And nor should you. This, she should understand! She is her own woman, as are we. We are old enough to lead our own lives, and this is the one I have chosen. What life will you choose, sister?"

My gaze falls soft, the room blurring. Never have I considered this before. Perhaps it is because I know I have no choice. For if I were to choose something of my own, it may not be to the benefit of either my sister or mother. It would be selfish, destructive, and I would be far too powerful without the fetters I keep.

"I must be going." I turn from her and stride to the door. "Good night, my sister. I know not when we will see one another again. I know not what will become of any of us."

Lirinda has the grace to show sorrow for me as I give her one final look over my shoulder, but I know that in a moment, she will rise from it and primp her hair before the looking-glass again. I wonder if the king will come to her here tonight, or if she will go to him in his rooms—if she will drop her pretty brocade gown for him or if he will tear it off her, now that she is his and he is hers, and there is nothing that can be done about it.

"Sirilda," Lirinda utters in a plaintive whisper. In her glimmering eyes I know she means to say many things, unspoken things I painfully understand. Then she breaks into a run toward me and wraps me in her tight, perfumed embrace.

I do not realize how angry I am in her arms. That my Current, always most volatile around my sister, and already incited from my encounter with the king, flares with a thousand furious tendrils, wrapping themselves around her in our embrace.

They do not harm her, and I know she cannot feel them, for she grips me still with a serene smile on her face, a deliriously happy heart beating with a slight sense of worry for my fading love for her. I can feel her emotions, the tighter my tendrils weave across her butter-smooth skin. I feel as though I am a part of her, like how when we would lie in our bunk and her dreams became visions before my own eyes.

I smell summer again; I feel the heat of a day long-since passed, where sunshine and a warm breeze glisten upon tall swaying grasses. Raging crimson poppies and periwinkle bellflowers. Mother's garden so near to us, chiming delicately with her moonbells that nod sleepily in the wind. Will this truly never be our life again? The ache of it…the anger…it surges beyond my fathoming.

Such anger I have for her, my sister, I do not even realize the enormity of it…but my Current does. My fury for her echoes far beyond this moment, from our childhood, from my infant days of longing.

In our embrace, Lirinda shifts uncomfortably as perhaps my Current, so charged with my emotions, thrashes and writhes like vines deeper within her fascia, her very network of life and memory, filled with sunshine, laughter, and play. I feel it all, seeing flashes of light and memory. These vessels are familiar to me, beating with her life's blood, hot and vibrant; it's all I can feel as I am wholly immersed within her.

Visions come to me now, moments within the castle I have never witnessed for myself. Memories, as real to me as if I was standing within them, smelling the perfumed shoulders of Honorables crowding me as they dance. I taste the residue of sweet wine, sweeter than I could dream of, lingering on Lirinda's tongue. The clean taste of a golden cup. These memories flash by without meaning or order, until I realize that the tendrils of my Current snake hungrily through my sister's mind, searching for what I am so desperate for, now, in this moment—comfort.

Briefly, we return to the warm flames of our home hearth, flames of our handcrafted candles lighting the mossy, leafy comforts of our cottage. Heat, laughter, joy, I feel again, my sister's heart kindred with mine. My Current searches her, imploring her for these comforts once more. But quickly they fade, for I find she has now her own comforts, foreign to me, beyond our life together. I can see them with my mind's eye;

for the first time in our lives, she has comforts and joys and laughter I have not been a part of. I see Lirinda as though I am there with her in the vicinity—the image she has of herself in her magnificent borrowed gown of blush pink velvet, the same hue as her own blushed cheeks, as she is seated within a massive oak-carved chair with a chalice of hot mulled wine held delicately within her fingers, in the midst of a grand wood-paneled chamber I can only presume to be the king's. And he is there, on his knees before her. So tall he is that his face is level with hers, and they gaze into one another's eyes after perhaps hours of revelry and flirtation.

How tenderly he reaches for the back of her head as he leans forward to kiss her. How quickly and heatedly their kiss becomes that her chalice falls to the ground in her abandon, the gold of the cup clanking, and hot liquid splashing with steam upon the flagged stone floor. How Lirinda becomes one of Mother's forest animals in heat as their kiss intensifies, and she yields hungrily to King Gastlin's exploring hands, her own hands reciprocating, until the back of her gown has been unlaced and the king's doublet has been removed and thrown aside.

The king picks Lirinda up into his bare, strong arms and chest and seats her upon his hips as he suckles at her neck then pulls down her bodice to suckle her abundant breasts as he carries her to his grand four-poster bed. There, slowly, the rest of her gown is removed to reveal her soft, complete nakedness, save for the controversial jewel glinting at her throat. The breeches of the king are unlaced so that he is as naked as she, and his round, strong buttocks flex as he mounts her and pushes himself gently between her spread, eager legs. How he kisses her hot mouth, then down to her pink nipples, licking at them hungrily. I feel the heat of their passion burn around me like a furnace, and in my repugnance for it, I retract from the vision. Hazily, as I wobble on my feet, Lirinda is before me now, standing in her bedchamber, a droplet of blood oozing from her nose.

She backs away from me, looking at me with horror mingled with pity for what I have seen and how I have done it—how I've used my moth-dance magic to violate her. She winces with pain and touches her fingertips delicately to her nose and sees blood.

I do the same. Blood trickles from my nostrils and streams warm to my lips.

"I did not mean to…" I say helplessly as I go frantically to wipe at my nose with the back of my hand, as always I have done, smearing the red up to my cheek—but before I can make a mess of my face, Lirinda pulls a kerchief from out her bodice and hands it to me.

"Keep it," says she, still uncomfortable, not meeting my gaze; the shock of oozing blood bright against her buttery skin. "May it help you to remember me, wherever you go. May it serve you as a reminder that you are always welcome here. Whatever our differences may be."

CHAPTER TEN

I lie upon my side in my borrowed bed. The linens are freshly laundered, crisp and fragrant. So heavily does the need to sleep weigh upon me, my frail-feeling body yielding, achingly, into the soft mattress, but still my mind thumps with questions in tandem with my rampant pulse. I had thought the mystery of Lirinda was one that would torment me still, but now I find her riddle is easily solved. It is the shadows surrounding her, surrounding Mother and myself, even, that keep me staring at the rising sliver of moon through the window.

Who are you, Mother? I wonder.

It is impossible for me to think that the guarded, strained woman I know as my mother would ever be the mistress of anyone, let alone the famously Honorable late Captain of the Guard. Could Lirinda and the king be desperately mistaken? What if they discover that Lirinda is no half Honorable and she is jilted back into rags…or worse?

For all my worry, somehow I know that Lirinda is indeed who she thinks she is; too easily does glamour and courtly courtesy come to my sister as though it's awaited her. With the most anxious spike of my adrenaline yet, I realize the only way for me to discover the truth in its entirety is to ask Mother myself.

It is not Mother's red hair I dream of, this I know. This hair is not so fiery red as the maple leaves soon to wither; it is even more wild and long, crimson-dark as fresh blood. So hazy is my subconscious that I cannot make out the face of the woman who walks before me, beckoning me to follow down a torchlit corridor, but I know she is beautiful in the poisonous way a snake might be.

Follow, she says without speaking. I feel her lure in the stone walls around me, a whisper like the damp drips slithering in through the mildewed cracks. Without seeing her face, I know she smiles.

I have followed her before, though I know not when. She is familiar to me, perhaps from dreams of long ago, or perhaps from conscious days unremembered. I feel I ought to know her—*is this familiarity only part of the dream?* In my subconscious form, insubstantial as the clouds drifting before the rising moon, I follow, though hesitantly, for I wonder if she can be trusted.

It is only a dream, I reassure myself.

However, there is something colder about this dream. Something of the atmosphere rises with urgency, pressing upon my bones in such a way that I feel them tremble and ache where I lay in the bed. I am aware of a moan that escapes me.

You're nearly there, she says again without speaking.

In my haziness, I realize that the woman carries a candle before her, a most unusual candle, bearing brilliant white light, like that of a star. Its lurid glow reveals the stone corridor before us—seemingly endless—but unlike a flame, I feel its radiance upon me like a touch. An energy, hungry and insistent, and it is not the woman whom I feel is desirous for me to follow, urging me on, but the light itself.

The light! Sentient, I feel it is, so gently aware with its tendrils of power extending to me like grasping hands of another being. I wonder if it was the woman speaking to me at all or if it was the light's conscious power. And my Current... my Current seems to reach out with its own tendrils and wrap with it in an eager embrace. How divinely they coalesce as though they are of similar matter. Both the pleasure and pressure of them both within me is agony! My spectral dream form fizzles and fades as I strain to wake.

Don't go! the words echo in my mind. By the time I'm conscious, they have lost their meaning.

The chamber I wake to is filled with the gray light of near-dawn. And my face, hair, and the linens I sleep upon are saturated in my noseblood.

I peel my face from where it sticks upon the linen.

"Dammit!" I hiss.

As I sit up, I find I am weak from the blood lost. There is a pitcher of water near a washing basin, and I stumble to rinse myself of the sticky muck that has soaked my hair and the nightshift I've borrowed. But just as I lift the ceramic pitcher into my hands, I find it has been cracked and the water drained of it. My bare feet splash in a puddle of the spilled water upon the stone floor. Still the pedestal upon which the pitcher rested drips with fresh water, and I recognize it as my doing.

I must do better to expel my Current, I think. *I have been keeping too much in me for too long, that it seeps from me in my sleep.* And I dismiss my strange dream as merely a manifestation of its need for release.

A gentle rap upon the door has me quickly setting the pitcher back upon the stand and trying to wipe my face of its blood, but it is too thick. As a young serving girl enters with a tray bearing food, she nearly drops it as she gasps at the red mess. I stand, resigned, before her, knowing how frightening I must look.

"Shall I call for Madam Morrie?" she breathes with fear.

I know not who Madam Morrie is, but I shake my head anyway, going to the linens of the bed and folding them so the mess is out of sight. I let my hair hang before my face so as to hide it from her. "Just a nosebleed. I'm sorry for the mess…"

"There's always some blood on the linens, with all the ladies and their cycles. Nothing to be ashamed of." She sets the tray of food upon the table. "Lady Lirinda had said you might be leaving this morning, so the kitchens prepared your breakfast early."

"Thank you," I murmur, looking away so she does not have to look at the crusted mess upon my face.

"I'll bring in some fresh things for you," says she. She hesitates before deciding to bob a small curtsy to me before exiting the room. I quirk a brow even after she leaves; how strange it is to be treated with unwarranted respect, for no reason more than my sister's fornication with the king.

I go to the breakfast tray and see the sausages and vegetables gleam with their juices in the pale light. I take one of the clean linens from the bed and wrap them in it, knowing Mother will need the nourishment.

A rap upon the door announces Tafton, who recoils at the sight of me.

"By the gods, Mistress. Whatever has afflicted you?"

"It is only a nosebleed. A servant is fetching me new water."

"It is bizarre, indeed, that you do not wish to stay," says he with a sneerish voice, inspecting the broken shards of the pitcher. "Wherever will you go?"

"I must care for my mother," is all I am willing to say, and I hope he has no further questions for me.

He makes a pinched face of curiosity but does not press me for more. I doubt he wants me here at all, so there is no persuasion to be had.

"The Lady Lirinda wishes for you to have this." He hands me a green velvet sack that is heavy and jingles slightly in my palm as he delivers it to me, a little unwillingly. "She hopes it will help you to fare well, wherever you go, and that you will one day return here to join her household."

I do not thank him as it is not his generosity. I nod silently to him, cradling the sack in my palms as I would a hot cup of tea. I do not count the coins before him, or check to see which quality of metal they bear, but wait for him to leave.

He gives a reluctant nod to me as he exits. Such a gesture seems to grieve him against his every pride. And he is gone without another word.

If there is any excitement I have in leaving the castle, it is that I will not have to be in his presence ever again.

The scents of herbs and hearth smoke upon my cloak are a comfort to me as I leave the castle, though the scents are not as strong as once they had been. They have faded with the days I have spent away from Haven, but will return…*I* will return. I feel a slight peace tickle in my chest at the thought of being back in Haven, but it is incomplete, knowing how different things will forever be.

As I descend the fortifying walls that border the sprawling castle grounds, I glimpse the fantastic castle gardens in the distance once more; the bizarre topiaries are partially lost behind cold swirls of mist creeping across the mountainside. I realize how longingly I stare out at them, and up to the castle towers where my sister sleeps, where balconies hang over the vicious sea that I may never see again, not in this steely cold morning light I find so lonesome and beautiful. My cloak whips around me with the salty wind that smells of the old stone surrounding me—the stone so deep in the earth that it beats with a strange, forgotten pulse seemingly only I can feel, like it yearns for me as much as I yearn for it. How foolish I have become, that I will grieve not being here. I almost feel I'm losing my home again.

"Aww ah-ah!"

I look around me for the familiar sound. High up into the steely mist encircling the battlements of the castle, I see the black figure of a crow soar. I narrow my eyes to try to see if it is any ordinary crow and figure it likely is. I cannot assume every crow in Glindor is Mother's one-legged companion. I walk on, securing my hood over my head to keep myself warmer in the cold chill, departing back through the gate house for the city, when in my periphery, I see the striking black figure of the crow fly on toward the city as though it follows my progress.

Perhaps that is Crow, I muse. Mother may have sent the bird to watch over Lirinda and me.

Mother...

The thought of her slack, miserable features fills me with perhaps more trepidation than I'd felt being in the castle of our mortal enemy. I feel ill to be returning to her, to see how she has fared in my absence—ill to be returning to her alone.

Once I have reached the Gander's Gullet, I am reminded of how truly splendid the castle was with its cleanliness and beauty. I pause a moment inside the pub downstairs, warming myself near the great fire, watching the gruff, rowdy people interact at the tables, how vile their mannerisms and filthy their flesh and cloth, that even their teeth and the tongues in their mouths are visibly unclean. Their unwashed reek is even more noticeable to me now than before, and I realize for the first time in my life how well Mother has kept Lirinda and me, that our teeth are whole and bright, our flesh smooth and radiant, and our speech clearly enunciated as any Honorable's.

I hesitate for as long as I am able, gathering courage to see what has become of Mother in my absence, before finally ascending the creaking wood stairs and standing before the door of our rented room. I listen intently for a sound, hesitating longer still before opening the door. My eyes wince bracingly as I push it open—but shock brings them to open widely at the near-complete darkness beyond, and how an arc of mice and rats scuttle from the light that pours in from the torchlit landing.

I jump back at the unsettling sight, chills prickling with disgust up my arms and neck. Tentatively, I advance into the room, a hand going to my nose for the increased stench of mold that makes me cough.

"Mother?" I scan the dark features of the small space and see a tangle of material where Mother had last been upon the floor. Her mold has stretched across the floor of the room, and a canopy of some gauzy material hangs from the wood beams of the ceiling. Vaguely, I make out a seated form beyond the ambiguous shroud, and once my eyes have adjusted to the dark, I see glints of light reflecting upon a pair of eyes as Mother turns to look at me.

I go at once to light a candle upon the dressing stand and discover, in the flickering bloom of light, that the gauzy material which drapes from the beams of the ceiling around Mother is a silken tapestry of spiderwebs. Her features are indistinct beyond the thick, silvery gauze, but there is no mistaking the recognition in her cruel gaze that I have returned to her alone.

I close the door, hiding away the magical monstrosity she's crafted, and light other candles of the small room for light; I eye the mold blanket suspiciously, for all the mice and rats I'd seen disappear into it. I swallow hard to keep myself from feeling sick.

Mother is manifesting her grief physically, I realize, feeling pity for her amid my disgust.

"I'm sorry for not coming sooner," I say softly to her. I go to kneel beside her bed of pungent flora and delicately lift aside a panel of spider silk, so I can better see her in the dancing candlelight; long-legged spiders scattering just beyond my fingertips. It has only been a day, but Mother looks even more wasted than before. One spider crawls across Mother's hairline. I go to gather it gently in my palm and set it up in the web canopy.

"Have you eaten?" I ask her.

She nods, her eyes on the empty fireplace. Only now do I realize how cold the room is. Mother must have crafted this bed of hers for added warmth, for thicker now is the mold as it sprouts tiny shoots of mushrooms and other pale fungi, like a fantastic little forest. But logs I had left beside the fireplace are gone, so it brings me relief to know she had gotten up and built herself a fire and tended to it overnight. I catch an acrid whiff of the pisspot, that it has been used but not emptied.

She's not completely without function, I think. *So she can rise from this and return to Haven with me.*

"Let's go home, Mother," I say softly, sitting near to her under the canopy of spiderweb. Her dehydrated eyes fill with tears. I take her cold hand and fold it into mine, something I have never been able to do before. The closeness between us is rigid and foreign. I feel in her muscles her urge to pull away, but she decides to surrender, for a moment, at least. But I know she smells upon my hair and skin the faint, lingering fragrances of the castle—honey mead and beeswax, Lirinda's lovely rosewater perfume—and I feel her resentment for it harden in my grasp.

"She has made her choice, then?" she croaks.

"She wishes for us to go live with her," I stipulate painfully. At Mother's dark expression I know it is something we will never do. Strangely, I feel a plummet of disappointment at this. I had not realized I had been hoping that we might live there, after all. That I might feel that enchanting familiarity again… as foolish as it is.

"I've brought something for you," I say, tearing myself from my sudden desire to return to those echoing halls and the memory of polished stone floors reflecting flames from pretty candelabras…so eerily like last night's dream. I reach for the linen bundle in my cloak and unwrap it for her, setting the meal before her, allowing the delicious smell to waft to her nose. It's still a little warm, for I ensured it was kept close to my chest all the long journey here.

She looks away from it at once. "I'll not have anything from that place."

My jaw clenches, and my fingers curl into fists. Taking a slow, seething breath in through my nose, I realize I've nearly lost all patience for Lirinda and Mother both.

"It's not so awful there," I say with spite, knowing how wicked those words will seem to Mother and feeling pleasure for it. Sour is my heart, cold and cruel my tongue, like a lashing sword, and the anger I've had for Mother boils my blood black. Before, I've been so cautious so as not to upset Mother past her fragile point, but now I wonder if perhaps that is all I'm left to do.

"From what I've heard, Mother," I say with slow viciousness, "you *have* had something from there before. An Honorable man by the name of Lirrus Fairfellow."

The way she flashes her eyes at me with panic, and how her teeth clench as though she represses the terrible urge to strike forward like a snake and bite me, reveals to me that I have struck a most tender target.

"Is it true, Mother?" My mouth wobbles with both anger and emotion that brings my eyes to burn. "All this time, Lirinda's father has been an Honorable? A *Pure?*" I swallow hard, shifting my teeth so my jaws don't burn so painfully.

"Do not speak to me of it," she hisses, her eyes wild. There is a madness about her that suggests she may flail her arms and strike me.

"So it is true!" I breathe a hysterical laugh. Overtaken, suddenly, by a sickening rage that indeed nothing has ever been as it has seemed in our life of Haven. Nor has Mother been to me as she has seemed. A *mistress?* Mother has kept the world from us, but not always from herself. What else has she not told us? What still does she keep from me?

I feel that my irises tremble with my fury, and burn with tears, but I force them away from Mother. I wish to run from her, from these insufferable feelings I know not how to contain, other than slinking off into the trees in secret and ripping their roots from the earth. Never to return.

It's a great effort to swallow down the bile that rises into my mouth with all the words I wish to say and remain silent. My mouth locks, so I speak no more treachery against Mother, for I know it will only harm her more if I do. Breathing deeply through my nose, I cannot bear the overbearing stench of mouse piss and mold, of being here in this room. Of being in this halfway place of trying to appease both sister and mother.

Rigidly, I begin to throw our belongings into our satchels, revealing anger in my aggression.

"Bundle up your foul growths, Mother," I command in a low, guttural voice, thick with my fury. I wince at the slice of sour pain that spreads up my jaw with my restrained cries, the burn of tears I reject. "I am going to build for us a fire, and you will cast your moldered horrors into it. It is time for us to be gone from this place."

Mother does not dispose of her grotesque creations willingly. After many roaring yells between us that blend in with the ruckus of the surrounding tavern, Mother and I throw most of the cough-provoking tatters of mold into the raging fire, but most the mushrooms and the spiderwebs Mother delicately, sullenly, tucks away into our satchels. Finally, once the disposed mold has burned away, and an herbal smoke pollutes the room like incense, and once the mice and spiders have melted seamlessly back into the walls from where they've come—but for those that have slipped eagerly into Mother's sleeves and pockets—the room looks as it had when we had first arrived. We part from it without a backward glance, and without a word to one another. Only a grateful murmur to Malinne as I generously pay her from the velvet sack given to me by Tafton, which Mother seems disgusted by.

We speak not for the hours it takes to climb the mountain. Hours longer into the night it accosts us with Mother's wearied slowness. I find the nourishment from the castle still fuels me as I hastily tear between bramble and rock and look down past my wind-whipping cloak to the pathetic image of Mother, hobbling with her head bowed slightly, up the unruly terrain.

Though we do not speak, I offer her my hand, but she ignores it. She labors past me as though I am invisible to her. I cannot tell if it is anger for me that she carries, or if she truly is so lost to her grief that she is not even here alongside me.

Blind she is even to the crow that soars above us, flitting its wings with our pace, and disappearing ahead into the mist-shrouded mountain of Haven.

I glimpse over my shoulder at the castle where my sister remains. The fate she has chosen for herself, the fate she has destroyed for us. So wrong it feels to walk away from her, the furthest from one another we have ever been, and though I ache with sorrow for this new life to be lived without her, I am more consumed with bitterness for her the further on I climb.

CHAPTER ELEVEN

Haven does not greet us with the familiarity of home. Noisy and wild it feels here, as if the birds and creatures of the trees have already forgotten us; the night is damper and more frigid than I remember. As I go into the cottage to light the candles and the hearth, my breath is visible in clouds of steam, and in the flittering light of candles, I glance around me to take in the new leaves that have grown upon the cottage walls. I wonder if the curling tendrils of ivy overtaking my bunk have always been there, for I've never noticed them before.

Is this really the place I have spent my entire life? Such a small space, so simple. How did we three women ever fit here once?

Mother unpacks her satchels in silence once she arrives. I watch her remove a silvery bundle of spidersilk, scuttling dozens of black spiders into our midst as she sets the weightless heap upon her working table. I wonder when at last we will speak. It feels we can go an eternity without uttering a sound to one another, and a great part of me would be glad of it. When she sits upon her chair before the hearth, staring at her flames,

I do not stand in her way. I do not protest.

I climb up to the bunk Lirinda and I once shared, but step back down immediately. I cannot lie there; the emptiness I feel would be even more realized; the extra space of the cottage, of all of Haven, is already too great. Instead, I lay upon the moss floor, gazing above at the ceiling of branches that flickers with shadow and spiders, and try not to think of my sister and whether she's thought at all about Mother and me.

In our days of absence, it seems our every habit here has been lost. Our garden has grown unkempt without Mother's constant care, the animals have grown suspicious of us and quieter, the land unfamiliar, and winter has stolen closer to life.

A crust of death has begun to crisp and curl the edges of the leaves, the vines. Already, the insects have gone quiet, the bees long since gone. The mornings of which I rise and fetch water, my footfalls upon the crunch of leaves is the only brittle sound. My breath is visible in the biting air, and the nights descend sooner, blacker, colder, with every day.

Mother works in the garden, but it is without her usual vigor. Before, she would so reverently bow her head to her plants and connect with their life force, her plants blooming or growing fiercely before our eyes, but now she hardly leaves her quiet defeat, and her plants seem not to change at all. I recall The Gander's Gullet, how Mother had said her power was diminishing. I wonder if it is so, even after returning home. Is this the end for Mother's power? Will she truly never recover?

When we first returned to Haven, Mother had not replaced her enchantment upon the Boundary. Though she said not a word of it to me, I know that she had left it open in her hope that Lirinda might decide to return home. Since, the phantom of Lirinda's arrival is never far from our minds—that we may see the bright shape of her coming through the trees, weeping with remorse for what she's done. But the days pass, and there is no sound of anyone coming. As the season fades, I do not think Mother would have the strength to replace the Boundary even if she desired.

When Mother is not working idly in her garden, she is seated before the fire. The work that always she has done to maintain our life I now do for the both of us. I am the one who cleans and cooks and prepares, while she sits outside amid her dying plants, doing nothing. Every evening when she comes in, I brew her a steaming cup of spiced fir needle tea, and we sit in an almost amiable silence, but still there is little conversation to be had. In the dancing flame light, I make out the silhouettes of tiny mushrooms sprouting from the shoulders of Mother's cloak, growing longer and more crooked with every passing day. Tempted I am to pluck them from her wool where they've embedded themselves, but I dare not touch her.

I know not how to remove her from this idle misery, nor how to tell her that I need her, now more than ever before. For every year, we spend these fading autumn days preparing for winter's deathly hold upon our world. We harvest and stopper and store deep underground. We reap the seeds from the fruit and dry them. We plant for spring. We commune with the fauna for the elderly who are soon to fall and we plan to collect their hides, their bones, and use them for our sustenance and warmth. But not this autumn. This autumn, Mother does nothing at all, and I work gruelingly hard to make up for it, but it is not enough. I wonder, sometimes, if Mother desires our doom.

Thankful I am, however, for the work that keeps me from thinking of Lirinda—from looking off into the distance where the castle rises into the dark rain clouds upon its mountain and imagining how her coronation has surely taken place by now. That my sister sits upon a throne as queen, while I smear handfuls of rendered deer fat across our iron cauldron. Cooking, always, for our mother who is lost to grief because of her.

In our empty nights, when I feel my lonesomeness strangle my throat, I try to forget my sister, though often I dream of her, of our days lost. One dream I have is that I slap her for her stupidity—a hard slap with the wrath of my Current, enough to make her eyes spin, enough to make her feel the pain that I do. I dream, too, of the castle. A frightening dream that wakes me with a gasp. The statues upon the castle exterior—how their white eyes stare at me while I sleep.

In my every moment, awake or asleep, I refuse my ache for the castle. How, if I were to allow myself, I would pine for it like a lost and forbidden lover—a dark and comforting love I've yearned for all my life. Still, in my refusal, I feel its call stretch to me even this far away. If only I could ignore the forest's every whisper and whine, every root curling into the earth, every stream's gurgle upon its stones, I might feel the chill of the halls, the white-glow tendrils so like my dream, reaching for me all this way.

One morning, Mother rises earlier than I, and in my surprise, I watch through the window how she treks slowly to the twig-trellis of climbing squash just outside our cottage. I breathe deeply with my hope that she has decided to rise from her misery and help me, that perhaps she has sensed our urgency at last. She extends a hand to a hanging fruit I've not yet cut, and rests the heavy shelled mass in her hand. Closing her eyes in her way that I know means she will make something flourish or grow, I watch with excitement at how the squash will swell with fatness and warm with rich color at Mother's magical touch, but when I see that, instead, the fruit turns steadily grayer, shrivels with blackening spots of mold, and falls into soggy pieces in her fingers, I feel my heart wither with it.

Mother looks down at the mess upon her hands with morbid regret. When she comes staggering back to the cottage, I slink my head back through the shutters of the window and lay back upon the moss floor as though I've not seen Mother's power fail. She enters through the door and takes a seat upon her chair. In the days that follow, Mother does not rise to work on her plants again.

A new resignation has befallen Mother since her killing of the fruit. Now, as she remains only in her chair, mold spreads from the very wool of her cloak, elongating across the floor like a trailing robe, and her spiders have cast yet more of their silken webs around her. As she sits there at night, the firelight flickers dizzily within the gauze. Spiderwebs fall from the rim of her hood and before her face like a veil, shrouding her from me, from my attempts at speaking to her, arguing with her.

Difficult she had been before, but now she is impossible.

Even our home has become overrun with webs and mold. I tear them from the shelves, from the bunk, even with my furious Current. I leave the cottage door open so the birds may come in to devour the spiders, but they seem not to want to come near Mother, and I do not blame them. Out of the corner of my eye, I see the flashing tails of mice scurrying about the cottage, beneath Mother's cloak, and when I scream my impatience for it all, I do not think Mother hears me.

I cannot help but feel that whatever this curse is that has been beset upon Mother is of her own doing and that she could reverse it if she so desired. The mushrooms, how they grow more greatly from her cloak, and she wears them like a weird mantle. Yet more manifestations of her misery I muse them to be. I await the opportunity to rip them off her, but I cannot bring myself to touch her. Hardly can I bear to look upon her even as I continue to serve her meals and steaming cups of tea.

The morning that I wake to the world beyond our cottage covered in sparkling frost, every individual leaf and twig etched in silver crystal, I know that Mother has forsaken me. For every year of my life, the first frost has been a day of completion, every supply gathered and prepared for the imminent snow. But so little has been done that we haven't enough to last a winter. Hardly enough to survive, and not without great suffering.

As I lie awake upon the floor that night, I realize my eighteenth birthday has come and gone. I need not wonder if the day has even touched Mother's mind, for I know it has not. I care not for the acknowledgment of something as foolish as a birthday, but the memory of once having it celebrated with spiced acorn cake and tea, and a trilling song from Lirinda, brings hot tears to my eyes that trickle into my ears as I lay, alone, upon the moss. I wonder how many more nights I will be able to comfortably lay here before Mother and I waste away with hunger and cold, or if I will ever hear her voice speak to me again.

The next day I rise to pull trees with my Current and stack them aside the cottage, hoping I will be strong enough to chop them with either our dull hatchet or saw away at them with my Current. Usually, it is Mother's power that has provided us with chopped wood for the winter, and we have run low of our store. I come inside to wash my face of my streaming noseblood, seeing how stupid Mother looks in her mournful seat before the low flames of the hearth, and I simply cannot bear it any longer.

I rub at my face with a rag, staring at her with hatred. I cross the small space of the cottage to stand before her, glaring down at her in her chair with my Current lashing around me like invisible snakes hungry to bite.

I'm consumed by an urgency to push her, shake her, pummel her with some force that might break her from this despair she's stuck in—powerful enough to knock the ridiculous mushrooms from her cloak. But instead, I take the rag in my hand and swipe the sticky curtain of spiderwebs away from her face so that I can look at her directly. Her eyes dart up to me, angry at my violation, then look immediately away, which infuriates me even more.

My mouth twists; my tongue licks at my teeth. All the words I've not cursed her with rise to the surface.

"If only I had a looking-glass, I would hold it before you to show you what you've become, Mother." My disgust growls low against the rumble of flames, but I know she listens. "For what you've become is not a mother at all."

Her throat tightens with a hard swallow. Her gaze in the flames ahead hardens with emotion.

"Yet you still have a daughter," I breathe. "One who has not forsaken you. But of course... I am not the one you wish to be here, am I?"

A darkness shifts in Mother's eyes that reveals to me that I am correct, though Mother looks away to hide it.

Such confirmation makes my Current flare with despair, and of course more anger at the injustice of it. My hands wring together, and I pace the cottage, circling around her chair, needing to move to better process the sting. I chuckle painfully.

"You are stuck with me now. The less-favored daughter. The shadow sister. And that is why you've surrendered, isn't it?

Why you've allowed us to run dry of honey and your medicines; why the tallow and wood are nearly gone? You do not care what happens to me. You do not wish to be a mother to me if you cannot mother her, too. For weeks, you have not so much as looked at me. But then, you never really have. Not in the way you've looked at her."

I stop my pacing and face her.

"Tell me, Mother, I beg of you." My voice quavers despite my rigid mouth. "Whatever have I done to deserve this? For you to never look into my eyes as you would *hers*." This, I say with a spit of venom, and the image of her, the ever laughing, golden image of my sister—so easy to love—blinds me, and my voice softens from my fury to sad pain. "For all I have ever done is seek to please you."

She will not look at me. But I do not relent from staring down at her.

"What is it I've done to you, that you will not love me?"

"Stop it, Sirilda," Mother hisses, teeth bared, as she looks up at me at last, and I feel a delicious sparkle of victory to have affected her so. To have gotten her to break from her wakeful slumber and look me in the eyes.

"Is it that I am not the daughter of Lirrus Fairfellow?" I press with a ring of pleasure in my voice, knowing this particular name is one to guarantee Mother's attention, and I am right. Mother's eyes widen with inscrutable emotion. The mushrooms upon her cloak squirm slightly. It seems her breath catches in her lungs.

"And what of my father?" The question pours desperately from me, a question I've never been bold enough to press for the obvious distress it causes Mother. But now her distress is my reward. Her darkened eyes narrow upon me, hardening with a dangerous glare. A glare that warns me to stop this pursuit, for she may rise from her chair and slap me. She does not understand that is precisely what I long for her to do.

To make it easier for her, I lower myself to my knees before her, so close I can smell something sickeningly sweet coming from her, from beneath her cloak of rotten things. But in my anger, I dismiss such a trivial stench. My mind reels with urgency to harm Mother out of her comfortable sorrow. My mouth frames to spit my cruelest question for her yet.

"Whom else have you lain beneath?"

Mother's hand whips through the air to strike my face, but I catch her wrist in my hand. My grip upon her is tight, clenched with all the days I have been at everyone's whim but my own, my fingertips squeezing with my burning Current.

I take her hand to my cheek and close my eyes, trying to feel some maternal comfort with it, but there is none. My eyes open again. They sting with hot tears of rage.

I've felt this rage blooming within me like a wrathful flower all my life, but tonight it breaks through the surface. For years, a sickly animosity has brewed within me like poison, boiling more each day with my jealousies and expended patience, which I've ignored for so long but will no longer. Never have I been so close to its cause as I am now. Mother's secrets, the ones that darken her eyes—they are my secrets, too. The reason Mother hates looking into my eyes when all I have ever done is seek them for approval. The reason she has always looked at me like I am a monster. The reason she looks at me with such trepidation now, how I grip her wrist like a vise, as though I am exactly what she has always feared.

And what is it you fear of me, Mother? I demand in my mind—my intent whirling with my Current—electric tendrils, desperate to understand why loving me has been so much more difficult for her than it has been for her to love Lirinda.

And just as before with Lirinda, my Current courses rampantly through my fingertips and past Mother's flesh, into her veins and life force, and I am once again being absorbed into a consciousness that is not mine.

CHAPTER TWELVE

D arkness. I am entombed in it.

It is not oblivion, however. This, I somehow know. This darkness is...*soil*.

Strangely, I understand that I am underground. And somehow, too, I know I've entered Mother's subconscious, and that it is forbidden, guarded; a secret world I have forced myself into.

Upon arriving at this darkness, I knew at once that it is vaster and deeper than Lirinda's subconscious. Such depth surrounds me, that I know I could spend years swimming through it in any direction. But most everything in this darkness is too rigid and uncompromising for me to penetrate. I press with my intent for answers, but nothing yields...except there are a few places in this forbidden darkness that are more pliant than others.

I want to know, I demand with more ferocity, and my tendrils of intent press through the softer grooves of Mother's resilience, seeking out what she guards least, until something begins to take form in this dark, seemingly bottomless world of Mother's, like a seed in the soil of her subconscious, spreading with pale roots. Growing, extending slowly to the surface. I know if I follow this root of my intent, it will take me where I want to go, the questions I want answers to guiding me to sunlight. And so I follow—until finally relief from the darkness comes with fresh air, sunlight, and sound spilling in from the outside world, like a flower opening its petals to the world.

The darkness opens upon a scene of forest. A world of trees I see, but it is not like the one I am used to. Rather than dense pine, these trees here bear leaves and pale white-gray trunks, and are spaced further apart; the earth is not hilly, rocky, and overgrown such as Haven, but a level ground of smooth grass. It is spring here, wherever this is…I can feel it, the new life, the greenness, growing fleecy upon silvery boughs. White flowers blanket the long, apple-green grass like wool. I feel—despite all my current despair—*bliss;* excitement. As though the emotions of the scene influence me.

Is this…a memory? I wonder.

"There you are!"

The sudden voice makes me reel around—and only then do I realize I have a dream-body and am standing. Just before me is a boy, the most handsome boy I've ever seen, with brilliant flaxen hair and hazel eyes; he is younger than me, perhaps fourteen. It is he who has spoken, and he smiles through me as though I am made of vapor. I reel around in the other direction to see to whom he speaks, and I see *her…*

She is young, younger than the boy but not by much; her beautiful, fair-freckled face is surrounded by a mass of thick fire-red hair, and her eyes are as lucent green as the leafy trees surrounding her. She timidly peeks her head from around one of the pale trunks, eyeing the boy through me.

"How did you know I would be here?" my young mother asks of him, taking a fragile step from behind the tree, revealing the tattered, soil-covered rags she wears for clothes. I see the tangly unkemptness of her wild red hair, the dirt smeared across her face, and want to laugh at the resemblance to myself, but then realize this unruliness of my young mother is more from the harsh neglect of a troubled childhood than my own wild habits.

The boy, in comparison, is very neat-looking. An obvious Honorable, if ever I saw one; I can tell not only by the quality of his polished leathers and finely embroidered doublet, but the way his fair hair is groomed away from his immaculate face, his expression that of haughty confidence. Only one of privileged upbringing could be so certain of their own great worth. And oh, how familiar he looks…

"You live near here, don't you?" The boy takes a step closer to my young mother, as if afraid to startle a delicate creature into running away. "In these woods?"

"You've been following me…" She shrinks timidly back to the tree trunk, but the boy raises up his hands in surrender.

"No! Don't go. I mean—*yes*. I followed you. But only to speak to you again."

She eyes him curiously, like an animal daring to trust the hands of man. But she flees not.

"Please, don't be afraid. I've not come to cause you distress. I come as a friend."

"A friend?" my young mother squeaks innocently. "Why should I believe you, when you—"

"Know you're a Magic?" the boy finishes for her, a little excitedly. She shrinks a little more to the tree in her timidness.

"I know who you are," she mumbles. "You're the young Fairfellow lord. My mother has warned me about you. Your father…he's the Captain of the Guard! He'd kill me if—"

"I won't tell my father!" the boy pleads with a friendly

smile. "I promise. On my Honor." He places a hand firmly at his heart.

"Your Honor?" she squeals disbelievingly. "The fact you're an Honorable is reason enough for me not to talk to you!" And with that, my young mother is gone in a flutter of long red hair. The grass and flowers are so long at her bare feet, she runs through their soft depth like water.

"I think it's wonderful!" the boy calls after her. She stops and peers over her shoulder at him. "What you did—" The boy pauses. "How you made that blossom open like that..."

I feel my anxiety seize in my chest, my corporeal chest, wherever it breathes in the cottage. Knowing this is truly my mother, by proof of her beautiful magic, makes me feel like weeping. This memory of hers, wherever and whenever it is, is sacred and haunting, and I am glad she has known such a day as this.

"And you're right," the boy concedes. "You have no reason to trust an Honorable. But I'm not like the rest of them. I think your magic is...well, I'm not afraid of it."

"What a relief." My mother turns to fully face him, and at once, I recognize the fierce woman I have known as my mother—the woman who can be so fearsome with just the concentration of her stare. "The son of the famous Magic hunter isn't afraid of my pretty flower tricks!"

The boy is taken aback by this sudden burst in her spirit. Mother does not dwindle in her ferocity.

"You must understand," says the boy with renewed modesty, obviously aware of his cocky blunder and desperate to mend it. "From the day I was born, I was raised to fear Magics. We all have been. Only, you have shown me what it really is!"

"And what is it?" She scowls.

"Freedom." The boy sighs, and by the starry, dreamy

flourish in his bright eyes, I instantly recognize Lirinda in him, and know this boy to be Lirrus Fairfellow.

"Freedom," Mother repeats solemnly. "For you, perhaps. But not for me."

Lirrus winces. "I did not mean that! All I mean to say is… this world is far more beautiful now that I've seen what you can do! There is freedom in knowing there is nothing to fear! The world…without its ridiculous rules and barriers…it's freer than I thought!"

She continues to stare at him for a long moment, weighing the naivety in his words, his ignorance, but also his intention for understanding and compassion. Finally, her mouth twitches as it suppresses a giggle.

Slowly, a grin emerges from her severe face, and the boy smiles, too. Soon, they both giggle, and I find myself grinning at the spectacle they make.

The flapping of wings and a flash of color interrupts their laughter as a red-breasted robin flies suddenly at the boy from above the trees, making him shield his head with his arms to avoid the attack. Unable to properly peck at him, the bird then flies to land upon my mother's expectant, outreached finger like a perch.

"It's all right," she mutters to the bird, who chirrups heatedly back to her, as if in scolding. "He's harmless…or so he says." With that, Mother flashes the boy a challenging glare.

"You can talk to animals, too?" the boy remarks in amazement, drawing himself up to his full height once more, though he's still shaken from nearly losing an eye to the bird's beak and looks as though he's ready to drop to the ground should the bird leave her hand.

"Most." Mother smooths a fingertip over the robin's gray head; the bird's eyes close slightly with pleasure. "Are you still unafraid, young lord?"

"Call me Lirrus!" says the boy eagerly, making his way over to the girl and her bird with slow caution. When he reaches them, he holds out his hand. My mother eyes it as if to inspect it for danger before holding out one of her own dirty hands to meet his.

"Mora," she says, quiet and shy, but I can see in her eyes that she is internally excited, as though she's fantasized about this meeting for some time and his touch nearly electrifies her when their fingers meet.

The scene of serene woodland dissolves in sound, color, and meaning until darkness surrounds me again. All perception is lost to me, as though I've been sucked into a lightless tunnel through which I travel fast, soaring through Mother's soil subconscious, until suddenly I arise again into another memory. The features of this new space are so dim, I can scarcely see them. Compared with the woodland memory before, hardly brighter this scene is than the darkness.

There is faint candlelight, flickering upon flesh—the flesh of a woman's bare back. She sits and covers the front of her with a cloth of some kind, shielding herself, though she looks somewhat at ease. I notice there is a bold black tattoo upon the blade of her shoulder, a line with a small 'x' at its center. A dusting of freckles upon her back and arms I am able to discern once my eyes have adjusted, that so resembles my mother's flecked flesh. Once I make out the vivid hair, red even in the dimness, pulled aside to reveal her bare back, I know it is her.

If this is Mother, why is there a mark upon her flesh I have never before seen?

"Burn it," she commands to the shadows in a guttural voice pained with disgust.

I see a red-hot tool come into view just at her back. A

circular shape that would more than cover the tattoo. I wince for the imminent pain.

"You're sure?" A man's voice, deep and low, carries from the darkness.

"I have never been more sure of anything," says my mother. I can still hear youth in her voice, though she is older now, much older than the last memory. A woman, though I see none of her features but her petite back, grown shapely with womanhood. "Burn it until I bleed."

The man with the tool hesitates before pressing the raging-red metal to her tender skin, and Mother, surprisingly, hardly flinches. Her head lowers, bracing against the pain, but there are no screams that tear against the sound of sizzling flesh, no fight to be had against the agony.

The tool removes, but she shakes her head.

"That will not be enough. More."

And as I continue to watch the tool burning away my mother's skin, her flesh oozing with the heat, chills raising upon the backs of her arms and a tremble bringing her to shake where she sits, I wonder desperately what this tattoo had been, and why ever she would want it distorted in so gruesome a way.

Rarely have I seen my mother's shoulders before. When we would bathe, of course I saw her bare, but I realize now she had always strategically placed her hair over this particular shoulder. Once, more than ten years ago, I saw the grotesque burn, with only a blur of ink beneath. As I was only a child, I did not think it would have ever been a tattoo. Still, I had asked her about it, her burn, and she had immediately replaced her hair over the lumpy pink scar, and simply said that she had been hurt once when she was small. Never had I seen it since or thought of it until now.

I wish to seek further into Mother's past to see where she had acquired this tattoo and why, but so thick is Mother's subconscious surrounding this memory, it is immovable, darker than darkness, her soil having become stone. The space between this memory and the woodland encounter with Lirrus is forbidden to my awareness, and perhaps even Mother's own.

The tendrils of my Current seek the next pliant memory to follow, and suddenly, another memory takes form around me. There is no sunlight, no trees here, either; dim firelight flickers but off timbered walls of a large room. A cozy ambience of home resonates through me as I take in my surroundings.

I now stand in what looks like the den of a great house—a house with gleaming wood-paneled walls and beautifully carved upholstered chairs. Is it the fire blazing hotly in the fireplace that fills me with heat, or is it the emotion seeping from my mother's memory? The feeling of most radiant and burning love. Not so unlike Lirinda's own passionate memory, but far stronger, worlds and years stronger. It is something I have never before felt, and it is stifling to me.

There she is! I think when the form of Mora, my mother, ambles into the room with an open book in one hand that she reads while taking a juicy bite of peach. Her vivid hair is unmistakably hers, though it's far cleaner and thoroughly brushed now, hanging freely in soft, luscious ripples that fall before her face and figure. She's dressed not in rags anymore, but a soft linen frock that tells me she has found comfort and care in this new life, wherever and whenever it is.

Years have passed since the first woodland memory. She has grown to be a very lovely woman, nearly as beautiful and voluptuous as Lirinda, and around Lirinda's own age of nearly twenty years; though her face is downturned as she paces the den, her eyes scanning the pages as she reads, I realize I have never seen my mother so happy, so at ease. Her coloring is radiant, not a line of weariness yet etched upon her face, and sadly I feel I hardly recognize her—that I have never truly known my mother happy. When she turns in her pacing, I notice a roundness of her abdomen.

She's with child! I remark at the unusual sight, which both excites me and fills me with unease.

"Beloved!" calls a man's voice from another room. Mora gasps in delight and tosses her book and half-eaten peach carelessly aside as an adult version of Lirrus comes striding into the den. I have little time to admire his handsomeness before my mother runs into his arms, and he bows his head to kiss her hair. Relief to be holding her in his arms softens his features. His shoulders sink with surrender for her, for this moment. When she looks up at him, their faces melt together in a passionate kiss that engulfs me in a dizzying warmth.

His flaxen hair has darkened somewhat with streaks of brown since his youth, and the stubble of a beard growing upon his strong jaw is golden brown. When he opens his eyes from the reverent kiss, and he looks down into my mother's eyes as she stares up into his, I see they blaze green-brown against his warm skin.

"Were your travels safe?" Mora sighs into his strong chest, which has also much changed since the last memory. Not only has Lirrus grown to be quite tall, but he's also built as strongly as I'd imagine a guard to be beneath the armor.

Never have I seen my mother so tender, so relaxed and surrendering. It is uncomfortable to witness, as though I am seeing something indecent. The two lovers caress each other's faces adoringly while gazing into each other's eyes. Lirrus takes her caressing hand and kisses the tender palm of it.

"I was not followed, I'm certain of it. Now, come and sit.

Rest. You have been carrying our child so bravely while I've been away. Now it is time I comfort you." Lirrus guides Mora to an upholstered chair before the fire. She holds a hand to her belly as she lowers herself to sit.

"Just you being home is comfort enough." Mora smiles at Lirrus as he pulls up a footrest beneath her bare feet and begins to massage them with strong weathered hands.

Why would Mother keep these memories from us? I wonder, feeling worrisome for the ultimate death I know Lirrus is met with. Why not even speak of his name? Of these happy days I know Mother cherishes so, for I can feel the love radiating all around me from within her.

"How is our child?" Lirrus asks, gazing adoringly up at my mother.

"She is strong and lively, like her father."

"*She?*" Lirrus's mouth splits into a surprised smile that is so very handsome, I find myself jealous of my mother's proximity to him. "You think we will have a daughter?"

"I do." Mora strokes her belly confidently, as though nothing could steal this happiness from her. "Intuition has never been my strength, you know, but I feel this child is a beautiful girl."

Lirrus kisses Mora's feet. "I will love her so. My two girls. How happy a man you'll make me."

"I thought of a name for her. Tell me what you think." Mora grins at his attentiveness. "*Lirinda.*"

"Lirinda," he repeats the name upon his own tongue and smiles at it. "I love it. Whatever made you think of it?"

"Your name." Mora smiles. "I wanted it to sound like yours. To honor you. But it is also of the Tarian tongue, *Lirin* meaning light, and *da*, meaning to give. For I feel already she wields such brightness, our little flame, don't you?"

"Tarian? The magic language?" He smirks at her conspiratorially.

I lean forward in anticipation. I did not know Mother knew other languages.

"The dialect is ancient and mostly lost," Mora explains with flourish. "Your Honorable friends would never recognize it."

Lirrus rises to his feet and leans over Mora's seated, outstretched body so that their foreheads touch. He presses gently into her, closing his eyes, nuzzling his temple with hers.

"I wish that they would. I wish that everyone would know and that we would hide nothing."

Mother sweeps a lock of Lirrus's blond hair from before his eyes. She looks too anguished to speak. She swallows hard.

"But, indeed," he says to her with slow tenderness, "Lirinda *is* our little beam of light. She will be too brilliant to hide." He lays a land securely upon Mora's belly. "And I think Lirinda will be the happiest, most beautiful girl in all of Glindor. For her parents are so in love, and we so love her."

The memory fades from this to another, but the cozy den has not changed, for Mora is seated in the same upholstered chair before the fire. This time, in her arms, she holds a swaddle of linen. Within it sleeps a baby. I see the small profile of my sister's face, and even as an infant is she soft and beautiful.

Lirrus comes into the room with his naturally proud posture. Quietly he lays a kiss on my mother's ear before stepping over to the drawn curtains and peering behind them into a dark night. When he apparently sees nothing of interest on the other side, he lets the curtain fall back into place and struts with satisfaction to the back of Mora's chair. He places a tender hand on her shoulder and stares lovingly down at the face of the little babe within the fine linen swaddle.

*The three of them…*I think with a pang of hurt…*They are harmonious.*

I feel my distance from them, an outsider. I might as well be outside of this house looking in through a window at a perfect family in a beautiful home. Such completeness, such love I know I will never know for myself.

But to see Mother so happy, so well cared for, her face flushed with warmth and pleasure, offers joy to my melancholy. To know that once she had known comforts as these, and love, and that she has not always stared grievously into hearth flames and willed herself to be consumed by mold and spidersilk, relieves me slightly of some of my own grief.

With paranoia, Lirrus checks over his shoulder at the curtains at his back, and I notice that in the deep cut of his linen tunic lies a familiar sparkle upon his chest. I recognize it at once as the necklace Lirinda inherited, the one that has since sealed her fate.

She is safe, I think. My sister is indeed who the king claims her to be.

So then is all else true, too? I recall Lirinda's appalling claim of Mother having been a mistress. I long to know how it all came about, but Mother's rigid subconscious around me will not yield.

Impatient I am to know more, to see—perhaps my own father will be revealed in these memories. Will I, too, have the satisfaction of seeing myself as a baby with my family, snugly swaddled and beloved? Knowing that my father is obviously not Lirrus, this precious image must surely change. And the ominousness of it, the imminent loss, chills me. The snaking tendrils of my Current are desperate to find a pliant spot of Mother's memories which might offer me the truth of who I am, but I feel trepidation for a much less endearing story.

CHAPTER THIRTEEN

When another memory comes into form, I am instantly consumed by pain.

Pain, whether from my own body or echoing from the memory itself, I cannot yet tell, for I feel it all before I can see anything. But I feel like screaming.

Then, I am able to make sense of what surrounds me; I am in the same den as before, but for some reason, I am now lying supine upon the hard wooden floor. And there is so much blackness—the shadow of Mother's subconscious—obscuring my senses like a tunnel.

There are voices…distant, echoing. I cannot make out what they say, or what even they sound like. So muffled are the details of this memory, I feel I'm trapped within a dark nightmare with no control, my senses blurred. I try to lift my head or legs to sit, but I am stuck to the ground, and the agony is too much to bear. I feel my corporeal body in the cottage may be screaming with the pain.

Is there not a boulder weighing upon me? Is there not a dark fog shrouding me from the true memory? For everything is so muffled, and I am powerless. A sharp cut of pain resonates through me, though I cannot quite place from where it comes. Where is Mother? Where is Lirrus or Lirinda? *Why so much pain?*

I strain to turn my face to the side, and with a gasp, I see that Lirrus lies upon the ground beside me, and he is dead. His eyes are open, dark blood spilled from his parted lips, his tunic soaked black with blood and torn where he has obviously been stabbed in the heart. A puddle of his life's blood spreads around him and across the floor to where I lie and beyond.

My eyes burn with tears. Who would plunge a sword into a heart that had been so loving? *How did this happen? Where's Mother?*

Fearful of what I'll see, I turn my face with effort to the other side and see Mother lying on the ground, too, looking straight through my diaphanous form; her eyes bulge with sadness as she stares at Lirrus's body across from her. The puddle of his blood has spread all the way to where she lies and has soaked her long, loose hair in what looks like thick ink.

But there is someone on top of her—a man, I realize with a sudden flush of hatred which has my fists clenching and my Current spiraling with such torrential power I have never before felt. But I know I must not let it rise with violence, for this is but a memory, and I might hurt Mother's supple subconscious if I do not contain my vicious power.

Who is he? I try forcing my eyes to look up at him, but no matter how hard I strain to see, my eyes cannot reach him through the obscuring shadow of Mother's mind, protecting her from reliving this monstrosity. But I need not see the man to recognize what he is doing to my mother, who lays rigidly beneath, though quivering with her shock for Lirrus's murder. Her skirts lifted, legs parted, his forceful hands pressing tightly, crushingly, down upon her wrists. I sense there are details about him, like rings upon his wicked fingers, but I cannot make out any of them; the memory simply will not allow it.

"Mother!" I whimper as my own hot tears leak from out my eyes. "Mother, I am so sorry!"

I have never felt such relief as I do when the memory melts away. The weight lifts off my body, and the pain ebbs, though I still can feel my heart drumming in my chest and my breaths quivering with horror. Breaths I can see, rising as steam. I now stand in a dark forest, cold and forlorn, a gentle snow falling upon already white-dusted trees, and a smooth blanket of untouched snow glows softly upon the ground in slow-fading daylight.

I look around—I know this place. I would always know it. After only a few blinks, I recognize the scenery as my home, Haven, but before it had ever known me, my sister, or perhaps even our mother.

How empty it seems here, before all our memories had embedded into the earth; before ever it had echoed with our girlish laughter or had our footprints pressed into its earth as we chased one another through the trees; before the routine of our work carved and cultivated the land. Before us, it was not a home, but a wild place that did not feel safe or welcoming. It was foreboding as any dark forest.

The familiar sound of one picking themselves through the underbrush introduces my mother before she can be seen. When she emerges from the tangle of branches, wrapped in bear furs with a plump baby Lirinda on her hip, I see my mother looks older, wearier, than she had not so long ago when Lirinda had been newly born. She has since lost her confidence of safety and love, that beautiful, healthy radiance of her skin and eyes has diminished. Instead, she is painfully alert, her gaze shadowed with secret pain. The shadow I now understand.

Mother's flame-red hair is sprinkled with the falling snow and no longer ripples freely in all its glorious, thick length but is confined to the stiff tassel-like braid I know so well. This weary woman who suspiciously scans the surrounding trees, as though something monstrous may suddenly spring out upon her, is now the one I recognize as my mother.

Her grief—I feel it aching from the very trees surrounding us. So pressing and heavy it is, I feel my bones might break.

She glances around, assessing the trees in the perfect winter silence. Despite her unchanging expression, Mother blinks the snow from her lashes and nods solemnly at her surroundings. She approves of this tangled place untouched by man.

"This will be our home now," says Mother to the babe in her arms.

She then takes Lirinda into one arm and wraps her tightly in the bear fur, propping her up against the trunk of a surrounding tree while she, dressed now only in a simple frock dress of cream linen, crosses the snowy ground to a great pine tree; it is the tree I recognize as her key to the Boundary, although it is younger in appearance; the trees surrounding it are much younger and smaller, too, than I know them to be now. Some of the trees I know so well as kin have not even yet begun to grow. Mother places her fingers upon the bark of this great, younger tree, and strokes it as if in greeting. Considering the next thing she'll do, she seems hesitant and almost fearful, as she looks at her fingertips splayed against the wood.

She then reaches into the pocket of her frock and pulls out her blade—the same blade I've always seen her use, and have used myself, but only in this memory—as the blade's sharp newness glints in the snowy light—do I realize it must have once belonged to Lirrus, for it is finely made. Time and much use has worn at the hilt since, but it had once been a handsome dagger with rubies set into polished wood. Mother must have since sold those rubies.

She takes this dagger to the tree, and after muttering a quick prayer of apology, gouges a small hole into the bark, deep enough so that the exposed sapwood beneath glistens with moisture. She then takes the sharp tip of the dagger to the palm of her hand and makes a deep cut through the tender flesh, only wincing a little at the sting. The blood that drips from her palm falls bright into the snow, melting in droplets at the surface but soon freezing into globs of garnets.

For a while she hesitates, looking all around her as though Lirrus might rise from the dead and stop her from doing whatever it is she is about to do. She waits with her hand held out, her precious blood dripping down her wrist and splashing upon the skirts of her cream dress, until finally, she presses her bleeding palm to the cut in the tree.

As her flesh touches wood, she closes her eyes and bows her head against the bark, muttering a few words I cannot make out but think they might be of the ancient Tarian tongue—and only after Mother says them does she shudder and gasp with more pain than when she'd made the cut, as though a great thrust of her life energy has left her. I can tell my mother is becoming suddenly weaker, her shoulders going slack, her balance unsteady. She drops to her knees but does not remove her hand from the cut in the tree.

Through my mother's memory, I can feel the rush of her unique magic—the chilling-sweet fragrance of herbs and earth, vibrating with the life of a thousand trees as it leaves her and weaves through the perimeter of Haven, interconnecting twig to branch and trunk to root, with each plant it meets. I feel her life essence, her beautiful magic, but it is mingled with something else. It is no familiar enchantment but perhaps a kind of sorcery I've never known. It feels slightly morbid and thumps with Mother's bloodpulse.

Is this blood magic? I wonder.

Mother goes slack against the tree and slides down against it—head resting back against the bark, eyes only slits in her exhaustion. Each labored breath is a cloud in the frigid air.

When Mother opens her eyes again, I see how drained of life they look, how much weaker her posture. Finally, she forces herself to climb to her feet and stagger to Lirinda where she has tried crawling away in the bear fur. She takes the child weakly into her arms and wraps the fur around the both of them again, swaying on the spot.

Encircled now in a thrumming enchantment, woven like the thread of my embroidered hood, Lirinda and Mother stand protected within a boundary that now seals them away from the outside world, so they might never be hurt again.

With the protective enchantment now in effect, zinging through the trees and roots around them, Mother staggers with Lirinda on through the snow. With slow progress, she weaves her way between the close trees, each individual twig outlined with white and sparkling in the muted light. Her gaze searches her surroundings as she walks—all perfectly silent but for the occasional coos and babbles Lirinda makes while wrapped snugly in the fur held against her mother's chest—seeing nothing of interest until she comes upon another tree, standing in the same place where I know our cottage to be.

"This one," Mora whispers weakly, looking up high to its lofty crown, squinting her eyes in her exhaustion. "This one will do."

Without setting Lirinda down, Mora raises her other hand—the one that does not seep blood that she wipes continually on her skirts—and places it upon the trunk of the tree. She closes her eyes in the intensely focused way that indicates she is connecting with a plant, commanding its roots, its growth, its every fiber to her imagining. Never have I seen her concentrate so painfully before that her teeth grind together and she groans aloud, but I begin to see why it is necessary.

Very slowly at first, so that it only looks like a trick of the disorienting veil of falling snow before it, does the tree begin to change. Twigs and leaves shudder, receding slowly into the trunk; the trunk stretches against nature into the round walls of our cottage home. Then, more quickly do the canopy of branches and leaves weave into a tangled roof, the topmost point of the tree elongating and hollowing into a chimney, and the bark separating into holes in the walls where windows belong, with one long opening for a door.

At the end of the transformation, Mother grips Lirinda close to her and, stumblingly, takes a few strides away from the deformed tree so she can view her great creation with grim satisfaction.

I stare at the place I've called home all my life with a tingle of both rapture and fear. Always I've known our cottage to be unnatural and have always assumed that Mother had somehow aided its growth with her magic, but never did I think it had been done with such desperation, such pain, such sacrifice.

With a pang of grief, I feel even more respect for the life Mother secured for herself and Lirinda; a life Lirinda has since renounced.

The cold snow surrounding me fades as another vision replaces it. I hear birds suddenly, the singsong pleasure of early summer before my surroundings come into focus. Startled I am to find that I stand in the same place as before, looking at the cottage just before me, but much has changed.

The trees around me are dark green after a spring of

torrential rain, and wildflowers speckle the ground. Already Mother has sown the beginnings of a garden around the cottage, for rows of small vegetable plants and herbs shoot from out the earth, and a few chimes have been hung from the cottage's roof branches and jingle in the slight, clean breeze. Most different of all is the cottage and how complete it now looks. Mother had fit a door inside the threshold and tree-bark shutters had been fit to the windows. A thin swirl of smoke issues from the chimney, and I assume Mother had learned to concoct the flame-retardant sealing paste, which keeps the shaft of wood from burning.

I imagine she had mice run up the flue to paint the paste with little brushes, as she employed them for most of her tiniest tasks.

The door opens, and I see Mother cross slowly over the threshold, checking over her shoulder to ensure, perhaps, that Lirinda is asleep before carefully closing the door behind her. Only once Mother has stepped out into the dazzling sunshine does she allow herself to crumble into quiet sobs.

She clamps a hand over her mouth so as to keep herself from letting out a sound that might wake her child. The more she cries, the more difficult it is for her to contain, so she runs from the cottage door and turns to the side to weep loudly into her hands. And I see, with an ice-cold trickle that seizes my entire body, that my mother's belly is large with child again.

Is that...me?

I stare at the swollen curve of my mother's stomach and feel myself go desolately numb, as though everything inside me has been sucked away.

I know it is so, that what I look at is me.

The timing is true. At the time of this memory, Lirinda would be nearing a year old by the end of the summer, and we are only a little more than a year apart in age. This growing belly upon Mother will be ripe just in time for autumn, the season of my birth.

The image of Mother pinned beneath that man scorches my memory. That horrible, monstrous man whose face I could not see. And I know it is him, that he is my father.

How it all makes sense…

The man to produce my seed was not a gallant, benevolent lover like Lirrus, not a lover at all, but someone lower than the lowliest of scum, of worms, of devils and evil. Someone who had harmed my mother so deeply that a shadow has forever been cast in her eyes. A shadow that is me.

"I cannot do this." Mother moans the words through her fingertips, shaking her head. Her fingers then go to claw at her scalp.

"It's his, I just know it! His excrement—his slime! I feel it still…growing inside me!" She lets out a shriek of deepest disgust and clamps her hand back over her mouth to keep herself from screaming.

"I don't know what I'll do!" she squeals through her hand, her eyes squeezed shut. "If it's his—I could not bear to look at it. To see *him!* How I wish I could just take it off! Take this belly off me!"

If I could shrink away to nothingness now, simply cease to exist, I would. For to not exist would be to restore the harmony of nature that had been violated with my conception.

How gruelingly I empathize with her yearning to destroy me. Yet, as I watch her now, I contrarily plead for her, as futile as it is, to spare me.

"I should have stopped it months ago, before I ever felt his growth squirm inside me!" Her squeal trails off to a thoughtful whisper and her eyes squint open as she looks around, considering. "I still could…" Slowly, her hand lowers from her lips. Her face, pinched with terror, falls soft. "But what if it is Lirrus's, after all?" she whispers tremulously. "Still, there is a chance. By the gods, please let it be his!"

The sunny summer's day is replaced by a cold autumn's night when the memory changes once more. Now it is a forest clearing in which I stand, a place of Haven I have always thought eerie, and by the generous light of the moon, I watch as my mother delivers me into the world.

Mother howls in the obvious physical agony of childbirth but also with her emotional turmoil, pushing mightily until I hear my own cry—an exuberant, hearty newborn cry. A cry that is hungry for life. Hungry to be cradled and loved. A cry I feel, even still.

I see how the moonlight shines upon the wetness of my tiny, wriggling body as Mother handles me for the first time. I wait for her to look into my eyes and feel love for me despite my features—despite *him*. But when Mother instead sets my wailing, naked form down in the cold grass and walks away, I feel as though my chest has been cleaved open.

I watch in disbelief how my mother trips and stumbles down toward the cottage. With the cold wind, I feel the guilt of her memory like a shrill howl, cutting and cruel as the driving of steel. She turns back to retrieve me only after it could have been too late. And it would have been too late, if not for Crow. *Crow*, of all creatures, who had kept me warm and protected.

If not for the strange bird who has always watched me so peculiarly, my mother would have killed me.

So consumed by horror am I that I hardly notice myself unraveling back to reality. That I am laying slack against Mother's lap, with a new growth of mold tatters and Mother's largest mushrooms yet growing around me from her cloak.

The wool of her lap, and my hair and face, are drenched in my profuse noseblood.

Mother and I blink to consciousness, as seemingly we had both fallen faint at some point. Her body is slackened back in her chair, head fallen aside to her shoulder, until her bloodshot eyes take in the sight of my bloodied face upon her lap, and she understands my doing, my power. At this, her eyes widen, wavering with tears and horror, as she struggles to recede deeper into her chair away from me—deeper into her growing forest of crooked, tall mushrooms. Mushrooms that have sprouted, twisted, since last we were conscious here together.

I rise to my feet, just as horrified to be near her. Mother holds herself tight within her arms, eyes shock-open and gaping mouth aquiver.

"How did you do that?" Mother whispers hoarsely. "Why would you... *how...?*"

I'm unable to speak, unable to feel. My eyes go unfocused.

"I never wanted you to know any of that." Mother speaks lowly as though she is ready to retch. Her bottom lip trembles. A shaking hand goes to cover her mouth as her eyes fill with tears. "But you saw it—*I* saw it. I lived it all over again."

Mother convulses empty chokes. "Oh, Sirilda, why?" Her voice has raised into a horrible moan. "Why did you do that?"

I glimpse the pitiful mess of my mother, trembling violently among her spiders who scuttle across her; my mother, whose lap is soaked in my blood, and whose pain-contorted face oozes some of her own amid her snot and tears. I don't know whether I pity her or blame her or blame myself for it all. For I am the very embodiment of her suffering, of her life's violation, and I have violated her just now.

I understand now, that is all she has ever feared of me.

I swallow. When finally I'm able to speak, my voice is hard, like the voice a statue might have; something cold and dead without the capacity to feel. "Forgive me, Mother."

I wipe my cloak's sleeve across my dripping nose and up my cheek. With the backs of my fingers, I wipe at my eyes, for I find they leak tears.

"Go!" she groans. "Just *go!*"

And I am eager to get away.

"Sirilda—wait!" she calls after me, but I have already closed the door behind me. My skirts are hitched into my sticky fingertips as I run barefoot across the prickly dead earth, the cold paining my toes. The trees are black before a midnight sky; I plow between them heedlessly, blind behind my tears.

"*Sirilda!*" I hear her cry echo distantly through the trees, but still I run, tears and blood dripping from my face. I am desperate to place enough distance between Mother and me that I may never hear her call again.

CHAPTER FOURTEEN

How much time has passed, how much distance crossed, I am unaware as I finally slow to a walk.

Haven is silent without animals to chirrup or squeak in the night. But I wish there was a choir of crickets, even a gust of wind, to detract from the noise of my mind, for the echoes of Mother's cries of pain, the sound of Lirrus's blood puddling across my ears, are all I can hear within myself, and I feel it reverberate through me still. The pressure, the pain, the things Mother has suffered and continues to endure.

It is no wonder why Mother loses her gaze to the flames every night, I think, recalling the nights she would never sleep but stare unblinking into the hearth. After a long day of ignoring the pain, perhaps, of forcing her smiles for her daughters to see, humming to keep from weeping. But only in this midnight silence has she ever been able to revisit her lost days of Lirrus, as painful as the memories are. For those memories are perhaps her truest happiness, too, returning to him in that spring scenery from when they were young.

"Call me Lirrus", *"Mora"*, I recall with a sting.

All these years, she has been living her torment. Never has she healed from it, never has she pried herself from its sickening grip. And her grievous mold and fungi in which she covers herself now, I realize, is far more than the grief of losing Lirinda.

Her precious Lirinda, who has always been her favored daughter. I know this now. No longer can I pretend I have ever been as beloved as she, the warm bundle in Mother's arms. Too well do I now understand the shadows in Mother's eyes that have kept them from gleaming whenever I reflect within them; the regret that I was not born with the golden hair and light eyes of her lost lover.

Instead, I am her dark reminder of *him*. Her every reason for terror and pain. Her every vile nightmare.

My father.

There is no escaping my tie to him. For even in not knowing him, I have been bound to him, and Mother has witnessed, perhaps, every moment I have looked like him, acted like him, spoken a word off my tongue like him. With a sickening burn in my chest, I wonder how alike we are. If my midnight hair and eyes had come from him, as I have always wondered. If perhaps I will ever see this man for myself.

"If he is even alive," I whisper to myself amid the dark trees, my breath a silver cloud. And I hope that, indeed, he is alive, so that I can be the one to kill him.

As I amble on through the forest weakly, my noseblood drenches the earth at my feet.

My blood, the only thing to warm me, like a hot kiss upon my lips, has never dripped from me this profusely before, for never have I expended my Current as deeply as I have tonight. I feel I may faint again, so exhausted I am to my wearied heart. I stop my walking.

In my exhaustion, I sway upon my feet, set off-balance by

my thundering heartpulse and by my limbs still trembling from the horror. I think I might fall to my knees and lay upon the cold leaves for all the days to come. Never to return to Mother. To be consumed by the falling leaves, eaten away with autumn. Dusted by the imminent snow until I am lost beneath it. I would disappear.

Mother would never have to look at me and feel violated again.

At the thought, hot globs of tears burn in my eyes, and I let them drop from me.

If ever I have achieved happiness or goodness in life, if ever I have smiled or been kind, it does not matter. Every laugh of mine to have echoed off the trees should never have been. My every meal, every breath, has been stolen from the earth. To disappear among it would be a slight repayment for all I have taken.

Numb to all but my thoughts, the memories of young Mora and her sad mysteries, I sit against the trunk of a tree until finally I make for myself a pile of leaves for a pillow and lay upon the hard ground, hugging my knees to my chest with my cloak wrapped around me like a blanket.

Dawn touches the forest with yellowy brilliance, shining in the newly laid frost like prismatic diamonds. My cloak shimmers with it. When I try to curl my toes, they do not move.

How long have I been away?

I think of Mother's plea for me to leave her but then her sudden call for my return. I sting with regret for it, for walking on, ignoring her as she once ignored my infant cry. But how ever will I face her again? To ever feel comfortable again in her presence feels impossible.

As the sun rises, the frost thaws, the trees dripping with it.

An icy drip upon my forehead is what forces me to rise up to my hands and take account of where I am, how long I've been away. And fear for what has become of Mother in my absence.

The forest floor is hard but slippery beneath my numb feet as I trot back to the cottage, panicked to a run when I see the chimney does not shimmer with heat.

Mother has not kept the fire, I think, my heart plunging with cold. *Something must be wrong...*

When I wrench open the cottage door, it is to find shadow deeper than ever I've seen here before and a rancid-sweet, but musty stench of Mother's foul growths. No light can penetrate through the windows, and there is no usual light from the hearth. When my eyes adjust to the darkness, and with mercy from the young daylight coming in through the opened door, I am able to make out a thick forest of mushrooms beyond. Tall, thin, pale brown mushrooms like young trees too dense for me to see through. And to add to the obscurity, any space between them is woven thick with spiderwebs.

"Mother..." I utter uncertainly, stepping forward and trying to squeeze between the mushrooms, breaking them as I press them apart. I rip my fingers through the gauze of spidersilk, feeling the spiders angrily scuttle over my knuckles.

"Mother!" I call, but there is no reply.

I suck in a deep, fearful breath, and a spiderweb clings to my nose and open mouth suffocatingly. I use a gentle thrust of my Current and, easily, space is created around me, mushrooms cracking and falling, allowing me to wade through to Mother's chair, where I see only mushrooms of the thickest, darkest, most twisted variety. My heart hammering in my throat, I reach upon the wall for a candle and a sprinkle of Flame Powder with which to light it. In the sudden bloom of light, I see what perhaps I have expected; Mother is indeed seated, still in her chair, and the horrific growths all stalk monstrously from her in an array of varying species and color. I clap a hand to my mouth, for this time the mushrooms have grown, it appears, from not only the shoulders of her cloak, but the flesh of her head, arms, chest, and belly as well.

I extend a trembling hand to my mother's flesh and feel that it is cold and inflexible. And just when my heart plummets with the despair that she is dead, her eyes open.

"Sirilda," her voice croaks, and at the sound of her crushed throat, I know something is morbidly wrong.

My mouth quivers, and my eyes shine with my tears as I lower myself to my knees again before her, and I take her frozen, stiff hand into mine.

"I'm here, Mother. I'm so sorry I left." I think of what Mother may have felt all the night long, that I would not return to her, and I feel somewhat warmed, delighted, by the pain she felt for my absence, though the ice of my regret is far deeper.

"I'm here now, though, Mother." I place my forehead to her hand then plant a kiss upon it. "I will remove these from you and free you as I should have done weeks ago."

"It is for naught," says she. "They *are* me."

I look her over with my mouth parted, my gaze upon her wavering with the ultimacy of despair. Without perfectly understanding how she has managed to create this monstrosity of herself, I do understand how she must have felt to allow it to consume her. Slowly, at first, with the small toadstools popping up upon her cloak, growing more jagged over the days of her spiral into inescapable grief. Then, with what memories I have evoked… how I had left her alone with them… she had lost all restraint against the growths. Willed herself, perhaps, to be consumed by them.

So, this is my doing.

I look over the horror of them with my mouth aquiver, knowing my guilt. I had not thought I could feel a lower, more stinging guilt than I had been flayed with last night. But, strangely, for the first time in all my life, even without speaking, Mother does not seem to project her blame, her ridicule, her unspeakable anguish, out at me. And for that, I feel a closeness with my mother I have never felt, even in such a despairing time as this.

"There must be a way to remove them," I say, horror having shredded my voice to a whisper.

I scrutinize a thick toadstool protruding from her neck, bowed upward, its cap huger than any mushroom I've seen grow around Haven, the width of my splayed hand, and this mushroom is one of Mother's smallest here filling the cottage. Beautiful though it is, with its reddish cap flecked with white, there is something that disturbs me about it; more than that, it grows from my mother's own neck. As I look closer to it, I cannot help but feel the stalk of it seems to palpitate slightly, almost with a heartbeat. And the gills beneath the cap…almost seem to breathe.

I lean away from them and swallow down my urge to scream.

"No," Mother answers me at last, in an exhausted breath. Her eyes fall closed. "They are too deep now. What you see… it is but the surface."

With a painful twist of my face to keep myself from crying out, I dare to lift the sleeve of her cloak. Within, I see that her flesh is protruding with polypores, like that of a tree. There is something unusually supple about her skin, I notice. It looks soft, like the rotting of a fruit.

Swallowing down the bile that leaks at the back of my throat, I part Mother's cloak at her chest and see that there appears to be some rotten tissue of her flesh, syrupy and dark, and I realize it is what I have been smelling for a while now. I wince to resist covering my nose, out of respect for my mother. As I hold open her cloak, a mouse slithers out over the hem with her whiskers soaked in the decomposing fluid. Gritting my teeth, I take handfuls of her cloak at the breast and tear it down the center to see the source; I find a gaping, moist hole where the mice have been gnawing at her, eating her—a hole where tiny furry white mushrooms thrive.

I fall away and cannot refuse the vomit that spews from me upon the moss floor.

"How long?" I speak hoarsely when I can, the vomit dripping from my teeth. "How long have you been suffering this?"

She does not answer. And perhaps I know the answer. I recall the first film of mold-fur she'd grown in the inn, the long night she'd sat with her mice and the first of her mushrooms upon the floor.

"Why didn't you tell me?" I squeak sorrowfully as I look up at her once more. "I could have helped you!"

The finality of my words confirm my fear, that there is no helping Mother beyond this.

"You could have," Mother says finally, slowly. "It is my own fault for not allowing you to. For not... allowing you closer to me."

I hear pain in her voice, remorse perhaps. Punctuating her words, the toadstool at her throat grows before my eyes, stretching, thinning.

I feel a flush of anger, irrational though I know it is.

"Stop it, Mother!" I rise to my feet. "You have to be able to stop it!"

And just as I shriek the words, another stalk at the back of the cottage twists and lengthens to the leafy ceiling. Mother's face looks paler, more shrunken. Her once-vibrant red hair, I notice, has steadily paled with her flesh to the color of ash.

I want to scream many more things to her but know they will only accelerate her grievous consumption. So my thousand pleas and arguments die within me.

"Please," is all I whimper.

"Sirilda," she says, and I am startled by the serene lilt of my name. "Won't you light a fire in the hearth?"

Blinded by tears and hurried by the urgent thundering of my aching heart, I crouch before the hearth and light a fresh log with Flame Powder.

"Sit with me, Sirilda," says Mother behind me. I look over my shoulder to ensure I have not imagined the invitation to intimacy I have never before received. "Come close to me."

Tentatively, I come near to her and lower myself before her lap. I am surprised to see one of her arms raise, breaking a cluster of mushrooms as it does, as she places a cold hand upon my face. A curling tendril of dark hair falls before my eyes and she sweeps it tenderly aside.

She is looking at me. There is no mournful shadow in her eyes. She looks at me as I have always yearned for her to. Like her child.

I hate my eyes for filling with tears and blurring the sacred image of her. Eager I am to blink them away for a clearer view, but they do not stop pouring upon my lashes, streaming down my cheeks made raw from the salty rivers I've run all night.

"Mother," I breathe. "What is happening to you? This is no ordinary illness…"

"I am no ordinary woman," she replies in such a way that chills me—to think of my Magic of a mother, a woman who could command a boundary of forest to radiate her living protection.

She considers what next she'll say for what feels like too long of a pause. I panic a moment and ensure she's alive, breathing still. But she gazes at the fire again.

"Magic is in every measure of me, and every measure is a mystery. Perhaps... it is like with your own power." As she speaks, I am reminded of the hoarseness of her voice, the effort she gives. I nearly stop her from speaking but know how vital her words are. "You know not the depths of how far it can truly go. For even deeper than this I feel my power aches, reverberates; I can only wonder what depths I would reach if only I expended it to its very end. But this"—she gestures to the sickening wound at her belly, the mushrooms twisting all around her—"*this,* I have not chosen. This expression of my power is not of my will, not like how I would grow the lilies and the pines. No, I've not chosen this, but perhaps what is worse is that I have allowed it. For to have felt my very skin rise and split felt a natural transition with what has transpired in my heart."

I am stung by how Mother must have felt, to have been so immersed in the grief of her heart, that the sensation of fungus breaking through flesh—of festering wounds and juices gnawed at by mice—would not contrast the pain but complement it.

"I want you to understand," Mother begins to say, "this is my fault." And with these words, a new pale mushroom breaks through her skin at her clavicle. Just as I protest Mother's apology for the sake of her health, she silences me with her other hand, holding it up with maternal authority.

"It is going to happen, Sirilda. The mushrooms...they will only continue to grow. You know as well as I how this will end. But I need to say what I must before it does."

My eyes clench too tightly with my onslaught of gushing tears. I lay my head upon her lap; her legs and knees are slighter and bonier than I remember, having wasted with her recent hunger. I feel her hand upon the side of my face, how she tucks my hair behind my ear. Relentless are my sobs that shake from my chest. Once I am subdued, calmed to a quaver, Mother goes on.

"You were born into my sorrow," says she. "And I've not known how to remove you from it. I hope that one day, you might forgive me for the pain my pain has caused you."

I glance up at her and see a tear has run slowly down her cheek and glints in the firelight.

I shake my head against her lap, refusing her plea. "I've never wanted to be removed from your sorrow." My voice is thick. "All I have needed was to understand it. But Mother… you keep so many secrets. Even still, I know you do."

Her eyes, heavy in the firelight, confirm this. There is more. What more could there be?

"*Why?*" I whisper emphatically.

"Ever since I went back for you, I vowed always to protect you. And protecting you has meant keeping you in the dark." Fleetingly, I think of my constant observations of myself. That where Lirinda is the child who is held and rejoiced with in the sun, I am the child who watches from a distance, living in the shadow. Lirinda was born to a warm, firelit home—whereas I was born to the cold night.

"I always knew it would be a burden for you, knowing what you know now, the truth of that terrible night. So I kept it hidden inside of me, even the things I loved."

Mother's throat struggles to swallow, both with the grief choking her and the mushroom growing near her trachea; her eyes glimmer with the firelight.

"I tried saving you from the truth. But perhaps it would have been better for you to have known it all along."

We are silent a long moment, as the fire of the hearth steals us both into mesmerized reveries, subdued by the warmth. As horrendous as the moment is, I cannot help but feel a comfort I've never before had. I revel in Mother's intimacy, the apology, the unspoken years of hurt. My mind tracing over the hard facts I now know and the blurred terrain of mysteries that have yet to be answered.

At length, I ask, "Why couldn't I see his face or hear his voice?"

I feel Mother's body tauten in our embrace, and I hate myself for reminding her, again, of him, my father, and that night. I wish I did not long to know these things. But I do.

"These eighteen years, I have hidden from him in my own memory. His smell, his voice…his face, I have worked to obscure from myself. They are but a fog now…though he will always be there beyond it, haunting me. Sometimes, the fog slips and his face will stare at me through it, smiling, always victorious…so I must never look up. And that—that is why you could not look up either."

Despite the heat of the fire, I am suddenly chilled with cold. His face, is that what Mother sees when she looks upon me?

I swallow hard. "Will you ever tell me who he was?"

Ashamed I am to ask such a question. It matters not his name or his face; I despise him and every trace of him within me, whoever he is. If I learned these things of him, his identity would only burden me more. His face and name would swim in my mind, rotting like some foul thing in a vial of liquid I could not rid myself of, but would carry it with me wherever I went, much like my mother has. Yet… I carry him around with me already.

This curiosity of mine… It leads to the mysterious depths of my own identity. For no matter how badly I wish my father was not the wicked man of my mother's shadows, he is still a part of me. And strangely, now that I know it, I can feel it—that other half of me, the one of black eyes and wrath; surely, it was his he had given me.

"No," says Mother with every heaviness of finality. "There is a reason you only saw those memories, Sirilda. The rest—the in-between, the fog—it is all a chasm. A shadowed space that will suck you in and never release you. My grief is a curse, as consuming as any dark magic. Don't you see what it has done to me?"

I blink in the image of her again but sobered now of my reactionary fear. What I see is that young Mora of the flowering forest, innocent as any doe, aged with misery and wisdom, lethally threaded through by stalks of mushrooms that twist and rise from her weakening body. She slumps under their weight, crooked to the side with the growth of one piercing through her abdomen, having worsened in only the last moments of our conversation. My mother—once such a ferocious being, with eyes like a hawk that could make me shiver with her influence and mass of red hair that was brighter than any autumn day, able to commune with any fauna, raise any plant to her creative will—was now weak, faded...dying.

"Saying his name will only reawaken what has been put to rest. And I"—she sighs—"would very much like to rest."

Her face winces softly as a mushroom presses through her face. I cannot look at it. My face screws up as I begin to cry again, this time a soft weeping. I rise to my feet and turn away from her. I cannot watch what it does, but I know I must. I turn back around to witness my mother's suffering.

"There are no potions?" I ask shrilly as I shake my head. "Nothing to save you?"

Mother's eyes have gone closed and her face relaxed, but

still she breathes.

"None that I know. Though even if we could concoct a potion in time, it would not save me. My power to grow and flourish the earth is all that could stop this, but I am already too far gone to even grasp my power. Even if the mushrooms receded, I would be left with holes."

It is but the surface, I recall Mother saying, and the imagery of the growths within her that I cannot see make me nearly retch again. How full of them she must be, that her every organ within may be slowly crushed by them, if they are not punctured and slowly leaking already.

"There must be something!" I plead, down to my knees again. "You used blood magic to transform a circle of trees into our Boundary. "Surely, there is magic that could mend you!"

"There is such magic, and there are those who have delayed death with potions and enchantments, just for another year, and another. It is darkest magic, and my life is not worth awakening it."

"I need you, Mother." Beyond the veil of my blurring tears, the form of my mother is pierced through with even more little mushrooms, taking more of her consciousness and brightness with them. I cannot imagine life without her, my constant mother, as I could have never imagined it without my sister. Now I will be without the both of them.

My voice wobbles with a sob. "If not for yourself, then for me?"

"You know not what you ask," says Mother in a voice strangled with growing stalks. I can hardly stand to remain near her as another sprouts out her ear, paralyzing half of her face. I close my eyes and clench my jaws against the sight.

I surrender, at last, and lay my head again upon her lap. I do not look. For hours, even as the fire dies back to embers, then ash, I do not look. But I am there.

CHAPTER FIFTEEN

I feel the entire world shift around me with the stalks of mushrooms, pressing around me, but still know my mother is alive. In the silence of the cottage, I become aware that each mushroom seems to beat with her slowing pulse and breathe with her crushing lungs. Then, out of the half-darkness of the fire having gone out, I hear her voice say my name. I think, for a moment, I've imagined it, such a choked sound, the sound of her throat full of fungus.

"Sirilda."

"Yes?" I raise my chin off her lap. There are mushrooms above my head, caps of them like parasols all around me. I cannot see Mother's face through them or through the darkness, and I am glad. I know it is horrifying.

"Promise me…something," utters she with her mouth filled.

"Anything," I whisper with a shiver.

"Promise me," she says again, "that you will not—" She sucks in a whistling breath and I cannot bear it. I bow my head forward with a cringe.

When Mother is silent, I open my eyes wide in the darkness,

desperate to know, desperate for the words to leave my mother's lips before they're trapped within her forever.

"That I won't *what?*" I urge in a panicked whisper.

"Pursue"—Mother sighs a jagged breath—"your father's… identity."

I gape at my mother in the darkness, bemused that her final wish should be *that.* Not bringing Lirinda home, not thriving within Haven and keeping her plants flourishing in her memory. Instead, it is for me to never discover the truth of my father's name or face. So trivial and unimportant it seems, but I can do nothing but agree.

"I—I promise," I say uncertainly.

After this, I feel Mother and her mushrooms sigh of relief, a sigh that seems to come from the deepest recesses of her wounds. A moment later, she does not breathe again.

Surprised I am that I do not weep. But I do feel that something in my chest squirms and dies, and that I will never be the same again.

Open-eyed in the darkness, I stare at nothing. For incomprehensible hours I remain here, wedged between a thin shred of consciousness and a horrific dream. I wonder if perhaps I have died, too. My eyes close but I do not sleep—I merely exist. Numbed by my unthinkable grief and the wintry cold seeping in through the open door, hardening the mushrooms with frost.

Silence.

Only my chest feels, weighed with an ache so deep, I think it may kill me if I have not died already. If I were to move from my tight embrace upon Mother's rigid lap, my very heart might fall out my chest and scorch the frozen moss floor to flames. So I remain, unmoving, hoping that in time I might dissolve into the earth as any of the autumn leaves fluttering from their trees to the crispy ground outside.

For as long as I can, I fight against my natural urges, until one moment I open my eyes and find myself crouched at the stream, desperately slurping the frigid water from my trembling, cupped hands.

With the rush of cold water streaming down through my esophagus to my belly, suddenly the sound and sight of all around me comes into crisp focus as though I've just come alive for the first time. I hear the brittle leaves of the deciduous trees brushing one another in the wind; see the gilt atop the western pines where the sun's light fades; notice the crystalline beads of moisture shimmering upon damp moss. It is evening; the evening of a different day, surely, for I can vaguely recall a night passing in my mourning vigil, half-aware of the moon's menacing grin traveling through the slivers of open space of the cottage, between the tangle of mushrooms.

I blink and blink. The world that surrounds me now is the same physical place I've spent my entire life, but I recognize it not as my home, not even as my reality. It is empty now, foreign, as though it is a mirrored realm mimicking the one I once knew. Even time itself feels like a lie. I cannot believe a day has already passed since I've last heard Mother's voice, those final words she'd uttered. It is unnatural, outrageous, that the mechanisms of the earth should continue, that the sun should continue to shine, when something so devastating has been wreaked upon the world. How do the trees still stand? How have the mountains not crumbled away? How do birds still chirrup into the sunset when my mother is dead?

I splash the cold water over my face, but it only stimulates my senses more. The frigid water awakens my flesh, and then comes the prickling of my hunger, more painful in my belly than it has ever been—a hole burning with fire. I know I must eat and cover myself in furs against the oncoming cold of night—start a fire, even. But I cannot bear to comfort myself when suffering is what I desire.

As the sky darkens over an even blacker forest, I have built a small fire by the stream. I've dared not go near the cottage, near Mother, for any supplies—no furs for warmth, no Flame Powder to ease in the building of my fire, no cookware or salts or dried meats. My fire has been built the natural way, with all the broken branches my weak form could gather, as I wove lonesomely between the skeletal trees. I gathered pine needles from the floor and sprinkled them into the flames for crackling light. Lichen off overhanging boughs I've gathered into a pile for keeping the fire alight. Though my belly roils for sustenance, I do not hunt. I care not enough for my life to take another.

Stars begin to prick through the velvety tapestry, my every breath rising in a cloud to meet the constellations. I shiver worse than ever I've shivered before but hardly feel the cold.

I wander without wandering too near the cottage for my fear of seeing it again, for plants along the forest floor I might eat. When I see a cluster of mushrooms upon a decaying log, something anyone would happily make a feast of in such a state of hunger, I am suddenly too sickened to eat. I resign to sit before the fire, clutching my knees beneath my chin, staring into the flicking wisps of flame, brooding with horror at all that I have seen and learned. All that has despairingly changed. How surreally I have come to sit here, in this moment, as though I've always been here and only dreamed my memories.

As another day rises, I am guided more by my hunger and do not think about it as I see a small fish in the stream. My Current simply wraps around the thrashing creature and breaks its form in half before it can come into my palm. With a peeled and sharpened stick, I cook it over the fire I've kept. The thin shreds of meat from around the sharp little bones are hardly enough to keep me from starving still, but I grunt like an animal with each tiny nibble of my front teeth.

Though I have sworn myself not to think of it, I cannot resist a memory of the castle. Of the juicy fish I'd been brought, served within the domed platter—the large, salty fish whose juices dripped down to my wrist. The fresh, honey-sweet mead I guzzled. My stomach, though less empty than before, growls with its hungriest cry yet.

I do not allow myself to think more of the castle, though I recall Lirinda's plea for me to live there.

I think not of the soft bed I had slept upon. Nor the clean linens. Nor of the cavernous halls consuming me as I walked through them, the hem of my cloak fluttering behind me, bringing the flames of the tall candelabras to quiver with my passing. Of the presence around me there that made me feel, for once in my life, that I was not alone. Not so different.

That I have a purpose.

But then I remember that this place I think of is no home to me. It is the home Lirinda has chosen for herself out of her selfishness when she forsook Mother and our life together, catalyzing this nightmare I now live. A foolish trade Lirinda made, for the castle and its pleasures will never belong to her, nor to me.

The stream upon its stones is the only sound.

In the days that pass, I do not dare face Mother's grave of mushrooms within the cottage for fear of seeing her. But Mother is everywhere. Traces of her essence linger in the places she had been the most. All throughout Haven her essence wafts with the memories that beheld her, and sometimes, I swear I can feel her power hum through the Boundary. A zing of mint leaves and dark, exposed earth surging around me. But it is a hallucination. There is no Boundary. There is nothing left of Mother at all, yet I am maddened by ghosts of her.

Upon the shrill wind through the trees, between crevices of stone, I hear her voice. At times it sounds low and guttural, like a moaning yell as if I've done something wrong, and I feel chills prick my flesh for it, my heart pounding with my fear of disappointing her. My belly roils with guilt. But then, at times, it is a thin whisper, and I eagerly look over my shoulder, hoping to find her standing among her trees, having risen from her mushroom grave and hobbled weakly down to the stream to join me. Of course, no one is there.

In one of my slow excursions for firewood, I think I see her. A most beautiful image before me, of my mother radiant again, brilliant red hair flowing before her face. But it is only a pale tree, white-trunked, etched with black scrawls upon the bark looking so like eyes. Willowy tendrils of red leaves fall before the imagined face, flowing with the breeze so realistically, so like her. When I walk to the tree and touch my hand to it, feeling the wood for its solid certainty, I know that I am going mad here, all alone. And that the longer here I remain, the more mad I will be.

I move the small camp I've accumulated over the days to the far reaches of Haven, past all the distant echoes of sisterly laughter—active memories of Lirinda and me chasing one another—and the flashes of Mother's green-hooded form sauntering through the trees. I travel to a place I've not been in years: a place of scant memory, its emptiness a sanctuary of unfeeling. A flat little clearing, set beside an abrupt face of rock, is where I choose to build my next fire.

One memory of this place is all I have. It had been midwinter, snowy and still—a time that Mother had been informed by Crow of a fallen deer in need of a merciful death. Mother had thrown her wolf fur over herself and packed her tattered buckskin satchel full of dried herbs and a slumber draught—a potion to numb one's body and fill one's calmed mind with pleasant visions. She ensured her blade was tucked away in her pocket by patting it before setting off into the snowy forest in her wooden snowshoes, dragging behind her a sled to carry the carcass back upon.

Lirinda and I had followed Mother, and Mother followed Crow to this place framed by the rock face where I sit now. And there was the buck, bleating in agony—he had leapt off the ledge and impaled himself upon a sharp, outstretched branch that pierced through his innards; it had not killed him instantly but would when removed. A dusting of fresh snowflakes melted on his hide—his hide which would become a new satchel and boots after he had been skinned and his meat portioned to sustain us women for seasons to come. Even his antlers would become hooks for the cottage.

Tenderly, Mother knelt beside the beast and stroked his head.

"Do you wish for me to ease your suffering?" she had asked him, and I could only assume that the deer had assented, for she then asked, "What is your wish for your body? Should you like to be buried whole in the soil, to live again in the spring through grass and rain? Or through blood, to sustain my family and live through our hearts and veins, until you are reunited with the soil again?"

The deer answered in what I could only understand as a painful groan. Mother thanked him and dripped the draught of slumber into the creature's mouth, who licked it off his lips with a long tongue. Within an instant, his eyes dilated, and his body relaxed, his head falling limply forward.

"Lirinda, would you like to perform the Release of Life?" Mother had asked, removing the blade from her pocket, and ensuring it was sharpened by touching the tip to her forefinger, drawing the tiniest bead of blood.

Young Lirinda, only eleven, whimpered behind her hands and shook her head vigorously.

"I would." I had stepped forward to take the blade from my mother. Something in her eyes was reluctant, but she nevertheless released her grip on the blade hilt to my ten-year-old self.

I then did what I had seen Mother do many times. I gently cradled the beast's heavy head in my arms, said my mother's words of *"blood of the earth, complete your circle"*, and slid the blade across his throat, spilling the steaming warm life from out his body in red-black sputters, melting the smooth white snow below.

I now stare at the place where the blood had once spilled and drained into the earth. A thorned bush has grown there since, bearing luscious, dark red roses. Flourishing, still, in the decay of autumn.

"Blood is never lost. It is ever flowing," Mother had once said, which I now recall with new understanding and awe of her blood magic. "In the wind and through the trees does blood continue. That is perhaps why the Pures burn the blood of the Magics."

Fondly, I remember the meal we'd made of the deer that night, the meat lightly influenced with the slumber draught. I felt so relaxed and pleasant when I'd finished eating it, Lirinda and I giggling ourselves breathless in our bunk for no reason; even Mother chuckled breathily at the sound of us. All the night long, Mother roasted parts of the deer upon a spit in the hearth while finally I drifted to sleep.

My stomach rumbles painfully at the recollection.

"What I would give for venison now," I whisper to myself wistfully, prodding the fire with a long stick. So long I've been without a true meal, I feel my body has weakened, thinned so much that my cloak hangs across my bones even more loosely than before. Indeed, I have diminished, for I have seen my reflection, an unwanted image shimmering upon the surface of the stream. How hollowed are my cheeks; how sunken my dark eyes have become. My hair a tanglier mess than ever before, with twigs and leaves I've not cared to pick out, with scratches from the trees across my colorless face.

I know that if I do not properly nourish myself soon, I will face illness, if I've not become ill already. And the long winter soon to come? I will not survive it like this. I ought to hunt, to prepare, if I am to not simply decompose where I sit. Despite the empty spasming of my belly, and my bodily weakness that suggests I shall not wait so long, I decide I will attempt a hunt in the morning. Yet, thinking of Lirinda being overindulged at her seat in the great hall, drinking deeply of sweet wine and chewing the flesh of suckling pigs, makes the thought of any effort seem laughable. I grimace with my rage for her. How she shares no grief in our mother's death, a death she ultimately helped to incite, and that she will not know a moment's pain or hunger in Mother's absence. I wish that Lirinda could see what has become of us while she sups greedily—how I slowly waste here in the open wild, and Mother, torn apart by her own wounds. Cold, rigid in her grave. Dead.

The sudden sound of rustling branches and a disturbance of leaves from somewhere beyond the imperceptible dark of the surrounding trees startles me where I sit, removing me immediately from my misery. My Current thrashes into my awareness, prepared to lash at the first creature to reveal itself. I scan the surrounding trees for a sign of movement, but beyond my campfire's bouncing circle of light, I see only blackness.

"Aww, ah-ah!" comes the blaring call of Crow as the bird swoops down through the dark. I hear the feathers of outstretched wings whistling before flapping to land. The bird, blacker than the night, balances on her single leg and hops toward me, stopping just before my feet.

"Oh, it's you." I breathe with equaled relief and dismay. When the bird does nothing but look at me, I murmur to her bitterly, "I suppose you've come looking for my mother?"

Crow only stands there, tilting her black head to the side to eye me more closely.

"Well, she's dead. Perhaps you know that. Mother always did say you creatures know more than you let on."

When the bird does nothing at all to respond, I realize how very long it's been since I've had someone to talk to. My throat tightens with grief.

"There's no use in talking to you. I am merely talking to myself." I bring my knees closer to my chest and rest my chin upon them. "And I don't need any more reason to feel as if I'm going mad."

When Crow continues to stand there motionlessly, my gaze wanders back to the bird, and I notice her beak and the small feathers of her head are dampened with thick liquid gleaming in the firelight. Besides ink or some thick potion the bird could have gotten into, I can only assume it is one thing.

"Is that blood?" I straighten up and peer closer.

At this, Crow hops away to the dark surrounding trees, but turns back to look at me, a red gleam of my campfire reflecting upon her jewellike black eye. The bird then hops one-leggedly nearer to the trees in a way that I feel, eerily, is an indication for me to follow.

"You…want me to follow?" I ask with a furrow of my brow, but of course the bird does not answer but simply waits for me. When I do nothing but continue to stare, Crow's beak parts as she releases an indignant yell of, *"Ahh!"*.

Hesitantly, I get to my feet, swaying a little with my weakness. Picking up a branch alight with flame from the campfire like a torch, I follow Crow slowly, uncertainly, into the dark trees.

"This had better be good."

The bird takes flight and guides me further into the wood, perching from bough to bough until I, careful not to catch any of the snagging twigs or leaves with the fire I carry, come near enough for the bird to take flight again.

"If you're guiding me to the cottage to show me Mother, I won't follow," I murmur more to myself than to Crow, for she flies out of earshot before I can speak. But I soon recognize that the direction Crow leads me is opposite the cottage, toward an edge of Haven I've never ventured past.

Caution prickles icily through my veins. Here, anything can encroach upon the land, especially as far as I am from the familiar grounds nearest the cottage. I remember the wolves I had seen in Mother's memory who had nearly claimed my newly born body. The thought of them peering through the darkness at me now makes my Current flare protectively. I do not know that I am strong enough in my exhaustion to defend myself.

Why am I following this bird? I ask myself, ducking beneath a low hanging branch. *Am I really that lonely, so desperate for companionship, that I've left my warm fire for a fruitless wandering through the night?* I am near to turning around, to conserve my fading strength, when Crow swoops suddenly down to a mass on the ground.

"Aww, ah-ah!" her cry echoes through brittle trees, but this time I do not wince at it. I am too curious. Once my fire illuminates the space, I see that lying upon the ferns is a petite doe—dead.

I lower myself to my knees and inspect the creature with my flame. The surrounding leaves are soaked with blood. The creature's throat had been slit—but not by a blade. It is a gruesome wound, looking as though it had been torn viciously open by teeth. But what animal would only chew open the beast's throat to kill it and not to eat it?

"You," I say, narrowing my eyes upon Crow, seeing now upon closer scrutiny that the bird's beak and feathers are sticky with the drying blood. "You did this. You killed her. Why?"

"Aww!" Crow hops to the carcass and begins pecking at its abdomen until a flood of innards spill out, still hot upon the cold ground. I stare disbelievingly at the bird and her expertise for butchery.

"How did you know I—" I begin to say, but suddenly recall the moonlit scene of my mother's memory, the night I was born and left to die in the cold of the clearing. It had been Crow who saved me. And now the bird has helped me again.

"Thank you," I say softly, extending a delicate hand to touch the bird. But Crow quickly nips at my finger with her sharp beak and flies up into a tree, cawing indignantly down to me.

I curse to myself, sucking the blood from my finger. Warm, metallic blood. Unexpectedly...delicious. Something I've not known I've needed. How its warmth floods into my mind, into my own blood. Nourishment, strength...

My eyes fall upon the open carcass before me; its gaping wetness reeks of death. Propping my burning torch up on a rock,

I use both my hands to stroke the wiry-dense fur of the dead creature's body. The stench does not repulse me. So hungry am I, my stomach growls monstrously.

Before I can consider the savagery of it, I dig my hands into the warm, soft innards and pull them out. I reach up through the ribs for the heart and bring the tough mass to my teeth to tear and chew. I eat nearly a quarter of the organ before sitting back on my heels and surveying the scene of my desperation. I can feel the blood dripping off my lips, my chin. I feel even the blood trickling down into my belly, and it is the most pleasurable warmth. But I cannot eat more. I am near to retching already.

I sit upon my knees, awed at what I have just done. Then I begin to laugh.

I laugh as I have never laughed before. My cackle echoes through the trees, and I can feel the sleeping animals around me open their eyes from their nests and question their safety.

I laugh until I begin to cry.

My torch flame dies once it is snuffed upon the damp ferns, and I am left in the total dark. I press my lips upon my knees, weeping more for the sound than for the actual tears, for I feel I have none left. It is the convulsion, the rhythm of weeping which reassures me of my pain, but I realize now even that is fading. I am beginning to harden from within. Too hard and dry to produce tears.

A full moon rises over the eastern trees, and I feel its glow upon me in silvery awareness. I see the morbid illumination of the doe before me, the half-eaten heart. Its eyes open and dry to the night, blood gleaming. A new swirl of a breeze catches the tendrils of hair that hang before my face, one I've never felt before in Haven. A breeze that smells unlike the forest.

Rising to my feet, I feel the wind flows easily through the trees here; it touches my hair, lifts it from my ears and shoulders.

Through moonlit trees, I see the timber grows thin before me, thinning before a great cliff of the mountain, wide and open to the bristling wind, an open chasm of sound and freedom. There is something pale out there that I see—something that I can feel. Something that doesn't feel like choking me with grief. I walk to it.

The closer I come to the mountain's edge, the more wildly my hair thrashes around me. I am aware of the doe's blood beginning to dry upon my face as I step out from the trees to the open rim of stone cliffs and stand at the edge before the wild, gusting chasm.

The perfume upon the wind is a sweet, invigorating blend of seawater and fields—a vast land I have yet to see or understand. Grassy farmlands and mint, cold and dying. A realm of which has always been forbidden. Glindor.

Far across the open space, into the distance, is, of course, the moonlit castle I see; there is a stark obviousness about it, like the center of a dream. So beautiful and small it looks from here, its sharp towers like pointed crystal—a tiny possession I might reach out for and grab, smooth its edges with my fingers. Upon the cold wind I feel its beckoning to me, tendrils like my own dancing with my Current. It is faint, here, but enough to make my heart throb with something other than my slow-decaying sorrow. My pulse rises in tandem with a dark thrill that blooms from deep within me.

"What life will you choose, sister?" Lirinda's words echo in my mind.

Like a river of images too quick to discern, I visualize myself remaining in Haven, walking among the bare trees along the frozen stream in winter, feeling the desolation of no kin, no purpose, my cloak upon the shrill snowy wind shredded and unpatched for I would not have the will to maintain my clothing for its futility. I would walk between snow-heavy pines to a sad structure of gathered logs I would have raised with my Current to build, but it would not keep away the cold. Damned in my loneliness I would forever be, never to be loved or known again. The face I see turn toward me, over my imagined shoulder, is as inert and pale as any birch surrounding me.

Another visualization is of myself carving my own path through the capital, though an uncertain path it is. Hazy is the image within my mind, of my cloaked form walking between the filthy buildings of the street or wandering among farmers and gardeners into the misty countryside, spending what yeor Lirinda had given me in the velvet sack to begin a life of my own. No one could ever truly know me. A name I may reinvent, my story to change with whomever I were to meet. But no matter what I might do, or how far away I might go, selling mullein tinctures in a faraway village or helping reel in nets with the fisherman, I visualize that there would always be the constant castle looming at my back, and I would feel its presence upon me, longing for me. In my spurning of its call, never would I understand it.

Then there is the visualization I have been refusing all this time, but now it appears easily before my eyes with the image of myself, dressed in a new cloak of fine linen, walking purposefully down the candlelit corridors of the castle—the very corridors I have been aching to surround myself within again. The white-eyed statues of Glindian kings who haunt my waking dreams would witness how I amble comfortably along with the courtiers in a castle forbidden to me, partaking of the fruits of their trees, their flowers, smelling their succulent sweetness as if they are all mine to enjoy.

Such purpose, such power I would feel there. The desolation I feel now, here in Haven, a painful contrast.

There is nothing for me here anymore, I reason with such sadness, aware of the enormity of Haven at my back and all the weight of my home with it, shivering with the fauna who watch me from the trees, and the trees themselves, aware of my betrayal—every memory of Mother and even Lirinda, between every crook of earth, to be relinquished. I wait for the tears to form in my staring eyes, but they never do. As I thought, my ability to cry has dried up, along with every other tenderness within me.

There is nothing for me here anymore.

But there is much that awaits me in Gillin's Castle.

I am a fool to deny my certainty, that every answer I yearn for is there. Though I am afraid of what it might cost for me to reap them.

Crow caws at me from behind me in the trees, either in a warning for my mortality, standing as treacherously as I am upon the ledge, or perhaps in uproarious delight, for as the wind grows stronger, fluttering my black hair with my cloak and drying the blood upon my cheeks, so too does an awakening of my purpose.

At last, I turn away from the ledge and cross through the pure moonlight back into the shade of trees. Through dappled rays of moonlight shining between boughs of pine, I drag the doe back to my camp. The fire is now only smoking coals. I toss lichen upon it, prod it with a stick, and add another log so that I am heated through as I brood over Lirinda's riddle.

What life will you choose, sister?

And this time, as I think upon it, there is only one answer.

CHAPTER SIXTEEN

It is not as difficult as I thought it would be to leave.

As I stand where the Boundary had once buzzed with Mother's enchantment, now open and empty, and I look back at the place I have called home all my life, I understand that perhaps I was never meant to stay.

The trees seem to sway with farewell. I know they will all grow taller without me; Mother's animals will live and birth and die without any of us to witness their cycle.

I turn from them and walk on before I can change my mind.

Before leaving, I had retraced the paths of my life. Where first I had learned to walk and run. The places I loved to play most as a young child. I stood outside the swell of open land where Lirinda and I would harvest with our baskets, the frost of early morning having outlined the remaining wildflowers in ice, a melancholic mist hanging in the atmosphere. And then, at a distance, I had given a final glance to the cottage, quiet and desolate. I felt none of the horror I had feared I would, only a sad peace. I had thought to go inside and view Mother one final time, perhaps take some supplies, but knew I would only violate the serenity, and thus, my resolve.

I do fear that one day, an unsuspecting traveler may enter Haven and discover the magical flora Mother had been cultivating—overgrown and feral, surely, in neglect. But there would be no way for them to link the outrageous, wild beauty of the flora with Lirinda or me. And Mother, in the cottage that is certain to crumble in the decay of mushrooms and mold, will shatter the potion bottles with it. The dried herbs will crumble to soil. And Mother's incredible body, capable of growing a forest of flora from her own sadness, will be soil, too.

Soil she will be, for her gardens and the forest beyond. In it the worms will thrive, and the birds shall rejoice upon their luscious fatness, and so the cycle will go on and Mother will still be a part of it all.

As I descend the mountain, slick with frost, I wonder at the possibility of ever returning—if Lirinda and I might decide to return to Haven as old women, after a long life lived in the capital city; to make dolls of hollyhocks for ourselves as we did when we were young, or perhaps for our grandchildren; to brew tea from Mother's forsaken flora. Our grandchildren, who would carry partial magic blood, could know in secret what they are—what the moonbells do in different phases of moonlight. Such a fond image it is, it relieves me of my guilt as I tread across the fallen trunks over gushing streams, meandering the narrow elk paths down the steep slopes, bringing myself closer to the jutting, sharp castle in the rain-smeared distance. However, there is a deep, sad knowledge within me that knows now that I've made the journey away, I may never climb this path again.

Nothing will be as it was. All is changed, and already I know I am not the same girl I had been. To choose to leave here, my home of moss and twigs, I choose instead a life of castle stone and silk. Where before I have been wild, I allow myself to be tamed.

Not for naught, I remind myself. *For a purpose...*

There is a place of roaring river where I stop for a drink. Long ago, Mother had taught Lirinda and me where to scoop the water between the rocks and slurp the bubbling-fresh liquid from our cupped hands. I do so now, looking up at the mountains I have descended, shrouded in mist. Fleecy yellow larch fleck the dark green wall of conifers.

There, among the pointed tops of the trees, do I see a large black bird soar from out the wisps of mist. Crow does not come near me; she simply soars on between folds of mountain, but I suspect this is not the last I will be seeing of her. She is free now, as am I.

A cold wind gusts, and I feel that a light sprinkling of rain has turned to the first motes of snow. There is something on the wet wind that feels so like Mother. A closeness of her skin, the smell of her sweat and tears I have already forgotten. I look up at the trees upon the river's edge, at how the crimson leaves swirl between boughs, breaking off their twigs to join the wind, and I swear she is somehow a part of it. That Mother is aware of me, of what I am doing.

Wildly, I think of spores. I envision them having spilled out from Mother's mushrooms and met the icy air surrounding the cottage. The breeze sifting them between ferns and the small needles of pine, swirling over the stream, down frothing waterfalls, between the velvety antlers of the bucks leaned over to graze on frosted forbs.

Do not pursue your father's identity, I recall her words as the wind gusts past me. A warning against the next steps I take beyond the river, out of the flatter woodlands, toward the meadowlands and farms before the great gates of the capital.

Evening settles early in wintry mauve hues when I arrive at the castle. A gentle snow has steadily fallen upon the slickened paved street and upon my hair that curls, tangled, past my waist. My breath as I announce myself to the guards is silvery as the clouds blotting out the rising moon. For how late it seems, the energy surrounding the castle is as lively as though the day is only beginning and much revelry is still to be had. Servants light the iron lampposts outside, and a trickle of courtly commotion can be heard from the balconies above, where I glimpse velvet gowns sweeping stone and fur mantles barricading ladies against the cold, their breaths of steam rising into the darkening sky like mine, with their chirruping voices remarking at the first snow. I feel a knot of unease at the sight of the Honorables I am soon to live among, but just as avidly, I wonder if supper has yet been served.

Once I enter the castle, past the white-eyed statues of whom I am not so fearful of this time as I enter their home, I am guided to my same temporary bedchamber by a young serving lad. When he lights a fire in the hearth, I go to it to warm myself at once. Standing before the writhing flames is where Tafton sees me when he arrives shortly after, a rather sour look upon his face to be seeing me again.

"You will be staying now?" he asks of me, and I do not even look over my shoulder at him. "Whatever has changed?"

"My Mother is dead," is all I say, and so grim an announcement it is, he pries no further. How haunting I must look, my drawn, wearied face before the flames, gaunter than he had last seen me. The tragedy I have suffered and the truths of myself and my conception I now know must be evident to him, perhaps my eyes even blacker than before. He watches me a while in silence. The little man must have thought himself rid of me. *Fool,* I think with a slight sideward grin.

"You have agreed, then, to vow to the Glindian Oath and join Her Majesty's household as a maid-in-waiting?"

I swallow hard at my sister's newfound title. *So there was a coronation.*

"I have."

"Then I shall have it arranged. A trunk of old gowns will be brought in for you as well as a bath. You must be cleansed of your impurities before listening to the Oath. Once you are dressed, I will have them read to you, then you may attend supper in the great hall as one of Her Majesty's maids-in-waiting."

It is not long after my agreement with Tafton that the bedchamber fills with servants. A horde of young men carry in heavy buckets of steaming water to fill the tub. Then, with their buckets emptied, they depart again for more hot water. Tafton stands by the propped-open door as they come and go, overseeing their progress, nodding to them as if he approves of their efficiency. When another set of servants haul in a wooden trunk, he waddles to it and heaves open the lid, murmuring an *'ah'* at the sight of the contents.

"The *old* collection," says he with humor mingled with pity. "These are the discarded gowns of the late Queen Jayna's household. There may even be some in here from the days of Elta of Yanderon!" He stops his rummaging through the fabrics within, and his eyes flicker up to find me. "Of course, you won't mind. You ought to consider yourself well looked after."

Between strands of damp hair, my eyes blaze at him for his continual snubs at me, as I am growing tired of them already. And as he leans forward into the chest to lift something from it,

I am tempted to kick his child-sized body inside and lock the latch. But my irritation is distracted when a gown of undyed silk, fair as a spider's web glinting in the autumn dawn, is hoisted up into his arms and laid out for me upon the bed. My mouth gapes a little in surprise. Without fully realizing that my legs carry me there, I sweep to it for a closer look.

I am reminded instantly of moonlight—and of the last vestige I'd witnessed of Haven etched in milky frost.

"Undyed silk," says he with disapproval. "I believe this was from Queen Elta's household, long before my time. For a while, there had been a desire to leave fibers undyed for their natural beauty…a desire that has long since been exhausted. No longer is it fashionable in our day, nor is it seasonable for this winter weather, but it will have to suffice."

I do not tell him that, though it is simple, I think it the prettiest gown I've ever seen, and that if I were to wear anything tonight, it should be so like delicate strands of spider's webs that would glitter white across Haven, entwining flowers to trees. I think of the white-eyed statues. Should they not witness me, a Magic, dressed so beautifully in their home?

The simple silk sheens pearlescent in thick, lustrous folds. Closer now that I am, I realize the bodice is embroidered with fine details of luminous white thread and tiny crystal beading. Aside from the intricate embroidery, which is an artful masterpiece in itself, I am appalled by all the lacings and tiny silver fastenings upon the back. It all looks so complicated. How could anyone dress themselves in such a gown?

"I do not think I could dress myself in this if I wanted to," I say with as much indifference for the gown I can muster, but it is not convincing. The thought of feeling silk upon my flesh excites me, but I dare not touch it with my soil-rimmed fingers. It is slightly worn and moth-eaten and obviously years old, but still breathtakingly grand, undoubtedly finer than any material I would ever see being sold in the market square, much less be intended to wear myself. *How many meals this must cost?* I cannot help but wonder.

"Dress yourself?" he laughs. "You are not a servant. You are not even low-status—not anymore. You are sister to the throne. Therefore, you must realize that after tonight, you will be living among the ladies in the royal apartments, and from hereon, all for you shall be a masque of courtly manners and luxury. You will not dress yourself—you may never dress yourself again, if you so wish. After you have been cleansed, a maid will help you into this gown. She will dress and lace you and help to pin your headdress into your hair," he says as he reaches into the trunk and pulls out a matching headdress, lined with large pearls and more crystal beading, to pair with the gown. I swallow hard.

"Who knows," says he, looking intently at my face with a new understanding, seeing a hunger upon my features he had not before. His disdain for me seems to soften. "Perhaps you may look the part after all."

When the tub has been filled with steaming water, the servants all dismiss themselves from the vicinity, except for three older women dressed in aprons with cloth coverings over their hair. One of them holds a bristled scrubbing brush at her side, another a molded bar of soap.

The old women stare at me, waiting for something I don't at first understand. Then, with a start, I realize they wish for me to undress. The steam curling from the tub tantalizes me, fragrant with rosemary and lavender. How long has it been since I've bathed? So many days I've spent wandering and hungering, sleeping a thin film of nightmares, exhausting myself to my bones; the salt of my tears crust upon my cheeks. I feel my weariness in all its miserable weight. I long for the steam, the hot water. My flesh itches for cleanliness.

They look me over with curiosity as I undress—the thinness of my limbs, the lines of my ribs beneath my slight breasts perhaps a sight they're unused to, as well as the scrapes, purpling bruises, and patches of dirt that speckle my otherwise pale flesh.

Once I have dipped my limbs into the hot liquid, the women begin scouring me with rags and harsh brushes, the water quickly darkening with my filth. The weeks of starvation and shivering, the lacerations of branches and the drenching of doe blood, rinsing from me.

My long hair, coarse and tangled, is painfully driven through with combs that make my eyes burn and leak tears. Twigs and leaves are picked from my mane, having been embedded in knots for the age it's been since either my sister or Mother have plaited my hair last. Each thick strand, once free of debris and clean, is examined for signs of lice, and to my relief, there are none. Then my nails, how aggressively they are scraped of their filth. My face wrenches with the sting, but I do not cry out at these women. I have not been groomed or touched by another in so long, and though it is not done with love, I cannot help but relish in the care.

They have lit candles by the time I have been dried and dressed, for the light out the window has faded with an early fallen night. I stand as they finish tightening the lacings of my gown, remarking amongst themselves how very thin, like a starved child, I am, that they need longer lacings to properly cinch me. To make my fitting more difficult, I am taller than any woman they've before dressed. *Tall as a man, thin as a foundling,* they remark with disbelief. I say not a word as they discuss how strange I am to them, how unusual my pallor, how even my hair is wretchedly thick that it broke one of their combs, but that with some warmed oils they have gotten it to smooth enough to comb through.

They scoot a taller chair to me so that one maid can pin the headdress painfully upon my scalp as another continues to work upon the tiny silver fastenings at my back. I wonder if all women who are dressed in this way feel as though they are being squeezed and pinched in a hundred directions. But as I stand, my heart pounding against the tight corset, I cannot help but feel I appreciate the rigid structure of it, and that it seems to suit my body.

The candlelight has rendered me into a flickering image upon the darkened glass of the window, and from where I stand, I can see the faintest outline of my reflection. Faint though it is, it is enough. I see someone else—a tall woman in a silk gown the shade of moonlight; her slender figure emphasized by the tightened bodice drawing to a point at the waist, the embroidery giving sparks of luster as she breathes her restricted breaths. The headdress upon her makes her appear all the more elegant—not at all the Sirilda from Haven.

But the hair beneath the headdress, still wild and thick in black ripples down her back, is the only clue that the woman is me. And I'm certain if I could look closely enough, I would see that my black eyes glitter fiercely with my fear for all that could go wrong in this castle, and the charade of living a Pure's life I must play, surrounded by those who would have me dead with just a slip of a detail about my life. Yet I know beyond my fear burns a confidence for all that I may discover here.

What would Mother think if she could see me now?

CHAPTER SEVENTEEN

"**I**t is your solemn vow never to defy Pure Law and to uphold Glindian tradition without falter. To ensure the preservation of Purity, you vow never to ingest any substance which has not been approved for its Purity, as well as to not have any contact whatsoever with anyone who has not taken the Oath. Leaving the castle without permission from your masters will result in your dismissal."

I agree to these horrible restraints with a nod. Yet my mind is faraway, down the halls where the stone exudes a clandestine coldness that feels so like magic. Something only I am aware of, surely—as though a voice, a whisper, urges me to meet it.

All I need is to wander the halls alone, I think with longing, and such a thought makes the fetters I place myself within bearable. As the Oath is read on to me, my thoughts wander to the dream I had the night I'd stayed in the castle. Of the strange woman guiding me through what seemed like interminable stone corridors, bearing the candle of brilliant light.

"Engaging in acts which have been prohibited by Glindian tradition, such as dealing in Demon Arts, will guarantee your immediate arrest," the drone goes on, and I continue to agree to what is now sworn law to me as a courtier of Gillin's castle. However, it is not the legacy of Gillin and his kings I ponder, but mine.

I ponder what ancient magic might have existed here before Gillin's dominion, and whether, perhaps, it has thundered through these stone passages these centuries since, unbeknownst to all who've dwelled here. All except, now, for me. For such an intimacy is strangely how it feels.

Could something still be here? I wonder. *Since before Gillin's upheaval of the old world?* I wonder what such a powerful thing could be, unless it is not a thing at all, but a being. The thought brings me to shiver; chilled I am by my desire to discover it. Once I agree to the Oath, I shall be able to live here, to spend my days in my quest.

"Madam," I hear them say to me. When I clear my vision, I see the royal scribe extend a feathered writing quill to me, the quill he had been scratching upon parchment all this time. I take the grand feather into my fingers and pause, not knowing what to do with it.

"You sign your name," Tafton indicates with an exasperated growl, though his impatience for me has improved since I've been bathed and dressed in a beautiful gown.

Lowering the tip of the quill to the parchment, seeing the empty space where I am to swear myself to the Glindian Oath, to King Gastlin, to Queen Lirinda, to the High Council—I remember how Mother taught me to scrawl my name with mud-and-berry ink upon dried buckskin. It is a far messier scrawl than what the scribe had done when I am finished with it. I tilt my head to the side to admire the large 'S'.

"No surname?" Tafton inquires.

It's something I've never thought much of before. I shake

my head.

He makes a face of interest. "I hope you are prepared for the discussions to be had as you dine at the ladies' table tonight. They have a tendency to be most...*inquisitive*. Surely your lack of surname they, and everyone else in court, will find most riveting."

Tafton slides a gold coin across the table to the scribe, who rolls the signed parchment to a scroll and seals it with wax. "Eliador Krom will be receiving that before he dines. Make haste to him," Tafton orders, and the scribe rises from his seat with the scroll and leaves us.

Tafton checks at the window and sees that the wintry night has fallen thickly around the castle. "Her Majesty and the Ladies will soon be seated if they are not already. We had best head there now."

Reality does not seem so like a dream until I am descending the castle stairwells, dressed no longer as a roughened outsider, but as any courtier. Never have I not worn the frocks and cloaks made for me by Mother. Never have I not been clothed in something to remind me of the faraway evenings spent sitting upon the moss floor with my sister as Mother sweat at the cauldron. Never have I not felt bound to that life by even the materials upon my flesh, perfumed with potions and smoke. But now, sauntering in silk, with no cloak to conceal my slender figure from the curious glances that follow me as I pass them, I know my vulnerability. My freedom. My fear—and also my thrill—that my life and purpose far surpasses the limits I had once known of cottage and forest.

Tafton returns us to the entrance hall, but we do not descend the grand staircase to the front doors; we walk around an interior balcony to a doorway, and as we make our progress amid the white marble, I notice a massive chandelier suspended from the high vaulted ceiling of the entrance hall that I had not properly admired before: gold-wrought and weighed with an impossible amount of crystal droplets, sparkling with the light of hundreds of candles I wish I could have witnessed a servant—or several servants—light. Tafton, so aware of beauty and his pride for the castle, is quick to indulge my interest.

"Diamonds," says he with relish, as though that might impress me, but it only makes me more furious for all the wealth that is wasted on glamour. For each strawberry-sized diamond alone could feed a family well for years, if not a lifetime. "Four thousand, two hundred and ninety-eight of them. I myself have counted," he concludes, and reaches for the handle to the grand door.

As he heaves open the door for us, immediately the merry din of fiddling string instruments mingled with laughter, loud talk, and the clattering of dishes erupts into the silent entrance hall.

I step through to the railing of another balcony, looking down upon the enormous, rectangular great hall. Here, tables are arranged neatly in aisles, and are each packed with chattering folk—mostly Honorables with their elegantly-dressed heads leaned forward in interaction. The tables have not yet been set but servants come around with carts, administering plates of pewter and silver to particular ranks of people. By the gleam of their silks, velvet, or worn cloth, they are easy to distinguish.

My eyes sweep over the grandiloquent details of the hall, lit brightly by torches, candelabra, and chandeliers dazzling their flickering light upon the glinting headdresses and jewels that shine upon the fingers and necks of the wealthy. Tall lancet windows line the walls from floor to ceiling, all the way up to the far end of the great chamber, where two high-backed chairs of carved wood are raised upon a platform above all others, the high dais, and occupied by none other than my sister and the king.

Sister…

My eyes burn a moment as I take in the image of her. How strange it is that she is here, queen of all that I see. In my pursuit for the castle, I have almost forgotten that she is the reason I am able to stand here, lucent in fair silk beneath chandelier light.

It appears Lirinda has not much changed in the weeks she's been without me, which seems surreal since I feel I've matured in that same time beyond years. She giggles behind her hand, ever a flirtatious little child, but now dressed sumptuously in a gown of crimson, with a crown upon her golden head, unmistakably that of a queen; and beside her is *he*, the king.

He is dressed lavishly in bear furs draped over a doublet of emerald silk, and a great necklace of jewels; he leans casually, though never failing to be regally posed, against the arm rest of his chair, as though his every effort exudes power even in languidness. He listens to someone before him speak, and I watch how his fingers toy with the stem of his pretty gold cup upon the table; how it all glints in the light.

There is a strange pull in my chest when I look at him. It is more than my usual flare of Current, which I do feel, too. But there is more, something more for him alone, that I do not understand. And it is somewhat painful.

Is it anger? Anger that he is an enemy to me—to Mother— as the descendant of Gillin? Is it jealousy that he's taken Lirinda from me and destroyed our life together? Or is it something else... some fascination—that uncanny connection I've felt for him before and again now.

Lirinda tilts her head to him and makes a comment; his

severe expression breaks with laughter, and he reaches for her hand to bring to his lips, and softly, so softly, he kisses it. He looks into her eyes now, and they speak lowly to one another, oblivious to the courtiers who have entered the great hall and walked down the aisle before them to bow and curtsy before going to their seats.

I watch the pair of them, entranced with my own disbelief, searching myself for happiness for my sister, but it is nowhere. Only a rage that roils sickly in my belly.

"Quite a turnout this evening," Tafton appraises, then looks up to me. "But you don't know who any of them are, do you?"

There is no use in answering, so I remain silent.

"I ought to spare you some discomfort, though it is inevitable, by pointing out to you those who matter. There, at the far table, are the ladies Her Majesty has acquired for her household." Tafton nods to a table just subsequent to that of the high dais. I see a group of ladies seated in extravagantly crafted gowns with such straight backs I think there might be boards strapped within their corsets. Their headdresses are far loftier than mine, horned escoffions decorated in sumptuous fabrics, and I wonder if such height and grandeur is a display of their importance, their richer blood ties to the king and his Honorables.

"Across from them are the king's gentlemen," explains Tafton, and I see just to the side of the ladies' table is a table of men wearing fashionable doublets and matching hats.

"And there is the High Council. They are the most important figures in the realm aside from His Majesty." I follow Tafton's eyes to a table closer to the high dais than any other. Each of them is a man, most of them old, and all of them dressed in flattering black robes as they discuss something quietly amongst one another. "Especially Eliador Krom, the Royal Advisor.

It is he who makes all the realm work according to the king's wishes."

"Which one is Eliador Krom?" I ask at last.

"He is the tall, thin one. Clever-looking but undeniably unnerving at times. The eldest of them all is the Great Receiver, surely you don't need me to point *him* out. He is the one true priest, the Receiver of the Gods, as certainly you've heard." I open my mouth to contest that I have not, but rule it wise to keep silent. Tafton does not pause for me anyway. "The others surrounding him are Ennick Fairfellow, Captain of the Guard—Queen Lirinda's uncle, in fact—and there's Tyvon Romnel; he deals in property and finance."

My eyes scan the table for the one he calls Ennick Fairfellow, and with ease, my eyes find a man so similar to Lirrus in stature and face, I think for a moment my mother's lover is alive after all. But the longer I watch him, the more I see that he is a different man.

Brothers, I muse.

Ennick Fairfellow is of a strong build—a flaxen-haired man with a few streaks of silver upon his temples. And much like his brother, he is handsome of face. I watch him closely, how he speaks to the priest, and I see it, indeed, the resemblance to my sister. *Fairfellow qualities.* A softness of the mouth, the angle of the eyes, their lucid brightness. A sunny radiance that defies the wintry gloom. I wonder if this Fairfellow brother, Ennick, had been promoted to Captain of the Guard after Lirrus's horrible death.

As Tafton prattles on about the rest of the court, my focus is upon the man who is so similar to my mother's lost lover, that I am swollen with a dull ache of grief. Does anyone else know about that night? Could any anyone here have witnessed Lirrus's slaughter?

Could anyone here have known my mother?

I am chilled at the enormity of the mystery, for whoever killed Lirrus may be the same man who forced himself upon Mother. Sickness fills me as my eyes rake over the hundreds of heads at the tables, wondering if any of them could belong to my father, but I know none of them are. Somehow, I feel a feeble Pure man could not have sired me nor my power. For I am coming to realize that there is more, much more, to me than an inheritance from my mother alone.

My mind fills suddenly with the shadows of my mother's sad tale. The horrific memory repeats behind my eyes, even as Tafton begins descending a stairwell which brings us to the floor of the great hall, and no sooner are we making our way through aisles of tables.

Heads turn to gawk at us. Eyes scan me from my headdress to the hem of my gown, and I am aware, suddenly, that it is rather short on me—that I am so tall, it reveals the pointed slippers I've donned and dares to expose my ankles. Some of the courtiers murmur comments to one another as I pass them, and I wonder if they've heard of me, who I am: the black-eyed sister to the sunshine queen. What must they think to see a foreign figure sweeping into their gilded, predictable world. So fair is the gown I wear, it is as though I have fallen from the sky with the snow itself.

I take a deep breath to calm myself from feeling affected.

This is my choice, I remind myself, trying to still my Current in my pulse. *I have come so far to play this Pure's game, and I shall play it the best I can so I might remain here and discover what calls to me.*

Tafton's short form meanders around the serving lads and wenches in our path. I follow his every motion, trying my best not to let my eyes wander to the staring faces beneath all the funny plumed hats and outrageous headdresses, no matter how badly I wish to stare right back at them. I avoid looking too closely at the tapestries and their embroidered depictions of beasts and magic folk being burned and quartered, their innards escaping them as evil snakes. Instead, I keep a fixed gaze upon Lirinda, who does not appear to have noticed me, for still she giggles primly, engaged with the king and now one of his amusing gentlemen.

"They have begun to take the wine around," Tafton mutters, though I hardly make out his words above the din of music and chatter. "You see, they go from the bottom tables to top when serving the drink, as it has been done for centuries. It's the benevolent king's way of showing his wish for good health and merriment to the people first." He seems to delight himself with this information, and when I turn to glance at the front of the hall where the lowest tables are situated, I see servants pouring dark liquid from pewter pitchers into the dingiest of pewter goblets.

When we are before the high dais, Tafton bends elegantly forward in a bow that Lirinda and the king are still too absorbed in conversation to notice.

I restrain myself from feeling a burn of hatred for her. That she should be so consumed in her silly charade that she does not even notice her own sister before her, a sister with whom she's shared all her life. How she cannot feel the magic simmering off me, reaching for her—nor feel my grief for our lost mother all the way from where I stand—beguiles me. I stand before her now, so near that I can smell the waft of honey and summer wildflowers exuding from her, an essence I had once thought forever lost from me, one I had been so desperate for. But she notices me not. She cares not.

So immersed I am in my burning-hot thoughts, my mind droning like a hive of disturbed bees, I hardly notice that I now stand before the table of ladies. Being so near to them now, I see how truly magnificent each of them are. How fine their gowns, each extraordinarily different from the next, and how their flesh and hair are so clean, they seem to have never known a moment of filth or discomfort in all their lives. Their faces are immaculate masks, amiably complacent at my arrival.

"Here you are, Mistress," says Tafton as he holds his hand out to a vacant seat at the table of women. They have the grace to nod to me with welcome, but I can read upon their rigid features how very unwelcome I am. How closely they watch me without revealing how closely they watch me.

I take his hand and seat myself delicately, with more grace perhaps than I intend; my gaze is limited so as to not reach any of those who watch me, looking immediately down at the silver cup and plate that await me, empty. My reflection upon the silver startles me. What had I been expecting to see? My tangled hair wild around me again? The tall pines towering at my back like how I would always see in the wavering stream? Not my hair so finely pinned beneath a glistening headdress, exposing my features, my sharp cheeks with no wild mane to distract from their harsh angles; my face a shade of fairest cream against the paleness of my gown; my black eyes and hair made to look blacker than ever before.

Suddenly dizzy, like I might swoon, I grip the chair's seat to keep myself steady, slowly bringing my sweaty hands to fold neatly upon my silken lap.

Like little fires, I can feel the heat of the intent stares upon me, from the ladies of the table to the hundred other tables of the wide great hall. Once I feel the scorch of another more penetrating gaze coming from the high dais, my eyes flicker eagerly to meet Lirinda's. Only, it is not Lirinda's eyes I find looking at me. I feel as though my insides have gone molten when I see that, instead, looking at me are the soft brown eyes of King Gastlin.

For an instant, I have not the reaction to divert my stare from his, and we look at one another for a time that feels too long for others not to have noticed. But Lirinda still giggles at one of the gentlemen, and the ladies around me resume a conversation I cannot hear. Finally, a servant comes to the king's side to offer him a bowl in which to wash his hands, and our connection is broken. However, his mind still seems to be fixed upon something; his dark brows are low with thought. Hastily, I return my gaze to my empty silver plate, my heart thundering in my ears.

CHAPTER EIGHTEEN

The sound of liquid filling the inside of my metallic goblet is what finally brings my attention from my plate to a serving maid pouring wine from a jug over my shoulder with practiced aim. Out of my periphery, I see that the king murmurs something to Lirinda, his lips so near to her cheek, framing words that resemble, *Is that not your sister?*

Curious, Lirinda turns her luminous face to the ladies' table, her fine crown of diamonds glittering like our favorite stream under the sun, and I cannot help but feel a flush of relief that her familiar face smiles at the sight of me—a glorious, beaming smile of wonder, perhaps, for how finely I am dressed and how clean my hair and flesh; a version of me, her sister, she has only yet seen in her fantasies. But just as soon as her attention is turned to me it is whisked away again, as she engages in more frivolous talk with the courtiers who vie for her attention.

I sit in reserved silence despite the ladies' talk around me, trying sips of my wine, which is bitter but sweet. The only wine I've had before was Mother's fermentations, sometimes of elderberry or rhubarb, even dandelion, but never this strong. And never before have I drunk from silver, which tastes pure and tampers not with the flavor of the drink. It is quite delicious, and I drink deeper still, nursing my discomfort.

Soon the servers come out with golden platters to lay upon the high table. I watch, as does everyone, as the servants lift the lids and reveal, beyond the veil of curling steam, dishes more opulent and ridiculous than I thought physically possible. My mouth threatens to gape at the sight of a great, colorful pheasant having been re-feathered and set upon a gigantic platter. Lirinda smiles at it, her cheeks rising coquettishly as she brings her hands excitedly before her chest.

I feel my stomach churn at such barbarity made beautiful, but Lirinda gasps with her awe and kisses the king full on the mouth, which the men of the table clap for, and for which the ladies at my table make sweet, chirrupy, birdlike croons, controlled and unfeeling. When the servants carve the creature and serve her plate, the king watches his wife's excitement with a smirk of satisfaction dimpling his cheek. Truly, she is his spoiled little doll.

Next, it is the table of the High Council that receives their platters. The men sit with severe, humorless faces in near silence, only muttering the occasional remark to one another. The priest is so old, with eyes draped with such wrinkles that I would think him asleep if he was not droning to the man beside him, the Royal Advisor, Eliador Krom.

Krom, too, is in old age, but in an alert, cunning way, age seems to only have improved him. As I am nearer to him now, I see he has a frightening face, drawn and cold, with dark eyes I hope never to see looking upon me. He leans to the priest droning beside him, mutters something that appears disdainful, then turns those malicious eyes directly to me.

My heart jolts with fear, and my hand grips my goblet's stem tightly, but again, just as with the king, I do not look away. Perhaps it is a foolish mistake that I continue to stare back at him, for in his cold, unyielding gaze is both disgust and contempt for me. Perhaps it is mere paranoia, but I cannot help but think that he knows I am a Magic—that he senses it from across the hall.

This man is my enemy, I understand at once. *My enemy, perhaps more so than the king.*

My trembling legs dare to stand and take me from this table, from the great hall, back through the castle doors and to flee into the snowy night. The way that he looks at me makes me feel as though he would like to watch me scream to ash at a Burning of the Blood ceremony, and if I am not careful, he may just succeed.

"Already have Krom on your scent, I see," says one of the ladies to me, and I am thankful for a reason to have my attention pried from his chilling black stare. The speaker I turn to instead is a woman a few years Lirinda's senior, with hair as pale as the innumerable seed pearls adorning her headdress and embroidering her rich plum gown. She sits with the countenance of an icicle, and the weak blue of her eyes only adds to her coldness. Looking at me with interest, she takes a rigid sip from her goblet.

"I know not why," I reply, stammering slightly with my nervousness, but immediately hate myself for sounding so dumbfounded to her, so plaintively pathetic. *Are my first words to these vulturous women going to be so vulnerable?* I punctuate myself with a deep swig of wine, too, to seem more confident. I will not allow any of these ladies to receive another such unpolished answer from me; they cannot know any vulnerability of mine. No one can.

Not even Lirinda…

The realization is a stab of pain.

"He does not take kindly to newcomers," the lady explains. "Nor to anyone, really." And with that, she erupts into a neat chime of laughter, which a few of the other ladies join.

"I've not seen him so harassed in all the years I have known him!" she continues with an unconvincing peal of delight. "So many *new* faces…"

I cannot help but conclude that she must be referring to my sister, seemingly appearing out of the woodwork as I have. With a flicker of my gaze around the table, I understand that some ladies seem rather uncomfortable at such a snub to their new queen, while others hide their smirks.

The ladies seem relieved when the servants carry platters to our table. In my anxiety, I have not realized how hungry I've been—how the last meal I've eaten was a bleeding deer carcass. Not until the servants lift the lids of the domed platters, releasing the steam and savory-sweet smells of the beautiful dishes within, is my hunger fully realized.

My mouth waters for meats of game, fowl, and fish, shimmering with their juices, and garnished with decorative sprigs of greenery. And for the pies with pretty crusts in intricate designs, and soups decorated with saucy embellishments upon the surface. Never have I seen such masterful food, and I think of the cooks who have surely spent all day crafting each little pie. It seems cruel when the servants carve knives into them and place portions upon our plates and bowls, and not a word is uttered by any of the ladies for their beauty before digging their utensils in, crushing the art to slop. And though my stomach gurgles for nourishment, starved as I've been, I feel slightly ill for the lavishness of it.

"Is the food not to your liking, Mistress?"

I glance up to discover it is now another lady who speaks to me, clad in a gown of ochre threaded with gold. Her auburn hair hangs freely down her back beneath a headdress to match her gown, and her sultry brown eyes blaze at me for how I've not yet touched my plate. She asks this as she delicately carves a piece of a vegetable tart and takes a bite.

It is ostentatious, as are all of you, is what I think. But with my back straightening in my corset and my posture raising, I reply in a mockery of her same charm, warm and fluid with the wine in my veins, "It is all so decadent, I know not where to begin."

"Do they not serve such dishes as these at Havenwood?" The ice lady cranes her neck over her plate to ask me.

I fight every urge not to burst with laughter. *Havenwood? Is that what Lirinda told them? A place where lavish dishes are served?* My lips twitch with a smile.

"Not at all. We keep our palates quite simple."

They glance at one another with interest at this, and I think that this parrying of wits and speech is not so difficult after all. All one has to do is saturate scorn into words and pretend they are sweet. To keep myself from smiling at the ridiculousness of Havenwood, I take a bite of my food, but I nearly lose it in a contemptuous giggle I do well to repress. As I swallow, I nearly choke.

"So, tell me, Mistress," the ice lady begins while dabbing at her mouth with a napkin. "You are the half-sister of the queen by your mother, is that correct? Has she been to court?"

"Yes, what is her name?" asks the eldest lady of the table. By the softness of her face, I think she may be old enough to be mother to all of us. She wears an elegant cloth wimple over her hair, adorned beautifully with sweeps of gold chain, which I can only presume means she has been married before. Perhaps she is a widow. She adds, "I likely know her."

Every humor within me dries suddenly. Everything around me, which has been so loud and lively, feels dull and quiet without Mother being alive. This world, void of her, is lifeless.

I swallow down my drying throat, my eyes too heavy to look up from my food. It feels disrespectful to speak of her here, in this place she vowed never to be. Yet I know that I will not uncover any of her mysteries if I do not so much as utter her name.

"Mora," I say with tenderness. Her name seems to echo from me, lonesome, like recalling a dream that has begun to be forgotten. "That was her name. She"—I think of a convincing way to answer her question without lying completely and tarnishing what sacred thread I have left of my mother— "preferred to avoid the dramatics of court."

"My condolences," says the eldest woman with soft pity, reading my grief.

"Well, I've never heard of her," remarks the smallest and youngest of the table, a girl of perhaps only thirteen years. Speaking to the ladies seated nearest her, so sweet-sounding and slight she is, her lowered voice diminishes to a mouselike chatter. "She wasn't an Honorable, was she?"

"No," the dark-eyed woman answers in a low tone beside her, taking a grape into her fingers and poising it just before her lips. "She must have been Lirrus's best-kept mistress." As if to conceal a smirk, she tosses the grape in. The lady in seed pearls catches her eye and smirks, too, whilst carving her fish and taking a bite.

Best-kept mistress? My eyes blaze at the woman for speaking so blatantly about my mother. If only she knew... if only she could see the things my mother was capable of, she would not reduce her to such a title.

But I cannot speak of Mother, not at all. I cannot defend her over-flourishing pumpkin vines nor her translucent potion that smelled of storms. Rather than boring resentfully at the woman, my eyes fall to stare at my meal, now looking more and more disgusting. I stab at it and take brooding bites, mulling over Mother's secrets. How she had not wanted me to come to the castle, yet I find traces of her here in this forbidden world.

Was my mother truly Lirrus's mistress? I remember their intimacy before the hearth in that handsome home, cradling Lirinda together. Was all of that illegitimate? And when this woman says 'best-kept mistress' does that suggest there were others—other mistresses Mother did not know about? Or perhaps did know? My stomach burns, and I wonder if ever I will have an appetite again.

"And your father's family?" the cold woman asks of me. "I'm afraid I've not heard a word about it. What is the name?"

A year ago, if someone had asked me this, I would have felt that I had no father to speak of. But now, I attempt to hide the shiver that runs suddenly up my spine, the secrecy of my father like a wicked chill emanating from the stone of the castle. The pulse of power throbbing with my own, intoxicating like the wine, tingling in my fingertips.

I do have a father. Nameless though he is—faceless, a malicious shadow—I sense his portion of me now as palpably as I sense Mother's. What, with my constant power, my deep, chilling call to the ancient magic of the Old World, I can only assume that my father is a Magic, just as my mother had been, and perhaps one even more powerful than she. That I, unlike Lirinda with her nonexistent power, am fully magic-blooded.

I feel strangely like grinning. Is it the wine? This sensation I feel—that I am more powerful than any of the ladies here, of anyone here, even Eliador Krom, even the king himself— intoxicates me. If I so decided, I could pull the chandeliers from their mounts and have them crash to the floor, setting flame to tablecloth, and sending everyone here into hysteria while I slinked out the doors. My gaze flickers to Eliador Krom, talking with the priest, and I think it a valuable plan if ever I needed to act upon it.

I am not helpless.

Poising my goblet in my power-roused fingertips, I blaze my eyes now upon the cold lady. "That is because there is no name," say I, rather brashly. "I've never known the identity of my father, and my mother herself had no surname to give. It was not so long ago that our *Queen Lirinda* was nameless, too."

The ladies show each other more expressions of interest, sharing amongst themselves nonverbal judgments and musings, suppressed grins.

"It is most curious how it all came about," the cold woman says, inspecting the engraved artistry upon her silver chalice, hardly caring to sweeten her disdain for me. "Our king simply picking his bride from off the street—a bride who just so happens to be the secret, illegitimate daughter of Lirrus Fairfellow. And how her sister here, who has no name at all to trace, is now seated at our table, amongst those who have taken great care to trace our lineage back to the Great Restoration."

"Ellaina," the wimpled widow warns.

Ellaina sucks in a deep breath for another hefty, and perhaps slightly drunken, spew of words, but is interrupted by Tafton appearing at my shoulder, just as her mouth opens to speak.

"Miss Sirilda, the queen wishes to present you to the high table," he mutters at my side, but loudly enough for all the table to hear.

If I was not slightly drunken, too, I might feel more afraid of the accusations Ellaina has been casting upon my namelessness, but for some reason I feel brazen—so brazen, in fact, that I look challengingly at her as I rise to my feet.

The wine has made me wobbly as I turn my back to the ladies, but as I saunter after Tafton to the high table, I quickly regain my awareness of motion, of every sensitive caress of silk upon my skin, though still my blood swims with heat, confidence, and an urge to laugh out of my spite. *Havenwood!* I cannot keep the grin from twisting at my mouth.

"Sirilda!" Lirinda beams down to me from her chair, which is set grandly above the floor level upon the dais. She extends a proud hand down to me at the side of the table, and I tentatively take it. Lirinda blinks expectantly; within her perfectly lighthearted mask of a smile is an expression that tells me I ought to be doing something.

Curtsy, Lirinda mouths silently, barely moving her lips from her perfect smile. Only because I have seen my sister form that very word upon her lips countless times as a child can I recognize it with ease.

Thankful I am for the wine that aids me in sweeping a surprisingly graceful curtsy, using my lithe strength and flexibility to dip very low, almost sensually in my warm mockery, while still holding Lirinda's extended hand. The fact I have seldom practiced this before does not show in my sudden, wild confidence. When I look up from my curtsy, a defiant glare burns in my eyes at my oblivious sister.

"Very well done, baby sister!" Lirinda claps. "Oh, how happy I am to see you here! I wondered if ever you would come! And now—*I hope*—to stay! How are you enjoying the castle thus far?"

"It is like a very strange dream," I say in my newfound false voice, which comes so easily to me, like a tree oozing sweet, sugary sap out of its wounds. "I expect to wake at any moment and find us still in our bunk."

Lirinda's smile never falters as though it is pinned upon her face like her crown is upon her head, immovably perched in her curling golden hair; but the sparkles in her eyes strain.

"You look so very lovely, sister," says she with the slightest tension. "How well that gown complements your skin tone. I cannot wait to see how well you will look, dressed in the other gowns from the old collection. And very soon, a collection of your own!"

I smile blandly at her.

"I have not yet formally introduced you to our king and my husband." Lirinda indicates beside her, to the one figure in all the hall whom I have tried to avoid looking at this whole time, for I know that when we look at one another, I will feel that strange tickling feeling again, and I know not what it means. And I hate it very much, the feeling he gives me.

When finally I turn my eyes upon the king, I see he is at first looking off to the gentlemen's table, but he then feels my glance upon him and slowly looks to me, as if he shares this secret, special ability to feel me.

Curtsy, Lirinda mouths smilingly again, and without breaking eye contact with the king, I perform my most beautiful curtsy yet, arms held wide out, dipping treacherously low. I hear the people at the tables behind me applaud, and I, numb and warm with the wine, feel my lips smile.

"Ah, yes. The little sister," says he, his voice so resonant and deep, that the tiny hairs on my neck raise. "Hardly recognizable you are with your curtsy, Miss, I should think you've long been a resident of our court."

His little remark at our first encounter, of my unwillingness to curtsy to him, prompts me to show him that such an unwillingness burns in my gaze, still.

"You have taken the Oath?" asks he, and I bow my head graciously, but not without my glare of defiance.

"I have."

"Well, then, welcome to court, Mistress Sirilda."

He sips from his goblet. As he drinks, his brown eyes do not leave mine. His gaze is not friendly, for it measures me with caution, and I find my black glare measures him in the same, cautious way. I feel we understand the threat of the other, each placed on either side of our golden, lovely Lirinda.

I wonder if anyone has ever made this king feel so uncomfortable as I do.

CHAPTER NINETEEN

Strange it is, how much colder a castle filled with riches can be than a crude cottage in a forest. When winter nights befell Haven, I never knew cold so long as the wood continued to burn in the hearth. Even a simple coverlet filled with down and dandelion and the company of my sister sleeping so near to me was enough to keep my cheeks flushed all the night, my bare toes peeking off the bunk rosy with warmth, despite the mound of snow swirling round the outside of the cottage.

The snow continues to fall this night, and the tower where I am now to live with the other ladies is frigid. The dark, exposed stone feels as though it drips with moisture through its cracks, and the wind can be felt in lonesome drafts. Even the sea—I feel rumbles of it crashing far below, striking the cliffs, its mist permeating the ancient mortar of the castle walls. The enormity of cold here can hardly be touched by the fires the servants keep. Mercifully, each of the four-poster beds in the ladies' tower are dressed heavily with thick velvet bedding and curtains.

Once a servant has unlaced me from my gown, I crawl

eagerly beneath the heavy coverlet, so exhausted I am from having come from Haven this morning. I am eager to be alone, to feel the weight of my bones sink into the mattress. How my scalp tingles with relief after having the pins of my headdress removed, and how freely I breathe without my corset.

As soon as I climb upon the bed, I pull the heavy velvet curtains around me closed against the chill—against the possibility of the moon creeping past the narrow glass of the window in the middle of the night, looking upon me, reminding me of how very far from home I've come.

How will the snow look now, I wonder, as it falls softly upon Haven; it is the first time I'm not there to witness it. I turn on my side and shield myself from the bloating grief I feel for my home, lost to me forever. My eyes burn.

Has Lirinda not felt this at all? This grief for home?

Perhaps she might, when finally I can tell her what's become of our mother. How all is lost to us. And perhaps, for once, she will sting with a portion of the pain I feel at a constant. Perhaps, for once, she will know her fault in this—her foolishness.

The ladies have come to bed later than me. While I had been brought to the ladies' tower room by Tafton, and the servants brought in my new-old things, the ladies themselves were attending Lirinda in her rooms, combing out her hair and helping her to dress for bed, as they are to do every night and morning—and as will I, beginning tomorrow. As I lay melting in my exhaustion into the mattress, I could hear the ladies downstairs; after attending to Lirinda, they spent some hours giggling out in the gallery with hot mulled wine, before stumbling up the tower stairs to this chamber and clambering into their beds.

"Oh yes...I forgot. *She* is here now," I hear one of them murmur about me, as I feign sleep with the curtains drawn around me.

The ladies continue to giggle and whisper in the tower. As I drift closer to slumber, their whispers begin to sound to me like the soft patters of snow falling upon Haven, the tall pines, the almost inaudible cushioned percussion. The entire world blue-white and still. Whispers—like the snow's gentle tumble off the trees. Sensual, almost. Like a whisper spoken from a lover, so near to the ear, it tickles the softest hairs of the auricle.

The white of the snow, brilliant. A brilliant light—I want to shield my eyes.

My Current pounds in my chest, and to each fingertip it throbs. *So near,* echoes the voice within my own heart, and it is agony. I reach out for the Source, for the blinding light that seems corporeal and tangible, but grasp only the velvet folds of curtain surrounding my bed.

I am awake before the servants come to rouse the flames in the brazier, standing at the slender window, staring out at the gloomy morning. A heavy rain has rinsed away yesterday's snow and beneath the dark morning sky, the castle lawns look slick and lush again. Although now, without their leaves, the trees far below have become black and skeletal.

I place my hands upon the cold stone of the tower wall, wondering at the familiarity of it to my dreams, evoking memories which I have already long forgotten. Stone...endless tunnels of it, dripping and cold.

As the ladies begin to stir, turning over in their beds with grunts and coos that betray their refinedness, I go to my chest and select a velvet emerald gown and its matching headdress.

The gown is frayed and aged from years of wear and storage, yet I find it beautiful. I attempt to dress myself, so as to not be gawked at by the ladies for my famished figure but cannot lace the back of my corset. Daringly, with my back to the shadows of the round chamber and my face craned over my shoulder, I attempt to use my Current upon the intricate lacings.

It is done horribly, uneven and loose, but I am glad for the release of Current, slight as it is. I sniffle at the small amount of blood that threatens to ooze from my nose, but it fades before it can drip to my nostril rim, and I realize that, since the night I had fallen faint after exerting so much of my power accessing Mother's memories, I have not suffered nosebleeds so profusely for small efforts. Have I grown more resilient to it?

When the servants arrive, I ask for assistance with my lacings. So furiously tight and expertly she pulls, sucking the very breath from my lungs, and then she laces me into my gown. I try to watch her over my shoulder so I might practice tomorrow.

With my headdress pinned to my freely hanging hair, I descend the tower stairs before any of the ladies have risen and await them in the long gallery, looking out the vast mullioned windows at the scenic castle grounds below enwreathed in mist and rain. From here, I can see stables and horses being led about to graze by servants. That strange tickling of my chest I feel when I see a familiar man riding in from the surrounding forest—the king, who, alongside his gentlemen of the court and their dogs padding around them, must be returning from an early hunt.

The ladies soon come downstairs to the gallery, yawning still and blinking in the abundant light here from the many windows. Although the light is dim with dark clouds, I think the amount of wine they stayed up to drink last night made their heads throb. I, too, feel like wincing from the contents of my cup, but have a pleasant enough expression painted upon my face where I stand at the windows, and as the ladies come sweeping by me in their far finer gowns. I do not speak with them unless I must, and they speak to me not.

I follow them into Lirinda's bedchamber for my new duties as her maid. Seeing her sleeping in her grand bed I thought would not be so surreal to me as it is, but the image of her familiar golden tresses spilled over silk pillows rather than our bunk fills me with another staggering realization that this is not just another of my strange dreams.

"Good morning," says she when at last she sits up in her bed and yawns prettily, raising her arms over her head like a dancer. "Sister... so good it is to see you in the mornings again."

My throat, too seized by a choke, cannot utter a reply.

The ladies and I comb out her long, luscious hair and aid her in undressing from her beautiful white nightgown into her even more magnificent and overly complex day gown of pale blue velvet.

"My, your majesty! So fair you are, you return the finest spring day to the sky," remarks the eldest lady who wears the wimple, who I now know to be named Lady Klaria.

"Yes, my queen," adds the ice lady Ellaina in her sweetest tone yet. "Your sunniness will be a delight to us here in the castle over the dreary months of winter."

And at this, with a horrible pang in my stomach, I realize that part of our assembly here in the mornings is to fill my sister the queen with flatteries. When all the ladies, and even Lirinda, look to me when it is my turn, I open my mouth while my mind works at an example as to how I might indulge her pride.

"How...beautiful your eyes, my queen sister." I pause my fastening of her fine ribboned slippers to say. "The tawny green of…boiled frog spawn."

"Ew…" Miella, the youngest, cannot refuse to squeak.

When the ladies and I are dismissed from Lirinda's bedchamber to await her in the gallery, so that we can all walk to the great hall for the breaking of our fast together, I ask Lirinda if we might have a moment alone to talk. The idea that we might need to be alone for such a thing fills her luminous, large eyes with alarm and, I think, dread.

"Whatever for, sister?" she asks as she fastens a necklace heavy with sapphires in the reflection of her great looking-glass. "Won't you help me?"

I go to gather her heap of luscious hair into my arms so she might fasten her jewels with ease. I see she still wears the Fairfellow jewel, always so long on her, secured within the crevice of her breast and unseen beneath the bodice of her gown.

"There is something of a personal nature you might like to know." I try to speak as patiently as I can, though my mouth grows tight with fury for her. I can see how her neck and shoulders tense as she assumes I must surely be thinking to discuss her old life of magic and soil.

Aye, Lirinda, that is just what I will discuss with you, and always will. You cannot escape our old life as perhaps you think you have. So long as I am around, I will be your reminder. Have you not once thought of Mother? I think viciously.

"Very well sister," says she. "After we break our fast with the court, let us partake of tea in my presence chamber, just you and me."

The great hall for breakfast was nearly just as magnificent as supper, and I pleaded within myself all the while not to allow it to strain me as it did. The rigidity of my back, the false expressions and conversations, the overly syruped food. I've had but two meals as part of the court and already I long for the peace of eating alone without celebration.

There is some solace when I return with Lirinda to her presence chamber, now completely furnished with a long table surrounded by the painted murals upon the walls, of time-faded swans and maidens and beautiful vases filled deliciously with cut roses. Upon the long table, servants have placed a painted tea set and a serving tray filled with cakes. I assist Lirinda in taking a seat at the grand chair at one end of the table, then seat myself opposite her. When the servants are not dismissed and go on to serve us, pouring us our cups, I clear my throat and indicate my scowling eyes at them.

"You may be dismissed," says Lirinda, concealing her aggravation with a delicate sip of her cup.

"So, sister," say I, rising from my seat and pouring a cup from the pot, and kindly offering her a refill as well. "How is married life?"

At once, Lirinda's anxious, stark face melts into the childish, warm expression I've always known, and I cannot resist a hot flush of my own heart feeling overjoyed to see it.

"Oh, it is greater beyond any loving dream!" she rejoices. "Never have I thought I might be so tenderly and properly loved."

"I am happy for you." I force the words out, but my voice is a thin, tattered thread. After clearing my throat, I sip deeply of my tea.

"I am happy for you as well, sister. For you being here! Dressed so beautifully, soon to be courted by gentlemen. In no time, I don't doubt, you will find a match of your own! And I've not yet told you the good news. I've an allowance for you. An allowance for your gowns and, if you were to marry, a dowry."

I nearly spray my tea out my mouth.

"Marry?" I choke out the word. "I've never thought of it in all my life."

"Perhaps you will now, with such suitable gentlemen in the king's attendance." Lirinda grins at me coquettishly over the rim of her cup.

Once, so long ago now it seems, I would have smiled back at her. But my face is hard, joyless. Would she have me come here merely to serve her as a maid and then be married? I look at my sister with a foreign gaze, for I feel the woman before me is not the girl I once knew.

"I feel quite incapable of such merry capacities," I say. "And to be honest, I find it unbelievable that you do not share in my feeling. For all the glamour in this castle, do you never feel the ache for all we have left behind?"

It is as though the clouds outside have come into this presence chamber and cast a shadow over the golden queen.

"No," she says simply. "No, Sirry. I do not. I ache not at all, not for anything."

For the first time in so long, I feel like I will break with outrage, my claws to dig into the table and a cry to erupt like an eagle's screech from my throat, but I fight against the urge and keep my features resilient.

"Really? You ache for *nothing?*" I spit the words. "What a privilege that must be! To not have witnessed every despair that I have in your absence. Have you not once thought of what has become of our mother?"

"Of course, I think of Mother!" Lirinda rises from her seat to project her voice at me, though still it is bated, quiet, as if she does not wish to alarm whoever may be listening outside the presence chamber doors. "But Mother will not come here. She will not help me as I have implored her to. She will not come to live here, though I would give her titles and riches beyond her any need. Estates grander than any mossy cottage, gardens vaster and sunnier than any plot of forest!"

"She would never come here," I say with a sad growl. "And now she cannot ever. For now, our mother…she is dead."

I have envisioned this moment since Mother's death—that when I told Lirinda of Mother's horrible demise, I might feel some malicious triumph for making her feel pain, a shred of the pain that I have, for she has gone so long without any. But how her eyes bulge with despair and confusion, and she claps a hand to her mouth, I feel no pleasure at all. As her eyes glimmer with the procuring of tears, I am reminded of my own grief.

"Dead?" Her voice is but a whisper. Tears stream from her eyes, over her hand. "Our Mother?"

I slump into my seat and look down at the table, fixated upon the grain of wood. "Yes."

Lirinda slowly falls back into her seat, too. Quivering-silent behind the hand pressed still to her mouth.

And she sobs. Into both hands now, covering her eyes and mouth, she heaves her cries. I watch her from across the long table, how her shoulders quake in her lovely blue velvet sleeves. I realize I've not seen my sister weep in years. Just as I feel an urge to go to her and console her, share with her in this pain I throb with, too, she muffles a squeakish plea into her palms. "Why did you not tell me?"

Easily, all sympathy I feel for her is washed away by my resurfacing anger.

"Have I had an opportunity before this?" I say with a snarl. "If you do not recall, you fled a world away from us, from our life. While I was caring for Mother until her final breath, you have been here…*dancing.*"

Still so much like a child, Lirinda wipes the tears from her eyes and cheeks, sniffling pitifully. She says nothing, of course, about her treachery to Mother and me. Still, I believe she is oblivious to the harm she caused us.

"How did it happen?" she whispers now, her sobs having receded into quickened breaths.

I shake my head and grimace a bitter smile. "You would not like to hear of it. It might spoil your enjoyment of your pretty little tea cakes."

Lirinda's bloodshot eyes glimmer furiously at me, and I understand that she insists I divulge to her the truth. After another pour of tea into my cup, with still that bitter smile perched upon my mouth and a thoughtful sip as I leer at her, I begin the story. I tell Lirinda every detail of Mother's grief for losing her beloved Lirinda to the Glindians—of Mother's growing shawl of mushrooms and the mice that ran up her sleeves. At this, Lirinda swallows hard and checks nervously at the door, as if someone might be eavesdropping. I tell her of our return to the cottage, how Mother neglected all she once cared for, but once I come to the part of how I lost control of my Current and witnessed her memories, I falter.

Mother's memories. As beautiful as some of them were, they were each entwined with the grim thread of my conception. Of my father who overpowered Mother as Lirinda's own lay dead beside her. How my own father may have been the one to kill Lirinda's. I cannot bring myself to speak of it, any of it, not even to the sister with whom I once shared everything. I take a brooding sip from my cup for a long pause as I think of the bright spring day Mother wished herself rid of me, and of the autumn night she birthed me and left me to die. There is nothing of my own I can share. When I speak again, my voice is broken.

I tell her only now of how Mother's grief had manifested so deeply, the mushrooms consumed her body. Even as I say it, it feels as though I am speaking a dream. How Mother's throat had been crushed with fungus—how I could not bear to look at her in the dark of the night as she breathed her final breath…

When I am finished, I grind my teeth while staring down into my cup.

"That is"—Lirinda's soft voice reminds me she is there, and that I am here, in a beautiful room so far away from the death and mushrooms of my mind—"a most…*horrific*…story."

I raise my gaze to the queen across the table from me, Lirinda. How distant she is, how unreachable from the truth; I do not think she believes me, or, perhaps, chooses not to believe me. I realize now that I am truly alone in this life. My sister would have languished with me in every magical detail and shared a wonder for how it was all possible. My sister would have wept for the Mother of Haven the both of us knew. But this woman is no longer that sister.

My family, my past, my home—all of it is lost.

"Aye," I say finally with a miserable croak. "Horrific…"

Lirinda rises from her seat and gestures with open arms for me to go to her and embrace her. I breathe in deeply through my nose with reluctance before standing from my seat and going to her. Our embrace as I fold into her is meaningless. Two stones pressed together would have more affection for one another.

"You have endured so much," Lirinda whispers into my shoulder, and I jolt with a small excitement that she may finally understand me. "I am sorry for losing our mother and that you were there to witness it all. But sister…"

She leans back so that she can look up into my towering face. "It is now the past. And the past…should never be dwelled upon. Let us move past our grief…let us speak of it not, not ever again. May such sorrows never touch this castle. And we can live happily here, together, in this paradise I have found for us."

My throat is unable to speak, perhaps ever again, I feel. My face is void of expression. Lirinda seems to accept my easy silence as agreement and is cheerful as ever. She holds my hand as we retreat into the gallery together where the ladies have been sitting in their chairs, embroidering panels of tapestry. The brilliance of stormy sunlight reflecting off the molded wall panels and marble fireplace reminds me of how very displaced I am. As Lirinda falls immediately back into her queenly charade, crooning over Lady Klaria's expert stitches, indulging in a laugh with little Miella, I wish myself far away. So far from this lie, far from any trace of memory, though I know not where I could go. Nothing belongs to me, not even my sister.

Only, perhaps, the cold stone passages that I have yet to find—the beseeching call of them more constant than any sister, any kin—and whatever secret they may lead to.

CHAPTER TWENTY

I rise from my bed the following morning while it is still dark as night, but the stars have begun to fade into an indigo sky, and the first cast of blue-gray light fills the frigid chamber. In my wooden chest is my old wool cloak, smelling still of cottage memories, which I don over my nightshift. As silently as I can, I wrench open the door of the ladies' tower and patter barefoot down the icy stone steps to the gallery, still residually warm from last night's fire. It is a beautiful space in this dark morning light. Through the vast windows I can see the shapes of hills and mountains of the castle grounds, blue-tinted and velvety, where deer have come from the forests to graze. And far beyond, I see the expanse of Glindor shrouded in wintry mist. In the distance, it snows.

The lush carpets of the gallery warm my feet before I leave the glorious long chamber for the rest of the castle. The gigantic guard standing outside the gallery door glares after me as I walk past him, pulling my hood slightly back to reveal my face, innocent and unassuming. He nods, and I do not think he suspects at all what I am set about to do, as I already think many of the ladies wander the castle at night, meeting with the king's gentlemen in vacant chambers, for they are always leaving and returning to their beds while they think I sleep.

When I am beyond the sight of the guard, faced with the entire sleeping castle to myself, with the shadowed stone corridors spread out before me, I feel myself choked with such thrill, and I realize I have not smiled so unrestrainedly in so long a time. I cannot remember if ever I have been more exhilarated.

My feet patter quietly over the flagstone as I steal down the dark corridors, with only the occasional guttering candelabra to illuminate the passages where there are no windows emanating bluish light. I know not at all where I am headed, and the more I explore, the more I worry I may get lost. There are more halls and stairwells than I realized, and the heartbeat within the walls, the lure I feel so strongly within my own blood, has no map. No direction.

Did I truly think I would find the Source immediately? If it is anything worth discovering, anything treacherous to the Pures, then it will not be easy to find.

And what if I never find it?

It has been more than an hour that I've wandered, and the gray light of the corridors has grown in brilliance. With the imminent dawn, I can make out more details sparkling on the walls—threads of tapestries, metallic armor on display, designs in the carpets that now reveal their color in the gaining light. But there are no indications anywhere of anything unusual—unusual for a Pure. Nothing, anywhere, like anything reminiscent of my dreams.

But it is there, faraway—an ache stretched across time and matter. I rest my hands upon the ancient stone of the wall and close my eyes, straining to visualize my friendly white light who dissolves so perfectly into my bones whilst I sleep, dancing with my Current. My friend is here, I am certain of it, but agonizing it is not knowing which way to turn to find it.

I hear commotion from the servants as they stoke the first fires and begin their day of work, and I scurry at once to find my way back to the gallery door, desperate to climb back into my bed before the ladies wake, but it is not so simple. My cloak flutters behind me in my rush up stairwells I thought I had memorized, but once I climb them, I realize they bring me to unrecognizable passages I had not been to before, and I am lost.

"Damn it all," I hiss to myself, pattering on my tiptoes back down the stairwell and ascending another, searching for familiar features that had once been shrouded in shadow but now glimmer with wintry daylight. Finally, I recognize the design of a carpet I run past and know that I am near. And at last, I see the guard who stands before the gallery door. I show him my heavily breathing face beneath my hood so he may recognize me.

Through the eyeholes of his polished helmet he leers at me with disapproval, but still he allows me to slither in past him to the gallery. I sigh with relief when the long chamber looks as untouched as it had upon first waking, the servants having not yet arrived. When I ascend the tower stairs and slip silently into the ladies' chamber, I hear their snores beyond their drawn curtains, rhythmic and thick with sleep. The lustrous folds of velvet unchanged from where I had left them; no one has moved.

In the silver light, I crawl atop my counterpane as I try to still my breath and battle with the despair I feel within. I had not thought trying to discover the Source would be so difficult. How long will it take me to discover it, if ever I do? Too many passages and chambers there are in this castle; it could take me years.

I would not last years… I think, feeling doubt swell within me, doubt for everything I have chosen. Should I never have left Haven? Why have I come here? Is it all for naught?

And what—I hardly dare ponder, for the ache is too much—*what if I have imagined it all along? What if there is no Source?*

As the servants arrive, and the ladies and I dress and go to wake Lirinda as we will do every day, every season of every year, I despair that I am here. The mountain of Haven, wisped in snow, haunts my vision. I see it framed within a tall window as the ladies and I descend the castle stairs on our way to the great hall to break our fast.

I cannot look upon it. I shy my eyes from my guilt of Mother's bones I have left there to crumble.

Every step I take, surrounded by the ancient stone, I beseech that strange pale call to prove to me in some substantial way that it is more than fantasy—more than a reflection of my longing for purpose, to belong. But there is nothing I am met with. Surrounded by the lively court and my own sister in all their merriment, I am desperately alone.

The evening is heavy with cold, the atmosphere pregnant with snow. After supper, I sit with the ladies in the gallery as I am required to do, while they play at cards, finish embroidering their panels of tapestries, or pluck the strings of a fanciful little instrument called a bandelon. Lirinda has already been put to bed like an infant, after we have combed out her hair and dressed her into her night gown, and so quiet and dulcet is the bandelon that, if Lirinda could somehow hear it between her chamber and the presence chamber, it would be so sweet a music she would be lulled to sleep anyway.

The fire in the enormous fireplace is my one comfort, save the pretty music, and I relish in it in my upholstered velvet chair as I work at stitching a panel of tapestry. Each of us are flushed with currant cider, and though I ache with grief for not finding the Source already as I had hoped I would, I am relaxed, for the first time in this castle, for perhaps months. But when the gallery door opens and I see it is King Gastlin's tall figure that enters, I instantly jolt to my most vigilant posture, ready to flee or fight, my Current flaring in my fingertips.

The ladies drop from whatever they are doing into desperate curtsies, and I bow my head over my embroidery as he walks past us all, nodding with a smile at those ladies whom he knows best, and lingering his gaze uncomfortably on me, making me swelter with adrenaline and that peculiar tingle where I sit. Just as suddenly as he arrived, he is gone through the door to the presence chamber.

My belly burns when I realize he is going to Lirinda's bed. I push away the imagery of it—those images of Lirinda's I had witnessed, of his strong buttocks and muscular back flexing as he slides himself within her—and resume my stitching with renewed fervor.

"Do you think she's able to sleep at all?" asks one of the ladies once the king is surely far enough away not to hear. "Beside the king? How could one not be wide awake all night?"

"If he *lets* her sleep," whispers another and all the ladies, except Lady Klaria, join in with whispered cackles. Lady Klaria simply shakes her head disapprovingly as she embroiders a new section of tapestry the other ladies have not yet begun.

"So terrified I would be that I might snore!" whispers another with a giggle.

"If you're in love, I suppose you might feel comfortable enough."

"And she most certainly is in love! And he with her."

"Did he love his former wife so?" young Miella squeaks innocently while sorting through her fan of cards splayed before her. "I've heard stories of her, the late Queen Jayna. How did their love compare?"

The ladies are suddenly wiped of their humor, glancing amongst one another solemnly. I gaze at Miella raptly; I had not known the king was previously wed.

"Were you not part of her court?" Miella asks of Ellaina innocently, unaware of the indelicacy in which she speaks.

"I was," answers Ellaina with a slow draw of her cards, where she plays at a table with Miella and the sour-natured brunette, Ilette. "He loved her very much, but it was a different kind of love."

"A love between children," adds another of the ladies. "So young they were when they wed. Queen Jayna was but twelve, His Majesty fifteen."

"Twelve is not so young," Miella says indignantly, as she is hardly older herself.

"I was there, too," says Lady Klaria, pulling her needle through her tapestry with a mournful expression sagging upon her face. "I served his queen mother, Elta, at the time. When his father was tragically killed, young Gastlin had to be coronated at only eight years old…and married far younger than a king ought to be. A boy still, he was. His mother was so concerned for the both of them—that they were too young—but the young king found friendship with Jayna. He confided his doubts and comforts in her, and, in a way, grew up alongside her. A turbulent time of uncertainty and perseverance we as a realm faced when young Gastlin took the throne."

The ladies are silent a long time. I realize I have stopped my embroidery to listen intently, but now I begin again.

"And she died…in childbed?" asks Miella in a whisper.

Lady Klaria nods sorrowfully. "Aye. After many trials of loss, Queen Jayna was lost, too. So we pray to the gods we will be blessed with a Glindian heir with our Queen Lirinda."

I breathe in deeply through my nose at the thought of Lirinda producing an heir for our enemy. A Glindian child, a prince or princess, product of those who had eradicated our Old World—our ancestors—albeit woven with a thread of Mother's magical blood. What a child that would be: a fusion of lies, warfare, and mystery.

The idea angers me, but there is more I feel. Something akin to what I had felt when witnessing Mother's memory of the babe Lirinda, swaddled and warm—the loving scene of family—*without me.*

"Our poor king…such tragic stories," remarks one of the ladies softly, fingers expertly rippling across the strings of the bandelon, sounding as sweet as a summer breeze wafting through tall grass.

"Tragic though they are," says Miella, growing in exuberance, sitting up in her seat with a broadening grin, "it *is* rather romantic, don't you think? Each of these tragedies have ultimately intertwined his fate with that of Queen Lirinda's!"

"You are far too much of a romantic, little Miella," drawls Ellaina, almost pityingly. "You ought to have that snuffed out by the time you marry."

"And what would you know of marriage or romance, Ellaina?" Miella retorts with a sugary smile. It is well known throughout court that Ellaina has so long remained unmarried that she disgraces her family.

Ellaina smiles coldly at the snub, slapping down a card upon the table, while the rest of the ladies, except Klaria, giggle.

"All I think of it is that it's a beautiful story," Miella's voice chimes again. "Both their fathers lost to the same horrific night, then the two of them coming together to wed after all these years. And him choosing her from his own heart. There's not another story like it in all of Glindian history."

Ilette, ever brooding and cruel, looks through her splayed cards and selects one. "There is nothing beautiful about what The Devil did."

My pulse quickens with this new information. *What The Devil did.* I remember now what Lirinda had said to me in her bedchamber my first night visiting, that she and the king had both lost their fathers to the same massacre.

So, King Gastlin's father, the king before him, was there that night, too? Murdered as Lirrus had been? By this Devil?

I feel a sickly cold sweat—albeit a forbidden bloom of hope— tingle my flesh at the thought that his name may be the one Mother pleaded for me not to discover. Setting my embroidery upon my lap to tremblingly nurse my cider, I listen intently to the ladies, while trying not to reveal too much interest in my widened, anxious eyes.

"No, of course not!" Miella exclaims. "By the gods! I cannot sleep some nights knowing he may still be out there!"

"I do not think anyone in the realm will sleep soundly until a Burning of the Blood is performed for him," Ilette says.

Burning of the Blood, the words reverberate in my mind. So this Devil… is a Magic…

I swallow down the sickening excess of cold saliva that fills my throat. A Magic man who was there the night of my conception? I set my chalice upon the table near me, for my hand trembles so, it has spilled cider upon my lap.

The walls around me feel suddenly colder. Chills rise up my arms and neck. I cannot hear what else the ladies discuss for they seem so far away now. I feel I might fall faint or vomit. This

'Devil'… could he be the one? My father?

"I do believe you made Mistress Sirilda ill with your talk, ladies," scolds Klaria. "One should not discuss such impure things, especially so near to the king and queen where they sleep."

I find each of them have turned their gaze to me, studying my pale shock; I do indeed seem to have gone suddenly ill. I stare back at them, my face drained of color, surely. In the moment, there is nothing that matters more than this terrible discovery of mine, but simultaneously I remember my obligation to act as Pure as them.

Swallowing down my saliva and taking a deep breath, I remove myself from my sickness.

"My apologies, Mistress," utters Miella softly to me. "Has the Devil Mellick destroyed something dear to you, too? It was long before I was born, but it was my family's town he burned… completely to ash. Not long before his attack on King Gasden."

Has he destroyed something dear to me? The words float in my mind like a spinning leaf on a river. He destroyed my mother, though she continued to live. And what is worse, is that in his destruction, he created me…

I open my mouth to answer, but too seized with horror I am that I'm incapable of sound. How pitiful to them I must look: a scared Pure maiden, unlearned of so many things, frightened at the name of an infamous Magic. I reason within myself that this impression of theirs is a far better alternative to them thinking I am the very child of the Devil Mellick of whom they speak.

Could I be?

"I, for one, am finished hearing of this," says Lady Klaria, rising from her seat and pressing her embroidery needle into her silk cushion. "It's late enough as it is. I don't wish for any such nightmares tonight. Good night to all of you."

And Lady Klaria gathers her things and ascends from the gallery to the tower as the ladies all murmur their words of good night. A few of the quieter ladies, who flock loyally to Klaria like she is their mother hen, dismiss themselves as well.

The remaining ladies and I sit in silence, but for a few murmurs of Ellaina, Ilette, and Miella's card game. I stare off into the distance of the room, revisiting the memory of my mother's—the pain I endured, radiating through her. Revisiting Lirrus, stabbed through the chest—revisiting the man atop Mother… the man I could not see; my father.

The Devil Mellick had been there. So had King Gastlin's father, King Gasden. And so was Mother. How could it have all come to be?

"Was the Guard there that night?" I croak unexpectedly out of the silence, surprising even myself. "The night the Devil Mellick killed the king and Lirrus Fairfellow both?"

Miella looks curiously to her elders. Ilette and Ellaina exchange glances over their cards.

"Some of them were," Ellaina answers uncertainly. "Others remained at the castle, uninvited."

"It was a hunting party," explains Ilette. "Lirrus had been visited by the king and his party at his hunting lodge in the woods. While they were there, making merry—being stupid, no doubt—they did not suspect they would be ambushed by Mellick."

"Ah." I nod, squeezing a swallow down my drying throat.

So Mother, the mistress, lived in Lirrus's hunting lodge, I deduce. So much more clearly this memory of hers is becoming…

"And…" I struggle to say without a quaver in my voice. "And how does anyone know for certain it had been the Devil Mellick who had ambushed them?"

"He burned everything down," answers Ellaina as though I am stupid not to know. "That is what he does, don't you know? Once he has had his fill of rape and murder, he sets everything aflame. It is his marking, his signature. He's done it before, many times in Glindor, like Miella's town of Shorn—tormented the women and killed the men before burning everything; it is a mockery to us Pures, I should think, for the burning of their blood."

A chill rushes through me at the powerful irony of a Magic burning Pures for their blood. Punishment, retribution, for all the damage they've caused over the centuries.

"And the Fairfellow lodge," Ellaina continues, "once it was discovered by the rest of the Guard, was nothing but sizzling bones and ash. None who had attended the party survived."

None, except your own queen and her mother, I wish I could say to her. *And the seed that is me.*

"Besides," Ilette continues with a draw of another card, "they say they detected strong amounts of magic from the fire. Surely, you've heard of *that.*"

I merely shake my head. My gaze has gone soft once more, staring off while I envision this unimaginable man, whose magic was so potent, it could be traced through ash and flame.

As I lie in bed soon after, my wide-eyed stare continues above at the chasmic darkness of my canopy as the ladies around me fall heavily into slumber. The memory of Mother I revisit, wondering whether that night she had been a part of the hunting party; if she had been known by anyone there as Lirrus's mistress; the beautiful red-haired woman with whom he shared a bonny golden child.

Had Mother perhaps baked one of her delicious gooseberry pies and served it to Lirrus's most trusted men? Could all have been a grand evening of hunting stories and a feast upon their captured game, until Lirrus drank too deeply, failing in his duty to protect his fellow men and the beloved mother of his child? Unaware that the Devil Mellick was about to burst through the door and massacre his king and then Lirrus himself, too? Destroy every dignity and love of my mother?

And sire me?

Mother must have escaped—escaped with Lirinda before the fire could trap them within their home, I reason. Or perhaps the Devil Mellick had spared Mother a fiery fate, only after defiling her first. Perhaps he somehow knew she was Magic, too, and let her go…

I imagine Mother tearing a baby Lirinda from her cradle and fleeing the fire that the Devil Mellick set upon the lodge. *And then, after she got away…*

My eyes burn with the image of a snowy Haven in my mind, how Mother had sought refuge there in her bear fur and baby Lirinda in her arms. *Mother must have fled there that very night…*

In my mind's eye, I revisit Mother's memory yet again, only now I imagine the terrible scene with renewed clarity. I know not what the Devil Mellick looks like, but I now have a name to place upon the mysterious man who plunged a sword through Lirrus's heart and looked down upon my mother's recoiled, trembling face from beyond the veil of fog.

The Devil Mellick. My father.

CHAPTER TWENTY ONE

Winter has descended upon Glindor in earnest and has transformed the world out the windows into one of Lirinda's frosted cakes, swirling with white tufts of cream.

With the snow, there is a merriness that fills the castle, one I've never known before. A merriness of celebration and play to combat the unchanging steely skies. But the joy of gifts being passed around, and the music and dancing of constant revelry, does not fill me as I constantly brood over riddles of the Devil Mellick, my recurrent dreams of the woman and the white light, the Source within the castle, and my own fate as a Magic sneaking through a Pure's world. Although, I do find myself, at times, enjoying myself despite my effort not to feel comfortable in my enemy's home.

One day in the midst of the revel season, Lirinda gifts me a magnificent coat trimmed with rabbit fur and a matching hat and gloves—as magnificent as any of the ladies'—and when I am urged outside with the court into the deep snow, I secretly relish in the luxurious furs about me. The massive hills and rolling landscapes around us seem endlessly high and sprawling when we stand among them and not from a high tower window.

The king's gentlemen have brought out a sled and convince a few of the ladies to slide down a small hill upon it with them; Miella is the most eager. Klaria refuses even to step into the deep snow. Lirinda wades into the scene in an ermine ensemble that looks as though a hundred spotted stoats had been slaughtered for her to look so fluffy and soft, and she laughs the most delightfully when it is her turn to ride on the sled with the king, who laughs when a spray of snow hits their faces. Beaded with snow, the two share in a deep kiss to the applause of everyone.

When the servants bring out cups of hot cider and mulled wine, the court becomes flushed with drink and begins to throw snowballs. I am eager to sneak away, hoping to slip unseen from the fray of snow so I might have an opportunity to walk the castle—an opportunity I seize whenever I can—but when I am struck in the cheek by Torren, a handsome gentleman of the king's, whose rust-colored hair drips with melting snow, his cheeks red with exercise, I am quick to dig my gloves into the snow and show him how very practiced I am in this sport. My aim as I hurtle the hard globe of snow toward him is precisely matched to his face, and the added jolt of my Current makes it so powerful a throw that he falls over when it strikes him.

He sits up in the snow and checks at his bottom lip, how it is smeared with blood. At first, my insides seize with fear that I've revealed too much, that everyone around us stares in horror at my precision, but I look around me to see that all others engage in their own play, and once I see that Torren laughs, I laugh, too; the teeth of his smile red with blood.

I know I am foolish to use my Current here, in sight of everyone, but I would rather conceal it in the open than never use it at all—than have it explode from me without control. Often, it feels it might. Often, it is unbearable.

I had not realized how frequently I used my Current in Haven. Now, I have no such practice—no silent breadth of forest to wander as I go to fetch water from the stream where I might fell trees and command birds. Now, my Current builds until I fear it cannot be restrained any more.

At nights here in the castle, after exhausting days spent dancing for Lirinda's unceasing revels and sport, I lay upon my bed wringing my hands together so as not to use my Current— to somehow keep it within me. But in my agonized restraint, I begin to hear groaning of the stone tower around me, and I fear I may bring it to crumble and collapse as I have in the city. So I jump to my feet and find something, in desperation, to use.

One night, in this desperation of my teeth clenched and my back hunched with pain for it, I see Ellaina's bed begin to rise off the ground.

"No, no, no!" I hiss silently, setting the massive wood bed down as gently as I can, but it is uneven and wobbles as it touches the floor, and I hear her grunt in sleepy confusion. Hastily, I flee the chamber for the gallery beyond and search the long room for something to use. Finally, I repetitively raise and lower a heavy marble vase to remove myself from the brink of destruction.

"I cannot maintain this," I breathe with defeat once I have, at last, quelled myself of my Current. "This…secrecy."

With each day I spend in Lirinda's service, I know I am nearer to my doom. Each moment around the ladies as we embroider in the gallery, or sup in the great hall as I am eyed by Eliador Krom and the king, is a gamble of my fate. I may have begun to act more like them, these Pures, and convincing now may I look in the fashionable new gowns and horned headdresses Lirinda has had fashioned for me, but I will never be them.

I cannot remain here. This courtly existence, this fool's charade, I cannot sustain for much longer.

I must find the Source before I lose the opportunity forever.

Every morning, before anyone wakes, I wander, aching but frantic in the bleak shades of silver through the corridors in search of the Source.

With each day deeper into winter, the mornings are darker and colder, the shade of night lingering longer into the morning. The servants rise later with the dawn, thus do the ladies, and I am given more time to slip secretly between corridors and follow new paths I've not yet followed. Over the weeks, I come to memorize them.

There are more forgotten passages I take, some I feel no man has walked in decades, leading to chambers abandoned and piled with dust and bones of mice—with broken-old furniture and empty chests that would make excellent firewood were they not so ornate. But these chambers and corridors lead me nowhere of merit. The only place I feel any strengthening in the pulse of my magic is when I descend the most decrepit-looking stone stairwell of all, leading me beneath the ground where there are no windows, only fiery sconces lighting the labyrinth of intersecting corridors, and the walls seem to weep with groundwater. But even here I see nothing, no doors or subsequent stairwells that indicate anywhere else for me to go. And whenever I am down here—so near to the call that echoes through my bones—I cannot help but feel a sickening prickle that I am trespassing into dangerous territory, and if I were to be discovered by one of the king's guards, I would have much explaining to do.

There is a balcony I often visit in the mornings before I must play the charade of Lirinda's courtly companion, and my only salvation is fresh air. This balcony, wide and massive enough to host a party for every courtier, overlooks a fanciful Outer Court covered in snow, and beyond, the shriveled expanse of gardens, dead and black beneath a sparkling blanket of white. The nearby forest called the Kings Wood, where the king often hunts, is still dark green with the pines topped with snow. This morning, I stare at it with such pain for the lost home I long for, the home I fear I have begun to forget. The perfume of pine I catch only barely, but it is enough to make my throat seize with a choke.

Many days I wonder why I've come here, if this Source I seek is not simply my imagination, my Current haunting me in its desperation to grow and destroy. For I am so angry.

Always now, I am so angry.

I wrap a hand upon the frozen railing and feel my Current seep into the stone. Icicles that hang like twisted swords from the balcony's edge fall and crack upon the Outer Court below at the small ooze of my power. This pain, this power, so easily shattering my surroundings, thrums within me at a constant, and I feel lately that I shall crack, too.

I lift my hand from off the railing, knowing that if I allow myself to release any more of my constrained Current, the balcony itself may break.

As I stare out to the King's Wood, I wrap my wool cloak tightly around me, desperate for a whiff of home, of Mother's hearth and herbs to soothe me—exhaling steamy breaths of my suppressed anguish and inhaling the scents of pine and fresh snow—when in my periphery I see something black swarm high around the turrets of the castle.

We seem to see one another in the same instant, Crow and I, and my heart lifts with delight.

The large bird swoops from the misty towers and comes to

rest upon the carved stone railing of the balcony where I stand, dusted with snow, balancing on her single leg as always. Her blackness a shock against the world of white.

"You've found me," I say, my breath steaming with every syllable. But then I check over my shoulder at the innumerable windows of the castle, how anyone could see me conversing with a bird and think me a Magic. Again, I am reminded of the hostility of this place, how I must hide everything, even my one remaining companion. I make to step away, to retreat to the gray gloom of the castle. My willing cage.

"Perhaps you will find me again," I whisper, and leave the bird upon the ledge alone.

As I step back within the castle and pull closed the massive glass-paned doors behind me as quietly as I can, I turn back into the shadowed corridor with my eyes downcast upon the floor. My mind is heavy with the mystery of Crow, and I am thinking how peculiar it is she has followed me here, yet again, when I notice a shift within the shadows ahead of me. I halt in my tracks and raise my eyes to the dark passage. I see two figures talking lowly to each other. So dim it is in the passage that I cannot make out their faces, only that the slighter figure is dressed in the livery of the king's personal attendants and the other figure towers with a strong physique, exuding an essence of power that affects me all the way where I stand. I need not see his face to know that I look upon the king.

Of course, it is him, I think, with a sickening rush of Current surging my veins for my enmity of him and another confusing flush of thrill for the dangerous mystery that he is to me.

"And the torches—they have been lit, Your Majesty," I hear the attendant say in little more than a murmur, but when they both sense my presence, they go suddenly silent, turning their heads to peer through the shadows at my silhouette. My insides lurch as I feel the king's unseen eyes upon me.

I wonder if he recognizes me, for how tightly wrapped I am within my cloak, with my hood obscuring my massive dark mane; but then I realize I stand barefoot, covered in motes of snow, and understand there is no other girl in this castle so wild and threatening than the one who came from ferns and moss without a father's name. Surely, he knows my silhouette better than any. I think it haunts him as he haunts me.

We stare at one another's form across the darkness as though into a mirror. The Magic-killer and the secret Magic.

"All of them?" asks he, his attention returned to his servant.

"The Ordained have seen to it that even the oil has been replaced."

"Then tell Eliador I shall meet him," the king says as he makes to walk down the corridor toward me, but I am hastily turning down another passage, then another, until it is certain his path will not cross mine. But I know I will see him again in only a matter of hours. So often we share the same spaces— the gallery, the great hall—even when the ladies and I queue through the corridors we pass him and his men, his Council. And always when the king and I see one another, between us is a strange, unspoken measuring of the other.

My Current, it has flared within me yet again. I know with frustration that I must somehow release it before I slip back into my role in the ladies' tower.

Another dream haunts my sleep, and this time, it is Crow who flies down the eternal passage before me, her image flickering like a wind-tossed flame, uncertain in my own subconscious.

In an instant, she is gone and replaced with the red-haired woman I've dreamed of so many times. In another instant, Crow perches upon the low-extending bough of an iron sconce and watches me with her critical black gaze as I pass down the corridor after the white light.

It is my most vivid dream yet, and when I wake, I find blood soaking the front of my nightshift. Horrified, I slide open my curtain to see if I've done any damage in my sleep, for so long it's been since my nose has bled, and I see that Ellaina is awake, too, in her bed, curtain open, quivering in horror at how her bed has somehow moved across the room at an odd angle.

All day, the ladies conspire as to what might have happened. Easy it is for me to act as horrified as they, but I tremble with nerves, panicked at how unaware I was of my power and how much worse it could have been. When they ask me of my attempt at an explanation, all I can say is that perhaps there was a tremor of the earth. Though they think it a stupid suggestion, as none else in the castle had been affected, the ladies then begin to speculate that all their beds do seem to have moved slightly, and that my bleeding nose might have been caused by such a force.

Somehow, even after having exerted my Current in my sleep, still it surges all the day, building beneath the surface of my flesh, thumping through my viscera. In my every task and conversation, I feel it hum in my fingertips, and so strongly I work against it that I feel cool perspiration beading under my arms. I fear I have become ill. So weak I have become with my Current like a deadly infection as I sit in the gallery stitching a shirt for the poor that at the obnoxious sound of Lirinda's false laughter, I hear one of the lovely painted urns crack down its center.

"I'm not feeling well," I say desperately as I set down the

heap of cloth and retreat to the tower room.

Never have I felt this way, so sickened by my Current that I must lean over the wash basin and heave my breaths, shivering with the weight of my power aching for release. I feel my eyes drip tears as I think of what I long for most, and how it is the fresh freedom of Haven to run and release my Current as I wish. I cannot sustain the imprisonment of this castle, nor my obsession with the Source. I will destroy something—someone—if not myself in my restraint.

Somehow, I sleep, but I dream again. I wander the corridors of my subconscious for an interminable time that feels like months, while my sweating body wriggles beneath my coverlet in bed, tossing in frustration and agony, sick with fever. My Current is rampant as electricity, as lightning buzzing in the sky; and when I feel it begin to ooze from me like poison, I wake myself with a gasp and sit upright.

I feel that my bed wobbles with an airy weightlessness that makes me feel as if I float among clouds. In my panic, I rip aside my curtains to see that, indeed, my bed hovers above the ground. Panting with my horror, I use my Current to softly lower my bed to rest its wooden posts upon the floor, then immediately I scramble out of the tangle of bedclothes and curtains, frantically digging in my chest for my wool cloak, throwing it over my shoulders and stuffing my feet into a pair of boots. All the ladies seem to be snoring as thickly as ever, and I have never been so glad for their nightly inebriation. They do not stir as I throw open the tower door and flee—flee through the gallery, down through the corridors and stairwells, to the front of the castle. The guards allow my departure but not without their yells of concern through the bluster of snowy wind so strong, it makes me walk sideways. I ignore them and walk on. I ignore even the chattering of my teeth. All I feel is a rush to flee as far from the castle as I can.

My Current as it pounds through my every extremity warms me like a sour, sickening liquor against the snow-flecked wind that howls into my ears and sends my hair blustering around me in the night sky. Through the falling flakes of snow—how they tumble so softly and slowly upon the city's streets as I come to it—I cannot discern if any of the buildings crack or crumble as I pass them.

There is no sight of anyone beyond the thick, disorienting veil of tumbling snowflakes, no figures shrouded against the cold, not even a stray dog whimpering in an alley. No one to see my lone hooded figure's pursuit through the snow. No one to witness my occasional wipe of my nose, which flows warm with blood, and my eyes which leak against the wet spray of wind.

Late though it is, the streets are brilliantly illuminated by the snow. As I pass a street lantern, I am partially aware of sparkles upon the snow underneath; they sparkle tenfold within a teardrop lingering upon my lashes. I feel the droplet fall warm upon my frozen cheek. Though as I pass the lantern, the glass panes shatter suddenly, the flame within dying once the wind can reach it.

I lower my head, knowing my destruction. Ought I to continue on back to Haven? Into solitude?

After hours of walking, shivering madly against the torrent of wind and snow, I feel I may faint, so exhausted I am, so internally cold, I can feel the wind driving ice like a knife into my flesh, whistling through the gaps of my cloak and through the thin silk of my shift, now wet. But I force my legs to keep traveling further, though I do not know where they lead me.

For an imperceptible time, I wander until finally, I can

walk no longer without feeling I may fall over, into the soft padding of the snow, which seems for an instant a comforting thing.

I stand without moving. Letting my frosted lashes stick slightly closed in my exhaustion, and frosted blood sticking over my nose and lips, listening to the gentle taps of snow striking my hood. Perhaps I've drifted asleep. Until suddenly I'm aware that I'm no longer alone.

My eyes jolt open with alertness. My heart thundering in my ribs.

I sense the presence before I see the figure appear from beyond the curtain of swirling snow. A hooded figure some distance away, too far away for me to not squint to see them, but I sense their eyes are upon me. And though the figure is far from me, I can feel a deep thrum of power radiating from them, palpable as a ray of moonlight in the dark.

A Magic, I think, both fear and amazement prickling through me, invigorating me to wide-eyed awareness.

There is only one Magic I think who it might be, and I recoil a little with fear, a shiver caught in my chest for the Devil Mellick. But as the figure hobbles nearer, I realize it is a squat, half-crippled old person, walking with a staff for support. A woman. Not a man at all; not someone who might be my father. It is a slight disappointment, yet I have never been more fascinated in my life. Fascinated and deathly afraid.

The woman's cloak is so black, it seems to defy the snow and emanate darkness. And when she lifts her face so I can glimpse it beneath her hood, I gasp at the astounding ugliness of it—as hideous as a half-rotten corpse.

For a moment, that encapsulates what feels to me like a void of timelessness, the stranger and I stare at one another, exchanging silence between our eyes. Then, the old woman turns her back upon me, peering over her shoulder, and with a long, claw-like finger, beckons for me to follow.

I am driven through with a trickle of ice-cold trepidation. I hesitate, watching the cloaked figure hobble on. My foot turns in the snow, in preparation to go the other way—away from danger, perhaps, but I pause, for I'm overcome suddenly by my curiosity.

So I follow.

CHAPTER TWENTY TWO

Down deserted streets rolling with snowy mist does the woman lead me. There is nothing I ought to trust about her, this hooded being, yet I willingly follow her dark silhouette through smattering snowflakes and a wind that seizes the voice from my mouth as I call to ask, *"Where are you leading me?"* and, *"Who are you?"*

She gives me no reply. Perhaps she's heard me not, perhaps she has, or perhaps she is incapable of hearing. I'm terrified, yet I dare not let her dark form wander too far ahead in the swirling snowfall, lest I lose the mystery of her forever.

Beneath bridges and the stone tunnels of the city she leads me, which provide me a moment's shelter where I pause to stand and rest before facing the wind again with my frozen hand gripping the tie of cloak at my throat, in an effort to keep it from blowing away, my eyes winced tight against the blast of snow. But on she walks without halting, and my curiosity for her has me trudging on after her like a fool.

After some time, it feels I've dreamed everything—even my own past—the days of sunshine and laughter, of drowsy flowers nodding in a soft breeze. I walk through a haze of white exhaustion. A dream where time does not exist and everything I have ever held dear feels it has never been.

In this numb blur of snow, it feels as though fate itself guides me through intertwining alleys. And so strangely familiar this is, I am overcome by the feeling I have done this before—though if I have, I know I most certainly would remember.

Perhaps in one of these buildings is her home, I muse, looking desperately through my frost-dusted eyelids after the buildings we pass, growing steadily sparser the further east she leads me. *Perhaps she'll invite me inside so I might be warm.*

But she goes to no building. Soon, the streets and buildings have thinned altogether as we come upon the very edge of the realm where the city meets the sea.

Salty wind with a fishy reek whistles between the gaps of the final buildings and swirls beneath the snow-capped eaves as I pass them, able now to see an unobstructed, infinite sky beyond. As I walk close to the edge, I am met with the perilous ledge of high cliffs, treacherously cut against a crashing ink-black sea.

Its enormity is enough to stir me from my dreamy daze and fill me with prickling adrenaline, reminding me of my mortality and of my foolishness. Massive black waves boom against jagged rock, and I pull my cloak tighter around myself as though to keep me from falling into the deathly cold waters below.

Misty snow clouds fade into the distant horizon in a gray blur. So immense is this sight, this presence of sea, I momentarily forget the mysterious old woman is here with me.

I turn to scowl at her, wincing through the wind that's thrashing so much more treacherously here than in the protected streets of the city. Why would anyone guide me here? Does she see my misery, as evident as the blood on my face, and hope I will walk off the cliff's edge? I nearly bellow angry words to the old woman, but I am shivering too madly, holding myself too tightly, to dare open my mouth, lest the frigid wind take even more breath from my lungs.

The woman's cloak flutters in the snowy wind as she goes on to take a step down onto a jagged tooth of protruding rock. I watch her with rapt fascination as she descends the cliffs with her walking staff as though this is a comfortable excursion. Motionless I stand, and the woman turns her ugly face up to me, her skin as pale and mottled as the moon.

"You have followed this far," the old woman calls powerfully over the spraying waves. I am startled by the strength of it, her voice; it sounds so deep, although it is cragged and cruel. It seems to echo through to my very bones, like she speaks to me through dream-tongue. I fix my eyes upon the old woman with renewed amazement. "Yet this is where your journey ends?"

The old woman stares up at me with such piercing knowledge as though she stares into my very depths—such depths not even I know, and it makes me shiver more than the arresting cold. I return a defiant glower despite the frozen pain of my face.

I do not trust this Magic woman, whoever she is. But she is right. Do I turn back so soon?

Where else have I to go? Back to the castle?

I assess the jagged black rocks, how she stands so powerfully among them, her tattered cloak flowing about her like a dark ghoul. I have climbed and mastered many such obstacles in Haven, some just as perilously high over mountain cliffs, but never have I been as weak as I am now; I stumble even on level ground.

I take a steady step out onto the rock. It is slippery-wet, I realize with a sudden jolt of fear, and I nearly slip as I take my next descending step. A small rock slips from under my boot and tumbles all the way down the jagged, dark descent to the foaming water.

The old woman says nothing more but continues down.

This must be a frequent venture for her, for the old woman seems to have no difficulty whatsoever with this descent. As there is no specific path etched in the rock, it mystifies me how the woman climbs down so easily with her staff. I struggle to follow her every step and grab of the rock with precise care. Nearly all the way down to the large waves that crash and spray menacingly close to our feet do we descend the sharp, wet cliffs, where tall skeletal trees sprout out of crevices in the black rock. Until, mercifully, an overhang of rock above provides shelter from the snow.

Here, I brave a daring glimpse out to the water, abysmal motion beneath a bright, silver-wrought sky; in my periphery, as if in punishment for my distraction, the dark figure of the woman seemingly disappears—melts—into the wall of cliff. I snap my gaze back to my pursuit but find that I am now somehow alone, with only the deafening rumble of crashing sea as my reality.

My heart, while too exhausted to hammer in my chest with fear, feels it will jump through my bones and hop away. Have I been dreaming again? The old woman feels like she was just a strange dream and that I've wandered here in my deathly haze of cold.

Did I imagine her? How familiar she was…

Numbly, despite the hungry waves eager to suck me into their frothing crest at any misstep of mine, I continue to the place where the old woman seems to have vanished, and there I discover a cave entrance so ambiguous among the rock, no one would ever be able to see it unless they already knew where to find it. And I know now that the woman has led me somewhere after all.

As I stand before the cave entrance, shivering with flecks of water spattering my cheeks, I look up the jagged climb of slippery cliffs and feel the weight of my stupidity for descending them here. For now, I am left with the option to climb back up them for naught, or to squeeze myself into a narrow crevice of rock after a terrifying old woman.

I crouch low and squeeze my arms to my sides to fit within the crevice of damp rock. Panic steals through me at the confinement of it, urging me to turn back, but I soon notice a source of light glowing faintly beyond, gaining in brightness the further I weave inward, until the passage opens upon an immense cavern, delightfully warm and brightly lit with orange firelight. Rising to my full height, my mouth falls open as I scan the surrounding space.

Stacked against the rugged walls of stone are chests and crates, all messily stuffed with damaged rolls of parchment, weathered books, dried bundles of leaves, and treasures that glint mysteriously in the light, giving winks of tarnished silvers and golds and pearly gleams of abalone. Crystals, too, of colors and formations I've never imagined possible, rest upon the crooked stacks of half-unrolled parchment and maps, as well as fat pillar candles, with their wax having dripped over the pages of books. They gutter lowly with their flames and fill the otherwise disordered space with an ambiance of comfort. Even the many animal skulls look at ease here, an ease I am familiar with. This glowing, crude space is surely this Magic woman's home.

I feel overcome with relief to be here among such comforts. Comforts, such as the bundles of dried herbs, hanging from string the old woman has tied to numerous stalactites jutting down from overhead. Beyond the stink of sea and damp cave, the perfume of herbs is enough to make me want to fall to my knees.

Upon the uneven ground of rock lies a scattered mess of feathers and bones, as though a vicious predator had torn through its prey and left about the inedible remains. And centered within the front of the dwelling is a cauldron over a crackling fire—above it, a hole in the concave rock ceiling serves as a vent for the steam and fire smoke that curls up from the cauldron, for the dark liquid within boils violently.

Without a thought toward courtesies, I leap to the fire and warm myself before it, shivering furiously, my teeth chattering. Slowly I extend my tremulous hands out for warmth. The crust of my blood smeared across my fingers reminds me that indeed I've not dreamed any of this night. That mere hours ago, I had supped on turkey legs and silk pies in Gillin's castle.

"Get undressed," snaps the old woman, again in that voice that is deeper and more powerful than I expect from someone so haggard and old.

I hesitate only an instant before removing my clothing as quickly as I am able with my violently shaking hands. I throw my boots off first; snow that had covered my feet spills out upon the stone ground, my toes upon the hard floor immovable as ice. I unfasten my cloak at my neck and drape it over a crate to dry, then lift my soaked nightshift over my head, tossing it to hang with my cloak. When at last I am completely naked before the fire, I have no feeling of shame, only awe at how jerkily I shiver. Small moans of distress escape my mouth unrealized as I rub myself down.

My eyes linger upon the woman who now rests her staff against a depression in the cave's wall and pulls back the hood of her cloak, and I refuse a horrified gasp at how much more hideous she is than even I had thought. A few patches of long hair remain upon her otherwise bald head, the hair as silvery-light and insubstantial as a spider's web. Her face is as wide as a toad's, withered and brown-blotched like a rotting peach, although she is as pallid as the dusty-gray bones upon her floor. And her eyes—horrible eyes the orange-yellow of old urine. Her hands that slip out from her draping sleeves are heavily wrinkled and spotted just as her face is, and her nails are so sharp and long that they curl inward like that of an animal's claw. She uses her hands to stir a long wooden spoon that protrudes so far above the cauldron, the stooped woman needs not bend over.

"The fur," the woman commands me. With one of her monstrous claws, she directs my attention to a great bear fur rolled up and propped against one of the haphazard stacks bordering the cave. "Take it."

I stare at her warily before going to it. Grateful I am for its added warmth as I unroll it and drape its heaviness over my naked shoulders. With it gathered around me, I sit upon the hard ground before the fire, watching in a daze of my exhaustion how the old woman dips a long ladle into the boiling cauldron and pours an opaque, crimson-colored liquid into what I can only assume is the cranium of a human skull. The woman then takes the skull bowl to one of her strings of hanging leaves and adds a few crumbles of dried herbs into it, where the liquid fizzles and spits upon contact. The potent smell of burned herbs transports me back to the cottage. Such fondness for it I feel, I can almost see Mother humming before the hearth, stirring at the cauldron.

I could dream of it now, if only I allowed my eyelids to fall closed as they wish.

I watch the old woman's silent potion preparation, tempted by the fire's warmth and familiar cottage comforts. *It is too good to be trustworthy,* I think hazily, desperate for a spike of fear to jolt me awake. *How is it this strange woman has brought me to a place so reminiscent of home? Is this a spell? A mere illusion of what I wish to see?*

Have I perhaps died? I think with enough fear to jolt me partially awake.

Despite my wavering exhaustion, I know this is real. And that if indeed this is an illusion of what I wish, then there would not be so many broken-toothed skulls that make me think of other lonely young women like me whom this stranger may have lured here to their deaths. Yet after living in Gillin's castle, surrounded by those who would easily kill me if they knew what I was, I am not so afraid to be here.

Strangely, I feel I am among kin.

"You have ice growing in your chest." The woman hobbles over, carrying the steaming skull in her claw-like fingers to where I sit, and offers it for me to take.

It's as though she was expecting me, I think wildly of the woman. *The fire was already aflame when I arrived, wasn't it? This potion, already aboil.*

I accept the skull into my hands and look down at the steam curling up from the curious red liquid, like a puddle of hot blood in the bowl of bone. Never have I seen such a potion nor smelled one of such deep magic. There are traces of herbs I can recognize, but beyond them is an inscrutable property I can only identify as magic unlike any I've known. Fleetingly, I think this may be a deadly poison, but I quickly bypass it, for I do not think this woman would have brought me all this way just to kill me.

If she wanted me dead, she had several opportunities to see to it on our journey here.

"Before it goes cold!" the woman snaps at me, and I quickly bring the hot drink to my lips and take a cautious sip; my tired, hooded eyes open wide at the first fiery drip on my tongue.

It is fire that I drink, liquid fire. It burns like flames…but it is not painful. I want to choke; I feel as though smoke wells at the roof of my mouth and issues from my nose, but I cannot stop drinking it. As the liquid pours down my throat, the most relieving warmth tingles through my chest. When I've slurped the final drips and taken my lips from the skull, I see that fine smoke curls from out my mouth and nose with every exhale.

The woman seats herself into a rickety chair before the fire—a chair of mismatched flotsam and driftwood tied together with plant fibers.

Discreetly, I study this strange woman from her blotched, balding head to her feet barely seen at the bottom of her long cloak, and I notice that only one of them is a foot wearing a leather shoe, and that the other had been replaced with a wooden peg, like some of the folk I'd seen limping through the capital. The immaculate descent down the cliffs seems even more surreal now, with her prosthetic.

Who is this woman? I gape at her blearily. *Or* what *is she?*

There is something I sense about her, only now that I'm calm and alert enough to understand; something like a radiant force is bound within her sagging, wrinkled flesh, nearly bursting at the seams. A most powerful kind of magic that makes Mother's magical presence seem slight in comparison. Overwhelmed I am by the layers of inscrutable essences this woman exudes. How old must she be? And why, unless I am much mistaken by my exhaustion, do I feel the Source so near to me here?

The old woman turns her large orange eyes upon me.

"You've stopped shivering," she drawls with a hint of amusement.

So many questions whirl in my mind but all I can manage is a stiff "Thank you."

The woman ignores my gratitude with a scowl of irritation. Such courtesy seems frivolous and unnecessary to her. I wait for the woman to speak more, but when she does not, and only stares ahead into the smoking fire, I feel my mouth open to unleash my many questions.

"What was that potion?" I begin with a small modest question, smoke issuing from my mouth as I speak. "I've never had one like it before."

"That is because no brewer is as skilled as me," the woman pronounces without moving her gaze. "I doubt you've known a master who could summon flame into liquid."

"No," I start slowly, a little startled by the woman's brusqueness. "I have not." My gaze lingers upon her, this woman who is so strange to me, yet that uncanny feeling of familiarity nags at me still, as though I ought to know her name. "Who are you?"

The woman turns her full face to me and smirks in a cruel way that makes me feel foolish for asking so impetuously.

"I am many," the woman begins with a tone to match her smirk. "But if it's my name you wish to know, I will allow you to call me Ama."

I feel a shiver trickle down my spine at the sharpness of her teeth as she says her own name. I cannot help the way I stare at her, measuring her every feature, my eyes large with surprise at every detail I see. My gaze rests on Ama's wooden peg of a foot, and I notice the hem of her cloak is peculiarly lined with black feathers as are her long draping sleeves. There is a strange crescent-moon pendant which hangs on a chain from out a pocket. I could stare at her for hours and still find details I wish to ask about. Even the wrinkles and innumerable spots like constellations upon her sagging face I look at seem to hold answers.

"See anything of interest to you?" Ama purrs with spite, and I realize I have been staring at her, dumbstruck, with my mouth having fallen open.

"I'm sorry, I…" I pause as I see she reaches into her cloak and draws out an impressively long pipe, then a sack of herbs from her cloak—herbs I have never seen or smelled before—and stuffs the dried leaves into the pipe's bowl. Then Ama holds out her hand, turns it over, and instantly, a flame appears upon her very palm.

I gasp.

With her palm cupped around the bowl of her pipe, she sucks until the dried herbs glow red. The flame in her palm then extinguishes, and Ama rests her flame-bearing hand to relax upon her lap as though nothing exceptional has just happened. I retract my gaze from her, but it is especially difficult not to look again, now that I've seen flames flare from her hand.

"It's just that…I've never seen another…" I break off, careful still not to reveal the incriminating word.

"Another…*Mage?*"

I furrow my brows. My silence alone is enough to reveal to Ama my ignorance for the word.

Laughter ripples from the woman; the most hateful laughter I've ever heard. Whatever softness in my expression I had recoils at my confusion for her nastiness. Anger begins to thump in my blood.

"Of course," says she with sweetened spite. "You would not know the term. You are more Pure than *Mage*… I can smell it off you. You reek of sweet things. Rosewater and *silk.*" She punctuates herself with a precise spit into the fire.

Despite the anger rumbling in my blood, a chill of understanding slithers through me. "*Mage*… that's another word for…"

"Magic?" Ama concludes easily for me, and though it is the very word I had nearly uttered myself, hearing another creature speak the forbidden word sends sparkles of fear and delight down my flesh.

I swallow hard.

"Magic is a Pure's slur for us. *Mage*—Magekind—is the true word for a Magic, though to use its proper name is to reveal your knowledge, and in this Pure realm, one must pretend to be stupid to survive."

"How...How do you know I'm a, a Magic—I mean, a *Mage?*" I stutter in my panic, eyes wide with awe. The fear I feel for sharing my truth with this stranger sends electricity through me.

Ama makes me wait before responding, taking a few exaggerated inhales of the pipe and letting the smoke harbor in her lungs before releasing dramatic exhales.

"How does any creature recognize one of its own ilk?" she answers slowly, the smoke curling out from her mouth. "Although you hardly look it. By the smell of you, you might as well have just come from Gillin's Castle."

I clench my teeth to keep myself from admitting she is right. She continues to smoke her pipe while I watch as distantly as I can, without revealing to her my interest in her every detail; my mind reels with all I have wanted to say to another Magic if ever I met one.

"It's as though you knew where to find me," I say out of the silence, wistful but accusatory.

"Aye," says she without looking at me. "I know more than you would believe."

"How?" I breathe with my excitement, sitting up straighter with my eagerness to learn all I can. "How did you know I would be there? Already you had this potion brewed as though you were expecting me..."

She turns now to look at me, her face slack while her

poisonous eyes measure me, my foolhardy exuberance, as if weighing her irritation, and whether or not I deserve to receive her answer. I swallow hard again but do not look away, my gaze reflecting hers furiously as my vulnerable excitement ebbs into determination. At length, her frown-drooped mouth raises to grimace wickedly, her yellow eyes burning back at me with a glimmering pleasure.

"I saw it," says she. "Before it happened."

"You saw it?" I raise a brow. I want to call her a liar out of brashness, but I do not think she lies. "You are a Seer, then?"

"And what would you know of Seeing, girl?"

"My mother once told me of Seers. That they are often wrong," I say, feeling braver with the heat of the potion warming me through my bones—excited by the words rushing out my mouth, speaking of magic, of things I have not spoken of in what feels like a lifetime. "She told me that Seeing is the most disastrous art of magic, with the greatest of liars. They See for they are incapable of other, truer means of magic. And to consult answers means you have no guidance of your own."

Ama seems deeply, darkly, amused by this.

"Was I wrong tonight?" she purrs, and I swallow again. "Of course, I was not! And grateful you must be to me for having not been, for my accuracy! You and your faithless mother know nothing," she snarls with smoke from her tongue. "But I know… I know what would have happened. I know All."

I am both mesmerized and maddened by this woman's strange self-obsession—her indulgent pride, which makes the ladies of the court and even Lirinda look modest. I do not know whether she is ill of mind, living here in sorcerous solitude as I surely would be, or if she tells some truth. She did find me tonight when I needed to be found. But does she truly know All? If she did, why would she not have found herself a place to live that is not so crude. If she knew All, surely she would not have a peg-leg.

"Fate has a curious way of unraveling itself," she says in a slower croak, almost to herself. "To a Seer such as me, I see every thread of the great tapestry, even the ones woven but never to be lived. I saw you tonight, wading through the blizzard, fated to die if you continued on your own path—aye, I saw that, too," she says to my horrified face. "Your death. The softest of your every possible death; you would have walked past every warm fire in your delusion and walked halfway into the forest. There, you would have fallen to your knees and lay in the snow, never to rise again. But no, it did not happen! Why? For in one of the possible threads of Fate, woven but not yet lived, I saw myself going to you."

I am silent. The heat of the fire, the warmth of the potion, and her words give me the dizzying sense I am dreaming again.

"Why did you?" I ask. "What am I to you? What do you care if I die?"

She takes a long draw of her pipe, making me wait another length for her to speak again. When she does, her voice is all smoke.

"There is still much to be unraveled. I know All, as it reveals itself to me. But like your mother, you are incapable of understanding."

I open my mouth to argue and bombard her with still more questions, but she speaks again, this time with the terseness of finality.

"My draught of flame may have melted the ice within you, but no good will it do if you do not rest. And no good will you do me if you're dead."

Ama takes one last suck of her pipe, the embers within glowing. After her long exhale, she dumps out the remainder of the bowl onto the ground and stows away the pipe within her cloak. She rises with only little strain from her chair and limps on her wooden leg to reclaim her walking staff from where she had left it and, without looking back at me, hobbles off to the back of the cave. She somehow dissolves away into the shadows, leaving me alone and naked with only a fur around me, a human skull still gripped in my hands, and a mind whirling with questions quite like how the snow flurries outside.

CHAPTER TWENTY THREE

I wake several times in the night to the sounds of fermenting gurgles from within jars and vials, and the papery scuttle of crabs creeping across stacks of parchment. Through half-closed eyes, I check the space for Ama but do not see her squat shadow. Despite the hard stone floor I lie upon or the fact that I am naked, I sleep deeply, comfortably wrapped in the bear fur, my exhaustion pulling me into the stone, into the earth. Somehow, I sense the Source here, too, radiating not so distantly from the stone walls of the cave itself—but I am too weary even in my sleep to care.

When I wake for the final time, I see the great fire in the pit has gone out, but the space is warm as though a fire burns still. The flickering flames upon the many candles have not melted down their wicks at all, and I assume they must somehow be enchanted never to burn, but perhaps to emit heat. I groan with pain as I rise with the bear fur heavy upon my shoulders, staggering with my dizziness from yesterday's strain, and go to one of the fat pillar candles, streaming with wax. I hold a hand up near to it and feel that it is warm as an oven.

What clever magic, I think delightedly.

I turn where I stand to take in the surrounding cave; how the domed ceiling and the far reaches of the cavern are too far to be touched by the bouncing candlelight, making the space seem all the more untouchable, vast, and frightening. I wonder where Ama has gone as she seems not to be here at all.

Clumsy with my soreness, I go to my nightshift and cloak where they hang, crisp and dried, and slip them back over my nakedness. Then I squeeze back through the cave entrance for a glimpse outside, checking for Ama and, perhaps, to remind myself that this bizarre cavern of magic is indeed part of the world I once knew. When I see the low-lying wintry sun glowing a smear of orange above black thrashing waters, and a few crying gulls alighting upon the slick rocks, I know indeed this is no hallucination of mine but more real than I have felt since Mother's death. I feel I've not seen the sun's light so clearly in the months I have been alone.

Of course, Ama is nowhere to be found here, either.

Ought I to leave now? I assess the nearly vertical face of cliff, and feel my bones fall weak at the thought of climbing them just yet. So I return to the warmth of the cave to the delightful smell of dried herbs and smoke amid damp stone walls, too pleased to be here to ponder what Lirinda and the court might think of my absence.

Lirinda might be glad of it… I think with a pang of sorrow that surprises me, for I did not think my wound for my sister could still hurt.

"Hullo," I call into the shadows, inspecting the makeshift shelves and surfaces as I pass them, pacing round the large space. Upon every visible surface are hundreds of unique glass vials, crammed disorderly beneath a thick layer of dust, many of which contain animal parts. Eyes of different creatures float within the murky fluid; some I recognize of goat, cat, eagle… even human. Fetuses of what look like small mammals have gone soft, gray, and bubbly in their vials; the only exception is a snake embryo, carefully extracted from its egg, which I pause in my stride a moment to marvel at. Horrid yet intriguing is an obviously deformed human fetus at which I frown with concern. As I pass the collection of vials, staring uneasily after their contents, I wonder what the old woman could possibly want them for—or yet, what kind of woman keeps such ghastly items as ingredients or keepsakes. In the half-darkness I inspect a long, narrow vial and realize it is filled with what must be blood.

"Ama?" I call again, but only a dull echo of my voice replies from the shadowed ceiling of the cave. A drip of water falls musically from one of the stalactites and splashes near to my bare feet. I walk on, stepping upon dried animal viscera, feathers, shells, and gelatinous substances with my toes; I study the perimeter of the cave's wall, stopping when I come to Ama's abundant plant collection.

The space is illuminated by a candle—thicker than all other candles in the cave—bearing a brighter flame that reminds me naturally of the sun. I wonder if perhaps Ama had enchanted that flame to bear sun-like light so the plants could grow here. My respect for the woman increases when I ponder what expert magic she must know to accomplish these things.

"Incredible," I whisper near an exotic fern I've never seen before; the soft touch of my breath exhaled upon it causing one of its fronds to curl away from me in response.

I step backward away from the fern so as not to disturb it further but collide with something at my hind. Looking over my shoulder, I see something shiny and black wobbles that I've knocked into—a polished slab of obsidian, about to fall off its pedestal to the ground. I catch it smartly in my hands, though it is slick and heavy.

I look down at what I cradle in my grasp and find my own dark reflection staring back at me upon the black glass. Though I stand perfectly still, the edges of my reflection shiver and twist as though I look into a black river. Something about this reflection does not seem like myself at all, but almost as though someone, some*thing,* else reflects me.

Tentatively, I set the slab back as it had been, propped upon an exquisite silver pedestal; the pedestal is wrought of metal to look like several long arms twisting together, interconnecting, their long, thin hands reaching out, fingers splayed at the top as though grasping for something to hold. The obsidian slab fits upon the silver hands perfectly, as upright and as reflective as a mirror; the pair of pieces together giving me an ominous sense that this object is very old and has been used before in sorcerous ways I can scarcely imagine.

"A scrying mirror," I mutter to myself, recalling the times Mother would tell me of them, of their dark power she much disapproved of. Never did I think I would see one for myself, and now that I have, I understand her concern, for I feel unsettled by the power of this mirror—unsettled, and fascinated.

I step before the glass again, unable to repress my curiosity for my reflection, how it seems to disfigure from reality, warping, moving slightly when I move not at all. Never have I seen magic so haunting and dark, warping outside of reality, of the earth's own natural laws, and I feel in a fearful way that perhaps I've never known true magic after all. The only force I've sensed similar to this is the beckoning white light of my dreams and the lovely woman who guides it.

A slithering sound tears my attention from the obsidian slab to a plant growing up the cave wall like a thick woven curtain. What I hear is the tangle of barbed ivy vines writhing peculiarly like a bed of snakes, and to my astonishment, the vines parting to reveal a cavernous passage beyond, imperceptibly dark but for a stooped, cloaked figure I recognize as Ama hobbling through with her walking staff.

As Ama steps through the doorway of ivy, she sees me at once, standing before her mirror, and something in her urine-yellow eyes narrows upon me that hasn't yet.

"I see you have discovered my mirror," she croaks as the ivy closes back up into a tightly woven wall behind her, concealing the passage completely.

I look back to the black glass, seeing its rivulets more now that Ama has come near. So powerful a Seer she must truly be that the image alters for her presence alone, though it only looks to me like splashed water, my reflection distorted.

"This is where you Saw me, isn't it?" I say mistily, my eyes lost in the rivulets. "How you knew where to find me?" My gaze slowly shifts from the slab to the old woman's saggy, spotted face, and our eyes meet. "And why you've not yet asked me my name nor where I came from. You already know all of that, don't you?"

The loose skin of the old woman's jowls rise, and her sharp little teeth show in a sinister grimace. I have forgotten just how horribly ugly she is, and I feel my small hairs rise in disgust for her.

"Want all the answers, do you?" Ama taunts. "I have them, you know." The old woman clanks with her walking staff to where I stand, the black glass becoming inscrutably wild with liquidlike motion at her proximity. Surely she sees things I cannot, for as she gazes at the chaos of rivulets, her grimace widens. Something within the mirror glass gives her great pleasure and she cackles. "I have them all, here, before me. Do you wish to see them?"

I hesitate, weighing Ama's enthusiasm as insincere. But my curiosity is too great, and ultimately I mutter, *"Yes."* I hear the secret longing in my voice and know my foolishness.

"Come, then!" Ama cries exuberantly, moving aside and indicating to the black mirror. "Unfocus your eyes. Gaze into your inner depths. Let the glass reveal to you what your eyes alone cannot See."

I move nearer to the obsidian slab and find my face reflecting back at me, my eyes like another pair of shining black mirrors. Part of me longs to tear away from the mirror, knowing that something sinister may come of this. But I am equally entranced and rooted to the spot. Perhaps it is the herbal aroma burning from the purple candle Ama lights upon the shelf just before us, for I feel my eyes unfocusing with ease. Despite my anxiousness, I relax, and it is easier to ignore the pounding of my heart, my internal urge to look away. Drowsily, I gaze past my own face in the dark glass and see only blackness, the blackness of my own mind, the blackness of unruly forest, of home. And where my face ought to reflect, I begin to see another's form.

It looks like my own face at first, but upon my wild, curled mane is the crown my sister wears. My heart lurches into my throat, and I suck in air at the excitement it makes me feel to see my gnarled, feral-forest silhouette carry the delicate crown of Glindor's queen, of importance—my features which have so long been regarded as a curse, an image of shame, to be regal and desired. Me—*a queen!* And what a powerful queen I would make.

But no sooner does the rest of the face quiver to reveal that of Lirinda's far more beautiful one, smiling her unburdened joy, the smile no one can refuse—not even the king of Glindor, not even our mother, not even me.

I grind my teeth, wanting to look away but unable to. Lirinda's face soon wriggles disturbingly with what looks like worms, but with horror, I realize they are mushrooms and that her face has become Mother's.

With a groan of grief, I close my eyes and turn from the slab, understanding I see nothing but my own jealous, grievous emotions reflecting back at me, induced tenfold by whatever aroma Ama burns in the candle.

Ama's cackle rings through the cavern. My chest burns with anger at the infuriating sound, my fingers squeezing into fists at my sides.

"Fool!" Ama bellows delightedly. "Did you truly think you would See?" She howls with laughter. *"You?* Only one trained in the ancient art of Divination can access the channels of Fate! That, what you saw, was only your own grief staring at you!"

I glower at the woman with loathing, stepping away from the mirror so I can see Mother's dead face no longer.

"There is much you do not address, isn't there?" The old woman tuts, still smiling wickedly at the mirror. "Pain you have not faced."

"You may guess all you wish, but you know nothing of me."

"Pretty little speech." Ama dismisses me with a wave of her hand. "Everything I need to know you've revealed to me in the mirror." She smirks triumphantly. "Your longing to trust is your weakness, girl. Now I have seen all your desires, your insecurities. That pretty girl, that was your sister, wasn't it?" Ama steps closer to appraise the obsidian slab as though she is able to study Lirinda's face in it still. "Not that you look anything like her. How must that make you feel? To always live in the shadow of such a radiant—"

"Enough!" I bellow, but Ama only cackles.

"So it's true!" She crooks her neck so her poisonous gaze

can glimpse me over the slump of her shoulder. "You're the jealous, hungry little wraith, but you've yet to accept it. And you're all alone—so far from home, aren't you? Was that your home I saw? That moment of darkness, the infinity of pines so quiet and pure, that not even the sunniest day can touch it? The capital must be quite a contrast for you. I can see you long for your home, but perhaps it is lost, and you know that. You know you will never go back; never will you face what it means to you. Never will you be so innocent, so naïve, again. And your mother—she's gone, too, isn't she? Did she love you very well?" Ama's widened eyes nearly glow with excitement at her own cruelty. "What of your father? Never knew him, did you? So many questions, so many mysteries…"

My throat fills with the urge to yell back, to deny all of this, but I am silent, scowling furiously at the woman, trying not to allow her orange-yellow gaze to penetrate me and read all my many yearnings—to see that she is right about all she says.

"I asked not where you came from, nor your name, for unless you have proven your greatness so that all of time will remember them, such things are useless to know. The world is a vast and intricate place, full of faces and names just like yours. Yet, of course, you must think you're special, don't you?"

I open my mouth to argue but she leers at me with disgust. "Don't you deny it. It's in your eyes, as true and black as my obsidian. I see it there, the typical spark of a girl who believes there is something greater out there, something for her alone."

She sees my expression soften and she chuckles indulgently. "Youth are always so hungry for purpose, to be *special*. Maybe you are special. Maybe there is some plan to all *this*." She indicates to the surrounding cavern with one of her claw-like hands. "Is that what you think, girl? You think you have a purpose in this miserable world? That I would have reason to come looking for you? You think you're *special?*" she finishes in a mocking simper.

I know better than to answer. Regardless of the answer I might have—regardless of how worthless and hopeless I feel—the spurned baby left to die in the grass, the lesser sister, the darker daughter, cursed seed of my father, rotten fruit of my mother, the shadow in the sun—there is a small voice within me that says, *yes,* I am special.

Instead of speaking, I narrow my eyes upon the old woman, resilient and impenetrable. I show nothing to her. Ama would only use my answers to laugh at me more.

Ama lifts her bald brows and smirks at my refusal to play along. She looks somehow pleased with this.

"You may be a fool, but you are learning," says she and hobbles away from the mirror, clacking down the aisle between glittering and dead oddities with her staff and wooden peg upon the stone ground. Tentatively, I follow.

"You cannot stay here, you know," says she without looking at me. "This is no home to you." Her pitiless voice echoes throughout the cave around us. Water drips from jutting minerals, chilling me despite the comfortable warmth. "By dawn, I expect you to be gone from here. Back to wherever you've come from or off to wherever you're going."

I glance around us and feel grief for having to leave this familiar space and all the mysteries within which I will not learn by dawn.

Over the hours that I spend with Ama, I am determined to ask as many of my questions as I can. As she busies herself with strange tasks throughout the cave, I remain out of her way, unassuming as a shadow so she will not be so easily irritated with my curiosities as I present them to her. Coolly,

I ask where she has come from, whether there have been any other Magics she has seen; most tentatively of all do I inquire after her knowledge of the Devil Mellick; then knowing I ask too much, I ask where the passage beyond the wall of ivy leads. Unsurprisingly, each of my queries is met with nasty snubs to silence me, if she does not ignore me completely. I understand now this Ama will tell me nothing of herself. Unfair it is that I've revealed much of myself to her when she remains a most obscure mystery to me.

I decide I will tell her nothing else about me, so long as I'm here, so long as I'm acquainted with her, unless she will oblige me. I'll tell her not even of my Current nor of my call to the castle, not of my dreams, or that my sister is the very queen of Glindor. Though, by the manner of which Ama perceives me, it is almost as though she knows these things already. Perhaps one of those reasons is why she has brought me here.

I think she means to ignore me more when she digs through several baskets of dried, dead things, like frogs, small lizards, birds, and even withered, eyeless rabbits, until she hands me a basket of them and orders me to bring them to her cauldron. There, she uses her flame-magic to light the fire and begins to concoct a most revolting potion.

"What kind of potion is this?" I try not to show such disgust in my face, but it is difficult, as she has me dump the dead, shriveled creatures into the boiling liquid, which turns to a lumpy gray once their bodies have disintegrated, the rabbits' fur, and all.

"Sustenance," says she with a pleasured whiff of the steam rolling off the surface.

"Oh, I"—I swallow the sickened saliva that threatens to rise—"did not think this was for…consuming."

"You sound ungrateful for my hospitality." Her teeth, sharp

like broken glass, catch a glare of the fiery light as she snarls down at the bubbling gray surface which she stirs with her long spoon. "Tell me, little wraith girl, how else do you think we will eat here in this cave? Should we go catch the gulls off the rocks outside? Chase crabs between crevices of rock? Are you going up to the city to bring us some hot potatoes and cuts of meat?"

At this, my belly, which has now become so used to the castle's indulgent eats at predictable intervals, growls loudly enough for Ama to leer at.

"Hand me that jar of Salted Salamander," she commands with an irritable nod of her head to the broken, half-collapsed shelves beside me.

I am glad for a reason to look away from the potion. I bend over to look for the jar amid the mess of rocks and parchment and find a soggy brown salamander floating in what must be a glass of brine. As I reach for it, I notice that beneath the jar rests a leather-bound book covered in decades of dust, and when I remove the jar from it, a near-dustless circle remains in its place, exposing a hint of a gilt title which instantly captures my interest.

Impatiently, Ama holds out a claw to me, and my attention is reluctantly returned to her potion as I place the jar of salamander within her grasp.

Once she removes the lid, Ama tips the glass so the brine spills into the potion, and the salamander drops into her outreached claw-of-a-hand, with which she then squeezes the soggy corpse over the cauldron so that a stream of brown juice sprays into the potion.

"What is the salamander for?" I nearly choke with nausea.

"One can serve a king a dollop of moldy, curdled cream with the Salted Salamander and it would taste to him like the sweetest butter," says Ama as she tosses the squished remains of the salamander into the gray boil.

"So it is a lie."

"It is survival."

I wonder how long Ama has lived off these potions of dead, dried things, for I do not easily visualize her seated at a tavern table, eating trenchers of bread and drinking ale among the Pures of the capital. Unless Ama has kin elsewhere; perhaps she dines with them upon her visits, but I feel she has none—that she has been alone like this for years. Tens of years. Perhaps longer. How important the illusion of the salamander's delicacy must be to her then.

As though she cooks an elaborate stew, Ama goes on to season the potion with dried herbs from her stalactites, and though I do not wish to acknowledge this, since her addition of the Salted Salamander, the stench of the dead potion has receded and been replaced with an appetizing, savory aroma, like salted, gravied meats. I resist a growl of my stomach with every measure of my being, for Ama's sorcery is so well done, I find I've begun to salivate over death.

Raptly I watch her obvious mastery of the art, with her flamboyant hand gestures over the steam. Ama reminds me of Mother in many ways I cannot name, but I reason it must simply be that I've seen no other potion brewer before now.

My gaze wanders from the hunched old woman to the innumerable treasures surrounding me where I stand, and I glimpse again the dusty book at my side. With a finger, I swipe gently at the dust to better inspect the leather cover, how it is enameled with gilt letters.

Gillindor, it is titled. I tilt my head with curiosity at the spelling of Glindor; how old this book must be that it is spelled for Gillin's name.

"May I?" I ask of Ama, indicating to the book when finally

she glances at me. She chuckles with distaste.

"That is but Gillin's narrative. Surely you need no more of that."

I lift the leather book into my hands and feel it sag with age, its pages so thin and worn I feel if I were to turn them, they would disintegrate to dust.

"This must be hundreds of years old," I appraise, unlatching the metal buckles upon the side and gently lifting the leather cover to see the pages within have been scrawled upon in neat hand, the ink faded but still legible. It is as beautiful as the artifacts I pass in the castle, belonging on a pedestal to be admired, preserved, not discarded among skulls and dripping wax in a damp cave.

"Aye, it is from the days of the Great Restoration itself. Gillin's own hand."

My mouth parts in awe. I turn through thick sections of the written text, wishing I could spend hours, days, fingering through every page, but feeling rushed to only glimpse hungrily what I am able. There are several illustrations and maps, signed by their respective artists. One such illustration is the cross-section of a mountain, wild and dark, with sinister-looking trees curling at the boughs; in the next illustration, the same cross-section looks leveled and unrecognizable: a prairie of small flowers.

"This is about how he changed the shape of the land," I remark, hoping Ama will explain it to me so I need not waste time trying to decipher the miniscule, coiled script. "How he reshaped the Old World."

"Aye, but he failed to illustrate the mass destruction to the Tarian folk. The *Mage* women and children sucked under the earth and crushed in its upheaval. The screams during the mass Burnings of Blood so not a drop spilled could touch the face of his new, improved earth."

I cannot speak. Too tight is my throat. Finally, with my voice dry with horror, I ask, "How is such a thing possible? Gillin had no magic, how could he have leveled mountains and opened up the ground? It would take a thousand men, a thousand years, to reshape the earth."

Ama's gaze, though it looks not at me, narrows, and a grimace pulls at the side of her mouth. I feel I've struck a delight of hers. In her urine-eyes something is alight.

"But he did have magic, don't you know?" She turns her wide, toad-like face to me. "Not magic of his own, but borrowed, when he was employed in the task of slaying the Shade King Rinma."

I quirk my brows at her.

Mother had told Lirinda and me many times of how Gillin had slain King Rinma, but not that it had been done as a hired job, nor that he had been given magic to do it. But always have I wondered how a man of no magic, a Pure, could manage such a feat, to kill a king of magic. With that knowledge, it is far less puzzling an achievement. I wonder if Mother knew this.

"Who would lend magic to a Pure king?" I ask.

"Gillin was not always a king. He was once a nameless assassin for the Pures who chased glory into the hands of a vicious Magic queen—*Mavet.*"

My heart slips into my belly at such a title as a vicious Magic queen. Never have I heard such lore of my own secret, forbidden world. Never of queens or their stories. Never of other lands. Not even of this land, Glindor, and how it came to be.

"Tell me," I command urgently, abandoning politeness, for I know it is wasted on Ama.

The ugly old woman's drooping eyes are reduced to cruel slits as she considers what to tell me, if I am worth her breath, perhaps. But I realize there is a nasty smirk in her gaze, as though she has hoped I might be interested in this tale.

CHAPTER TWENTY FOUR

"**I**n that age, and for ages prior, Rinma was the sworn enemy of Queen Mavet," Ama begins. "Too powerful he was becoming, and unlike all other kings of the world, she was unable to keep him under her thumb. The King of Stars, he was also named in those days, with otherworldly power Mavet wanted for herself. So she rallied the Ancients of the world in her cause to see him destroyed.

"She employed the greatest miners, smiths, and craftsmen from every realm to forge the sword Hallath, strong enough to slay the King of Stars; it was crafted of metals so powerful, so dense with magic, that only a Pure's hand could wield it without being utterly destroyed.

"Mavet had been waiting to employ a Pure to this task, to wield the sword and destroy the King of Stars, when one day, Gillin, a foolhardy Pure bent on seeking glory, had attempted an assassination upon one of her High Priests. Gillin awaited execution in her dungeons, but instead of meeting his demise, he was brought before Mavet's throne and made an offer not even a stubborn Pure could refuse. She promised Gillin a kingdom in exchange for slaying her enemy, which made him a most perfect puppet—and thus his descendants, his kings, her placeholder puppets for all the ages to come."

I remember the painting, the vast mural within the castle Tafton had looked upon with such fondness, with the goddess's eye and the sword Hallath.

"I've heard of this sword," I say. "But the Pures say it was a goddess who had given it to Gillin."

"Mavet is no goddess," says Ama with a sneer of disgust, tossing a leaf of sage into the cauldron. "Although to Gillin, she may have seemed as such. And for all anyone knows, perhaps that is what Mavet told him she was. Powerful beyond comprehension, beautiful beyond compare. Her court and throne sophisticated of magic and technology beyond what any little Pure had witnessed before, it may well have seemed to him derived of the heavens. Gillin told tales of Mavet's gift to Purity with such embellishment, the legends have taken on their own ludicrous depictions of her, of what happened those centuries ago. If the Pures only knew their precious goddess was no more than the *Mage* they seek to destroy."

I turn the page to another. I see a sphere—a crystal perhaps. And though it is drawn, it seems to bear light. At the top of the illustration is the word *Il-lar.*

"That," says Ama with that same spark of delight as before, seeing the page I look upon. "*That* is the object of your curiosity."

"What is it?" I furrow a brow and tilt the book so it might make more sense. Turning the page, I see a detailed illustration of a strong, dark-bearded man holding the sphere in the air while trees are airborne around him, levitating earth. I feel a chill surge up my spine at the sheer power.

Gillin, I muse, studying the bearded man with burly

features, the sphere balanced upon his palm. *It must be this—this magic he used to reshape the earth.*

Ama seems to delight in this subject very much. I have not yet seen her smile so widely; a horrible smile it is. I wonder what about this tale could be so thrilling to her, unless it is my ignorance for it that amuses her. I swallow hard.

"Killing the King of Stars alone would not be of much merit to Mavet now, would it? Not when he was exceedingly powerful—more powerful than she. So of course, Mavet would desire a way to destroy his body but keep his power—his spirit essence—for herself.

"Mavet had spent years seeking such a vessel, plundering every ancient landscape and mining deep into the most sacred earth for a medium that would succeed in imprisoning the king's power. At last, she had discovered a perfect crystal, so delicate and pure of light and magic that one's spirit essence, even one so powerful as that of the King of Stars, could be sealed within, unharmed; their power able to be harnessed and commanded at whim. The *Il-lar*," Ama says with relish.

"She presented it to Gillin along with the sword—the *Il-lar* empty, but soon to be filled with Rinma's spirit upon his execution.

"Mavet then enchanted a seal upon the *Il-lar*, as an indication of her promise that Gillin and his sons would be the only kings of this new Pure world. This seal allowed only Gillin's hand to touch and wield the *Il-lar* for all eternity—Gillin's hand and the hand of his descendants alone, for all others to place so much as a finger upon it would instantly die. So no one, not even Mavet herself, could lay hand to the *Il-lar* without meeting an instantaneous demise. Perhaps Mavet trusted that her puppet kings would always wield it as she commanded."

I think of King Gastlin, striding as he does down the

corridors, arrogant and seemingly unaware of these ancient mysteries. Does he know of this? That he, as a descendant of Gillin, would be able to wield the *Il-lar?* If, in fact, the *Il-lar* still exists.

"So with the sword Hallath, Gillin slayed the King of Stars and sealed his spirit essence within the *Il-lar.* But not without a drastic change in the plan—for in Rinma's final moment of life, he had used the last of what power he possessed to alter Mavet's seal upon the *Il-lar,* so that his spirit essence may one day be released."

"Released?" I look up at her. "Rinma... his spirit can be released?"

"Aye," says she with a pleasurable glow in her orange-yellow eyes. "But not so simply. For in order to do so, the beholder of the *Il-lar* must first bear the blood of Gillin—but to release his spirit essence of its prison, the beholder must, too, carry the blood of the King of Stars himself. The one to release him, a descendant of both Glindian and Rinma's bloodlines, the one to undo all Mavet has done."

"Both bloodlines?" I laugh with incredulity. "A Glindian Magic." I smirk at what a preposterous image that would be, a king of Gillin's throne and a Magic consummating an intimate bond? Then, I realize—with a jolt of my heart—that my sister, my Lirinda, has done just this.

"But...you say this Magic would have to be a descendant of King Rinma," I stipulate. "Are there such descendants?"

"You would know them as well as I," croaks the old woman.

I feel a slight chill up my arms suddenly, but surely it's due to the dampness of the cave, the occasional sea wind whistling through a crack in the stone bringing the enchanted candleflames to gutter. I turn the page.

I see an illustration of Gillin's castle: the image of the pale, pointed structure that has haunted me all my life, perfectly detailed in faded ink—but it is not poised atop its mountain; instead, the illustration reveals a vast network of intricate, ancient citadel beneath. Sprawling fantastically far and wide beneath what must be, now, the modern Glindian capital, are enormous arched passages, held up by ornate columns. So foreign in design and architecture are they, and so very elegant, it is obvious Rinma's thronal chamber dwells within, just beneath Gillin's own throne. A lost world, buried beneath Gillin's new construction, their interconnectedness one massive structure.

The citadel of the King of Stars lies beneath Gillin's castle? I wonder with an added beat to my pulse. *The entire capital city?*

I recall my dreams of ancient stone corridors, the white light beckoning me to follow. Deep, deep within the castle. Within the walls. A presence like a heartbeat, a pulse.

My throat has gone dry.

"And where is the *Il-lar* now?" I utter in little more than a choked breath.

"Whispers of the *Il-lar* are now that of legend, myth. No one but the Glindian kings themselves know where it is kept, if it is kept."

I blink into the distance of the cave, overwhelmed by the enormity of fear and fascination I feel for unraveling more of this mystery. Ama, I see out of my blurred periphery, watches how I ponder painfully over this new information. Hungry excitement flares in her orange eyes, but when my gaze meets hers again, she looks back down to the cauldron.

"You will be needing your strength," says she with a croak, ladling the soupy concoction of the cauldron into two bone bowls and handing one to me. I fold the book closed at my side and thank her with a sickened mutter, taking the skull into my hand, my mind still upon the secret citadel buried beneath the castle of my sister.

I remember once asking whether my sister or Mother felt as I did.

We had been carrying our wares back up the dusty cart road from having spent the long, hot summer's day selling at the market square. I staggered up the cart road after Lirinda and Mother, sweating beneath my hood and cloak, the lush, shade-enfolded mountain of Haven set squarely before us, the terrain growing wilder the further we wandered from the capital.

"What *is* that?" I had asked. Impatience and exasperation strained my young voice, for I had been agonized by the question for hours, and now it was strained more with the pair of baskets I carried, nearly half as large as myself, for I was still a small girl, no older than eight years. "That heartbeat feeling coming from the capital?"

Mother looked back over her shoulder, her hood concealing half her wary face as her emerald eyes assessed me.

"You sense something?" she asks.

"It is almost alive," said I with wild emphasis. "Something alive in the capital."

She quirked a brow at me. I'm certain there were many such odd things I said at that age, things Mother must have dismissed as parents need sometimes do.

"There are many things you might feel," explained Mother wisely. "Many lives with beating hearts."

"It is more than that," I argued. "It is like magic. Could it be?"

Mother pondered this as she hiked on, her cloak catching a late-summer breeze carrying the smells of hot tavern-food from the city, which subsided and was replaced by a cool scent of the nearby frothing river. "There may well be magic around us still. But I do not feel it."

"It is right beneath our feet!" I squeaked indignantly, heaving one of the baskets onto my tiny shoulder. "As real as any root of tree."

Mother smiled, perhaps thinking this was one of my many games for attention.

"How about you, Lirinda?" Mother asked with an air of play. "Do you feel the heartbeat of which your sister speaks?"

"Only my own," replied my sister with a wistful sigh, thinking surely of a handsome boy she had laid eyes upon that day or perhaps a ribbon she was unable to buy.

No one heard my rationalizations as we climbed the meandering mountain path home, and in my frustration, I glared over my shoulder at the castle at my back, squinting my young eyes in the brilliant sunshine as the castle reflected diamonds of suns upon every window. The castle seemed the only other structure in the land to mirror my affliction, to understand.

I wondered then, but wonder even more now, why I have felt the deep magic pulse when they did not.

Could it be the *Il-lar* I've felt reverberating from wherever it is kept? The very spirit essence of the Shade King—the King of Stars? Imprisoned for centuries, awaiting release? I feel I do know, in the marrow of my bones, that it is so. What more could explain the starlight of my dreams than the *Il-lar?*

And why then does it beckon, of all people, to me?

When it is dawn of the next day, Ama is nowhere around

to see me leave. I stand at the entrance looking for her shape among her odd treasures, but I know she's gone again to the mysterious passage she's disappeared to before. I do not wish to overstay my welcome, but I do feel strange not having said farewell to her, this unusual woman who is but feels not at all like a stranger. As I turn to leave, I glance a final time at Gillin's book, where last night Ama had tossed it negligently among her forgotten, broken keepsakes. I wonder if she ever takes notice of it, how it wastes there beneath the mildew and gathering dust. If she will ever read it as I would.

Would she notice it missing amongst her hundred other deteriorating books?

With another glance around the cave, I stalk toward the book and slip it discreetly beneath the arm of my cloak. And slowly, not too quickly to attract any attention if she were to happen upon me, I slink through the cavern passage to the violet dawn beyond.

Dawn is still, but for the thrashing of waves against the cliffs. I climb them with more ease than descending them, although clamping the book beneath my left arm hinders my speed. I had been weak, exhausted before, but this time I am energized and purposeful as I scale the slippery dark stone, wet and crumbling at my fingertips and beneath my boots, my cloak billowing behind me in the low air. Continually, I check at the bottom of the cliffs where Ama's cave had been, fearful of seeing the woman's hunched cloaked form, her frightening amber gaze narrowed viciously up at me, but I see naught but gulls fluttering down in the pinkening light and silvery spray from the crashing waves below.

I am gone from her. I wonder if ever I'll see her again.

This morning, the capital is slow and quiet with trade and commotion. The people draped in their tattered shawls, trading baskets and pushing carts of firewood on the now-hardened snow, tread carefully so as not to slip and fall, their steamy voices muffled by the thick snow that pads every eave of every building. Every chimney shimmering with heat. I scurry past them all with my hood obscuring my downturned face, weaving my way back up the mountainous swell of city streets leading up to the castle. My every fall of foot as it presses into the frozen snow reminds me of the illustration of how the modern capital and castle had been constructed over the ancient and extensive citadel of the Shade King Rinma. The very ground I walk upon the roof of a lost world.

My lost world.

A smile creeps across my hidden face as a bloom of hot purpose grows in my chest.

I knew it, I murmur in a steamy breath to myself as I meander between children at play upon the slippery road. *I knew it.* I had always known there was something hidden here—something resonating like a living pulse.

But what I feel cannot simply be the inert passages of a citadel long suffocated. What I feel is vibrant and voracious—alive. *What I feel is the* Il-lar.

I close my eyes and recall the visualization of glowing white light luring me down a stone passageway, as familiar as an entity who has pursued me all my life. *I dream of it most every night,* I recall fervently. *My very bones ache with it, for it calls to me. Not to my sister, not to my mother.*

Me.

Why not them? Why not my sister, who is beautiful enough to be hand-picked off the street to be a queen? Why not my mother, who can raise life from soil, weave her organic matter into creation, and commune with fauna?

How could I in any way be unique to the *Il-lar?* To the King of Stars?

The only difference between us, I ponder, *Between my mother, sister, and me, is my father.* My father—my mysterious, powerful, Magic father—may well have some obscure tie to this. I wonder if he has felt the same beckoning I do, the throb of ancient power. If he, too, has been haunted by dreams of sentient white light.

Perhaps, I consider with a flutter in my belly, *Could he be a descendant of Rinma?*

Such a thought makes me giddy and fearful at once—and desolate with despair, for I know I'll likely never know the truth. Likely, I will never know anything, for Mother had never revealed my father to me. My own father, whom—regardless of his evil acts—I have a right to know. I've no source of my father's identity to trace, even if I desired; none but the one fiery clue of the Devil Mellick, whom I may never encounter.

For the first time, but not without origin, do I feel the heat of hatred for my mother's neglect of me. In so many ways my mother failed me, and even in this, swearing me to an oath not to hunt down the truths of my paternal ties, did she leave me isolated and in-the-dark as ever. Even in her death has she left me in the grass on a cold autumn's night, alone.

"All I can do is find it," I swear to myself under my breath, feeling my downcast spirits rise with my secret ambition. "I must keep seeking the Source—the *Il-lar*—until it is found. Until I have followed the labyrinth of my dreams to its center, for I know now it exists."

CHAPTER TWENTY FIVE

As I make my return to Gillin's castle, with his sacred book clamped under the arm of my cloak, unseen by the guards at the gatehouse who nod to me upon my reentrance to the castle's snow-bright, lovely grounds, I recall the reason I left so heedlessly into the blizzarding night. An illness of my magic. Suppression of my truth. My Current seeping from me like waste from a dead man. I feel that same illness encroaching again the nearer I ascend the outer fortifying walls of the castle. But it is not the proximity to the Source that ails me. It is something far more difficult to bear.

I realize it is the thought of being so near to Lirinda, having to endure the sounds of her laughter, to smell her summery smells, which fills me with such rage that I feel the first churnings of illness again. It is my intolerance of her, her falseness, sickening my belly with dread and rousing my Current with slithering tendrils of loathing. It is my servitude to her, my submission at her feet—when I am far more powerful than she—that provokes me so.

I am not here for her, I remind myself. *Perhaps I was before.*

But now… I am here for myself. And as I enter the castle and am surrounded by its strange, blinding-bright marble beauty once more, with the white eyes of sculptures upon me, I think for the first time that I wish Lirinda was not here at all—that I could have this castle to myself without her dictating my life.

Nothing I do is for her. My every stitch of the tapestries, my steps in her stupid dances, my curtsies to her and those of her court—they are all my disguises, so I may continue to wander the sleeping corridors in delicious solitude, unsuspected by the guards who watch me slither out the gallery into the shadows; unsuspected by the king himself, when he sees me among his halls, that he does not think I search for his ancestor's fantastical tool. Now, as I ascend stairwells and saunter through corridors to the royal apartments, all the gilt thread in the tapestries and the gold candelabras lustrous in the morning light, makes me long, hungrily, for the velvety winter darkness to consume this space, so that I may begin my search anew, with this fresh purpose I feel burning with my pulse. But these disguises of mine, I can only assume them so long as I do not succumb to illness as before.

My Current, I vow to myself, *I will not lose control of again.* Just as important as my pursuit of the *Il-lar* must I prioritize the safe expulsion of my power, exercising it to exhaustion nightly so it will not be volatile as it had been. Most important of all, I must distance myself from Lirinda as much as I am able.

But I cannot keep myself from her presence, though I am desperate to. For immediately, once I return to the ladies' tower am I summoned to her bedchamber.

"What ever for?" I demand of the ladies who have informed me of this.

Servants bustle through the room as the ladies are prepared for the day, fastened into their gowns and headdresses. Ilette's long auburn hair is combed out delicately by a servant; Klaria's wimple is applied with care. Each of them refuses to glance at me, and if their eyes happen to meet mine, there is scorn in them.

"You left the castle grounds without permission," squeaks young Miella almost pitiably when no other lady wills themselves to answer. "You have broken your Oath!"

"It is most merciful of the queen to discuss this with you herself, first, before alerting the High Council of your absence," Ilette drawls once the servant finishes combing her hair. "You ought to consider yourself fortunate."

I scowl bitterly at my freshly made bed; how inviting it looks; how I wish I could crawl upon it now and not have to speak of my blizzard ventures to the one who prompted them.

"I was ill. As you all know," I declare in a low voice.

"And we told her you had been," Miella says uncomfortably. "How you lay in your bed for hours that day."

"Even still," adds Ellaina coldly, with a suspicious leer that passes from the hood of my cloak to my boots and back up again, "it is rather odd how you simply disappeared!"

I wait until the ladies have exited the tower in a tumble of velvet and perfume to remove Gillin's book from under my cloak and slip it into a cobwebbed crevice beneath Ellaina's four-poster bed, knowing she will always be too drunk at night to notice it and too prim in the mornings to ever put her hands and knees to the cold chamber floor. Evidently, it is not a place the servants notice either. And if by some chance they ever did notice, I reason that the book, Gillin's own, would not incriminate anyone of magic, although its rarity may raise questions as to how Ellaina came by it. I suppose, too, one may even presume the book could have been hidden there for far longer than Ellaina's possession of the bed.

Finally, I dress into a gown of dark-blue velvet with black embroidery and its corresponding headdress. Only then do I amble as slowly as I can to my sister's chambers.

The morning sun, now fully risen and shining through the windows, reflects off the many mirrors here, glaring in flecks upon pretty spun glass and in dizzying prisms within facets of jewels, and even upon the lustrous golden hair of my sister. So brilliant is the room that I wince away from Lirinda; it relieves me not to look at the beautiful image of her, how she stands in the midst of her chamber freshly dressed in a thick velvet gown of winterberry red, making the natural blush of her cheeks and red of her lips all the more evident.

"Sister, where have you been?" Her shrill voice squeals when she sees me. "I've been so worried!"

"Surely the ladies told you I was ill." It is not a full lie, but a withholding of the truth. Like vomit rising in my throat do I feel the need to expel all that burns within me. How I wish I could tell her of Ama, of her cave and her potions, of all I have discovered—how the throne of King Rinma remains intact beneath the earth, beneath her very dining table, and how the *Il-lar* may call mysteriously to me. Oh, how helpful the Queen of Glindor could be in my quest! How helpful to have a sister who could aid in my pursuit. But I know I cannot tell her anything, not even of the book belonging to her husband's ancestor. Saddened I feel, how the one person in all this life I have remaining, one with whom I once shared everything, is now just as much an enemy as the king himself.

I swallow down any urge to divulge these secrets of mine to her.

"Ill?" she exclaims, measuring me with confusion for the obvious wellness I am in.

"You knew I was ill, didn't you?" I ask. "I had dismissed

myself from your presence that day."

"But to run away in the night! Into a snowstorm! And not return for a day? I had sent pages looking for you!"

I am glad for the sun that keeps my eyes from hers as I lie fiercely now. "I could not risk exposing you to my illness, Your Majesty." My voice is dry as I croak bitterly, "Too important you are."

She breathes a little laugh, and I am not sure she is convinced; I am unsure she hears the resentment bittering my tongue.

"You have broken your Oath, sister," says she with frustration trembling in her soft voice. Gently, she shakes her head. "Only weeks after swearing to it. This is no light thing…"

"What will you be doing about it, then?" My eyes pierce hers despite the brightness. "What fate awaits me for my unspeakable treachery?"

I see her smooth throat flex with a swallow. The pout of her mouth hanging fuller as she considers my innocence.

"If indeed you've acted out of benevolence as you say—for the safety of me your queen and thus the realm—I cannot have that punished. But by the gods, sister, next time you are ill, you must see Madam Morrie!"

"I shall," I grunt.

"You are well now?" She looks me over anxiously.

"Fresh air is medicine," I answer with raised brows. "Mother often said that, did she not?"

Lirinda looks down as her eyes weigh with heaviness. "Indeed, she did. Perhaps such medicine may be of help to me as well." Lirinda goes to one of her pretty leaded windows to unlatch it open. A rush of icy sea air, mingled with snowy pine of the surrounding mountain, spills in and rustles her long hair and puffed sleeves of her gown with the breeze. Something about it, her vulnerability, fills me suddenly with a melancholy I did not think myself capable of feeling for her.

"You are ill?" I cock a brow, realizing I've not seen my sister so docile in years, restrained enough not to be dancing about at any opportunity. But a slight smile raises her cheek.

"Not ill, no," says she softly. "I've never been more well. But I cannot take any risks. Especially not now…"

A protective hand goes to the flat velvet of her stomacher.

"You're…" My mouth falls open, eyes blinking. Elation, jealousy, and desolation fill me all at once, and I struggle to speak. "You're with child?"

Both of her hands now flatten themselves over her abdomen as a brilliant smile beams across her face. "I think that I am!" Tears glisten in her eyes, along with the diamonds and crystal of the room. "The midwife says I have missed my course and show the first signs of pregnancy. She advises me to wait, but I cannot. I will be telling the king tonight."

She glides to me and slinks me into her embrace as always she does, and I am stunned as I am pressed into her fragrant hair. I say nothing. I cannot speak.

"A little prince or princess, Sirry," she murmurs happily into my hair. "Our family." She retracts from the embrace and looks up to me. "Your own nephew or niece will be heir to the throne of Glindor. All that was once before…it matters not, for this, this child, is our future."

With Lirinda's news, the entirety of the castle and its court has surged into a tumult of celebration. Any whisper of my disappearance has faded from the castle; indeed, most everything has been forgotten in the midst of the announcement of a Glindian heir. The uncertain fate of my sister's womb is shouted from every balcony, across every hall, and sung in a hundred songs across the realm, likely filling even the taverns and the smallest, most threadbare hovels of the poor. *The little prince,* they all say it will be. How long awaited an heir has been.

Up in the high towers of the castle, a nursery is readied. Gifts already are brought in like offerings from the wealthy families hungry for royal favor: little gold statues and pretty jewelry boxes, heavy with family sapphires, rubies, and emeralds, all things an infant could never use. Treasures fill the bright room in useless heaps. Treasures for who will certainly be a greedy little child, I think with revulsion. New servants are hired, nursemaids, and half the castle's workers are dually obligated to rush up the many spiraling stairs and assist in the care of Glindor's heir.

I've not seen the king so happy, so easy to smile, in all the months I've glanced at him. Always grinning among his men and High Council he now is, boasting of the son he will have to hunt alongside him soon. It seems that even Krom, with his cold eyes, has begun to smile, too. To Lirinda, King Gastlin is even more doting and syrupy than ever before, kissing every measure of her hands, between her fingers and up her wrists, while looking at her as if she is his most prized dessert. She knows this, that she has indulged him beyond any worldly desire, and the sultry gazes they share before all the courtiers is enough to heat the room without the ever-raging fire.

I cannot look at it.

The winter months seem not so dreary and cold when the castle is swathed in constant decoration, ringing with joyful music, and overflowing with bountiful, beautiful feasts,

Lirinda and her ladies marinading in the cheer. But dreary and cold it still is for me as I slink unbeknownst to them all in the shadows of the corridors, following my secret pursuit.

Easier it is for me to disappear within the castle with so much celebration to distract everyone's gaze from my discreet form, slithering by where no one walks. Especially as the days warm and brighten with spring, when much of the court lingers out upon the balconies or within the Outer Court, bundled still in their coats in the fresh air, where they celebrate the Glindian prince or princess who will be born this summer.

I know now that what I seek is near. Far below me, in the old stone. When I obsessively trace my finger across the illustration of Gillin's castle built above Rinma's throne, I see where they join. But how to reach that deep, secret place, I know not. If not for my dreams reassuring me of a passage I must follow, I would think it nonexistent, impossible. Sometimes, still, I am riddled with doubt and think it impossible indeed.

Only in the darkness of earliest morning do I return to the underground stairwell that seems to lead nowhere. Cold and damp is the subterranean passage, reverberating strongly with the beckoning that pulls at the very fibers of my Current, reminiscent of the tunnels of my dreams—but with nowhere to go—no doors, no contiguous halls.

"Dammit." I have breathed the curse more than once, feeling frustrated enough to slam my fist into the stone wall when I have ventured again to the dead-end, lingering too long in the futile space, wasting my precious hours of shadow, having to return too soon to my charade with the ladies. With the ever-celebrant Lirinda in sow.

Fruitless. A waste, it feels. Until one early morning, gray still before the dawn, I am about to descend to the subterranean passage when I hear the voices of the king and Eliador Krom and their footfalls as they ascend the stairs toward me.

I slink quickly behind a tapestry and listen to them as they pass me, murmuring too quietly for me to fathom. Gastlin's voice, however, is distinguishably sleepy, and he stifles a yawn, as though he has long been away from his bed.

So there is something down there, I reason with an eager bite of my lip. For why else would Krom and the king venture so far, so early, to merely stand amid a useless passage. There must be some door, some other place for them to go. *But where?*

Every free moment that I'm not seeking the Source—the *Il-lar*—by sneaking through the castle, I spend hungrily flipping through the pages of Gillin's book. Obsessed with it I've become, although I must remind myself that every word and illustration I pore over is corrupted through his own victorious perspective. I cannot deny how it captivates me, though I despise Gillin all the more with every page I read by moonlight through the window in the ladies' tower—or by a candle as I sit in the velvet privacy of drawn curtains around my four-poster bed.

One evening, after supper, Lirinda and her ladies fraternize among the gentlemen and king in the gallery. Sunset falls later now and paints rosy hues with the fading light, still wintry and cold, but generous to us captives of the court who have been kept so long within castle walls in elongated darkness. I find myself willing to grin at Miella and Ellaina's sharp-tongued banter before the gentlemen they play at a game of cards, and how Klaria blushes as a handsome young lord asks her to teach him an expert chord of the bandelon, plucking strings before her and inviting her hands to join, but she keeps them stuck upon her lap.

I smile, partially, until Lirinda asks me to join her and the king in a game of cards.

Absolutely not, I wish to say, but instead, I rise stiffly from my comfortable seat by the fire and go to sit before her without a word or glance to her, only a slight nod of my head to the king. Sidewardly, our eyes meet in a mutually vehement gaze, and he looks away as abruptly as I do.

Sitting so near to him feels disastrous to me. For there is an electric sensation, like a sky pregnant with lightning, that brings the fine hairs of my flesh to stand on end. My Current begins to thump with my pulse at our proximity. I study my cards and we play.

Thankful I am for the practice of cardplaying with the ladies over the winter, that I have learned the strategies of the game and easily make a fool of Lirinda—that I am competition enough for the king.

When I win a round and gather the wagered gold coins, slipping them into my new silk coin purse, Lirinda claps her hands for me, delighted by the heat of our game.

"Oh, Sirry, how wonderful it is to play with you like this again!"

"The two of you played often?" The king asks as he deals a new hand of cards.

"Oh, daily!" Lirinda chirps with a beaming smile. "Especially at night before the fire, much like this." She gestures to our surroundings—the grand firelit gallery—and I lift an eyebrow at the lie.

He smiles so his cheek dimples, his eyes blazing upon his wife as he expertly flicks her a card. "I am glad that you are able to play again as you once had."

"Sirry, won't you tell His Majesty how well we once played? Card games were a favorite among our household."

"By card games, do you mean the stick game?" I remark with a brightened voice and a smile stretched across my mouth to match hers. "When we would pass the stick to one another while Mother sang, and whoever held it when her song ended, lost?"

The king erupts with a laugh, loud enough for the nearest courtiers to turn to listen to our conversation.

"The stick game?" He slouches back within his chair and looks from Lirinda to me with amusement. "Why ever are we playing cards when we can play the stick game? Shall I have a servant bring one in for us?"

Lirinda's eyes smolder at me though her smile falters not. "I've no recollection of *that* game. Truly, we must have been very young. Unless, of course"—she ripples a delighted giggle— "my sister's memory deceives her, and she actually remembers playing with a servant!"

I rise to stand from my chair. "I thank Your Majesties for an exhilarating game. I know when I am ahead in my wagers, so I must decline another round. Good night to you."

With a deep curtsy, I clench my skirts with my Current-tingling palms and swish through the gallery to the door for the tower stairs. The tower room, once I reach it, is cold and silent as its stone, soothing me from my inner fire.

With my surging Current, I raise one of the several lit candles illuminating the tower into my hand as I storm past, the flame flapping in the wind I cause. Then, my tendrils of power slide Gillin's book from its cranny into my grasp as I climb upon my bed, using my Current to angrily whisk the curtains closed around me. Frequently do I use my Current here now, for I know I will hear the ladies ascending the stairs to the tower before they arrive. Usually now I am perfectly at ease with my Current, exercising it every day, but there are occasions like this, when Lirinda is too insufferable, and I must excuse myself before I reveal my hatred through cracking pottery and splintering walls.

I open the book to where I last left off reading, the scent of Ama's briny cave upon the ancient pages reminding me of my treachery for having it in my grasp. My fingers upon the soft, dust-textured pages are chilled to touch it.

If only the king knew what I held in my hands. I smile tersely in my solitude, still furious with Lirinda but feeling sated now for the expulsion of my Current.

I must find the Il-lar *soon. I cannot continue this falseness much longer. That is why I cling to this book; so near it brings me to the past, the truth—so near to the* Il-lar. *It is my only purpose in this life.* I feel my mouth tighten again with my anger, and my eyes burn with sadness that something invisible, untouchable—something I cannot speak to—should be my one companion.

I am lonely, I realize. I've not been any less lonely, being here in the castle, than I was alone in Haven, starving among the trees. I wonder if ever I've not been utterly alone.

I cast aside these foolish feelings of mine as I press my face nearer to the open book and read more of the destruction to the Tarian folk, the Magics of this native land—the land of Taria before it had been renamed Glindor.

How would Lirinda feel if I were to read her this page? I muse with a wicked grin as I read Gillin's account of how he urged the Tarian folk to gather in the forest so that he could torch the trees around them, leaving them nowhere to run but into Gillin's expectant army. *Would she be so proud of her Glindian heir then?* I read on, learning how the mothers with their children at their breast howled through the smoke a word in their language he did not understand until his translators later told him. *"Siril!"* they cried, meaning mercy.

My throat goes suddenly dry like I might choke or retch. Slowly, I close the book upon my finger to save the page.

Siril. My heart hammers, dizzying me. I am reminded of the memory of Mother's where she names Lirinda from the Tarian words *Lirin* and *Da,* which together mean *to give light.* I open the book again to view the word *Siril.* Mercy.

Siril Da.

My eyes burn for the name my mother gave me.

I hear a bleat of laughter as a few ladies come running up the stairs and into the chamber. They slam open the wooden door against the wall and giggle together as they dig through a personal trunk for a special deck of cards, murmuring to each other that they wonder if any of the gentlemen will ask to meet them tonight. They do not seem to notice the bounce of flamelight upon the stone ceiling above my bed. Not soon enough are they gone, giggling again down the stairs, and I clutch the book to my chest with a grunt of agony, bowing my head over it, thinking with dry, stinging eyes of the night Mother stumbled back up the mountain for me.

Mercy.

She had wanted me dead but gave me life. A tender sentiment that burns a hole in my heart.

I lay back against the silk of my pillow and stare up at the ceiling, pursing my lips into a straight line, remembering the gushing stream of vile creation my very blood is, existing without ever truly being loved. A shadow, second best, sister to the queen, her servant in the same ancient magic space I feel, strangely, belongs to me.

"What mercy you have shown me, Mother," I hiss spitefully in the dark to myself. A sting radiates in my jaw. "Spared, like a mouse beneath a hammer. What a kindness."

CHAPTER TWENTY SIX

With the blooming of spring flowers, so, too, does the child blossom beneath Lirinda's silk gowns. It is a sight that fills me with trepidation and reluctant joy, seeing my sister's belly grow round and heavy like fruit upon the orchard trees.

Before spring, however, for many long months, the ladies, Lirinda, and I had been trapped within the gallery, stitching clothes for the baby soon to arrive; with many conversations—infuriatingly upon the heir—concluding with a sudden burst of Lirinda's retching into a bowl held by servants. The constant rain slithering upon the window glass was, for a good while, beautiful to watch as the world beyond transformed from dead and brown to luscious emerald, but in time I began to feel imprisoned, remembering how it felt to be free in the rain, to hear it fall upon the trees of the forest—how it sounded when the stream would rush with melting snow and flooding rain. But all I heard in my waking days was the prattling of the ladies, and rather than breathing in the fresh air of wet pine and earth, all I had to fill my lungs was the gallery's shared, stagnant breath and the stink of Lirinda's vomit coalescing sickeningly with the bouquets of fresh-cut flowers brought in by servants.

But now, after the months of dark rain, when a summer sun cleanses the gloom and weariness from the chambers with warm light, Lirinda begins to regain her energy enough to venture outside the castle. Even I, in my bitter aloofness, am eager to leave the cold castle corridors for the fresh, warm flowery air of outside. We flee our stone captivity as often as Lirinda is able, with the ladies and I carrying the hem of her sweeping, extravagant gowns so that she does not trip.

So beautiful are the castle grounds against a cloudless sky, sometimes I find it easy to forget King Rinma and his throne beneath my feet. I want only the fresh bird-chirruping air, sea-sweet as it rustles through my tresses, fluttering my sleeves. Desperate I am to ignore etiquette and sprint up the velvet hills and roll upon soft grass as I did so often as a child. There would be no luxury greater to me than spending the day among the insects upon the ground, having them crawl up my arms and into my hair; frazzling my tresses with pollen and setting my headdress askew; I long to laze about so unabashedly upon the ground that soil smears the silk of my gown; to run at my full speed, barefoot in the grass, and explore the mysterious hedge maze in the distance; to jump without hesitation into the ponds—floating upon my back among the swans. But instead, we spend most of our days in a marble pavilion set within the lawns, dancing and singing and continuing our agonizing needlework as Lirinda bids us. She joins us in the dancing as the energy comes to her, and much energy she still has. There are days I long for her spontaneous bouts of vomiting—how they kept her, for once in her life, quiet and still.

By midsummer, so heavy is Lirinda with child that she is unsteady on her feet. The ladies and I assist her in descending the castle staircases by holding her hands and elbows, though I do suspect her wearied waddle to be exaggerated. These excursions outside we make morning and evening now that Lirinda is near her delivery, for the midwife, Madam Morrie, has instructed such for the benefit of Lirinda's endurance and for the positioning of the child within her womb.

Today, so strong is the summer's sunshine that we all carry parasols above us as we walk. I wear a flowing gown of pale green silk; my long hair tumbles down in black curls to my buttocks. As we pass through the Outer Court and archery butts to the lawns, I notice a few of the courtiers admiring me when they hadn't before. Gentlemen practicing archery turn to look at me, but I only scowl at them so they will not think to ever approach me.

Gardeners are seen into the distance of the polished mountainside, reaching with ladders to trim the many topiaries into their desired shapes of magnificent animals. A tall arthritic man of old age ambles out from among them. I recognize him as the Master Gardener. He removes his hat and bows to Lirinda as deeply as his bones will allow, then partially to us.

"My most gracious queen, have you come to visit your new garden?"

"Master Dagellas!" Lirinda beams at him beneath her parasol. She extends a white gloved hand, and he bends again to kiss it. "I did not think it was yet ready."

"It has still only just begun to grow—such a cold spring we've had! But if it pleases Your Majesty, your company would only make the space more beautiful."

She purses her rosy lips, smirking at each of us at the old man's flattery, as though we find it absolutely inspiring to hear.

"Perhaps my fertility will aid in its growth!" She smooths

a proud hand over her roundness. "Come, ladies—Sirry." And Lirinda guides our pastel procession beneath a carved stone archway I've not passed through before, to a fleecy green garden flourishing in shoots of young plants, with fat buds beginning to unfurl.

"The Queen's Garden," Lirinda appraises of the green space with delight bright in her eyes.

As we walk along the paved path, Lirinda explains to me in particular, as the Honorable ladies already know this as common knowledge, that here it is tradition that the presently reigning queen has the garden designed to her liking.

"I had been brought through here just after my coronation in autumn," says Lirinda with fondness, reaching out to stroke at a new leaf of a growing sunflower. "I decided then I wanted my garden to rage in all colors of the earth. Foxgloves and poppies, lupine and lilies, bellflowers and violets and daisies—buzzing and humming at all moments with bees and hummingbirds, their song of pollination to ring in every ear that passes by."

I glance at my sister, for so dearly has she described the garden of our Haven. Perhaps, foolishly, I wish to connect with her over our lost past in a brief glance, but Lirinda does not look at me.

Down the paved path is an even grander archway that Lirinda leads us beneath. Once beyond, I gasp a little in awe of what surrounds me, learning at once that Lirinda's plot is only the ante-garden before the Queens' Memorial Gardens.

Terraced throughout a cleave of mountain is a manicured network of nearly a hundred small gardens, bordered with stone walls laced with flowering climbers. Several pretty fountains can be seen sparkling with water, each placed sporadically about. There are also womanly statues I see, and I assume they are of goddesses or perhaps the late queens themselves.

Lirinda tells me the Queens' Memorial Gardens are a collection of every Glindian queen's beloved flowers, all to regrow again with each year. Those who had reigned centuries ago were still remembered by the trees and flowering bushes that continue to flourish even now, and that if the plants are ever to die, they are replaced in an identical fashion. A morbid contrast it is for me to learn that buried beneath the gardens are their queens.

The first plot of garden Lirinda leads us to is Queen Jayna's: a simple but neat plot of rose bushes surrounding a small spurting fountain, with a stone plaque, still freshly carved, marking her grave. I glance at the earth, the grass, thinking how King Gastlin's first wife lies there beneath. I wonder how decomposed she is while her replacement strides above.

"What can you tell us of my predecessor, Lady Klaria?" Lirinda tenderly asks the eldest of her ladies, who has been reading Queen Jayna's plaque with reverence.

"Oh, Your Majesty," Klaria begins grievously, "the young Jayna was a softer spirit than most. A lovely little thing, quiet and demure as her roses. She would have made a tender mother, had the gods not taken her before she could fulfill her earthly duty."

Lirinda places a hand to her heavy belly, as she so often does throughout the day, and makes a mournful face for the woman who had gone and died in her same role.

Our gowns sweep the path as we continue on. Lirinda, with nothing better to do to waste the beautiful day, has each lady take a turn and read a plaque. There are seventy-eight of them in all, with some queens having reigned for decades, others only a matter of weeks. The drone of bees and garden birds in my ears make me feel sluggish and drunk beneath the heavy midsummer sun.

As we wander through the gardens, I notice there is a great amount of space for the queens yet to come and wonder what women will succeed my sister upon Gillin's throne. Lirinda's unborn child, perhaps, or more plain girls from Honorable families. It is an invasive thought, but fleetingly I envision the garden I would plant here, if I could. Wild it would be, twisting with ivy and ferns, brightened by trillium in the mists of spring. If I did not have to hide the magic flora, how beautiful it would be to plant moonbells and scryflowers here—to grow my own fire lilies for Flame Powder.

By now, too exhausted is Lirinda to walk back through the gardens and invites us all to rest by a pond. We travel a level path lined sweetly with flowering trees, leading to a bean shape of water reflecting the blue sky above. There, we assist Lirinda in sitting upon one of the surrounding benches and fan her as she watches swans float placidly upon the water, surrounded by their fluffy cygnets.

Too lovely the day is to spend it seated beside Lirinda. Idly, I walk around the pond, admiring the flowering trees of varying color and fragrance, not too far from the ladies or Lirinda should they beckon for me as always they do. As I fondle a leaf in my palm, tracing the vein down its center, my mind drifts to Mother and her plant magic, which feels now so long ago, like a lost dream.

What would Mother think if she knew she was soon to be a grandmother? I wonder. *Her grandchild, heir of all she ever hated, feared.*

I glance to where Lirinda sits, her hand as always resting upon the large swell of her belly tight beneath her primrose-pink gown. I think of the child within, my own kin, and how they, with their Glindian blood, could touch the *Il-lar*—behold it, and wield it—just as Gillin had. I think of the illustration of

Gillin in his book, with the *Il-lar* in his grasp, and feel chilled.

"Oh, what a most welcome surprise!" I hear Lirinda rejoice and the ladies croon in agreement. When I look, I see a crowd of servants carrying in trays of tea and pretty pastries. Lirinda lifts the domed lid of a dish and discovers within a pudding embellished with a pansy, which makes her giggle.

"My dear Gastlin sent this, didn't he? Only he knows what I crave!"

Laughter and the clinking of little cups on saucers dances across the pond as I continue my walk away from them. I relish in cool solitude and distance, tucking myself slightly within the luscious blooms of a pale blue hydrangea, but I am panged, too, with a loneliness I wish I did not feel.

Cupping the heavy blooms in my palm, weighing them broodingly, I ignore my pain as always with my obsession of the *Il-lar.* I promise myself, with the *Il-lar's* discovery, that it will cure me of all I feel.

Won't it?

Will it find for me a home? Will it recover all I've lost? Will it give me family?

I glance again to Lirinda and see her completeness with her heavy womb, her fruit. The ladies and servants who fawn over her, and her husband who will fawn over her tonight as he always does. This beautiful land, which is hers, her home. She has forgotten all else, though those long-forsaken people and places still belong to her, too. I envy that she can forget what is hers, while I, even with them never belonging to me, cannot relinquish the strands of their memory.

I pluck a little cutting of hydrangea into my fingers and twist the petals until they shred. Then, suddenly feeling like I am being watched, I glance up. Within a blooming rhododendron tree just behind the hydrangea shrub is Crow, perched upon a crooked limb, staring at me.

I stand motionless, startled, my breath bated in my lungs. Concealed she is behind folds of clustered flowers I had not noticed her familiar shape. Her measuring eye upon me like a polished bead, making me feel suddenly cold and naked in the hot sun.

So many times, for so many years, I've seen this bird look at me like this. Why now does she unsettle me so? It is not so much that she's seemingly guided me and saved me in the past, with the night of my birth and the offering of the doe. No, it is something more, a familiarity in her gaze. A mirroring to something I've seen before. I swallow hard.

Commotion of Lirinda and the ladies stir me back to reality. They are withdrawing now from the pond, about to embark upon the garden journey back to the castle, to be dressed in their finer evening gowns for supper, the servants carrying out all their cups and platters in balanced towers.

As I make to walk away to join them, I am reminded vaguely of a time I've seen Crow perch like this recently. Not in a tree, not in Haven, but upon a torch sconce mounted upon the wall of my dreams. With an identical, expectant gaze with which she looks upon me now had she had looked upon me then, too. A chill slithers into my very heart at the realization.

That was the last time I saw Crow, though that was not really her...

Of course, in the strange way of dreams, it did seem the bird and I truly were there together for what felt like hours. Tangibly, I can recall how, for those hours, she'd flown down repetitive corridors ahead of me like a guide, flickering insubstantially into the same form as the beautiful walking woman.

As I walk on, the layers of blooms twisting us from each

other's view, I continue to measure the large bird, who still has not relinquished her expectant stare from me. Of course, it was only a dream, and it was ludicrous as dreams are.

But those dreams… I parry in my mind against myself. *Those dreams are not simply dreams, are they?* For if not for the dreams, I would not have ever visualized the ancient halls which call to me, nor of the white light. The dreams…it is as though they're a manifestation of the *Il-lar's* power, reaching me through my subconscious. But why then should Crow be among it?

As I follow the path back to the castle at the flowing hems of the ladies before me, the serene, colorful gardens all around me looking far too easy and beautiful to exist in the same realm as the one of such deep ancient shadow, I think that if Crow should appear in my dreams again, I will pay closer attention. Perhaps, like with the doe in the wood, the bird wishes only to lead me somewhere. Though making a connection with the real bird and the figment of my dream seems ludicrous, I feel a heavy, eerie sense that if the opportunity should arise again, I must follow her more closely than ever before.

Since that day in the garden, more lucidly has Crow appeared in my sleep, and I have followed her as I vowed I would. No less tangible are her iridescent feathers in my dreams than the very sewing needle and thread I stitch with in the day.

So closely have I paid attention to the bird's every dream-flickering motion, surrendering myself utterly to this subverted reality, that with each night, I fall deeper into the fabric of my dream. So deeply I've fallen, I'm convinced I am truly there with Crow and the mysterious red-haired woman—she, who sometimes materializes before my dream-form like the lighting of a flame, as though she's always been there, beautiful and oddly sinister.

With each dream I have, the more real to me they become. I have begun to reach out and touch the stone of the walls, memorize the grooves, feel the cold dampness, and look at my palm in the firelight of the burning torches and see that it shines with wetness. I have even wondered if this subterranean darkness is true reality and that the languid months of passing summer is the dream. I feel a mounting pressure now while I explore the dreamscape, as though I am on the precipice of discovery. I look up at Crow's shining eye as she perches upon the iron torch sconce and see in her reflective gaze something like impatience.

With each dream I intently follow, the more they seem to advance with detail. In one dream, after Crow and the woman both have guided me down unending stone corridors, and after the bird has alighted upon a sconce, does she do something new: furiously, she cleans her beak upon the iron bough.

I furrow my brow up at her, at the scraping realness of the motion, curious if there could be some significance to this new progression of the dream. Desperate I am to search every subconscious surface for clues and compare them with the real halls of the castle in my waking hours, but I have little time now in the sweltering days of late summer to explore as I once had. With Lirinda taken to childbed in the anticipation of the heir's arrival, seldom am I able to leave her royal apartments.

The ladies and I wait upon her in her chambers, knowing any day her waters will break, and she will need our immediate assistance. So huge she is with child she can hardly move, and groans in earnest now when she must stand to use the pot, which is every few moments it seems. Unbearable are these weeks. The castle, how it swelters with a late summer sun all the day long, but chills deeply at night and early in the mornings with the taste of autumn in its elongating shadows. I ache for winter's long nights again, the promise of darkness in which I can enrobe myself to my secretive task, my augmented freedom. Yet I cannot wait that long.

One morning, I rise as early as I can to sneak about the castle before Lirinda will need me. But just as I tip-toe into the gallery, bathed in the pale glow of receding night, I hear the door to Lirinda's chamber open. I freeze where I stand, trying to compose myself to look as though I've only been gazing innocently out the wide window, expecting to see one of Lirinda's many servants carrying water, or perhaps to announce that she is in labor, coming out from beyond the door. When I see it is instead the shadowed form of a tall man exiting, stepping into the gray gloom as he crosses the gallery, revealing himself as the king, with bed-messed hair and dressed in a linen shirt beneath his open robe, I decide quickly that I shall not flee as I wish to.

Merely I stand there, a statue of serenity, though my pulse and Current panic. As he nears me, I catch the spice of autumn upon his warm skin. I mean not to, but my gaze goes immediately to the strongly sculpted chest cleaved in shadow at the low cut of his linen shirt, the terrain of collarbone at the base of his muscular neck. Realizing my folly, I look quickly up to his face, desperate to keep my expression impassive, my furious gaze terse and impenetrable as ever.

His eyes narrow curiously at me.

"You are up early," muses he in a voice deep with sleep.

I look to the window glass, out at the misty lawns, resolute to not glance at him nor his chest again. My heart, how rapidly it beats, I fear he may hear it.

"I could not sleep, Your Majesty."

"Perhaps you should see a physician for your sleeplessness. For I hear you wander most every morning."

My eyes, though I do not mean for them to, widen with my obvious surprise.

So he knows of my habit.

Unable to stop myself, my gaze leaves the window for the king's downturned face again, to measure his expression; I am curious to know if he is upset or amused, but there is no emotion to discern. Never have we stood so near to one another before. I can feel the heat of my sister's bed radiating off him. How cold I am in contrast.

Perhaps the guard outside the gallery door has told him how often I slink past to wander the halls. I swallow hard as I think of what next to say.

"The castle…it is beautiful in the morning," I admit.

Silently, he evaluates me, then the long chamber subdued in the soft gray glow. Colorless are the upholstered chairs, formless in shadow are the paintings upon the walls.

"It is," he agrees, but still with a question hanging in his voice.

"And quiet," I add, looking out the window again, to where mist devours the trees and mountain, swallowing the faces of the statues far out in the gardens. What I don't say, which I think we both understand, is that it is quiet without the chatter of the ladies and Lirinda, for so like hens in a coop they are.

For a long moment, the two of us stand together at the wide glass, raptured by the beauty of morning, our eyes on the King's Wood, which must smell so sharp of pine at this early hour before the sun evaporates the delicious dew.

Finally, the king nods his head in farewell to me and mutters "Good day, Mistress Sirilda."

I curtsy to him, almost disappointed that he leaves my side.

"Majesty," I whisper.

I keep my head bowed until he is gone from the long chamber, and only once I hear the door close in his absence, do I breathe again.

I do not dare leave the gallery now. Not this morning, when the king wanders the very halls I long to haunt. I patter back up to my bed and lie in the regret that I had, for a moment, not hated my enemy as I ought.

"It's time!"

The ladies and I bustle maniacally about once Lirinda's waters have broken and her contractions ensue. The midwife says all is going very well.

Much of the court has flooded the gallery, especially those of the Fairfellow family I've never seen before, using Lirinda as their tie to royalty. Apparently, they, like everyone else in the excitement of the king's heir, have conveniently forgotten Lirinda's illegitimacy—forgetting that, less than a year ago, she was the unknown daughter of a forestine mistress and a topic of scandal. In my frantic passing for more linens and water alongside the servants, the pretty flax-haired Fairfellows grab at my forearm, calling me kin, and asking for updates on the queen, but I shrug them off and tell them nothing. Hours I spend at Lirinda's sweaty bedside, mopping at her head, allowing her to squeeze my hand.

"I wish Mother was here," she groans to me. Though she trembles with pain and fear, she smiles still with her joy. I smile wanly back, dabbing at her forehead with a cloth.

"Who is to say she is not?" I reply, though I do not truly believe my words. They are comfort enough to Lirinda, who rests her head back upon the pillow with a peaceful smile, though her breathing is jagged and fast.

Once it is time for Lirinda to push, Madam Morrie and her servants urge the ladies and me to leave the chamber. I stand by the door, listening to the sounds of my sister's straining and the midwife's encouragement, thinking perhaps what everyone in the realm is thinking, too: that Queen Jayna before her, in the very same chamber, had gone into this task but did not leave it alive.

I wring my hands together as I wait, picking at my nails, then chewing them. What if Lirinda dies?

The image of Lirinda—with her long hair flowing like golden water off the bed around her, lying dead with her large eyes open—burns my imagination. I chase away the horrible delight I feel deep and wickedly within me, that if such a tragedy should happen, my own life would be much improved.

The gurgling cry of a babe pierces the air, and the ladies and I collectively gasp and sigh at it. Klaria weeps into her kerchief. The ladies join her in her release of emotion—so, too, do the servants, who have all waited within the presence chamber. My throat is so dry and choked, it feels I've swallowed a bundle of tinder. Everything, with this child, has been made permanent. Changed.

She did it. Lirinda has given the king a child.

"A little princess!" I hear the midwife croon proudly from beyond the door. "The most beautiful babe I ever did see!"

It is not for hours more that I am allowed to visit. Only after the king himself and the High Council have gone in, to witness and make record of the historic birth of another descendant of Gillin, am I able to weave in through the happily warbling ladies and have my moment with my sister alone.

Sunset glows in peach hues upon the scene of my sister, sitting up in her massive canopied bed with the windows open to the fresh sea breeze. Swallows swoop by, their evening melodies sweet enough to sound melancholic; the curtains around Lirinda's bed flow with the soft wind. And if I am not mistaken, there is an essence of magic in the air.

I see the sea sparkling through the windows, matching the crown upon Lirinda's golden head. One of the servants must have dressed Lirinda for her royal visitors, for she looks as beautiful as ever in a soft robe of forget-me-not blue. With her crown and her hair lusciously combed through, she looks every measure a queen. Her cheeks flushed with her exertion and a smile, more serene and wise than ever I have seen upon my usually playful sister, she looks down at something small swaddled within her arms.

"Here she is," Lirinda whispers to me once I've sauntered before her. "Your niece."

She pulls back a sheer wrap of linen to reveal the baby sleeping within the small bundle.

For a moment, every ill emotion of mine diminishes at the sight of such innocence. For a moment, I am reminded of what is true, what purity really means.

"She has red hair." I swallow down my dry throat, noting the wisp of copper hair peeking from beneath the white bonnet.

Lirinda lets out a pleased chuckle. "It seems that is my gift to her, from Mother." Tenderly, Lirinda strokes a finger upon the babe's new skin, delighted at her own creation. "From His Majesty she has received pretty brown eyes. I'm tempted to wake her so you can see them."

I say nothing, only stare down at the little princess, who dozes against her mother's chest. Full, rosebud lips part peacefully, looking so much like Lirinda and the king already, with dark lashes and plump, rosy cheeks. Her soft little face twitches as if she dreams of milk.

"She's beautiful," I remark throatily before turning my gaze away.

"Would you care to hold her?"

"I shouldn't," I croak, and I don't understand why I cannot feel happier in this moment, why I feel so like crying, the marigold sun blinding my eyes. Why I am so internally distraught that I wish for nothing more than to be alone, to leave my sister to her happiness.

"She is too fragile," I blurt. "I—I wouldn't want to drop her."

Lirinda does not seem to care that I do not wish to take the child into my arms, as she seems perfectly content to keep the child close in her own. I do not think Lirinda has once looked up from the babe.

Seeing my sister cradle her own young in such a way reminds me of Mother's fondest memory, how she lovingly cradled Lirinda as a babe not unlike this. My eyes burn. Whether with happiness or woe or both at once, too heavy is the emotion to withstand.

"Has she a name?" I screw up my face so my voice is impassive but thick.

"Not yet. As she is a girl, the king has entrusted the task to me. But I cannot think of a name sweet enough. Can you?"

Another warm breeze wafts through Lirinda's chamber, and upon it, I sense magic indeed. I had thought, perhaps, it was merely the atmosphere of the moment—my sister's pain and sacrifice energizing the air itself, but it is more. What I sense is the child, like a waft of spring air defying the crisp undertones of autumn. *Magic.*

I think instantly of the flowers in Mother's wild garden, sweet as nectar, sweet as their honey. How I wish we could go back now—live as if we had never left, with Lirinda's babe for us to raise among snowdrops and crocuses as we had been. For us to laugh and play without restraint.

This little child, my niece, with her red hair and brown eyes, and quarter of magic blood, will know only cold castle walls, corsets, and courtly courtesies, and for that, I pity her. Never will she have the free splendor of a childhood that Lirinda and I had to run and play wildly, our only responsibility a harvesting basket filled with dandelion down. This child, with her grandmother's blood in her veins, how she will ache for trees and soil and not know truly why.

"Alilta," I say, recalling Tarian words I had read in Gillin's book, another phrase the Magics had pleaded, *'to be'* and *'free'*. The words another prayer against Gillin, the babe's own ancestor.

Lirinda smiles and strokes her child's skin again. "Alilta," she whispers fondly. "Princess Alilta. It's lovely. My little Alilta."

I force a smile.

Until the sea out the window dazzles with the emeralds and indigos of the darkening sky, and the servants come in to light the many candles and close the windows against the chill of a fallen moonless night, I remain by my sister and her child. Meekly I speak to Lirinda of spring rain and new flowers, of the freshness and pristine beginnings Alilta inspires me to think of, and how I agree with Lirinda, indeed, that the little Alilta is destined for glorious things, but I tell her not of the name's secret irony.

CHAPTER TWENTY SEVEN

The week after Alilta's birth, the princess is taken by her wetnurses up to her tower nursery for her cradle of gold and new, foreign breasts to suckle. And Lirinda—recovering still but returning swiftly, too swiftly, to her exuberant energies—is once again dancing and hosting parties out upon the balconies, in the Outer Court, and even the gardens. And I, with Lirinda's diminished demands of me, return to my dreams. Return to my search for that which calls to me.

Crow is more prevalent these late summer days, perched always within the trees of the gardens when I amble along the path with the ladies and Lirinda, as if a solemn reminder of what I have promised to pursue and that I ought not dawdle in it. Once, even, the bird finds herself a perch upon the open window of the ladies' tower room, her gleaming black eye an unsettling stare upon me as I comb out my long hair at the looking-glass. I gasp as my relaxed gaze finds her stare within the reflection, and when I spin to regard her with my own eyes, she has flown away.

It is a few nights later, after enduring a long day of perspiring in my tight corset out in the pavilion of the gardens, practicing a dance Lirinda has choreographed for the ladies and myself, that I lay in bed in my silk shift, eager for a cool retreat to the damp stone of my subconscious wanderings. We are to perform the dance tomorrow at the princess's royal reception, and the ladies around me all retire to their beds early. All is silent but for the rhythmic rushing of the sea out the open window, and I slip easily and powerfully into my dream.

Just as before, Crow flickers uncertainly in flight down the long stone passage, a spell of horror and interest as the red-haired woman glances almost amusedly at me over her shoulder. Then the woman is gone, but Crow is upon the torch sconce. The same sconce as all my other hundred dreams, I think.

With my dream-eye, I glance down the long corridor and see an infinite trail of fiery torches dancing into oblivion. *But this one*—I perceive for the first time with such a shiver that I feel the gooseflesh prickle upon my body where it lies upon my bed—*this one is not lit.*

Crow aggressively cleans her beak upon the iron bough of it, insistent at my discovery.

I reach out for the bough, and Crow takes flight. The dream becomes suddenly real, more real than before. The iron cold, scraping in my fingers. Am I not truly here?

I push sideways slightly, and the sconce clicks and turns like the opening of a lock. And once a door before me opens, I lose all perception of the dream. All I witness is a chasm of darkness, followed by a shine of light so brilliant that my dream eyes are blinded. The light pulls so intensely, so deeply within my bones and blood, that I gasp awake in bed.

Sunlight spills in a line across my counterpane where the curtain of my bed has parted slightly. The hour must be late:

never in my life have I slept so long that daylight has touched my bed whilst I've been in it.

I throw open the curtains and am stunned to see the ladies have gone and already their beds have been made. How did I not wake to them dressing? And of all days—this is the reception of the princess Alilta, and I am to partake in the revels.

But I am still panting where I sit. The dream—it echoes painfully in my bones. My teeth chatter with my fear and exhilaration; my arms are sprinkled with chills. Did I truly discover something? Or was the dream merely that: a dream, and I will be disappointed when next I wander down to the subterranean halls. I raise my hands before my face and see they tremble, and they are smeared with blood.

I scurry out of bed and my reflection captures my attention. The shocking white of my panicked face is smeared scarlet with fresh blood up my cheek. I must have strained my Current, for so long it's been that my nose has not bled, thanks be to my strengthening exercises. I plead within myself that I did nothing more to reveal myself as a Magic in my sleep.

I dress with fumbling hands into my dark green gown with sleeves that drape with my skirts to the floor. Being alone, I use my Current to hastily tie the fastenings of my corset and the back of my gown. Too hasty I am to comb out my wild curled hair or care to fasten in a headdress, so my thick mane hangs freely, albeit wildly, at my back and over my shoulders. Quickly, I rinse the blood from my face with the fresh water from the pitcher. My pale cheek is rubbed red as I look into my reflection, wondering what I will do, imploring my own black gaze for an answer as to whether I shall attend the party for my niece as is my courtly, and familial, obligation…or if I shall defy all and sneak immediately into the shadows. For I long to know if what I've dreamed is true.

What if I tried moving one of the torch sconces in the passage below, and a door of darkness before me opened?

Without even using my eyes to guide it, for so often do I reach for it now, I use my Current to slip Gillin's book from its hiding place and whisk it through the air to my outreached hand. I tuck it under my arm, for my heart throbs with a peculiar sense I may be needing it.

I still have not made up my mind as I saunter through the corridors and descend stairways, my gown and long sleeves flowing behind me with every step. Every measure of the castle is deserted, and strange it feels to have it so empty while filled with summer light. The high arched windows cast columns of brilliant light upon the stone floor, which is warm beneath my slippered feet. The sunny halls echo with my hurried footfalls.

With each window I pass, I have a view of the festivities outside. The lower I descend the stairs, the more I can hear the muffled shouts, applause, and laughter roaring from the gathering crowds outside. Games of swords and skill are beginning to be played in the lawns by the lower-ranked gentry, while the Honorables bid upon whether or not any of them may injure one another. Indeed, I had wanted to sit among the ladies and spectate.

I still can.

Some force within me desires to return to the ladies' tower and return Gillin's book, so I can go freely to join the festivities. The flowers ought to be full and fragrant at this hour, before the scorching late summer sun has dried them of their morning luster. There soon will be a luncheon with the courtiers out in the lawns where the servants have set up tables and hung flowing white curtains and banners in honor of the princess. There is a desire I feel, contrary to my urgency for the Source; a desire to stop chasing; a desire to be still.

A desire to accept this new life of courtly bliss as my own.

For today I could try to forget my silent rebellion and simply enjoy this life which has opened before me—and what a lovely, pleasurable life it is. Today I could be at peace with the Glindians, indulge my aching heart upon their wealth and splendor. I could smile and giggle as I drink sparkling wine and eat delicious ice-cold oysters and sea cakes at the luncheon. I could flirt as all the courtiers do, for sometimes I long to cast lingering sideward glances at the handsome gentlemen in their riding coats and gloves. I could sit on a bench in the Outer Court and coquettishly spin my parasol while gazing fiercely back at them, perhaps smile, perhaps allow myself to feel something for one of them and allow them to, perhaps, feel something for me. I could be a Pure, just as Lirinda wants me to be.

I pause in my tracks to consider the warm sun spilling onto my face through a tall, curvilinear-traced window. Among the rays of warmth embracing me is a tendril of coldness pulling at my chest, beckoning me on, downward, to my dark dreams.

What life will you choose, sister?

I already know the answer, even as I near the window glass and glare down upon everyone, like jubilant, colorful insects far beneath me. Lirinda, the queen of them. I catch a gleam of her crown where she does a silly jig near the ladies. The musicians who fiddle and flute furiously down in the Outer Court, how slowly and eerily their sound seems when it reaches me where I stand, echoing lonesomely through the halls, dulled by the window glass. All of them out there, the courtiers, the gentry—the Pures—are ridiculous the more I look upon them. Insignificant in the scheme of time, of history. Their very existence a display of frivolity. But everything I burn with in my veins as I cast my gaze down upon them, everything I desire, the horror of my flesh and history that haunt me, is the substantial truth that could crush them all.

My gown rustles as I follow on. Past the tall doors to the balconies, past the windows, past the daylight, past the white-eyed statues who watch me slink by to uncover their secrets. No one crosses my path as I descend stairwell after stairwell, following rib-vaulted corridor after echoing corridor; the sweeping of my gown eerily loud in the darkness now lit necessarily by ornate sconces bearing torches.

I descend the final stairwell to the long stretch of corridor that leads seemingly nowhere. The air here—it is thick, cold, and so far from the merriment of my sister. Here, no one comes. I feel the ancient heartbeat of stone reverberating through my bones. I can visualize a phantom of the red-haired woman walking into the distance here, giving me an almost disdainful smirk; Crow's feathers belong here, flapping as she soars ahead down the passage and landing upon a sconce, but she is not here. I am alone, in an echo of my dreams, and the weight of the Source's cold gravity aches my teeth.

I walk along, my hand grazing the moist stone, just like I have many times without being here, physically. The grooves upon the cold wall are familiar like a friend to my fingertips. I look up to the torches, all lit. Every one. I despair momentarily for the loss of my dream-discovery, until my hand passes over a groove of stone that I remember. The torch near to me burns with a flame like all other torches, but this one—this is the one Crow had perched on, I know it!

My fingers at my side wriggle with my Current; I glance furtively in all directions around me for any presences, but there is nowhere for anyone to spy, to witness what I am about to do.

I stare at the burning torch and, with my Current, raise its burning mass of fat-soaked reeds from its holder and hover it, a burning fireball, before me. Then, tentatively but breathing in deeply through my nose, I reach a hand to the sconce arm and feel its rough iron bough in my grip, and before I can reconsider, push it forcefully aside just like in my dream—and it turns. Something within the stone wall before me clicks, and I step backward with a quivering intake of breath.

My hand goes to my mouth.

So it is true. My dreams. Everything...

Trembling, breathing shuddering breaths, I scan anxiously around me once more as my hands grope the stone wall. The groove within the stone, the one my fingers always catch upon in my dreams, I give it a strong push and a door from the wall of stone groans inward.

Darkness breathes beyond—cold, musty darkness. The flaming ball I hoist beside me, and the torches all around, flicker into a wild dance as a cold gust of underground breeze wafts in. The wet mineral air reminds me of Ama's cave, deep within the earth. I stand before the black chasm, shivering that indeed my dream was true. All I have suspected can no longer be denied.

I have been led here.

I swallow hard as I face the chasm ahead of me and wonder if I should turn back now while I have the chance. For if I go ahead, I do not know what I will find, but I do know it will change everything; everything about life as I know it; everything about me. I have a chance, still, to run up the stairs and dance with Lirinda in the sun.

The blackness before me swirls. What if I lose myself in the dark? What if I become trapped within? What if I am caught?

No, I reason furiously. This is for me to follow; I have been led here.

I remember Ama's words, *You have followed this far, yet this is where your journey ends?*

I hoist the fireball ahead of me to illuminate my steps in the darkness as I walk in. With my Current, I heave the door closed behind me, and hear the torch sconce click back into place.

Have I sealed myself forever within, to die with my dreams? I shiver a terrified breath. Could this be a trap? A trap set by the Glindians to lure a Magic—a possible descendant of King Rinma—to their demise? I close my eyes briefly and swallow down the terror that seizes the sinews of my throat. *Would Crow guide me to my doom?* I ask myself. *I do not think so, not after she has saved me...*

Crow. The constant bird of my youth. How is it possible she's led me here through my dreams? I wonder, but cannot linger in thought too long. Not here.

At first, I see naught but the orange arc of firelight burning from my ball of flame. Once I blink my eyes, squinting in the dark, I make out a close tunnel around me with steps descending at my feet. A stairwell of rough, rounded ancient stone. A rat scurries in the shadow; I see its long naked tail whip out of sight as I descend carefully down.

Maneuvering the ball of flame before me, its arc of light touches the wall at my side. It appears lumpy and rough at first, but then I recognize that what I see are human bones. A skull's face mortared with the stones of the wall brings me to gasp and nearly lose my footing upon the stairs. Ten skulls, a hundred skulls; bones of the dead panel the walls in a way that might be beautiful if it was not so macabre. The dusty odor I've breathed and tasted, like dull salt on my tongue, I now understand and wish to spit upon the ground but restrain myself for whatever my respect is worth here.

I wonder whose skulls these are in this catacomb. They

could not be my kin, the ancient Tarians, could they? For they were all burned in the Burning of the Blood fires, and I think the Glindians would have proper tombs. Regardless of to whom they belong, I cannot fix my gaze upon them too long. Their broken smiles and gaping voids of eyes are, I think, filled with rats, and I sense I am being watched. Uneasily, I quicken my pace down the poorly illuminated stairs before me, leading me into impenetrable blackness.

The darkness squeezes me. Asphyxiating is the pressure of the earth and the magic I feel I'm so near to. It closes around my chest as though I am drowning in cold water.

When my arc of light illuminates an unlit torch mounted upon the wall, I hover the ball of flame to it and nearly laugh with relief when I see it catches fire; the flame spreading down a trench of oil to light a downward spiraling passage beyond, lighting innumerable torches into the distance. Suddenly, everything comes into full, fiery illumination: skulls and neatly arranged bones for as far as I can see, twisting with the stairs out of my view, with only columns to separate segments of wall that meet at a barrel vault.

For an unsettlingly long distance, I descend the spiraling catacomb with my fading fireball hovering before me, until at last, the repetitive walls of bone cease, and beyond a final pair of columns lies a vast, open space.

Columns grander than any towering oak tree surround the great open space—columns that are smooth and elegant, unlike the complex and ornate sculpting of the Glindians. I know instantly these structures are more ancient than anything found within Gillin's castle. Older than old this place is—there is no comparison within time, for it is of another world entirely. The arched columns unlike any architecture I've seen before, apart from what illustrations I've seen of Rinma's citadel.

I pause in my stride, for so surreal this reality has become that I cannot tell whether I am back in my dreams. But it cannot be so, for my every measure of flesh is invigorated by the wet, deathly air. I have never felt so aware, more awake in my life.

I look up to where the ceiling might be and see only a darkness the firelight cannot reach—the darkness of enclosed earth. Beyond and above the open columns is Gillin's constructed world, a casket of mountain rock; I wonder if this vast platform lined with beautiful columns had once been open to the sky.

With trembling fingers, I fish Gillin's book from beneath my arm and flip to the page with the illustration of Gillin's castle having been built atop the crumbling ruin of Rinma's citadel—how the two had been crafted into one, joined seamlessly by a single passage.

I trace my finger over the ancient ink and feel a great chill slither through my innards as I locate the space in which I presently stand. *I am there.* After so many months of searching for this place, I have found it.

I hold the open book to my chest as I gape around, breathing heavily with rapture and fear. My throat is so filled with the tension of my excitement and terror, I cannot swallow. It feels as though my heart has risen into it, choking me. And my Current—never has it felt so energized in all my years of its power.

Delicately, slowly, so as not to miss a single detail in my progress, I cross the open space, between cracked, ancient columns and down the continuing passage, wide and smooth, illuminated still by the burning trench of oil and its excitedly blazing torches, offering little heat here in this frigid place. The expanse of mountain surrounding me, unseen, I can sense around me like a vast open cave, breathing with cold and the air of minerals. If I had known that in my quest I would be venturing so deep into the earth, into Rinma's ancient world, I would have dressed warmly in furs.

A tingle in the air here makes me feel even more awake and inspired than before. The dense sensation of magic makes me feel as if I am coming home, albeit to a home I have always ached for but never known. All that has beckoned to me all my life through the very earth of the capital flows through the air here like an unseen river of power. If I was weightless enough, I might float atop it.

At last, the passage I follow ends at the foot of a great and otherworldly stone edifice, like the highest turret of an ornate palace—and towering above where I stand is a pair of magnificent arched oaken doors, so tall and looming that I must raise my chin to behold them. *The* doors, for I can feel so strongly here that the cold, brilliant presence of my dreams and waking years of yearning, lies beyond the ancient carved oak.

Torches here illuminate statues receded against the walls at either side of the doors. Glindian statues nearly as tall as the surrounding columns, staring down at me with their sightless eyes, cast in shadow beneath their strong brows. Gillin must have built them here after his conquest. I feel a sense of knowing from them, these great statues, as if they know what—*who*—I am. A flush of pride burns within me, that I have come so far to arrive here, despite history and its violent centuries keeping me away. I have defied the Glindians, and now it is only this wood which separates me from my great mystery and purpose in this world.

My hands flex nervously before I wrap them upon the heavy iron handles and pull.

CHAPTER TWENTY EIGHT

In all my dreams of all my years, a white light has reached for me. I have known it to have a sentient presence, to feel as though it has whispered far beyond the auricle of my ear, into the deep untouched caverns of my heart. Its wisps like a hundred hands, reaching deep within me for crevices unexplored. No dream, vivid as they've been, has prepared me for the bone-crushing gravity I feel as I come upon the source of my every mystery, bright as a white sun—a *star*—blinding me with the purest luminescence upon the earth.

Light is all I can see, at first, as the doors part and a sliver of eye-burning brightness grows in the space. My smarting eyes drip tears down my face, but I will not look away. Not as my vision begins to adjust to the brilliance…and like a ball of sun do I see the form of the Source in the center of the light, at last. A beautiful sphere of glass no larger than a small serving plate, fitted within a stone pedestal.

My eyes, they leak all the more now with my emotion. For so simple, so delicate is this ball of light, yet I know at once it is the source of every beckoning I have ever felt, reaching for me from the walls of the castle through the lonely breezes of Haven. My face, as I strain still to look upon it, contorts desperately with pain and awe.

I've found it.

My Current releases the fading fireball, and it falls to the floor. I step on it in my passing and crush the remaining smoking embers to ash as I cross the space of the chamber to the light. I look not away, not even at what surrounds me, simply drinking in the image of this ball of light, its validity— trying to understand that, indeed, my being here is real, though I still do not understand how. I do not breathe as I go to stand before it, for the radiation of its power is almost too much to withstand. Such blazing pain I have never before felt; my Current pulsates on the very cusp of my flesh. My breath, when I suck it in again, is staggering and painful.

I hear the strikes of blood upon the stone ground before I notice my nose drips. But I will not wipe at it, for nothing so inconsequential matters anymore. So powerful is the lure to the sphere that I am overcome with a sudden desperation to escape my body and join with the glow, exist with it. As though I am only a sliver of a completeness, and some unseen force within the sphere is desperate to combine me with my remainder; everything I have ever lacked, this beautiful sphere possesses, and everything this sphere needs, resides within me.

Agonizing is my desire to put my fingers upon the round, smooth glass. How I long to touch it, to release my overwhelming Current, buzzing so strongly that it burns me, almost to the point of yelling out in torture. I can feel now how powerful my Current truly is, and I know my body has not the capacity to contain its entirety, how it presses upon the very confines of my flesh, threatening to spill from out my seams. I know I would feel serene relief if only I put my hands upon the sphere.

I wonder, would it be cool or warm upon my fingertips…

Hardly aware I am of my hand as it reaches for the ball of light, serene and pretty like an immaculate moon. Mesmerized, I watch how tendrils of white smoke dance off the surface and encircle my suspended fingers, as if the very essence of the sphere reaches for me, too.

I feel their cold, cloudlike essence, these tendrils. I have known them for years, but now—now we have no dreamspace to distance us. They dance around my fingers like that of a friend. The tendrils want so much for me. For me to know the mightiness of which I am capable. They understand me, they know my secrets. They know I am lost in loneliness—but that I would be no longer, not if I lowered my hand and pressed my skin upon the glass.

The tendrils know my anger, that my heart has begun to blacken as perhaps it was always meant to, being born what I was. They know I am jealous, so very jealous, and impatient for a destiny of my own. The tendrils want for me to release them from their captivity. And I—I, too, want release…

"I would not touch that."

The sudden deep voice from behind me makes me freeze up in fright. I gasp, removed from my trance, and at once, the smoky white tendrils recede back into the sphere. With jagged, frightened breaths, I slowly pull my hand away into my long draping sleeve. My heart pounds furiously as I turn around to face the king.

I know my face is blanched with fright, with a fresh stream of blood over my lips. With a few blinks and an intake of breath, I draw myself to my full height and wipe at my nose with my long sleeve so that I am wiped clean—not a trace of my guilt left upon my skin.

"How did you get in here?" the king demands, his eyes

fixed intensely upon me, jaw clenched and a vein visible in his forehead.

I swallow hard, tasting blood. Truly, I do not know how to begin to explain myself to the king, the very man to whom this all belongs. I know I have been reckless, coming here with only the whim of a dream and preparing no plan or story to explain myself should I be caught. Lirinda's sweet influence over the king is likely not enough to save me from this, if even she is willing. More than any urge, any desire of the lucidly glowing sphere I feel tearing at my bodily seams, do I wish I had the power to disappear from this moment—to wake again in my bed.

"Your Majesty, I—" My throat goes dry. I strain to swallow again.

For the first time since entering beyond the great oaken doors, I am sobered enough to see that I am surrounded by a round, high-domed chamber. Massive statues of horned and winged figures encircle the space, terrifyingly great and menacing in the shadows; the white light of the sphere a glint upon the black stones of their eyes. And most impressive of all the sculptures, set back against the curve of wall opposite the great doors, lies a magnificent raised seat of polished stone—a throne chair.

This is not a place anyone would want to be discovered by the king, least of all people, me.

My anxious gaze roves over the elegant architecture of the chamber: how the tall rounded walls meet in a dome ceiling. With my Current, I believe I can bring the ceiling of this place to collapse, and if I am quick and slippery, I can attempt an escape—but it is a foolhardy plan. Not only would I likely be crushed in the destruction, if I survived, I would be guilty of murdering the king. Worse even, I would never be able to return to this place.

I must be clever, for the best way of saving myself is to somehow appeal to His Majesty. I must play at my innocence. I must lie. And I must say something soon, for the longer I hesitate, the more visibly his anger clenches in his jaw.

"You best explain yourself, Mistress!" he snarls, the deep voice stirring the chords of my panic.

"I..." I breathe again, blinking up at him as I calculate what I must say, but only a shred of truth arrives foolishly at my lips. "I have read of this place, Your Majesty." The words slip from me in a breath I cannot retrieve. I bite my lip as if to keep myself from saying more, but it is futile. I have incriminated myself with Gillin's book.

"You lie," growls the king. "That is impossible. None but I and The Ordained know of this chamber."

I suck in a breath of confidence, my gaze burning with sudden ferocity.

"It *is* possible," I contest. Reluctantly, cursing myself inwardly, I slip Gillin's book from its place at my side and reveal it to him. His anger diminishes at once and is replaced with confusion.

"What is this?" He takes the book, my precious book, into his hands, feeling the cover with his fingertips, turning it over. Recognition arrives at his eyes when he sees the ink scrawling upon the first weathered pages. Amazement brings light to his eyes. His gaze finds mine.

"This is Gillin's," states he in awe. "Where did you come by this?"

I breathe in slowly through my nose to keep myself calm, raising my chin with dignity.

"I found it," I say simply.

"*Where?*" he demands with a growl, coppery eyes alight with furious impatience. Though my body nearly jumps at his voice, I strenuously still myself to appear as resolute as the beastly statues behind us. With all the might to save my life, I carve my expression into one of self-assured innocence. My voice, as I speak, is that of a courtier.

"An old woman had it in her possession. I relieved her of it."

He squints at the pages with fascination and fury. "I will have this book examined," says he with a determined growl. "And I would have this old woman of yours investigated for having it in her possession."

I feel a wild urge to smirk at the thought of Ama being investigated. I do not easily imagine the Guard in their clanking metal suits descending her sea-frothed cliffs and locating her impossible cave entrance. Try as they might to search for her, they would never find her—for even if they did, somehow, discover her cave, she would not be there to be caught; she would have disappeared beyond her wall of ivy vines. In all her Sight, she would have foreseen it coming.

"I would think that wise, Your Majesty," I say agreeably.

"Why had you not turned this book in when surely it ought not be in your possession?"

My gaze drops to the book, open before me but in another's hands, and I cannot help but mourn for it. Knowing now that it's in the king's possession, I will never take it into my own again.

"It has…fascinated me." I soften with my longing for the book in his hands. "You see? There are illustrations, Your Majesty." Carefully, I extend my fingers to the book he holds and flip easily to the page I have turned to so many times, the diagram of Gillin's castle built upon the citadel. "Most beautiful drawings of the bowels of the castle."

He glares at me with mistrust before returning his attention to the book in his hand, his long fingers, bedecked in onyx and gold signet rings, delicately turning the ancient pages as I have done every day. I feel a strange, slippery feeling in my belly that the very person I've dared not discover this book of mine is the one who tenderly touches the pages, *my pages*—and yet, they, too, are rightfully his. It is forbidden and intimate at once, and a part of me feels relieved that I have shared my secret book with someone who cares for it as I do. Although this someone is my most dire enemy.

"As informative as these illustrations seem to be," says he as he turns another page. "I see no indication of how you managed to find your way *in*." Suspicion hardens his voice, making my heart thunder with renewed fear. I raise my eyes from the page up to him. He cocks his head at me and raises his thick brows, awaiting my excuse.

"That is the mystery of it, Your Majesty," I say, summoning my sweetest innocence into my wide eyes as I attempt now to lie as any courtier, never betraying their true emotions beneath a cool mask. "I had been fixing my slipper onto my heel and merely rested my hand upon the sconce for balance. In the next moment, a mechanism within the door somehow unlocked. Accidental though it was, once the door opened, I could not turn away. Too curious I was not to follow."

"And why would you follow?" asks he, still riddled with his impatience for me. "The catacombs, the darkness. Surely any woman would find such a descent frightening."

"My sister your queen perhaps would," I cannot help but say with a cruel smirk. "But I? I had to see where it would lead me."

His eyes become slits as he glares at me, his suspicion still as ripe as before. "How unusual you are, Mistress Sirilda, that you have managed to slip here so easily, so conveniently, when all others are attending the luncheon. Why have you decided to wander the frigid underground of the castle, chasing illustrations in an ancient book, when you could be partaking in the revels outside?"

I stifle a smirk, but still it twitches at my lips.

"But I already told you, Your Majesty. I have been fascinated," I say with as much innocence as I can, for I am innocent; there is no lie in my fascination. "Discovering this chamber has been my one true purpose all these months I've been here. I've devoted hours to it, losing myself within your halls, hoping to find myself here."

His examining gaze narrows still upon me. "Tell me, why does the sister of the queen have such fascination for the ancient secrets within my castle?"

"I've been desperate to see if it all was true." I glance over my shoulder longingly at the glowing sphere behind me, letting the king see my innocent wonder. I feel his severe gaze surveying me closely, inspecting the line of my clavicle and the quickened breath of my smooth, pale throat, as if for treachery, but finding only my passionate innocence. "To know if it was real..."

I walk to it. I can resist it no longer; the glowing sphere before me fills me again with its insistent energy. The fingers of my hands fidget with the overwhelming surge of my power, so close to release but stoppered and still ready to burst; they pinch at the folds of my skirts to ease their disquiet.

"This is it, isn't it?" I whisper, more to myself than the king. I know the white glow of the sphere pales my already ashen features. "This is how Gillin destroyed the Shade King."

Gastlin closes the book and tucks it at his side, sobered now of his anger but not of his suspicion. Another emotion furrows his brows—interest.

"You know what this artifact is then, do you?"

"Of course," I breathe. "It is the *Il-lar*."

The king is startled by my answer, but his suspicion softens.

"The *Il-lar* has become legend to Glindor." When he speaks now, his voice is not a boom of rising anger but gravelly and level, his true speaking voice that is not proud nor showy. I've not yet heard him speak this way. "A legend no one speaks of. Not even those closest to me in my court. No one, other than I and The Ordained, and our fathers before us, knows it exists still. And now, there is you."

Neither of us speak. By the relaxed features of the king, I do not sense that I am endangered still. I allow myself to gaze at the *Il-lar*, thinking of Rinma's spirit within. Aware partially of how the king watches me, my fascination.

"Who *are* you?" he asks, and the abruptness of it makes me look up at him.

"Sirilda," I answer simply.

"No, you are much more than that." He shakes his head, growing agitated again. "You are—" He breaks off, uncertain of what to say, irritated at his own confoundedness. "Why do you haunt me so?"

I stare at him, taken aback by his sudden honesty, his vulnerability. Neither of us look away for a long moment. Indeed, I've felt haunted by him, too, in a way I've not been able to comprehend. He's been familiar to me, almost as though I've dreamed of him before, known him in another lifetime. Somehow, just by our unspoken moments in passing through morning shadows, I feel I could know him better than Lirinda does, but how could that be?

"I don't know," I admit in almost a whisper.

"From the day I first saw you, you have looked at me as

though I am not your king." As he says this, what fear of mine that has receded rises again with the thundering of my heart, thinking he will condemn me for magic after all.

"What's more outrageous is that I've allowed it," he continues, and by his anguish within himself, I know I am safe still, so long as I continue to act as I have.

He goes on, "And not because you are the sister of my wife, but because you seem to see within me the very fissures in my sovereignty I've been so keen to hide. Curtsy to me all you wish, call me Majesty, but I know it is reluctant! You have haunted me so, and it's made me eager to convince you that I *am* your king."

I am overcome by a rush of tingles through me. Gastlin may never be my true king, but I have certainly come to accept him as Glindor's king, my temporary king, and for that I do think his effort has been successful.

"When I think you cannot haunt my thoughts more, you are everywhere I turn when I think no one else will be there. Always I find you, lurking in the same places I go for peace. And now I find you here! Not often do I visit the *Il-lar*, but today, I've come here in need of reflection, to ponder my kingdom, my sovereignty, my inheritance of this world...and my heirs who will follow. Yet I find you already here! Why is it you're everywhere I turn? Why is it I cannot escape you?"

I do not know what to say, but I know at this moment, it is best I say nothing and look resiliently back at him, though still demure and soft as seems to appeal to him. I do not wish to appear too intimidating, else he might suspect me again. With just the right amount of delicacy, with my mask of innocence, I might be like a rose to him, beautiful and soft and able to be possessed. Men, from what I have observed, enjoy a small challenge of defiance, a slice of pain, of sport—a contrasting bite of thorns which make the soft petals all the more lovely to behold…a trait Lirinda possesses not. I try portraying these things to him in my face and posture and watch as he surrenders even more to me.

"I ought to be angry," says he with cruel humor—an empty laugh. "But for some inexplicable reason I'm—" He breaks off, shaking his head with outrage at himself, going to stand before a lofty statue of a winged woman. He studies the statue a moment, considering his own thoughts before turning to face me again. Then, once his eyes take in the image of me, aglow and perfectly innocent in the white light, he scoffs another laugh, which turns to slow, deep little chuckles that echo thunderously through the domed chamber. Thrilling is the sound, making both my fear and desire whirl, my Current flare, the *Il-lar* sing within me.

"Damn it all to the gods, I do try not to be so easily amused," says Gastlin darkly, a grave humor upon his handsome face. "But amusing this is." He leers at me with playful suspicion. "My wife's little sister, sneaking around the castle, in the hope of finding the *Il-lar*, of all things."

I remain silent, my expression unwavering, as the king considers the harmlessness of my intrusion.

"I don't know why this chamber ought to be forbidden at all. Why so secretive this entrance has remained," he muses. "It's not as though the *Il-lar* can be stolen."

Unable to resist any longer, now that the king has relented, I return my attention to the brilliant moon before me. Slowly, I hold my long blood-smeared fingers above the sphere again, watching the smoky white tendrils leap from the glassy surface of the *Il-lar* and entwine insistently around me.

Gastlin watches with pride how mesmerized I am with his object and continues, "You know why, don't you?"

"Because," I begin, my voice throaty with my longing for

the *Il-lar* as I toy with its moving tendrils between my fingers, like that of a living creature—a serene playfulness upon my face, a slight smile. "Anyone but a descendant of Gillin to lay hand to the *Il-lar* would die."

Gastlin pauses in affirmation. "It ought not be a secret to anyone, especially those passionate about the conquest of my ancestor, of the power that has crafted this realm. Besides, there are only two living who can wield it. Myself, and—"

"Alilta," I finish for him, looking up at him at once.

I've thought of it before, but not until now—seeing the *Il-lar* for myself, knowing it truly exists—has the revelation struck me that my own flesh, my own kin, the babe who so resembles Mother, could wield the *Il-lar*. Any child sired by Gastlin could. But could Alilta, a mere quarter-magic, free Rinma of his prison? That, I wish I could know.

But if even she could not release him, if perhaps no one could, with Alilta's hold upon the *Il-lar,* other changes could be made. She could unearth the old citadel and bring magic back to its rightful realm. How many of us would no longer have to hide. What retribution there could be for us all.

"I heard once," I begin carefully, hoping my steady innocence will coax any answers Gastlin might have to seep out. "That King Rinma had made it so he could be restored. That someone of his own kin could free him from the *Il-lar.*"

"Where did you hear that?" asks Gastlin, suddenly severe.

Quickly, I think of another lie. With a timid shrug of my shoulder, I say, "Country folk have many stories they tell, gathered around their tankards."

"Well"—Gastlin raises a brow with amusement—"you should know tavern talk is not to be relied upon. However, there is some truth to what you heard. Few know the secrets of the Shade King's defeat, but I suppose, if rumors have been passed around the realm, I ought to oblige you with what The Ordained have told me, so it might ease your concern.

"There is record of the Shade King having announced that one of his own kin could free him of the *Il-lar*. That was in his final moment, before his body disappeared, so no other evidence could be gathered. But you need not fear, for it is impossible."

His body disappeared? I think with a sparkle of astonishment. Always I have imagined that Rinma had left behind a body when his power was drained, to be burned or buried. But if there was no body, how can anyone say they ever truly conquered Rinma?

"The Shade King had no kin," Gastlin continues. "We know this from records of his centuries-long reign. He thought himself too divine—his immortality too great to deny—to ever pass on his blood. He thought it would only shame him to procreate, for to procreate was to invest in a legacy an immortal did not need.

"He'd claimed he was too far above the carnal pleasures of flesh to even touch a lesser creature in lust. So it has been deemed only a lie that he could have ever been restored; that his proclamation to change the enchantment on the *Il-lar* was only for Gillin to relent out of fear for his threat. As you can plainly see now, the lie did not hold over my ancestor, and the Shade King still was drained of his power. And his power has remained within the *Il-lar* since."

The king steps nearer to the *Il-lar*, opposite me. I pull my hands delicately away from the sphere, and for a while, he and I both gaze in silence down upon it, our every detail thrown into utter whiteness. His every metallic lacing of his doublet, the garnet necklace hanging at his chest, the rings upon his fingers, and the very irises of his dark eyes illuminate with stars.

Then, to my most shocking delight, Gastlin extends his free hand to the glowing ball and grabs it out of its basin within the pedestal, as light as a glass sphere of air. My eyes, I know, widen at him with rapt amazement. So similarly he resembles the book's illustration of Gillin brandishing the *Il-lar*.

"But...say there was a way," muses Gastlin in his most severe voice yet, inspecting the glowing ball at rest upon his fingers. "Say the Shade King had indeed a secret heir, and that creature was some unearthly scum like the *Devil Mellick*," he spits with hatred, making me take in a shudder of breath at the blatancy of the name of who may be my father. "I would like to see a demon-blood wriggle his way into this room."

The thought amuses Gastlin's handsome face into a smile, and fleetingly, a smile flickers on my lips, too, at the humorous, empowering thought that I may well be the bearer of the Devil Mellick's blood and have indeed wriggled my way here. That I, the probable product of the Magic who killed the king's own father and the father of his queen, have splayed my hands above his one weapon.

"And even *then*," Gastlin continues, turning the *Il-lar* thoughtfully in his grasp, "this figurative descendant of the Shade King would die as soon as he laid his filthy claws upon it, as he would need to carry the Glindian lineage. Laughable it is to imagine such an impossibility coming to pass: a filthy Magic weaving bloodlines with mine."

I stare at him. Hatred mingled with amusement at his stupidity. How lowly he speaks of magic when he has so easily slipped himself within it and ejaculated his progeny.

"Laughable," I echo, trying to suppress the wicked smirk that dares to beam across my face.

Gastlin, you wonderful fool! You are the laughable one. I keep my coolly composed innocence. *You dressed your doom in jewels and guided her into your private chambers! Your golden-haired, sparkle-eyed doom. And you let her birth you a Glindian Magic. Whether Alilta can restore Rinma or not, she still can wield the Il-lar. And if I have anything to do with it, she will know her true allegiance lies far below, where the true castle and the true king are to reign.*

All of your children will.

As he places the *Il-lar* back within the pedestal, I cannot remove my eyes from the sphere, for I notice that no white-smoke tendrils encircle Gastlin's fingers as they do mine.

I force my hands to clasp before me, to restrain myself against reaching out for the *Il-lar* again.

No, I cannot touch the Il-lar…*but he* can.

With a flicker of my pained, aroused gaze up at the king, I realize profoundly that my purpose never has been to eradicate him but to utilize him. Him and his descendants, the ones I can influence to use the *Il-lar* myself.

How clearly now I see, as though the veil of my dreams has been lifted. With the thrilled throbbing of my Current does my energized sense of purpose and pride pulse through my very heart and veins.

Standing opposite Gastlin, with the *Il-lar* between us, I feel the usual gravity to him I've not been able to understand. A riddle of attraction—of chemistry I know we both feel. So alike we are and yet opposites. I am drawn to him, I feel I know him, understand him, see him, and by the way he has glanced at me and been haunted by me, I know he feels similarly. I realize now that we are of the same position; he is king of the new castle, and I am queen of the old and true. We mirror one another. Powerful, matched in many ways. We are different but meet here, at this center, at the *Il-lar.*

I had thought it was Lirinda who was my counterpart, my mirror image, but it has been the king all along. Lirinda has only been an instrument in delivering me here. Her maneuvering into the king's bed has been my steppingstone to my home, my destiny.

I offer the king a half of an alluring smile.

Slowly, his light-filled eyes raise from the white lumen ball to mine. Something has yielded in his expression that had not before. Perhaps there is a trust he now feels for me after having divulged to me such forbidden things. History and secrets, which I doubt he has ever uttered to Lirinda, or anyone other than his 'Ordained'. Certainly, Lirinda has never been here to witness her husband take into his hand an ancient sphere possessing the spirit energy of the King of Stars. Surely, she has never so much as learned of the *Il-lar*.

Perhaps Gastlin feels the same slippery way I feel about having shared Gillin's book with another who appreciates it. How it is not so lonely a life when one shares with another, even when that person is last to be expected.

All suspicion he's held for me has melted away; I see it in his softened gaze, his mouth. And why wouldn't it? I am, after all, only the curious little sister of his wife. The feral, untrained girl from the forest. What threat could I possibly pose? He smiles back, unrestrained for the first time since we met; warmth in his starlit eyes and a dimple upon his cheek; a smile I am certain only few in his regal show of a life have witnessed.

I feel a sudden, dark bloom of desire deep within me. With it, I wonder so startlingly that I nearly gasp, how powerful the two of us could be together.

The thought brings my throat to dry again. I cannot swallow.

"Have you seen enough for today, Mistress?" the king asks of me with dark and playful amusement. "I think I have contemplated what I've needed to. Why don't we ascend back upstairs now and fulfill ourselves with lighter matters. Surely the court is wondering where we are."

I force a dry swallow and nod.

"A prudent suggestion, Your Majesty," say I, unable now to view the king with the fear and dislike I once had.

CHAPTER TWENTY NINE

I walk alongside the king of Glindor up through the fiery-lit catacombs, feeling strangely empty and changed within. I have lost Gillin's book to its true owner; I discovered the *Il-lar* at the cost of being caught, perhaps never to return again. I should be whirling with despair and anger, and yet…I am strangely content, walking beside he who feels to me like a new and unlikely companion. I feel assured that, so long as I maintain a kindness with the king, I may have all I could ever desire at my disposal.

As I ascend away from the *Il-lar*, I still feel its beckoning upon me like a lover's hand, but it is not so insistent as it was before. Instead, it remains patient and stable, deep within my blood and bones.

The *Il-lar*, how it now seems to reside, *live*, within me, even when I am away from it.

I gaze around at my surroundings with longing before they are gone from my view, even the frightening faces of the skulls, flickering red with the firelight. The king glances curiously at me as I take in the details, and I realize he may never have seen anyone take interest in something other than the gold and glamours of his court. We speak not to one another until we are back in the corridors of life and daylight, of sound and air.

"I will not speak of your trespassing to anyone," says Gastlin lowly as we amble together through the deserted halls.

"Thank you," I mutter quietly. Our hushed voices are so much more unfamiliar here now than in the ancient depths of Rinma's throne room. Here, the sound of our conversation echoing between historic tapestries reminds me this is not merely fantasy. Today, together, we have stood beside the *Il-lar*. Stranger than a dream it is now, that the king of Glindor and I walk side-by-side through the halls I've so long wandered alone.

"If Krom ever learned of it, he would be keen to have you arrested—or worse." Gastlin sharply looks down at me. "If I were you, I would not speak of it either."

My eyes widen up at him, reminded that Gastlin is not the one who I've most to fear here. "But you are the king."

"I am. But there is power Eliador possesses of his own," he warns.

When we exit the castle through the immense glass doors to the deserted balcony, I go to stand at the railing, resting my hands upon the warmed stone. The king, glistening in plum and gold brocade in the full sun, raises a brow at my deviation from our journey.

"I think I'll wait here a moment…if it pleases Your Majesty," I say softly to him.

He hesitates briefly before descending one of the mirrored staircases from the balcony to the Outer Court, and at once, all who stand in his imminence part for him and bow lowly. As always, announcements are proclaimed at his arrival, *"His Majesty the King!"* After only a few of his majestic strides is he then approached by the black swarm that is his High Council, who steals him away in severe conversation. I am glad to have avoided such a trap.

Perhaps I should feel fearful still, of all that remains threatening to me, but in this moment I do not. For standing in the bright sun, after having embraced the tendrils of the *Il-lar* itself, I feel beautifully invulnerable and accomplished. I look out at all that lies before me, wreathed in flowing banners and curtains, with thousands of summer flowers harvested and strewn among the decorations. Nothing about this surface world seems so treacherous to me anymore. There is only a frivolity I now feel quite like enjoying—*celebrating*.

With purpose in my unhurried stride, I slink down the smooth stone stairs to the Outer Court, then slither through the crowd of liveried and aproned servants carrying away the half-eaten platters from the luncheon. As a servant passes me by with a plate of pear tarts, I delicately grab one off the plate and bite of it. I nibble contentedly as I walk on across the sunbaked lawns, between groups of Honorables and gentry, all dressed in their richest dyed fabrics, plumed hats, and ornate, towering headdresses of horns and gauzy silks. Laughter, chatter, and music resounding at every angle.

Such a contrast is this fine day to the stone depths where I've just been. I cannot help but carry a slight smile upon my lips at my utter satisfaction with it all. Across the mountain, the late summer sun contrasts with elongating shadows and the crisp looming of autumn. The season of change, of death, I can taste like a new spice upon the air, upon the light breeze that flutters my loose-hanging curls.

So much is different, I think as I glance toward Alilta's curtained pavilion, filled irksomely with flaxen-headed Fairfellows. *And so much is still to change...*

Down the winding garden path I walk, out into the spiraling dances where the gentlemen have taken the ladies as partners upon the pavilion. Upbeat music rings between flowers and willow boughs by the heartily playing band of musicians. It does not matter that I am unadorned without my headdress when I slip between courtiers, already drunk on their summer wine, for a prancing Miella comes up to me and places a coronet of fresh dahlias upon my head. In the sun, the painted and embroidered silks of gowns and capes flash around me like a living mosaic. I join in their action as though I have been a part of it all along.

It is easier to slip into my charade as a Pure when I feel my purpose has been realized. I step in graceful poses through practiced dances, feeling my skirt spin around me like a bell, brushing my ankles. Finally, at last, I can close my eyes and enjoy the feeling of the sweet garden air, knowing now that the *Il-lar* has been found, and that it awaits me still. Knowing that I am where I belong.

I look over to Haven, opposite where I stand. A watchful presence just as the castle had been to me not so long ago, but now feels like a lifetime. How is it I am now here, so changed, dancing in the Glindian gardens with my sister the queen, while the magic flora grows wild over Mother's bones? I wonder, with the small pang of grief for her that remains now, if any of her own faunal friends have nibbled her bones clean, and if the moss of the cottage has grown to cover her as a gentle grave—if still, even in her death, flowers bloom from her. How disturbing, yet pleasing, a feeling it is to look upon the place of her bones now as Lirinda and I dance at the very place she pleaded for us never to go. With me knowing, now, so many of the things she vowed for me never to discover, yet with so much still to understand.

Did she know about Crow, her closest animal companion?

How the bird would guide me here?

How I wish I could ask her.

Amid the motions of my dance, I glance around at the boughs of the trees, but I do not see Crow perched among them. I hope that the bird will return. Will I dream of her again? Will I ever understand how she stole into my subconscious?

Now that I have followed where she has led me, will she fly away as she ought to have long ago? Or, in the reflection of her dark eye, have I still much to accomplish?

Looking still for a sign of Crow, my eyes pass over Lirinda. She dances in a shining gown of deep violet silk that sets her golden hair ablaze. How beautiful and radiant she looks, appallingly even more beautiful now that she is a mother. A foolish but pretty queen, unable to do anything more for this realm than prance and preen. My sister, who I feel is hardly kin to me anymore. Memory is all that binds us to one another, and the memory is a thinning shred. It has faded, as have our footprints upon Haven's soil—overgrowing, surely, with forbs and grass.

I do not mean for them to, but my eyes rove now to the image of the tall king who approaches Lirinda, bowing to her as she curtsies to him before leaning into his open arms. She pecks a quick kiss upon his cheek then draws him by the hand nearer into the tumult of dancers, but any reverent kisses he hoped to pay her are lost, for now Lirinda skips like a silly child around him, giggling with the ladies at such a rapid dance. Over her bouncing head he glances softly at me.

The breeze seems to strengthen as we share a glance, smiling at each other only through our eyes. Upon the gust that billows my dress and hair around me, I catch the spice of his essence—smoke and autumn, so like the spice of change.

Together, I know we think of the bright white room with the

Il-lar at its center; this significant artifact no one here around us cares to know. Our unspoken alliance. Our unusual bond. I understand him. He understands me.

STEPHANIE ESCOBAR is an author of fantasy and Gothic fiction. She first wrote *Mercy of the Crow* while living off-grid in a dark forest with only candlelight to write by. Much of her inspiration for Haven came from this wild lifestyle she lived for several years. Currently, she resides with her husband and their two daughters in a historic home filled with antiques and the smell of fresh coffee, where she homeschools, raises chickens, and enjoys having champagne with her husband in their flower garden. She invites readers to her website (sescobarauthor.com) and to join her on Goodreads, so they may be informed of the sequels to come.